THE GOLDEN
CENTIPEDE

THE GOLDEN CENTIPEDE

Louise Gerard

COACHWHIP PUBLICATIONS

Greenville, Ohio

The Golden Centipede, by Louise Gerard
© 2014 Coachwhip Publications
Louise Gerard, 1878-1970.
No claims made on public domain material.
First published 1910.
Cover: Centipede © Emmanouil Filippou

ISBN 1-61646-254-X
ISBN-13 978-1-61646-254-3

CoachwhipBooks.com

CONTENTS

CHAPTER 1

"Across the tractless seas I go,
No matter when or where
And few my future lot will know,
And fewer still will care."

THE S.S. *ASABO*, OUTWARD-BOUND for West Africa, swung idly in midstream with steam up ready to start as soon as the London passengers and mails were on board. The day was almost tropical. The early afternoon sun danced and scintillated on the highly burnished brass of the vessel and rendered the white-painted iron hot to a degree of discomfort. The deep blue sky reflected in the Mersey made the usually thick and muddy water appear clear and vivid. Nearly all the ship's officers had donned tropic garb, and the remark: "It's more like Africa than England," was freely passed round. Most of the passengers were on the upper saloon deck watching the tender that fluttered round the Prince's landing-stage in a state of obvious agitation at the delay caused by the lateness of the London train. They were rather an assorted crowd. The majority were holidaymakers *en route* for Grand Canary, the remainder mostly traders and engineers, with a sprinkling of civil servants and military officers bound for some more or less salubrious place on the West Coast of Africa. Although not more than an hour on board they were already broken up into cliques, and the highest, those in His Majesty's service, were grouped round the *Asabo's* captain.

Leaning against the rail, with indolent, half-shut eyes, was a tall, powerfully built man of about thirty-five. His expression was that of supreme indifference, of one whom life bored to the verge of extinction. Few people had seen Major the Hon. Tracy Sinclair exert himself; he appeared to meander through his allotted span in a state of chronic somnolence. Hurry was unknown to him, and whatever happened his eyes never opened to their full extent; he spoke with a sleepy drawl and his movements were slow and languid to a degree of irritation. In spite of his seeming laziness he had always managed to come out top in all the examinations that led to his present position and in any game of skill, if anyone had sufficient patience and energy to rouse him from his habitual comatose condition. Notwithstanding his apparent dislike to anything approaching exertion he had, in the days of his captaincy, seen a good deal of active service. At his father's death, however, when he came into a very comfortable inheritance, he retired from the army, and for the last few years had done nothing but a little shooting in out-of-the-way parts of the world. He was an enthusiastic, if such a word could be applied to so lazy an individual, ornithologist; hence his presence in search of rare and unknown birds in districts and countries where Major Tracy Sinclair in his official capacity might not have been made welcome. Shortly after retiring from the army he went to South America with the object of ascertaining whether a certain member of the feathered tribe, said to be extinct there, could still be found. What the name of the bird was he did not divulge to his friends; but soon after his return to England a bald-headed eagle that had fluttered down from the north and hovered over a small and somewhat defenceless country on the southernmost borders of the American Confederated States flew back rather hastily on receipt of a letter handed in at Washington. Major Sinclair's return to England was in no way connected with the incident; in fact among the juniors of the various embassies he was voted "a muddling ass" where things diplomatic were concerned.

His present expedition was to German West Africa, the region lying somewhere south of Rio del Rey. There was nothing extraordinary in this because, as all the world knows, the birds in that part have been woefully neglected, and probably many hitherto un-known specimens would be the result of the little trip.

It was Major Sinclair's first visit to the West Coast—Captain Morton of the *Asabo* marked that at once. Sinclair had not troubled to contradict him; it would have been too much exertion, and be-sides, in a way, Captain Morton was right. If he, Sinclair, under the name of Danvers, had visited the German West African hinter-land by way of Mombassa to make a few inquiries about a big gun-running affair into Northern Nigeria, and returned by the same route without reporting himself at the Government house, it was perhaps as well to say nothing about it.

As he leant there idly against the rail he appeared to notice nothing beyond the end of his cigarette, yet his languid gaze was resting on a man who stood some little distance away—the leading spirit of the lowest stratum on the boat. This was a big, fair man of about his own age, with a bloated red face and an air of self-indul-gence and dissipation; his eyes were deep-set and had a cunning, shifty look; an expression of latent cruelty lurked in the corners of his selfish mouth, and the sharp teeth his frequent smile displayed gave him a curiously wolfish aspect.

Captain Morton's eyes wandered alternately from the waiting tender to the man who had aroused Sinclair's interest, and his weather-beaten face depicted obvious concern.

"How long before we start, Captain Morton?"

The speaker was a slim girl with a wealth of deep golden hair, rich and red like raw West African gold. Her skin was pale and her eyes a soft, dark brown. "Pretty, but too frail-looking," was the usual comment passed on Marjorie Sinclair, the major's eighteen-year-old half-sister and ward. As a matter of fact she was just recovering from a long and severe illness and was going with her aunt, Mrs. Onslow, out to Grand Canary to stay there until her brother's return.

"We should have started an hour ago, Miss Sinclair, but for the lateness of the London special," and again his eyes wandered un-easily towards the big, fair man.

"Who's our big friend, captain?" Sinclair drawled, noting the glance.

"Carl Langfeldt, chief agent for Schmutz & Co.; German Camer-oon. Biggest rogue on the coast bar one!"

"Really? I'd no idea we traveled with such distinguished com-pany. Which of that lively looking crew holds the first?"

"He's not on board yet."

Sinclair lighted another cigarette and waited: rogues apparently did not interest him; occasionally they sought him out as an easy pigeon to pluck. At times he humored them. "Rooks," of course, come under the notice of an ornithologist.

Soon after the tender left the landing-stage Morton turned to-wards the bridge, and at his invitation Sinclair accompanied him. The captain leant against the rail, scanning the passengers as the little steamer approached.

"Umph! I thought as much. His name wasn't down on the pas-senger-list, but the young devil doesn't advertise his comings and goings more than necessary."

"Who's that?" Sinclair asked with a suppressed yawn.

"The Babe."

Had Morton's gaze not been fixed on a slight boyish form in grey flannels, a broad-rimmed soft felt hat, blue cummerbund and long loose tie, who perched negligently on the tender's side, he might have noticed his companion's eyes open about an eighth of an inch more than was their wont.

"Who is he?"

"Claude Wentworth, the cleverest blackguard on the whole of the West Coast. Langfeldt is his right-hand man; that big villain I pointed out to you a little time since. What's his game now, I won-der? The young jail-bird!"

Captain Morton's voice sounded, to say the least of it, un-friendly. Nearly six years previously, when he had numbered Claude Wentworth and Carl Langfeldt among his passengers, a matter of some two thousand pounds in specie, drafted to a bank in Sierra Leone, was missing. The episode had nearly cost him his certificate. "The Babe" had been seen hovering in the vicinity of the strong-room, and Carl Langfeldt had developed malaria to such an extent that it necessitated his being left behind in Grand

Canary. The pair were accused; but all evidence against them fell through. "The Babe" brought an action of defamation of character and wrongful detention against Captain Morton and won. Then followed the "Bacuto" mine swindle; for which, much to Captain Morton's delight, Claude Wentworth had to undergo six months in the second division and only escaped that number of years on a plea of youth, undue influence and first offence. Things West African were quiet for a time and then there was a big ivory raid in Spanish territory. Much underground friction ensued between the two governments and a little rubbing of the golden ointment into the injured Spanish palm. In spite of all efforts the leader, who answered to Claude Wentworth's description, could not be brought to book. True, he had landed there one evening, but, much to Captain Morton's disgust, he had to give evidence as to "The Babe's" return the following morning and to his being on his vessel a week later when the raid took place. Strange as it may seem, shortly afterwards Schmutz & Co. shipped an inordinately large quantity of ivory to Hamburg; but unfortunately the links between were missing. There were several affairs of a similar nature in other districts and more doling out of the golden salve. The leader was known to be English; but Claude Wentworth always proved a satisfactory alibi. Guns of the latest pattern leaked through to North Nigeria for the arming of a chronically rebellious tribe, as the British found to their cost. Schmutz & Co. flourished and prospered. "The Babe" traveled about with a broad and innocent smile. The thorn festered in the British epidermis. Then Major Sinclair decided to hunt for rare and curious birds in West Africa, more especially in the German Cameroon.

"Which is 'The Babe'?" he asked presently; he knew the reputation but not the man.

"He's coming up the gangway now."

"That infant!"—surprise cut through Sinclair's habitual drawl.

"He looks a very innocent child, but he was just the same the first time I saw him nearly six years ago. He seemed about sixteen then and not a day more now."

Sinclair made no comment, but watched the slight figure coming jauntily up the gangway. A welcoming shout and wave from

Langfeldt made Claude Wentworth look up. The floppy hat was taken off for an answering wave and the sun glistened on a mop of dark chestnut curls. For a moment Sinclair had a glimpse of a slightly tanned, round face, with big dark eyes, rather full lips and a surprising dimple that lurked in the left corner of a smiling mouth.

"It's a wondrous pretty babe," he drawled.

"He is, the young demon!" Morton answered grudgingly. "Sitting up all night drinking and gambling doesn't seem to mar his complexion. He told me so once; the night I swear he lifted that two thousand. I was rather anxious about him in those days—fancied he was a young and tender pigeon Langfeldt & Co. were plucking."

"Who is he?"

"I can't find out a word of his history previous to his first voyage with me. The devil's own spawn, I should say!"

The youth under discussion passed along the lower deck and was lost to sight for a time. Sinclair's gaze wandered to the head of the stairs leading to the upper saloon deck. Just near, lying back in a long cane lounge, was his sister. Seated beside her was Mrs. Onslow. From them he glanced to the opposite side where Langfeldt stood surrounded by a few kindred spirits. Close to them a brawny negro deck-hand was cleaning a brass rail. Sinclair noticed his gaze wandered from the German to the head of the stairs. Presently, with his hat well on the back of his head and cigarette between his lips, Claude Wentworth came up. He glanced round quickly. The negro stood stiff and straight, and to Sinclair's surprise the man's eyes were not fixed on "The Babe," as he expected, but on his own sister, Marjorie! His astonishment did not stop there. Claude Wentworth's eyes followed the negro's; he started, and then, after a moment's hesitation, threw away his cigarette and approached the two ladies. At Marjorie's side he stooped and appeared to pick up something from the deck. The sun glittered on a threadlike piece of gold that lay in his hand as he spoke to the girl. Her attitude was that of denial; the youth's insistence. He appealed to Mrs. Onslow and then the glittering little object was placed on Marjorie's book and with a graceful bow he left them. As he passed the negro a ringing, defiant laugh reached Sinclair; the answering scowl on the man's ebony face was not good to see. On nearing the bridge "The Babe" looked up and caught Captain Morton's unfriendly stare. The laugh rang out again.

"Hello, captain! Ain't you glad to have your 'curly-headed babby' on board again?"

"Damned young skunk!" was the amiable reply.

When a few minutes later the pilot came on the bridge Sinclair left. An unnecessary circle round the upper deck brought him to where "The Babe" leant carelessly against an upright ventilator, talking in an undertone to Langfeldt. As he approached and passed, he was conscious that the youth's gaze was on him.

"Who's that sleepy-looking josser? I don't remember seeing him on the westward trail before," a clear young voice inquired.

Sleepy or not, Sinclair had noticed the eyes that watched him were a deep, dark blue; also their expression was defiant, but behind, carefully screened, was a world of anxiety and care.

CHAPTER 2

"I wish I could guess what sense they express,
There's a meaning doubtless in every sound,
Yet no one can tell, and it may be as well—
Whom will it profit?—The world goes round!"

THE STEAM-SYREN GAVE OUT three ear-piercing hoots as slowly the S.S. *Asabo* got under way. The pleasure-seeking portion of the passengers crowded to the side for a last glimpse of Liverpool. Mrs. Onslow got up to join them. She glanced at her companion, who sat gazing at the curious little object on her book.

"Why it's just the colour of your hair, Marjorie," she remarked laughingly, and then, "but what a vicious-looking little thing it is; one could almost swear it was alive."

"It's certainly not beautiful, auntie, but it's very weird and fascinating and creepy-looking. That boy seemed so positive I'd dropped it. I'll show it to Tracy when he comes along, and he can give it to the captain. There'll soon be someone asking for it."

Marjorie turned to look for her brother, and the book on her knee moved. The glistening object lying on it seemed to become imbued with life and crawled an inch or so higher. Mrs. Onslow shivered.

"I do declare it's walking up your book, Marjorie. Don't touch it whatever you do. I believe it's alive!"

"Nonsense! auntie."

14

However Marjorie evinced no desire to touch it, and a look of relief came to her face when her brother sauntered towards them.

"Oh, Tracy, see what I've had given to me," she said, holding the book up.

He gave an almost imperceptible start—The Golden Centipede! He had seen it once before near Blenka's Land in the far-away German West African hinterland. Whilst traveling across a range of rocky hills he had found a skeleton. A glint of gold in the gaping jaw had attracted his attention. Inside was a weird golden insect. He had buried the time-worn bones and the golden symbol now reposed, with other small treasures, in a secret drawer of his curio cabinet. Now a similar token rested on his sister's book.

"Who gave you that diabolical little beast?"

"One of the passengers saw it lying on the deck against my chair. He thought it was mine. I assured him it wasn't; but he said it may have belonged to someone who had been with me, and I was to keep it and see."

Sinclair picked up the centipede carelessly. It was about three inches long. Every joint of the flat repulsive body wriggled at his touch and the thin antennae on the vicious-looking head waved to and fro. He laid it on its back on the palm of his hand and forty tiny golden legs started to move.

"Are you sure it's not alive?" Mrs. Onslow asked nervously.

"Quite sure, auntie; but it's marvelously lifelike and a wonderful piece of workmanship."

"What shall you do with it?" his sister asked, seeing him slip the wriggling piece of gold into his pocket.

"Give it to the captain, and if no claimant turns up return it to the one who found it. Now, auntie, would you and Marjorie like to have tea on deck? If so I'll give the order; I'm going below to straighten up a few things in my cabin."

When Sinclair entered the saloon the chief steward came up to him apologetically.

"I'm sorry, sir, but I've had to put a young gent in your cabin. He came on board unexpectedly and wanted a berth to himself. I said such a thing was impossible this side of Grand Canary. I had hoped to manage a clear cabin for you, sir—"

The chief steward sighed, he fancied he saw a promised ten-pound note vanishing into space. Sinclair lovingly fingered the golden centipede reposing in his pocket, and blessed his never-failing luck.

"That won't make any difference, steward. Will you see three teas are sent to the upper deck."

Sinclair went along the corridor leading to his cabin. When he entered, "The Babe," who was busily engaged in unpacking, looked round airily.

"So you're my stable-mate? I'd no idea I was to be stalled with an elephant."

The other glanced at him sleepily, yawned and then drawled: "No? I suppose a monkey would have suited you better."

"The Babe" laughed.

"You're a sharp old bird, ain't you?"

The sleepy look on his companion's face became even more apparent. Was it only fancy, or did this precious young bounder lay more than ordinary emphasis on "bird"?

He sat down and watched the youngster who, from the depths of his portmanteau, brought forth pyjamas of a highly vivid stripe and calmly deposited them on the upper berth.

"I say, that's my crib! I thought I left my mark and seal on it," Sinclair exclaimed.

"Oh! was that your loose gear I found flung all over the place? I'm a tidy boy myself and the sight hurt me so I shoved it all in there," pointing towards the lower berth.

"Did you?"—grimly.

"I did,"—serenely.

"Well suppose I said I'd a decided preference for an upper bunk?"

"Lots of us have decided preferences for things we can't have."

Sinclair was sorely tempted to take the precocious youngster by the collar and put him out of the cabin. He refrained, however, as such a proceeding was hardly in keeping with his assumed character. "The Babe" went on unpacking, at the same time whistling the latest popular ditty. For a time nothing was said. Presently he glanced at his companion. A provoking dimple lurked in the left corner of his mouth.

"Well! have you come round to my way of thinking?"

"Thinking! What about?"—Sinclair's voice was intensely bored.

"The berth palaver."

"Have both if you wish. I'd be sorry to inconvenience you in any way. I daresay they'll allow me to tuck up in the smoke-room."

A quick glance was cast at him. He, however, appeared to be deeply interested in the shape and formation of his right deck shoe.

"I'm not greedy. One will suffice. Besides I'm a bit of an owl and I guess you know their habits." With this parting shot "The Babe" left. Sinclair sat lost in thought until the ringing of the tea-bell aroused him.

It was nearly dinner-time before he had an opportunity of showing the golden centipede to Captain Morton. He met the latter coming off the bridge and was invited to partake of a cocktail in his cabin. Sinclair said nothing about his find until they were alone with the requisite appetizers on the table between them: then he brought the insect out and laid it by the captain's glass.

"Can you tell me anything about this vicious little brute?"

Captain Morton whistled softly as he turned the tiny wriggling object over gingerly.

"Where did you get it from?"

"It was found lying by my sister's chair."

"Did you find it there?"

"No; it was that young reprobate Wentworth who saw it and, naturally supposing it was my sister's, picked it up and gave it to her."

"The devil!" Morton ejaculated.

"Have there been any inquiries about it?"

"Half-a-minute and I'll find out."

He rang for the purser and chief steward and asked if any of the passengers were inquiring for lost trinkets. In both cases a decided negative was given. After the two men had gone Morton sat gazing at the glittering little object in silence. A shadow fell across the room. Sinclair glanced round quickly. As he did so a dusky face was hastily withdrawn from the porthole, so hastily in fact he could hardly swear to its having been there.

"Seen the beast before, captain?"

"No,"—and after a pause—"but I've heard of it though!" Morton took his cocktail at a gulp, picked up the centipede and going to his safe unlocked it and put it in.

He sat down thoughtfully and after a few minutes' silence said: "It's a wild yarn I'm going to spin and more than forty years since I heard it: I was a youngster of twelve at the time. Seeing that fearsome bit of gold brought it all back to me. It must be about a hundred years since it happened. My old dad was over seventy when he told me and he was not more than twenty when it occurred. He had charge of a trading hulk then, well up Rio del Rey. In those days it was a bit risky living on shore: the natives were not as amiable as now and he only saw his own sort about once in the proverbial blue moon. You can imagine his surprise when one morning a fancy pleasure yacht came sailing up the river. There were about a dozen Europeans on board, including one woman. I remember how my old dad used to rave about her. She was the most beautiful woman he had ever seen, with hair like raw West African gold— the same colour as your sister's. He saw her only once. The men were a riff-raff lot: educated blackguards of every nation, and their leader, Devereux, the very devil! They stayed out a week at my father's place. What their little game was he could not discover. But that was not the end! Some two years later, when he was on a trading expedition into what is now the German Cameroon, a rumor reached him that a white man was dying in a village near. The man was no other than Devereux! He died before the night was out, the whole time raving about 'Chrysanthe' and 'The Ghost Bells.' For the sake of his friends and purposes of identification, my old dad searched the corpse. Like a tattooed mark on his left upper arm, running from elbow to shoulder, was a huge centipede; and on his chest, just over his heart, with its forty vicious legs embedded in his flesh, was—a thing like young Wentworth gave your sister! My old dad took it out, careful not to touch it.—There are many devilish poisons wandering about in West Africa.—He put it in a

box with several other bits of native jewelry. The next day, when
he went to look at it, it had disappeared. Nothing else was touched.
Only the golden centipede had vanished!"

For a time both men sat lost in thought.

"And if you have no claimant, what then, captain?"

"I shall think that young skunk dropped it purposely against
your sister's chair and then pretended he thought it was hers."

This had been Sinclair's private opinion all along, but he did
not say so. Instead he asked: "What motive would he have in doing
so?"

"It would be difficult to give a reason for all Claude Wentworth's
actions. However, if no one turns up to claim it within three days,
he shall have his devil's toy back again."

Sinclair got up for a turn on deck before dinner. It was a beautiful evening, the sea still and calm as a millpond. Far away in the
west the sun had all but reached the water's edge. For a moment it
poised like a gigantic ball of molten gold and then took a sudden
plunge into the ocean's depths. A cloud rose as it disappeared, covering the sea with a misty veil of mingling blood and gold. Then a
ray of deep red light came slowly over the water. Mechanically
Sinclair watched it as it crept towards the ship. It trembled, almost disappeared, and then shone out a deeper, more vivid red
than ever, full on "The Babe" who was perched on the rail watching the sunset. It paused, wavered, and crept on again until it
reached to where he stood. A soft breeze came moaning over the
water, whispering and sighing among the iron ropes of the vessel.
He was not superstitious, but in spite of himself he shivered. A
ghastly trail of blood seemed to join him and the youngster. How
long he stood there he did not know. Slowly the red light died away.
A low evil chuckle reached him. He looked round quickly. The upper deck was deserted save for himself and the boy. With an effort
he pulled himself together and went down to dress for dinner; but
it was some time before he could throw off the uncanny feeling
that had assailed him.

He dressed quickly, having promised his sister to be in the
music-saloon a few minutes before the gong went. On entering,

his mouth hardened. Sitting in a low chair, a picture of frail beauty in her soft white dress, was Marjorie. Leaning carelessly against the piano, with one slim brown hand swinging his felt hat, and the other thrust deep into his pocket, was Claude Wentworth. The saucy mouth dimpled when he noticed Sinclair's obvious disapproval of the situation.

"Well, Miss Sinclair, here comes your brother to rescue you from my evil clutches. I told you I was no end of a bad lot, but you were good enough not to believe me," and with a laugh and a bow he went out of the room.

"Who's your new friend, Marjorie?"

"Why, Tracy, that's the passenger who thought I'd dropped that little insect thing. He was in here when I came in and he asked me if I'd found an owner yet. He says if I don't I shall have to keep it."

"Did he? Well there's plenty of time yet for a claimant to turn up and—er—if you don't mind my saying so, little sister, I'd rather you didn't get friendly with that youngster. He's a very bad character."

"Is he? I'd no idea. I thought he was rather nice."

He smiled and pinched her ear. Simultaneously the dinner gong sounded and Mrs. Onslow entered.

About eleven o'clock that night Sinclair strolled into the smoke-room. A grey cloud encircled the table where Langfeldt, "The Babe" and a few others were playing poker at a ruinous rate. "The Babe" glanced up as he passed and made some remark to the German. An hour later, when he passed them again, with the idea of having a stroll before turning in, the youngster looked up with a provoking smile.

"Good-night, old chap; don't sit up for me. I'm a late bird and not often caught napping."

Langfeldt & Co. roared. There was no mistaking the emphasis on the "bird" that time.

In the small hours of the morning, nearer three than two, some-one falling into the cabin roused Sinclair. An over-powering odor of whisky permeated the atmosphere as "The Babe," apparently a trifle unsteady on his legs, groped round in the dark. Behind the curtain Sinclair lay low and said nothing. Presently his companion climbed up into the berth above. As he did so something fell noiselessly to the ground. After waiting until all was quiet, Sinclair put his arm out and felt round. The result was a handkerchief saturated with whisky. He lay back thoughtfully. Evidently the youngster was not as intoxicated as he had at first imagined him to be!

CHAPTER 3

"At home or abroad, by land or sea,
In peace or war sore trials must be,
And worse may happen to you or to me,
For none are secure and none can flee
From a destiny impending."

IT WAS THE *ASABO'S* THIRD DAY out from Liverpool and a pitch dark night. Away on the horizon the lightning played fitfully. There was a stifling, oppressive heat over everything and the sea had an ominously oily look—the smooth, dead, stagnant calm that comes before a storm. The silence was broken only by the measured, monotonous panting of the engines. A group of passengers stood in the flood of light that streamed out from the open companionway, and close by, in the shadow of a suspended lifeboat, Marjorie Sinclair and her aunt were talking to Captain Morton.

"So you have found no claimant for that horrid little insect, captain?" the girl was saying.

"No; to-morrow I shall return it to its owner."

"The finder, you mean. Mr. Wentworth is very anxious I should keep it; he says evidently it was for me since of its own accord it crawled to my side."

"You mustn't believe all young Wentworth says, Miss Sinclair. He has the reputation of being the—er—most beautiful—prevaricator that ever traveled by this line. I know him of old and, if my age will excuse the remark, he's not exactly the companion for a young lady."

"So everybody says and I wonder why. I've only spoken to him about half-a-dozen times but he always seems very nice."

Captain Morton smiled grimly.

"Oh yes; he can be very agreeable when anything hangs on it."

"But nothing could hang on me."

"I sincerely hope not, Miss Sinclair."

As he turned to reply to some remark of Mrs. Onslow, Marjorie went to the ship's side. She leant back against the lifeboat in the secluded corner between it and the rail. Something stirred in the boat above her; but lost in the weird beauty of the distant playing fire she noticed nothing. A dusky face peered over. A moment afterwards a hand appeared and in it a long glass tube. As she moved suddenly to the side something long and wriggling, that otherwise would have fallen on her breast, caught in the lace at the back of her dress. For a moment the dusky face watched, in doubt whether the squirming object would retain its hold or not. Little by little it crawled up and the waving antennae touched her bare shoulder. She put her hand to her neck as if to catch a stray hair. The thing stopped and then crawled on again. At the second touch she went quickly to Mrs. Onslow.

"Auntie, I do believe there's something crawling on my back."

When the light fell on her the group started. Mrs. Onslow screamed. The men's faces whitened as, fascinated, they watched the object that slowly crept on the girl's bare shoulder. It was a huge six-inch centipede of the deadliest variety known in West Africa!

"Take it off! Oh, take it off!" and her horror-stricken face was turned towards the men.

In a moment Captain Morton had recovered his presence of mind.

"Don't move, Miss Sinclair," he said hoarsely. "Stand still and try not to be frightened. Wait till it crawls on your dress again and then we'll knock it off and settle its evil career. It won't hurt if you don't touch or frighten it."

She gasped, and the soft white flesh seemed to shrink and shrivel as slowly the many-legged creature drew its repulsive length on to her shoulder. It stopped there and its antenna played lightly on her pale, drawn face. To attempt to remove it meant almost certain death to the girl: at the least touch the deadly jaws and forty poisonous legs would be embedded in her delicate flesh. For a moment she felt she must tear it off, whatever the consequences; and then the horror of the thing seemed to freeze her and she stood white and still like a marble statue. The light made the insect's scaly body glisten as if it had been flecked with gold-dust. For a time it lay quietly on her shoulder, pleased with the soft warmth. A sob broke from her lips as slowly it began to circle her neck, finally crawling into the little hollow beneath her chin and, forming an ill-shaped S, stayed there motionless.

"I shall go mad," she breathed.

A clear, ringing laugh echoed along the deck. The creature raised its vile head, alert and listening, with antennae waving backwards and forwards and its whole body stiffened in an attitude of expectation. "The Babe" and Langfeldt came towards the frozen group.

"My God! Look at that!" the German gasped.

Claude Wentworth's face went ghastly. The light played on his chestnut curls, bringing out a glint of gold, and on the listening insect. That was chestnut and gold too! Marjorie's wild eyes met his imploringly; without hesitation he went to her side.

"Don't be a thrice-damned fool, Claude. Don't touch it. Let that devil's messenger alone!" Langfeldt gasped.

Ignoring his friend "The Babe" said quickly: "Don't be afraid, Miss Sinclair; I can entice him off in no time."

As he spoke, the centipede turned slowly with raised head and poison jaws working menacingly.

He pulled up his left sleeve till the arm was bared to just below the elbow, so that the tightness of the shirt cuff would prevent it from crawling underneath, and then very stealthily he laid his hand on the girl's breast, an inch or two below where the creature lay. There was no sound except the youngster talking to the poisonous legged worm in a low crooning voice as he watched it with strained eyes.

"Good God! What devil's game is this?"

Sinclair's hoarse whisper cut through the silence as, on coming up from the saloon, his gaze fell on the weird picture. The low chuckle he had heard once before came out of the darkness: then from over the still, black water an awful, death-like wail:

"Oh, Golden Flower, it is the doom!"

"The Babe's" face went more ghastly than the tortured girl's. There was a convulsive movement in his throat and the slim brown hand trembled a little as he answered, "Great Asquielba! To all the end comes soon."

Sinclair and Morton exchanged glances: the wail and answer were in the Blenguta tongue, an almost obsolete West African dialect.

Something thrown from the upper deck missed the girl's shoulder and rolled to the captain's feet. He turned to the purser.

"Go and see what nigger is on the upper deck."

Sinclair came to where his sister stood, his height and width screening the two from further assaults.

Slowly the insect uncurled and crept towards the slim hand. It hesitated and the antennas flickered round the fingers lying on the shrinking white flesh. "The Babe" gave a quick, short gasp when six inches of death crept on to his hand. A sigh broke from the crowd. Marjorie stood with her eyes on the centipede as it crawled up the youngster's arm to within a few inches of the cloth barrier and stopped. For a good five minutes it stayed there motionless. Sinclair's eyes were on the boy's strained face.

"Hold up, Wentworth; it'll soon start crawling again and will be on your coat in no time," he said hoarsely.

The words were hardly out of his mouth when a thin rope thrown from the lifeboat fell across the glistening, copper-colored body. A low moan broke from "The Babe's" lips as the hideous creature buried itself in the soft flesh of his arm. The horror of the thing petrified the watchers. There was a thud of bare feet on the deck. Sinclair glanced round quickly to see a form disappear into the darkness. The sight roused him: the boy's life depended on promptness of action.

"Go to the doctor's cabin and tell him to have a good supply of strong ammonia and a carbolic needle ready."

A dozen willing messengers flew at this command.

"Come, Wentworth, pull yourself together; you're not dead yet."

Watching the dazed face he drew the youngster to the ship's side. In spite of the cheerful tone there was a very anxious look about his eyes. He had been in more than one land where centipedes were over-numerous. Making the boy hold his arm well over the water he struck a fusee and ran the glowing, red-hot head up and down the back of the embedded insect. To attempt to tear it out meant leaving most of the poisonous legs in the flesh and a terrible festering wound would ensue, most probably resulting in the loss of an arm or even death. As the match ran up and down, one by one the pointed, crab-like legs were withdrawn and in less than half-a-minute a wriggling, twisted mass dropped into the sea.

"Thank goodness that awful creature's off the boat!" Sinclair said hoarsely.

Taking a handkerchief out of his pocket he tied it just below the elbow with a strength and tightness that made his victim wince. This ligature stopped the flow of blood and confined the poison area to the lower arm. As quickly as possible he hurried the youngster to the doctor's cabin and stood watching his white face while the wound was being treated with strong ammonia and carbolic injections. After a few minutes "The Babe" brightened up a little and began to take an interest in the proceedings.

"I say, you're making a pretty mess of my arm," he said feebly.

"I shall have to, my lad, if you want to keep this side of 'Kingdom Come.'"

"How many more of those beastly injections are you going to stick in?"

"Quite a few yet! Why? Feeling a bit sick?"

The ghost of a dimple lurked in the corner of the boy's white lips.

"Oh no, never felt more healthy in my life."

The doctor went to the locker and measuring out three fingers of brandy brought it to him neat.

"You don't expect me to take that beastly stuff raw?"

"Why I thought you could take it by the tumblerful."

"Did you? Well let me tell you I've turned over a new leaf. I'm going to be a good boy in the future; no end moral and virtuous. Quite a plaster saint!"—the defiant laugh rang out very shakily—"I guess you chaps are bursting with curiosity as to what game's on now. Shall I tell you? I'm a missionary this trip, a pious and holy devil-dodger." Then lifting the glass, which had been returned to him with the addition of water, he looked at Sinclair mischievously. "'Good hunting,' Major Sinclair, and many thanks for returning me to the broad, smooth way that leadeth to destruction."

"The Babe" was getting back to his normal state of impudence. For a time he watched the doctor quietly.

"Will it leave a mark?" he asked presently.

"Yes, for a time."

"Oh!"

For some moments he chewed the cud of reflection and evidently found it not to his liking.

"For how long?"

"I daresay it will be a matter of a month or two before it dies away properly."

The information did not appear to be received with any great delight.

On removing the ligature the doctor suggested one or two injections in the upper arm. The victim got up unsteadily and hastily pulled down his sleeve.

"I'm hanged if I'll have any more! I've been made enough of a pincushion for one night."

"As you will; but let me put a bandage on."

"I've been mauled about sufficiently, thanks. I guess I'll turn in now, though it's a bit early for me to go to roost."

When he left the doctor remarked: "I shouldn't be surprised if that youngster is a bit light-headed tonight. His arm is pretty certain

to swell and give him a deuce of a time for an hour or two. Who's
he berthed with, I wonder?"

"He's in my cabin, so I can keep an eye on him. You'd better let
me have a cooling solution in case he gets uncomfortable."

"I'll send two; one for internal and the other for external ap-
plication. If they don't work let me know pretty quickly; he's not
out of the wood yet."

Sinclair left the doctor and went to inquire how his sister was.
But for "The Babe's" courageous action the night might have ended
with her death. She was not in a state of health to battle with in-
sidious poison, however prompt the remedies. Having satisfied
himself of her welfare, he went along to the captain's cabin. The
ship was one buzz of tongues discussing the averted calamity, and
all inquired after his sister and Wentworth.

"Well, captain, what do you think of to-night's affair?" he asked
as he seated himself.

Morton filled up two glasses thoughtfully.

"You must keep a sharp watch on your sister, Major Sinclair.
Don't let her wander in any dark parts of the deck at night. In my
opinion there's some fearful underground 'ju-ju' business going
on. I shall be quite relieved to get Miss Sinclair safely landed in
Grand Canary. What puzzles me is why young Wentworth should
interfere when he's up to the neck in every vile negro ceremony.
I've had all the niggers on the boat in front of me, but I can't put it
to any one of them. The whole thing was some awful fetish rite."

"It seemed vastly like it. How do you account for that voice and
laugh?"

"Easily enough. A case of ventriloquism; an art the nigger 'ju-
ju' priests are well up in and use to befuddle their flock. 'Golden
Flower!' That might mean your sister: it's the sort of name the
niggers would soon christen her."

Sinclair sipped his whisky with a thoughtful air.

"Didn't you say the man your father found about a hundred
years back raved a lot about 'Chrysanthe?'"

"Yes: why?"

"It's a Greek name and means 'golden flower.'"

Morton sat up and looked at his neighbor in blank astonishment.

"The devil"—the knotted hand round the glass trembled visibly—"I'd like to drop young Wentworth overboard. There's always hell to pay when he's about."

"He saved my sister's life at the risk of his own; and the fear of death was on him when he answered that ghastly wail."

A strong wind was getting up when some time afterwards Sinclair left the captain for a final stroll before turning in. Most of the passengers had retired, anxious to be in their bunks before the storm broke. After a few turns he went below. On entering the cabin a cold breeze blowing through the curtains of the upper berth took his attention. Switching on the light, he drew them aside noiselessly. As he leant across to close the port he glanced at the sleeping youngster who lay there rather flushed and hot-looking. For a moment he studied the face: there was a wistful innocence about it entirely out of keeping with the boy's villainous reputation: an anxious, careworn little face with a touch of mischief, but no vice.

"The Babe" awoke with a start, sat up suddenly and Sinclair's extended arm struck him full across the chest. The bored eyes opened to their widest extent and the strong, sinewy hands fastening the port stumbled over their task, for the contact had been feminine in its softness.

"I say, youngster, don't jump about like a pea in a pan, winding yourself in this manner," he said unsteadily.

One hand went through the dark curls in a dazed way.

"Oh, it's you"—with evident relief—"I thought . . . I . . . I don't know what I thought. What are you doing?"—sharply.

"Closing the porthole. You don't want to be washed out of your berth in the night, do you?"

"I left it open. It was so hot. Hot as hell!"

"You'll cool off in a bit. Now lie down and go to sleep again; you'll get a chill sitting up chattering."

"Will you get me a drink? I feel like a furnace, and my head throbs like the dickens."

Sinclair was about to turn away when a step sounded along the silent corridor. "The Babe's" hand clutched his wrist. Something

in the nervous grip moved and played on chords in Sinclair's being that had never been touched before.

"That's Langfeldt. The fiend! Don't go. He's coming here. I'd
like to shoot him. Shoot him and the whole of Schmutz's lot! I'll be
even with them yet. There's one card in our pack they don't know
and—it's my deal this time."

Sinclair's disengaged hand groped round in the berth below and
brought out a light rug.

"Look here, youngster, if you're going to sit up all night inter-
viewing people, you'd better let me put this round your shoulders."

Rather wild eyes watched him as he slipped the wrap round.

"You won't go, will you? He's coming here, I know. I'm afraid
of him. What rot I'm talking. We're all rotters and I'm the biggest."

The grip on his wrist tightened when a knock fell on the door.
He watched the youngster's face as the door opened and saw the
obvious effort to retain reason. The German glanced at Sinclair
who had never looked more dense. Under cover of the rug, the hot
hand clutching the latter's wrist trembled.

"Well, Claude, how are you feeling now?"

"A1, thanks. Having no end of a time keeping this old bird hopping round waiting on me."

"You'll play the fool once too often, and we can't afford to lose
you just yet."

"The Babe" laughed.

"I'm a valuable asset to the company, ain't I? But there's no
need to worry your hair grey over me. The devil looks after his own!
Now go to bed quietly like a good boy, Carl, and don't forget to say
your prayers. We're a holy, pious lot this trip. Glory be!"

The German laughed and went out. The youngster's eyes were
fixed and listening till the heavy steps died away; then he fell back
weakly and lay watching his cabin-mate with dazed, nervous eyes.
Sinclair mixed a cooling draught and gave it to him; then, tucking
him in carefully, turned off the light and sat down on the couch
opposite, his head in a whirl. It was too incredible! Yet he was not
mistaken. But for Claude Wentworth's six months in prison the

thing might be feasible, wild as it seemed. The whole business was too uncanny; and this latest development beyond all!

For a good hour he sat trying to make head or tail of the affair. A restless movement in the upper berth made him switch the light on. He glanced at "The Babe." Beads of perspiration stood out on the smooth young forehead and the face was very pain-drawn. The poison was running its course, and the time the doctor had spoken of was coming on. He mopped the wet forehead carefully; the heat of it reached him through the handkerchief. One of the soft curls coiled round his finger. He looked at it, loath to let it slip off again. A gasping little moan roused him.

"Why, youngster, what's the matter now?" smiling into the blue eyes that were watching him in a helpless way.

"The ghost bells! Can't you hear them? They woke me up. The golden ghost bells! Ringing, always ringing! Ringing to eternity. Ringing till the devil claims his own again! Ten thousand of them— ten thousand devils! That arch-fiend Mungea, what's he doing on board? I can't keep up this killing pace much longer. I can't! I can't!"

"Steady, child! Don't go babbling on at this rate. Let me get you another drink. How's the arm feeling now?"

"It's agony. Just as if it were on fire. But I must see this deal through and then— Can't you do something to ease it off a bit? I feel as if I were going mad."

"Let me bathe it for you; I've got some stuff here that will cool it down."

"The Babe" looked at him with the same strained, striving clutch after reason that had been on his face at Langfeldt's entry.

"Oh, no, it's not as bad as all that. Have I been talking rot again? Get me another drink, will you?—like the last; it seemed to clear my muddled head. And don't go fooling round or sending for the doctor. I'm as right as hops."

In spite of being "as right as hops," Sinclair had to lift him from the pillow. The small hand seemed uncertain where the glass was, and then its hold was so unsteady that a much bigger one had to come to its assistance. He watched the pain-drawn face anxiously, hoping he would be able to carry "The Babe" through the worst hour single-handed. The feeling grew and pressed on him that the fewer who knew the true state of affairs the better. This was a turn in the game he certainly had not looked for, and it left him breathless.

For a time all was quiet. Sinclair stretched himself fully dressed on the couch, listening for and noting every movement in the berth opposite. The wild impossibility of the whole thing struck him with redoubled force and he shook himself to make sure he was not dreaming. As he lay there all the weird mid-ocean noises reached him: the sigh and splash of the rising sea on the ship's side filled the cabin with a menacing ghostly hiss. The memory of the first night's sunset came back and he shivered.

Faint hurt moans made him start up quickly and turning on the light he looked sharply at his charge.

"What is it, child? Can I do anything?"

Bright fevered eyes gazed at him blankly.

Very carefully he felt the arm that lay on the coverlet. It was burning hot, and swollen right up to the shoulder and farther. Low sobs of pain came at his touch.

For a moment Sinclair hesitated, undecided what to do, and then he took the law into his own hands, only hoping that when "The Babe" got over the brief delirium there would be no recollection of this hour. He lifted the moaning youngster gently. The curly head rested on his shoulder as he unfastened the highly striped coat and drew the hot swollen limb carefully out of the sleeve and buttoned the garment again, leaving only the arm and shoulder exposed. In doing so he moved a little and the light fell on the limb that had previously lain in the shadow. He started violently. The whole of Captain Morton's story came back to his mind with a rush. There, like a birthmark, running from elbow to shoulder, was a huge centipede! The same as the one seen on the long-dead Devereaux! Down the body, each letter tattooed in one of the well-marked divisions, was the Greek word "χ-ρ-ι-σ-α-ν-θ-η"!

"CHRYSANTHE!"—in his astonishment Sinclair repeated the word aloud. The fevered eyes opened. With a sudden wild effort

"The Babe" sat up.

"Great Asquielba! I come!" and he fell back unconscious.

For a moment Sinclair's heart stood still. He took the limp wrist between his fingers and heaved a sigh of relief. Presently the low sobs broke out afresh. For the next hour he stayed by his charge laying and tending the injured arm until the worst of the swelling subsided and the moans died down. Then he carefully slipped the coat on again and very gently coaxed a draught between the parched lips. Laying the weak, pain-racked form back on the pillows, he stood watching the white little face with a strange anxiety, until the delirium gave place to fitful, feverish slumber and then to quiet, soothing sleep. Having assured himself that all was well, he drew the curtains and left the cabin. Day was breaking when he gained the deck; till the first gong sounded he paced up and down, his brain in a whirl, trying to convince himself the whole night's work was not some wild dream. What weird, barbaric mystery lay round the golden centipede? Who was the daring little sprite he had left sleeping in his cabin? What had Claude Wentworth to do with the man Morton's father had found nearly a century ago?

CHAPTER 4

"Things were to have been, and therefore
They were, and they are to be,
And will be,—we must prepare for
The doom we are bound to dree."

BREAKFAST WAS NEARLY OVER when Claude Wentworth came into the saloon. There was a very washed-out look about him and the jaunty air seemed forced. The comments on the previous evening and inquiries concerning his welfare that hailed his appearance obviously annoyed him. His replies were brief and curt to the verge of rudeness as he ran the gauntlet of the tables and eventually reached his own. He sat down limply, grunted something to Langfeldt and then glanced across at the captain's table. Marjorie's place was empty; the event of the night before had been a little beyond her strength. His eyes went to Sinclair anxiously, but that lazy individual's whole attention seemed devoted to the arduous occupation of buttering toast. "The Babe" ordered coffee and refused all else. Sinclair watched him covertly as, one after the other, in evident mental abstraction, he dropped fully a dozen lumps of sugar into the beverage. Langfeldt suddenly appropriating the basin aroused him. He started visibly, glanced at Sinclair, laughed, and ordered a fresh cup. This he stirred thoughtfully and for a length of time its sugarless condition did not demand. Again his gaze wandered to his cabin-mate. Then, forgetting the drink entirely he got up and left the saloon. It was very apparent something worried the

34

youngster. The keen eyes that had watched from under half-closed, sleepy lids smiled to themselves.

Sinclair finished his breakfast leisurely and then went out. He noticed the object of his search stretched out on a lounge-chair with attention divided between a fairly stiff whisky and soda and a sixpenny novel with a highly sensational cover. As he came along at his usual indolent crawl, he was conscious of two blue eyes watching him with nervous apprehension. "The Babe" finished his whisky at a gulp, closed the book and waited.

"Why, Wentworth, you're just the one I wanted; I owe you a few thanks. I'd no chance last night, you left the doctor's cabin in such a hurry. I was going to when I turned in, but Langfeldt came; after he went you looked so deadly tired I thought it kinder not to worry you, and you were sleeping like a top this morning when I got up. I'm truly grateful for what you did. My sister was about at the end of her strength when you came along and enticed that brute off. It was a bold thing to do and I cannot say how much I am indebted to you." Then leaning carelessly on the rail, "How are you feeling now?"

Some of the anxious, scared look left the youngster's face as Sinclair's languid drawl went on with just a shade more animation than usual as the circumstance demanded. The fingers that were carefully tearing the book cover into long, thin shreds, and then into neat squares, ceased their wanton destruction.

"I'm quite fit now, thanks"—then with the air of one making a final, desperate plunge—"I'm afraid I kicked about a good bit in the night and disturbed you. I—I seem to have a sort of idea I did." Sinclair drew out his cigarette-case slowly.

"No fear of that. A shipwreck wouldn't disturb me once I got to sleep," and he laughed lazily as he offered the case to his companion.

"No, thanks; I'm off smokes just now."

"The Babe" sounded quite chirrupy again, as if a considerable weight had been lifted from his shoulders. He sat up with his hands clasped round one knee. Sinclair noticed the left was still a trifle swollen.

"How's your sister? She doesn't look strong and that thing must have been an awful shock to her."

"She's all right now and I expect will be out and about before lunch."

Then Langfeldt appeared and "The Babe" got up and went to him.

It annoyed Sinclair that the youngster left him with such cheerful readiness. He watched the two as they went along the deck together. From the first moment he had disliked the big, shifty-looking German; but "The Babe," with his unbounded cheek and saucy smile, had only amused him, and now— He sighed and picked up the mutilated novel that had been thrown carelessly on the deck. As he opened the arm of the chair marked "Wentworth," with the intention of putting the book in, a debris consisting of old sporting papers, boxes of matches, odd cigarettes, a pack of cards and a few scattered chocolates in silver paper met his eyes. Somehow the sight of the last named pleased him. He picked one out, not with the intention of eating it—he had lost his sweet tooth years ago—but he felt he must have something belonging to "The Babe" and that was the only feminine thing there. Then putting the book in carefully he resumed his morning crawl.

It was getting on for lunch-time when Claude Wentworth, who was in the smoke-room watching Langfeldt plucking a couple of pigeons with a professional ease that aroused his admiration, received a polite message to the effect that the captain wished to see him. He gasped. Through the flying feathers the German glanced across at him.

"What does old Morton want with you, Claude? Our lot are not on visiting terms with him usually."

Claude appeared to be wondering too, apparently overcome by the honor. Perhaps after all that sleepy-looking josser was the man he had first imagined him to be, and had been playing a game with him this morning, smiling up his sleeve all the time. And now—

Sinclair was standing with Morton just outside the latter's cabin when the youngster came along. The weight of anxious care and misery on the round, childish face hurt him. There were depths in the case he could not fathom, but it struck him the forlorn little figure coming towards them was playing a lone game and a vast

amount hung on it. He smiled when the blue eyes met his defiantly. It was not his intention that either "The Babe" or anyone
else should find out the extent of his knowledge. He had come down
to hunt out the knave of spades and found the queen of hearts
instead.

"You sent for me, Captain Morton?"—in spite of all efforts the
voice trembled.

"That you, Wentworth? Come into my cabin, will you?"—the
invitation included Sinclair.

"The Babe" entered, feeling the hour of execution was at hand.

Morton seated himself leisurely, so did Sinclair. The third party
wondered how much longer the agonies were going to be prolonged.
The sleepy eyes watched him as he stood there, white-faced and
defiant.

"Sit down, youngster. What can I order for you?"

The curt invitation came from Morton as he leant across to ring
for the steward.

"The Babe" seemed to breathe again and a little of his accustomed impudence returned.

"I don't drink in the enemy's camp, captain." Sinclair laughed
and drawled: "How pleasant and amiable you two are."

"Ought to be. We appreciate each other's good qualities, don't
we, captain?"

Morton growled, and going to the safe took something out and
laid it on the table.

"That's your property, Wentworth. I don't want any of your vile
'ju-ju' charms in my possession."

"The Babe" looked at the golden centipede with preternatural
innocence and turned it over gingerly with a slim forefinger.

"Why, it's the thing I found against Miss Sinclair's chair! I
thought you'd got an owner for it long ago."

Morton looked at the youngster with blatant unfriendliness,
and Sinclair, who up to now had cherished a great regard for the
Asabo's captain, found himself rapidly growing to dislike that person.

"I'm prepared to swear you put it there."

"Don't swear, captain. It ain't seemly. Beside it's sometimes costly. You once mislaid two thousand and swore I'd taken it. It took quite a good sum to soothe my injured feelings."

The veins on Morton's forehead swelled. The dignity of his position forced him to keep his temper; but for that he would have taken the youngster by the collar and kicked him out of the cabin.

"You precious young bounder!"

'The Babe" leant negligently against the cupboard and smiled sweetly. Then he picked up the golden symbol, examined it carefully, swung it between two fingers and watched it wriggle with evident surprise and delight.

"Cute sort of customer, ain't he? Ever seen anything like it before, Major Sinclair?"

Sinclair agreed as to its cuteness, but forgot to reply to the latter part of the query.

Morton watched it with distrust, and then said, "Well, you'd better take it out of my sight. You found it; nobody claims it, and I'm sure I don't want it here."

"The Babe" slipped it into his pocket with a laugh, and as he went out said, "Well, I half made Miss Sinclair promise to have it if no claimant turned up; I guess I'll go along and give it to her now."

Morton gasped.

"Whatever you do, don't let your sister have anything to do with that young heathen or his uncanny gifts."

His companion smiled.

"I can't explain how it is, captain, but I've a feeling he means well."

A disbelieving grunt was the reply.

A few minutes later Sinclair left the cabin and strolled along towards where he knew his sister was sitting. Once before he had found her tête-à-tête with The Babe" and the situation had displeased him intensely. This time, however, it gave him a feeling of inward satisfaction. Marjorie was looking very frail and worn, but the youngster's chatter seemed to amuse her. He was rattling on at a great pace, evidently delighted with the situation and himself. The same saucy smile greeted Sinclair's approach.

"Look, Tracy, I've promised to keep this"—holding out the little golden insect that lay coiled up in her hand—"Mr. Wentworth has been telling me quite a lot about it. He says it's very lucky and that I must keep it and wear it always and never lose it, and all manner of good things will happen to me."

Sinclair took up a position by the youngster's side and noticed he watched Marjorie with obvious relief.

"Why, Wentworth, I thought you knew nothing about the beast?"

"Perhaps I made it up as I went along. I've got a reputation to keep up, you know." Sinclair thought he managed it very well.

Marjorie looked at him straightly.

"I believe you made me promise under false pretences."

"Never mind if I did. You promised, so that's enough."

She laughed. After a few minutes Sinclair strolled off again, leaving the two together. Later on, when at the sounding of the luncheon gong Morton came along, he decided Sinclair was the sleepiest fool he had ever met to leave his sister alone with that young reprobate.

As the afternoon wore on a strange restlessness seized Major the Hon. Tracy Sinclair. This increased as the daylight waned and the shadows lengthened. After dinner he paced the deck in a state of irritability that made him difficult and dangerous to approach. A problem confronted him, the like of which had never entered into his life before. He was learning the true meaning of "the horns of a dilemma." Each horn was studied to a nicety and found equally uncomfortable. If he suddenly cleared out that foolish little babe would suspect immediately, lose its nerve and the end might be the deuce! If he stayed—! This horn, in spite of its unconventionality, seemed to lead into less complications—at least, he could see the end of it. It only meant three nights. After the Canary passengers left the vessel there would be nothing suspicious in him shifting his quarters: it was the usual thing to do. Looked at all ways this was the wisest decision. He smiled as he thought over the days since leaving Liverpool. Now he understood the youngster's late hours and why he never stirred in the morning until he was well out of the way!

The object of his thoughts came along—looking very washed-out and weary. Sinclair hailed him as he approached—last night's affair was a good excuse for friendliness.

"Will you join me in a whisky, Wentworth?"

"The Babe" hesitated. He had had a trying time and several severe nerve shocks within the last twenty-four hours, was fagged out and wanted to go to bed. Then he bethought him of his reputation and agreed a whisky was the very thing he was looking for.

"Have it out here or in the smoke-room?"

One sacrifice at the altar of reputation was as much as he felt equal to.

"I'd rather have it out here. The smoke-room's beastly stuffy to-night."

This decision pleased Sinclair. He went along and gave the order to the first available steward. When he returned, "The Babe" was listlessly dragging two deck-chairs into position. He felt an over-powering desire to assist, but deemed it more diplomatic not to. There was still a look of latent nervousness in the tired blue eyes.

Seating himself leisurely, Sinclair watched his neighbor, who sat in silence gazing straight ahead. The promised storm of the previous evening had gone off in another direction: only a little extra breeze and motion had fallen to the *Asabo's* lot. The sea lay like a stretch of heaving silver with a broken, ragged edge that tossed and mingled into a sky of soft, transparent indigo. In the cloudless void the full round moon hung like a globe of brilliant whiteness and its cold, pure rays marked out the ship's deck into shapes and patches of black and white with startling, clear-cut distinctness.

For some time "The Babe" sat with hands clasped round one knee and eyes fixed on the peaceful scene, and then he said suddenly, "I like watching the moonlight. It's so jolly nice and clean-looking—pure and fresh and wholesome, like a drink of clear cold water. It knows just what's what—no talking round your hat with the moon. It draws a keen straight line and one side's white and the other black, and there's no mistake about it"—with a laugh—"I'm talking rot again. I do sometimes when I'm tired!"—then with ill-concealed anxiety—"Did I talk rot last night? I felt off my chump a bit at times."

"You were not at all 'off your chump' when Langfeldt came. When he left you asked me for a drink and that's as much as I can tell you."

There was a faint sigh of relief.

"I felt viciously inclined towards Langfeldt last night. I thought I might have raved at him and said something to hurt his feelings. He's a good sort and would not have mentioned it. Carl wants knowing to be appreciated. He's full of surprises. Full of surprises!"—slowly and thoughtfully.

The arrival of the whiskies aroused the youngster from a mental survey of the manifold virtues of his bosom friend: Sinclair proffered cigarettes with a choice of cigars and watched the slim fingers that picked out the former. "The Babe" was no novice at cigarette smoking; he neither choked nor coughed nor chewed the end into a hopeless pulp of sodden paper and wet tobacco. He went at it like a man, not as if it were a task to be completed in the shortest possible time, but with lingering enjoyment and a quiet sip of whisky in between. The absurdity of the situation brought Sinclair to the verge of hysteria. In spite of all efforts to the contrary he laughed.

A quick, suspicious glance was cast at him.

"Why are you braying like a full-blown ass?"

"I was thinking of the captain's face when you told him swearing was costly."

A dimple lurked in the corner of his companion's mouth.

"At first I was struck speechless with the honor of being invited to his cabin. I've traveled with old Morton a good many times during the last six years and such a thing had never happened before. I make a point of getting on his boat if possible; we understand each other and know what to expect. Last voyage up he brought me most of the way home in irons. A few of us came on board at Dwala, a trifle elated at returning to civilization. In the exuberance of our natural spirits, and a good addition from outside, we fired the saloon. I'm sorry to say it annoyed him and"—in

an injured tone—"he pounced on me as the ringleader. Kept me in
irons as far as Grand Canary! That's why I'm so smug and proper
this trip"—then with evident pride "I've been able to walk to my
cabin every night so far. That's a record"—contemplatively—"I
wonder if I shall be able to keep it up. Langfeldt pulls my leg no
end about it. He's got a bet on I shall be carried down before we
reach Canary, but I may surprise him yet," and "The Babe" smiled
with sweet innocence as he flicked the ash from his cigarette.

For some time there was silence and Sinclair watched his companion as the smile died away and an anxious, careworn look took
its place. He felt he must take this babe on his knee, make it put
its curly head against his shoulder, tell him all its troubles and let
him smooth them out. Then the youngster brightened up with the
obvious intention of doing the polite and indulging in small talk.

"It's your first trip to the coast, Major Sinclair?"—the remark
might have been either statement or question.

Sinclair knew "The Babe" had once looked upon him with suspicion, but his languid sleepy manner had worked successfully, for
after the first day the youngster had ceased to bother about him.

"Yes, why?"

"I thought so. There was a chap named Danvers answering to
your build birds' nesting up in Blenka's country a year or so ago.
Tall and broad, but sharp as a razor; no end keen-looking and eyes
like gimlets. The first might be you, but the second ain't though,"
and "The Babe" laughed.

The sleepy lids drooped a little more than usual. "What were
you doing in that ungodly part, youngster?"

"Picking primroses."

"The Babe" got up, refusing a second whisky.

"I guess I'll turn in now. It's a virtuous hour to retire, not ten
yet! But everybody says I'm looking seedy, so perhaps I need a little
beauty sleep."

Sinclair watched the slim figure as it went along the deck and a
weak voice echoed in his ears, "I can't keep up this killing pace
much longer. I can't! I can't!"

CHAPTER 5

"And I cannot break my oath, though to leave thee I am loth,
There is one that I must meet upon the moor."

ON THE SEVENTH DAY OUT from Liverpool the *Asabo* steamed slowly
into the harbor of Las Palmas, Grand Canary. Those of the passengers who had not visited the place before gathered on the upper
deck to view the island that lay basking in the broiling sun like an
inverted saucer of parched mud relieved here and there by a cluster of palms or a few white houses. The "Coasters" did not give it
more than a casual glance as they passed in to breakfast. To them
it was not altogether a happy sight, for it represented the last link
of civilization they would see for a period varying from eight
months to three years according to rank and position.

Immediately after breakfast Langfeldt & Co. gathered near the
gangway watching the departing passengers and discussing how
the day should be spent. The *Asabo* was not due to sail until the
small hours of the following morning. Perched on the rail, a cherub
in white drill, was "The Babe." There was an air of perturbedness
about him: it was evident he did not approve of Langfeldt's plan
for the disposal of the time on hand. His seemed to be the only
dissenting voice. The three others appeared to enjoy the situation
immensely. It was not often "The Babe" was nonplussed or got the
strings of his bow tangled; but it happened now. Since the moment of his arrival on board he had shown a decided preference
for Marjorie Sinclair's society. This, however, her brother had

prevented for the first day or so, then, much to Captain Morton's disgust and the amazement of the most select clique, he had ceased to interfere, it might even be said he encouraged intimacy between the two. A strong friendship—flirtation the company at large called it—existed between Claude Wentworth and the major's pretty sister. Behind his hand Carl Langfeldt smiled, and now, the morning of the *Asabo's* arrival at Grand Canary, he launched his bomb. It appeared a certain young lady, one Rosetta Millon, was staying in the island. "The Babe" did not seem so anxious to see her as the German assured him she would be to see him, and added to the youngster's discomfiture and the mirth of his companions by remarking on the virtue and necessity of being "off with the old before being on with the new."

"The Babe" sat on the rail and whistled dolefully, wondering how he could escape this undesired young person without creating suspicion.

"I thought she'd left the island months ago," he said in an injured tone.

The German grinned.

"She wrote to me some time since, telling me all you had promised, etc., etc., and had not done. Did I know your address? She seemed rather wroth. I wrote back saying you were on the chronic move and I couldn't say where you were. Also that you were returning this way very soon and she had better wait here and interview you personally."

"The Babe" rubbed his chin and looked at Langfeldt viciously.

"You villain! Why didn't you write back and say I was dead?"

"I didn't want to break the poor girl's heart. Oh, Babe! you'll get your curly head combed this time, and more than ever if she hears of sweet Marjorie."

Then "The Babe" swore—swore with a length and strength of adjective that surprised and for the moment disconcerted Sinclair who, coming slowly and quietly along, heard Langfeldt's last remark and the youngster's lurid and fancy reply. When the latter paused for breath before plunging into deeper and more fiery depths, he saw his cabin-mate beside him. His astonishment and dismay were such that he nearly fell from his perch backwards into the sea. Only Sinclair's hand grabbing his shoulder with a quickness entirely out of keeping with his usual languid movements saved that babe from an unexpected douche.

"I hope you haven't made your arrangements for the day, Wentworth. We're driving into the country to where my sister is staying and she wants you to join us. We're starting at once; the carriage is waiting on the quay."

"No, I hadn't fixed anything up yet. It's jolly decent of your sister to ask me and I shall be very pleased to come"—perhaps how pleased no one but "The Babe" knew.

As he slipped off the rail Langfeldt said, "Ta-ta, Claude. I'll give your love to Rosetta, but I expected she'll be looking you up personally before the day is out."

Claude made no reply but went along by Sinclair's side, it might almost be said, subduedly. It was very apparent something troubled his mind.

Presently he said, "I don't often let off steam like that, but Langfeldt had played me no end of a lowdown trick and it riled me."

"Were you letting off steam? I hadn't noticed."

"The Babe" smiled again. Since the night when the two had partaken of whiskies and cigarettes together their friendship had increased apace. The same thing had occurred the following evening and then Langfeldt came along and induced the major to join in a quiet game of cards. Sinclair submitted to the plucking process with a graceful ease. The youngster watched and felt rather sorry. The next night, when at the termination of their drink the German came along, he tried to put in a hint; but "the sleepy-looking josser" was so dense and went like a lamb to the slaughter. "The Babe" did not play but watched with big, sad eyes. Sinclair would have willingly paid a much higher price to have his cabinmate sitting against him taking such a heart-felt interest in his welfare.

"The Babe" was in high spirits during the drive. He knew the country by heart and was a veritable guide-book. He sat, as befitting his masculine gender, by Sinclair's side on the smaller and less comfortable seat of the carriage. Whilst he talked and laughed with Marjorie the look of anxiety left the back of his eyes. Sinclair registered a vow not to let this one small babe out of his sight, to follow it up to the end of its journey and keep it out of harm. He had started this voyage with the intention of searching for and classifying rare birds, and on the way had found one he once fancied would never fall to his lot. He wanted to catch it without frightening or hurting it or even ruffling its feathers; to hold it in his hands, feel its heart beat and teach it to take things from his lips. He would have to go about it very warily; it was such a cheeky, saucy little bird. Such a daring young customer that it might get hurt in the snaring.

At lunch and dinner that day Claude Wentworth seemed to forget his reputation. He refused all strong drink and showed Marjorie how to make an excellent "kid-reviver" out of ripe oranges, soda-water, sugar and ice, taken at a certain given angle through two straws. He was "off" smokes too, forgot to whistle, and once or twice neglected to retrieve Marjorie's tennis balls, when during the afternoon they had a set together. Her brother rectified the latter error as he watched them in his usual indolent manner. By-and-by "The Babe" let him do all the running about for both himself and his opponent. Mrs. Onslow remarked to her nephew that she could not understand how it was the boy had such an unsavory reputation. It was a pity he had got in with bad companions; and being a kind-hearted woman with no children she made her nephew promise to look after him and use his influence towards the youngster's ultimate regeneration.

At ten o'clock that evening when "The Babe" took his farewell of Marjorie he held both her hands in his and said, "Don't forget you've promised to wear the golden centipede always. Don't give it away to anyone, or ever be a moment without it until you get back to England."

As the carriage started its four hours' drive back to the port the youngster sighed.

"This is the jolliest day I've had since I don't know when," he said, drawing out his cigarette-case and borrowing a match from his companion.

Richard was himself again.

When they reached the *Asabo*, only a few minutes before it started, a sleepy steward informed "The Babe" that a Miss Millon had been on board to see him and had waited some considerable time, until midnight, in fact, and had left a note. He read the heated epistle and thanked his stars for a lucky escape—Rosetta was as cute as the devil and would have spotted him in a minute.

The approaching atmosphere of West Africa appeared to have a very deteriorating effect on Major the Hon. Tracy Sinclair. He neglected his former companions and consorted more and more with "The Babe" and his ill-conditioned few. Langfeldt approved of this heartily and made a steady income out of him. Claude sighed often and thought, "The sleepy-looking josser was no end of a good sort, but very innocent-like and not capable of looking after himself in such a wild and sharp-fingered community." When Sinclair played too recklessly the youngster would come and take him gently by the arm and lead him away from further temptation. The German did not mind; it kept the victim from getting suspicious and privately he applauded Claude on his tactics. In the seclusion of his cabin Morton shook his head over Sinclair and thought he had never been so deceived in a man; but he had seen many a good sort led astray by that fascinating young reprobate of a Wentworth.

A week after leaving Grand Canary the *Asabo* reached Sierra Leone and then continued its voyage slowly down the coast, landing one here and two there, until on reaching Old Calabar only "The Babe," his friends and Sinclair were left on board. At this place the latter went ashore with the object of gathering together sufficient porters to carry the paraphernalia necessary in the sport of bird-hunting. He came back with a scratch-looking lot of about thirty. Langfeldt remarked that if he had searched the whole of the coast he could not have found a more mangy set of niggers. No doubt about it, Major Sinclair was a fool! Strange as it may seem, when the *Asabo* left Calabar, thirty of the smartest men in the local Hausa regiment were missing, and more curious still the officers appeared not to notice their desertion.

One thing Sinclair had not learnt was "The Babe's" destination. Langfeldt & Co. were landing at Dwala, the capital of the German

Cameroon. The youngster had paid his passage to the far end of
the journey, some five hundred miles farther on, and said he would
get off when the spirit moved him.

Early in the afternoon after leaving Calabar the *Asabo* steamed
carefully over the mud bar and entered Rio del Rey, the southernmost of the oil rivers. The scene was typically West African—a weird
stretch of mangrove swamp and mud as far as the eye could reach.
A veritable nightmare of a place. All around was a tangled mass of
bush, creeks and foul lagoons, the home of crocodiles and the
dreaded malaria fever. The heat was sweltering and an overpow-
ering smell came in gusts from the poisonous swamps around. The
mangrove was a fitting tree for this scene of desolation; tall and
gaunt with coarse, leathery leaves and bleached roots starting some
two feet above the slime, like skeleton hands grasping the mud.
Thin white shoots came from the branches, straight as a. plumb-
line to within a foot of the water and then split up into groups of
thick fingerlike aerial roots. The foliage formed a home for scores
of noxious insects. Among the roots dwelt loathsome hairy crabs,
blowing great bubbles and watching the passing vessel with uncanny waving eyes. There were openings between the closely growing mangroves; narrow waterways, dim and ghostly, shadowed by
the meeting branches and a mass of matted creepers. On the mud
banks huge crocodiles slept; others floundered in the black, slimy
water that oozed down to the main stream. A few "dug-outs" (canoes), made from the hollowed-out trunks of trees and propelled
by scantily-clad, wild-looking savages occasionally passed along
the darkened waterways, bound for some squalid village away in
the midst of the swamp.

The *Asabo* proceeded slowly, often touching the soft mud bottom, and worked its way with great caution through the difficult
channels of the river. Very often the vessel was within a few feet of
the mud banks; occasionally the rigging caught in and shook the
boughs of the overhanging trees and a shower of foul and repel-
lent insects fell on the deck. Here and there was a tiny patch of
sand with a few palms and a profusion of beautiful ferns with

perhaps the addition of a solitary hut, a frail structure of bamboo interlaced with coarse grass and thatched with palm leaves.

For some hours the vessel proceeded on through this scene and eventually anchored in what appeared to be a lake surrounded by mangroves, for neither the entrance nor the continuation of the river were visible. The still heavy air was impregnated by the stench of the fever-giving swamp, and the silence engendered by the excessive heat only broken by the harsh grating screams of flocks of grey parrots flying towards their roosting quarters. There was no sign of civilization there beyond two trading factories, one on the English and the other on the German side of the river. They were built on piles in the slime, like tin arks in a waste of mud.

It was sunset when the *Asabo* anchored. Already the brief twi-light was waning and the stealthy night mist crept in patches and long streaks like uncertain, giant, fevered hands, out to where the vessel swung at ease. Standing on the upper deck with anxious eyes fixed on the German side was "The Babe." One slim forefinger was rubbing up and down the rail in a gradually lengthening straight line. The youngster's whole attention was on a spot to the left of the factory; a ghostly, mist-wreathed water-way that looked as if it might lead straight to hell. A strong, sinewy hand laid suddenly on the rail stopped the finger's perambulations. "The Babe" looked up with a start, then down at the finger and hand side by side, touching in fact, and drew it away hastily. It was a very soft touch and a very small finger, yet it made the whole of Sinclair tingle.

"Admiring the view, Wentworth?"

"Yes; it's not beautiful, but it has a charm of it own. The attrac-tion of the fantastic, grotesque and unknown. It's like the Styx; you want to know what lies beyond it. It always reminds me of a bit of the world God forgot to separate when the water and earth took shape to themselves, and has been forgotten ever since. It's peopled with vile, uncanny things that don't grow in other parts. We've a saying out here that there are only three feet of earth be-tween West Africa and hell. I believe it too, yes, I believe it!"—passionately.—"It's an uncanny place. The devil's own land! It has

an awful fascination, like all evil things have. Once you get into it
you can't leave it. You have to come again and again until you
finally slip through. We've been 'Coasters,' all our lot, for generations and generations, and we're bad. Rotten! Rotten as the country! Rotten through and through! I was born out here—had a black
mammy for a foster-mother. All the mother I ever had! Lived out
here until I was twelve like a wild piccaninny. Then they sent me
to a school in England. Kept me there for nearly five years; I played
hell the whole time. They said I was the very devil—I believe they
pray for me there still. A lot of good that will do! We're past praying for—have been for generations—since an old ancestor sold himself and posterity to the devil. The devil keeps him to his bargain
and—"

"The Babe" broke off abruptly with a conscious air of having
let himself go a bit too far. The nervous forefinger started its per-
ambulating again.

"I'm talking endless rot, but you're such a sleepy sort of chap I
like to see how many lies you'll take in without opening your eyes.
I've told you a good many and you suck them up like a sponge. And
once I thought you might be the sharp-eyed josser who was prowling round in Blenka's country," and "The Babe" laughed at its own
foolishness.

Darkness fell like the dropping of a blind. Out of the swamp came
the sudden, ear-piercing shriek of the tree-devil. Weird and long
and flesh-creeping, like a woman being slowly tortured to death.

The youngster started and then said, "That brute always gives
me the creeps. Everybody says a sloth-like little beast makes that
awful yell; yet no one has ever caught it at it. The niggers say it's
old Nick himself."

Presently, a second time, the hideous, awful wail cut through
the thick darkness. "The Babe" shivered and stood with both hands
clasping the rail. Shivered and waited. For a third time, commenc-
ing like a long, panting moan, then louder, now dying away to a
sigh, then with a tortured, agonising scream the thing wailed and
sobbed. Sinclair shuddered as the pain-stricken cries echoed and
re-echoed through the murky darkness and died away in one final

shriek of agony. The youngster's hands dropped. He turned away and rang the deck-bell for a steward.

"I guess I'll order two cocktails."

Side by side they sipped their before-dinner drinks. "The Babe" was unusually quiet. Generally he chattered nineteen to the dozen and Sinclair answered in sleepy grunts, occasionally summoning up sufficient energy to drawl out a sentence.

"That brute has given you the blues, youngster," he said at length.

His companion came back to earth with a start.

"Yes; it has a bit. It reminds me of a lot of things. It's funny how we two have got so pally. You're the sleepiest josser I ever met, and I'm the sharpest rogue in these parts. I've done a lot of thinking this trip. Generally I go on the booze and it stops all that sort of thing, but I had to lie low this journey; I'd been going the pace a bit too much and for the price of two pins old Morton would clap me in irons. He has had his orb on me the whole time waiting for the ghost of an excuse, but so far I've surprised him. I'm certain to break out soon though"—then confidentially—"Have you ever noticed how things alter when you get older? What seems no end of a lark when you're seventeen changes its shape and looks quite different when you're twenty-two. What seemed square and all right then, gets a funny wavering look and leaves you wondering."

The youngster stopped with a sigh. Sinclair watched the small, thoughtful face and felt he must take this one foolish babe, wrap it up in a rug and send it back to England and safety. He wanted to hold it in his arms and tell it all sorts of things, but he knew this would only scare it and he might lose it altogether. He must follow it on and when the mystery was solved try and entice it into his trap.

His companion finished the cocktail with the air of a connoisseur and then got up.

"I guess I'll go and have a wash and brush up before dinner."

Sinclair stayed on deck until the gong aroused him. On entering the saloon he went to his accustomed place, sat down and glanced across at "The Babe's" table. The youngster's seat was empty. For some time he waited with ever-increasing nervousness.

"Where's young Wentworth?" he asked presently.

Morton looked across with a grunt.

"Left the vessel, I expect, like he always does, for some vile negro orgies away in the swamp. I'm due to sail at four a.m. tomorrow, and if he's not on board then I'm hanged if I'll wait a minute for him."

Sinclair's dinner suddenly seemed to choke him. An icy hand clutched at his heart and the tortured, wailing moans he had heard earlier in the evening rang and echoed in his head. He left the saloon and went on deck. Somewhere out in the savage waste, swallowed up in the blackness, was that child! The night was full of low, spiteful hissings. The red lamp at the foot of the gangway cast a ghastly sheen on the thick, oozing water. From the side streams came the hoarse bellow and splash of floundering crocodiles. Uncanny whisperings and rustlings filled the surrounding bush. The lights of the two trading stations gleamed like eyes in the darkness. Wafted faintly on the breeze that blew from the English side came the strains of a wheezy, hoarse-voiced gramophone, and it played a coon song—"Ma Curly-headed Babby." He groaned. Whilst he had been sitting there dreaming of her, that daring little girl had slipped through his fingers!

Until three the next morning he paced the deck with strained eyes watching every shadow on the water, listening for and starting at every sound. Presently out of the darkness came the splash of native paddles; a tiny canoe loomed up from the mist and made for the gangway. In the shadow he watched, afraid to show himself lest "The Babe" should suspect. A moment or so later a slim figure in white drill and floppy felt hat came up the steps and disappeared along the lower deck. He breathed again; then he went below cautiously and retired without noise, conscious of faint sounds in the adjoining cabin denoting "The Babe's" presence.

The next morning at breakfast Sinclair was helping himself leisurely to iced fruit when the captain's voice made him glance round with a suddenness unusual to him.

"Young Wentworth looks as if he had been on the tiles last night."

Sinclair was conscious of his hands shaking as he watched the figure entering the saloon. It was the same slight graceful form, small hands and feet, mop of chestnut curls, saucy smile and lurking dimple, but over the whole a subtle air of dissipation. In the dark blue eyes that met his so coolly was not the anxious look he knew so well, but behind them the devil sat and smiled. Morton's voice droned on in his ear.

"I've noticed that with the young skunk before. He'll behave himself quite decently for a time, but one night's orgies among the niggers and there's hell to pay. Last voyage home I had him in irons to Grand Canary. I let him out there prepared for any devilment when he returned. It did him good; he behaved himself quite decently for the rest of the way home and this trip out too—but look out for squalls now!"

No one unless in Sinclair's hypersensitive condition would have noticed the difference. In a quick sharp shuffle in the dark, someone had taken his queen of hearts and left him with the knave of spades. He studied "The Babe" at the opposite table and knew he was dealing with no ordinary rogue. He felt he had met his match this time and the knowledge of his loss made his hands shaky.

What had that smiling young devil done with his sister?

CHAPTER 6

"Is my secret known to thee?"

To SINCLAIR THE BREAKFAST seemed never-ending. He endeavored to wade through the dishes in his habitual dawdling manner and take his usual sleepy interest in Morton's pet subject—the manifold sins and wickednesses of "that young skunk"—conscious the whole time of the latter's close scrutiny. The young fiend had calmly left his sister in the midst of a "ju-ju"-haunted swamp. Those three yells last night had been the signal. Now he understood her silence afterwards! Why had he not thought of it sooner? How those tortured cries rang in his head! Those and the dull monotonous thump of the engines whose every turn took him farther away from the child. He had intended to follow her on and if possible catch the brother red-handed. Now he had been out-witted and the only clue to her whereabouts lay with the young villain opposite.

As Sinclair watched the face so like the one he had loved since the night of his amazing discovery, he had his first lesson in fear, and of the very worst sort; not the fear that shakes for itself but that trembles for the fate of another; the sort that squeezes all blood from the heart and sends an icy chill to the marrow. There was not one sin in the whole human category that smiling young devil would stop at.

"The Babe" looked up suddenly, caught his fixed gaze (Sinclair's loss had left him with not quite such a good grip of himself as usual) and smiled across at him—a shy little smile that had sometimes

54

fallen to his lot when they had been alone together and "Claude" Wentworth had for the moment forgotten his reputation. He was conscious of "The Babe's" renewed scrutiny; the shy little smile became broader and the blue eyes twinkled with a wickedness that had not been in the others. Sinclair wondered whether the devil's son suspected him of having learnt his double game or whether he had recognized him as the man who had visited Blenka's country?

The grumbling remark of the first mate, "One of the nigger deck-hands deserted last night," made Sinclair, "The Babe," and Langfeldt glance up as one man.

Then the youngster's attention wandered to the German and the devil behind his eyes grew very thoughtful. Langfeldt looked at "The Babe" and his glance was blatantly perplexed. In the deep and kindly interest these two friends suddenly evinced for each other, Sinclair's look of inquiry passed unnoticed.

The breakfast came to an end at last. Sinclair went on deck like one dazed. Every plank and portion of the vessel had some tender recollection—every day of the last month stood out sharp and clear, every little incident and word that had passed between them. With a groan he leant on the rail. Behind, like an ominous black cloud on the horizon, was Rio del Rey; ahead, a green dome in the sea of sparkling blue, the island of Fernando Po. How the whole scene mocked him! In the black swamp behind that stretched for hundreds of miles, a maze of undiscovered ways, was his little girl swallowed up in the ghastly waste! To go back would be madness. The only thing was to follow the young villain until he did what had been done before—met and substituted his sister for himself. The chief mate's words haunted him. He thought of the doom that had been proclaimed; of the rope thrown across the slender arm; the thud of bare feet directly afterwards and the form that had disappeared into the darkness. His mind went back to the first day on board—the negro's look at Marjorie, the gift of the centipede, the ringing, defiant laugh and the answering scowl. What did it all mean? Why had the nigger followed her—his little Chrysanthe? He stood with drawn, haggard face and eyes on the distant, shadowy land until a voice roused him.

"Shall we do these photographs now, Major Sinclair?"

The powerful hand on the rail tightened and the knuckles stood out clear and white on the surrounding brown. It was his own babe's voice speaking, but through it ran an under-current of devilish laughter. Only yesterday afternoon they had taken those snapshots of the river! He was a skilled photographer; Chrysanthe only a novice, and since the *Asabo's* arrival in African waters one of their daily amusements had been the taking and developing of these same negatives. Now this smiling young demon was asking his help just in the way his sister used to do. He had wanted to develop them straight away yesterday afternoon, but the little girl had proposed leaving them until the morning and he had wondered why the round, childish face flushed when she made the suggestion.

With an effort Sinclair pulled himself together and answered in his usual manner, conscious of being narrowly watched.

"I'm ready any time, youngster. Go along and fetch the things; I'll see to the water palaver."

All morning they sat with the solutions and water between them, in the throes of daylight development, printing and fixing. "The Babe" chattered away as usual, but without the occasional and quickly suppressed little bursts of confidence that had lately marked their conversations, and watched him with a disconcerting sharpness. Sinclair noticed when his companion splashed about in the water he did not turn his left sleeve up quite as far as usual and knew why: beyond was not the faint red scar, and he wondered if farther still lay a giant centipede. Now and again "The Babe's" hand was laid impulsively on his arm. Once upon a time the touch had thrilled him; now it left him with a desire to choke the owner. Claude Wentworth had studied his sister to a nicety and knew her every action and movement.

The developing over, Sinclair issued his customary before-luncheon cocktail invitation. This was readily accepted. Lately his babe had refused and he had not pressed or remarked on it. Evidently although she had apprised her brother of their friendship she had not gone into fullest details. It pleased Sinclair that she should not have done so. This was the only slip "The Babe" made during the morning.

Lunch was over when the *Asabo* dropped anchor in the harbor of Fernando Po. There seemed an unusual stir in the town and the attitude of the natives towards the British flag was the reverse of friendly. A minute steam launch came snorting indignantly out to where the vessel swung shimmering in the broiling sun. Claude Wentworth sat on the rail and smiled. Captain Morton went forward to meet the two irate, gold-plated individuals who came up the gangway as quickly as their circumference and the heat would allow. It appeared they desired information concerning the whereabouts of someone, at present unknown, but undoubtedly a British subject, who a week ago, single-handed, had removed from the treasury of the local cathedral goods to the value of five hundred pounds in gold and jewels. The thief—may he burn for ever!—answered in description to the one who had headed several ivory raids in other parts of their territory. In appearance he was slight, height not more than five feet six, wore white drill clothing, a floppy felt hat and a black mask.

"The Babe" sat on the rail and listened with a hurt look as he rolled a cigarette backwards and forwards between his hands.

"Lord! it might be me," he said presently, gazing at Morton with the innocence of an angel. "There's some villain down here playing the deuce with my reputation. Major Sinclair here has come to hunt him out, and a very good thing too! I'm surprised the British Government didn't take it up sooner. That sort of thing breeds no end of ill-feeling between the two countries. A chap of his description ought not to be allowed a free range in these parts. He's a shy bird though and on the chronic hop. It's damned hard lines I should answer to his description so neatly; it keeps me out of tip-top society altogether."

Whilst he was speaking, a stout old monk, who had some difficulty in negotiating the perilous and uncertain void that parted the bobbing boat's side and the swaying gangway, appeared on deck. His eyes fell on the figure perched on the rail: he gasped, choked, fought for breath and his fat red face assumed an alarmingly apoplectic look. "The Babe" slipped off the rail and going quickly to him gave him several vigorous and friendly claps on the back which only added to his discomfiture.

"Madre de Dios! This is the man!" he blurted out, overcome by his own emotions and the youngster's sturdy pummelings.

Two gold-plated individuals swung round and a moment afterwards Claude Wentworth was in the grip of the Spaniard. A hot, unfriendly hand grasped him by each shoulder.

"I say, don't do that, you'll spoil my nice clean clothes. Captain, tell them to take their greasy paws off."

Much as Morton disliked and distrusted "The Babe," and though it went against the grain to say it, he had to give evidence to Claude Wentworth being on his vessel in Forcados River when the robbery took place. The Spaniards seemed inclined to doubt his word; thereupon he was very wroth and consigned those two officials to a much hotter place than West Africa. "The Babe" translated the captain's good wishes into excellent Spanish with an even freer flow of adjective. Relations between the two nations were very strained for the next few minutes; there was danger of an immediate outbreak of hostilities. But it was the word of one monk against an entire ship's company. They retired, silenced but not convinced. The youngster saw them off the premises; regretting his likeness to the man they sought and sorry to be so disobliging as to have been so far away at the time of the outrage. He helped the ancient priest into the bobbing boat with really loving care.

Sinclair listened to it all longing to give his version; but the fact that the clue to his little girl's whereabouts lay in the young villain's hands, kept him silent.

At dinner that evening Captain Morton was in high dudgeon. He was not fond of quarrelling with port officials. Things can be made very uncomfortable thereby.

"I swear the young skunk was at the bottom of it," he grumbled. "He planned it out and left some trusted lieutenant to carry on his nefarious designs. The greatest pleasure of my life would be to sling him up to the yardarm."

This and much more Sinclair listened to, having never thor-
oughly understood or appreciated Morton's ardent dislike for the
youngster until now. He glanced across at the opposite table where
"The Babe" was drinking large and long "King's pegs" in competition with Langfeldt. The former caught his eye and hailed him.

"I said I couldn't be good for much longer. I've been on a milk
diet over long. We're all getting off very soon, every man jack of
us, aren't we, Carl? Then good-bye to home and all kind friends
for we've to sweat and stew for Schmutz & Co. Morton would never
forgive me if he hadn't the pleasure of putting at least one black
mark against my name this trip. I'm a kind-hearted chap and hate
disappointing people. It cut me to the quick to disappoint those
Spanish johnnies: they seemed so cocksure they'd nabbed the right
man"—then lifting his glass and smiling at Sinclair—"Here's to the
girl I left behind me!"

Langfeldt & Co. roared. Sinclair heard Marjorie's name whispered, also that of Rosetta, with much chaff. He knew "The Babe"
meant neither of these, but, having recognized him and guessed
his mission, was anxious to find out how much he knew, if anything. The youngster watched him narrowly and then laughed.

After dinner he invited "The Babe" to the customary drink.
Claude sat with twinkling eyes and talked as usual, inwardly thinking his sister a bigger fool than he had imagined her to be for not
recognizing the man he had spotted in a minute. True, she had only
his description to go by, and Major the Hon. Tracy Sinclair did not
altogether tally with the big, keen-looking chap who, under the
name of Danvers, had been making uncomfortable inquiries concerning him in Blenka's country. He watched Sinclair speculatively
and felt he still had the ace of trumps hidden up his sleeve.

Late that night a scrimmage just outside his cabin door aroused
Sinclair from his anxious musings. There was a steward's voice
mildly expostulate, another that in its cups lapsed back into German and a third that even through its drunken hiccough reminded
him of the one he had lost.

"Steward," it hiccoughed, "why shouldn't a man walk on all
foursh if he wanth? I'll race you, old chap, up an down the corridor.

Go and fetch the captain, he can be umpire. Carl here will hold the stakes; honest sort; wouldn't take a penny that wasn't his, would you, old man?"

Again came the steward's voice imploring something he evidently upheld to go to bed quietly.

"Must I go to bed? Well, good-bye, Carl, shake handsh; you'd never go back on a pal, would you? Good-night and good-bye again. I bet you all the drinksh you can carry you can't walk down the aisle and pick out your own pew first shot."

A roar of drunken laughter and then heavy clumsy feet went uncertainly down the corridor and tumbled into a cabin about half-a-dozen doors away.

"Never mind, steward, he's tumbled into the wrong crib. Let him stay there, poor devil, he's tired and so am I. I'll go to bed like a good boy. I've been a treat this trip, haven't I? First time I've needed your arm. Good-night, steward. God bless you! Best friend I ever had bar one."

Someone was escorted into, and then dumped on the floor of the adjacent cabin and stayed there in silence. Sinclair lay listening. For the next hour all was quiet save for the occasional deep and sodden snores of his neighbor. Presently they ceased and there were slight movements as "The Babe" apparently in stocking feet, opened the cabin door with an ease and lack of noise that spoke of recent oiling, and then went stealthily along to the cabin where Langfeldt was sleeping off the effects of his late carouse. Sinclair sat up with every sense alert and ears strained for any sound. After a time came the quick metallic click of a latch and then all was silent except for the sudden sharp creaks of the vessel and the occasional slam of some distant open door. For quite half-an-hour he waited and then he heard the soft sounds of unshod feet and a moment or two later the next cabin was occupied. There was a sharp click, a rustle of papers, another sharp click and then someone climbed into the upper berth with surprising agility considering the condition he had been in less than two hours previously. Sinclair lay awake and thoughtful, wondering if he would ever fathom the mystery, and if so, at what cost?

It was a little after daybreak when the *Asabo* steamed into the Cameroon river. As Sinclair came on deck the imposing Mungo Mah Lobeh, the highest mountain on the western side of Africa and one of the highest peaks in the whole continent, met his gaze. It rose sheer out of the sea to a height of nearly fourteen thousand feet. A striking and magnificent sight after the low shores and foul mangrove swamps usually comprising West African scenery. The vivid light of coming day touched the silent, snow-capped peak and trickled and ran in tiny red streams down the mountainside. It was only the fantastic playing light, the brilliant rays creeping out from the east, yet the effect was ghastly. It brought back the uncanny, eerie feeling of the first evening. He had come on deck early because his lost little girl had so often spoken of the beauties of "The Throne of Thunder," as the picturesque native name ran. He watched the flickering, lurid beams and a cool, soothing breeze reached him from the white heights, pure and cleansing, different from the ordinary swamp stench. It cleared his head and took away the dazed feeling that had been with him since the previous morning. His glance wandered to the north-east. On the skyline stretched the deep, trackless forest reaching away to the unknown, to the very heart of Africa. Somewhere, hundreds of miles inland, on the uncertain boundary dividing German territory from Nigeria, lay Blenka's land. To the north-east of that, belted round by a waste of unexplored country, was a silent, wooded hill, a green cone against the blue sky. On the topmost height, like a colossal fist rising out from a cuff of green, with an immense forefinger pointing to the heavens, was a mystic peak. Sometimes clear cut against the blue sky, it pointed to so menacingly, now blood red in the lurid sunset, or mist-wreathed and hidden when the clouds lay low on the land. Often, from a range of hills more than fifty miles away, he had watched it, wondering what secret lay within the clenched hand. The gloomy, tangled, lifeless, waste of matted forest and swamp surrounding it had baffled him. He could never reach it. It was one big "ju-ju" mountain—the devil's hand stretched out from hell—the natives told him.

An old legend, whispered to him one night over a convivial cup in the hut of a friendly and loquacious chief, came back to him—

"Arru! But the white man had seen it? He had traveled even to the edge of the great 'ju-ju' forest? It lay right in the depths, a distance of six good marching days. In the time of his father's fathers, told by their grandfathers and back into the mist of ages (Sinclair calculated something like three hundred years), there was a time, whisper it low, when that awesome hill was not. But there was one walking in the country, someone whom the devil wanted but who came not, someone who was even the colour of this stranger! Arru! but it was so! Then one night the earth moved as with a violent pushing underneath and behold when daylight dawned, that giant hand! These many moons it had waited, and was waiting! It was not good to dwell in the shadow of that hand. Would that the devil's fist would claim its own and the blighting curse be taken off the country!"

Sinclair stood musing and thinking over the old legend until the breakfast gong roused him. On entering the saloon he noticed Langfeldt coming along. There was an unusually anxious look about him, as of one suddenly apprised of the illness of a near and dear friend. They seated themselves at their respective tables awaiting the arrival of "The Babe." The meal went slowly through its courses but he did not appear. Presently Langfeldt sent a steward to inquire as to his whereabouts. After some considerable time during which the German's anxious air grew apace, the man reappeared. Claude Wentworth was not in his cabin and he could not be found anywhere on board the boat. For a moment the German seemed stunned, then the saloon resounded with lengthy and vigorous oaths, German-English edition.

Sinclair sat dazed. In the darkness of the night, when the *Asabo* had slowed up to negotiate some difficult river passage, the second "Babe" had slipped through his fingers!

CHAPTER 7

"Where has he gone? or far or near?
Good sooth, 'twere somewhat hard to say."

A WEEK LATER SINCLAIR SAT on the veranda of the governor's bungalow still wrapped in the cloud of thought that had enveloped him
since Claude Wentworth's disappearance. On the balcony of
Schmutz & Co.'s factory, rather more than a mile away, Carl
Langfeldt sat similarly affected.

"The Babe's" mode of departure had been explained. The *Asabo*
had slowed up off the little town of Victoria, that lay just at the
mouth of the river, to deposit a passenger taken on at Fernando
Po. One of the sailors had seen a half-decked native canoe come
alongside, but thinking it had only come to do some trading with
the nigger deck passengers, had not troubled to mention it. By the
time the youngster's absence was discovered the craft had disappeared. It may have slipped down one of the numerous creeks and
landed him immediately, or it may have gone on up the river where
it would soon be lost among others of its sort. One thing was certain, Claude Wentworth was no longer among his friends and nothing had been seen or heard of him. Meanwhile two men sat in the
town of Dwala, each waiting for the other to move first.

Sinclair thought over the conditions of the case: so far the game
was about equal. Although he alone knew the secret of "The Babe's"
successful alibis, the latter had recognized him and guessing his
purpose would be more wary than ever. He felt confident some new

scheme was afoot; something quite different from the usual dep-
redations; some private deal of the young villain's of which
Langfeldt alone had an inkling, and this worthy had in some way
overreached himself. "The Babe's" duplicate had discovered this
and come out to warn her brother; with the result that Langfeldt
was now left in the lurch. He was fully aware of the German's continued presence in the town; also of his sudden and violent dislike
for his former friend and ally. The cause of their quarrel interested
him greatly, he felt pretty certain the youngster had abstracted
papers of considerable value from the German; the episode of the
last night on the boat and Langfeldt's attitude the following morning pointed to it. Probably the lack of these caused the latter's long
stay in Dwala.

Sinclair sat ruminating on the shady veranda, and he felt the
best course he could take was to wait until Langfeldt moved and
then follow. At least the German knew two things, his, Sinclair's,
object, and some of his late friend's future intentions.

When the cool breeze that hails approaching sunset blew up
from the sea, Sinclair rose for his accustomed afternoon stroll.
Curiously enough his steps always turned in the same direction—
towards Schmutz & Co.'s factory. Just opposite the premises a
couple of loafing niggers were playing a game with a wooden board
and some beans. He glanced at them in passing, but they continued their occupation apparently oblivious of his gaze. Langfeldt
was still at home. He sauntered on to the native town, through rows
of palm-thatched huts built on foot-high mud platforms. In front
of each the evening meal was cooking over a stick fire. Every second interior boasted a highly colored print of the Kaiser and
Kaiserin, an elaborately carved wooden stool and a well-burnished
frying pan hanging on the wall for "dandy" (ornament), not use. A
circular route through an avenue of palms brought him to the bungalow again. He strolled on under the shade of some magnificent
mango trees whose cools dark leaves were set off by the flaming
red of the acacias that blossomed by the side of them. To the left
was a patch of squalid, oozing swamp and in the middle of it, tall,
straight and pure against the surrounding foulness, was a white

lily. For a long time Sinclair stood looking at it. Its roots were deep in the mire that gave it life and support; yet in spite of the filth it sprang from it was in no way tainted. Something hidden in its lower leaves moved, and a moment afterwards, a loathsome, hairy crab looked at him with spiteful eyes. The sight annoyed him. Picking up a stone he threw it at the creature. His aim, usually so true, missed and hit the flower's fragile stalk. The pure white head dropped and slowly it sank into the mud. The crab scuttled away, lost in its native element. He continued his walk, but the lily he had accidentally destroyed because of the vile creature hiding in its flowing green skirts haunted him for a long time.

A few more turns brought him once more in the vicinity of Schmutz & Co.'s bungalow. Langfeldt came out of a corrugated-iron shed close at hand which was shop and depot in one. He greeted Sinclair with unusual friendliness and invited him to come up and try a special lot of whisky that had come out by the *Asabo* and had only just been rescued from the grasping officials, at a "dash" (coast parlance = gift) of three bottles in the dozen.

Schmutz & Co.'s prosperity was not shown in the bungalow or its appointments. It was a battered old wooden place with a leaky-looking tin roof, surrounded by a wide balcony reached by rickety steps. Its furniture consisted of a few dilapidated wicker chairs, a couple of warped tables, a parrot, a bunch of bananas, and a bell. Sinclair seated himself in the most weight-resisting of the chairs whilst Langfeldt clanged the bell. In response to its chimes an un-prepossessing black, attired in a dirty loincloth and a singlet to match, came loafing along from the back premises. Presently, with the aid of a reeking kerosene lamp, that appeared to attract all the winged inhabitants of the place, Sinclair sipped the whisky and pronounced it good. He knew Langfeldt wanted something more than his passing judgment on that drink. For a time nothing was said. One by one the lights of the distant dwellings sprang out of the darkness. Schmutz & Co. seemed singularly isolated. Even in West Africa, where much is forgiven, there was an un-savory odor about them and a general anxiety that the shadow of their dwellings should not fall on less successful and more scrupulous traders; or maybe the firm encouraged these uncommonly lonely sites. There was a lot went on in the dark round Schmutz & Co.

Sinclair glanced at his companion. So deep and earnest were his thoughts that the whisky stood untouched at his elbow, which was somewhat unusual. Suddenly without any preliminaries he unburdened his mind.

"You've come down here, Major Sinclair, to inquire into the ivory raids and one or two things of that sort?"

Considering "The Babe" during his brief stay on the *Asabo* had made Sinclair's business common property, it would be foolish to deny it, so he admitted it was so.

"Well, what I'm going to say is only supposition on my part, and for the reputation of the firm I represent I sincerely hope it will prove without foundation. I'm boss of the shipping department out here. What happens up country has nothing to do with me; my concern is to see all goods are shipped off to Hamburg. Wentworth, damn him!"—the viciousness of the German's voice pleased Sinclair—"is a trader up in the wilds. He's young for the job, but he knows the natives and the lingo as if he had lived with them all his life. Practically the whole of our up-country produce comes through his hands. But for that little slip of his over the 'Bacuto' mine, I should have no reason for doubting him. That sort of thing leaves a bad odor"—there was a virtuous look on the speaker's face, which, however, seemed a misfit. "Somehow I can't help connecting him with those ivory raids you've come to see about: I'm not going to say he heads them, because we have every proof to the contrary, but he has something to do with them. He knows as well as I do that the firm I represent would have nothing to do with goods other than legally procured. But it's funny how he always sends a big dose down here when the thing has fizzled out a bit. I feel it is my duty to give you every assistance in rooting out this villain who so resembles one of our best traders, and through this likeness the firm is getting into ill repute. The way Wentworth slipped off the boat makes things more suspicious. He must be well on his way up country by now, and we hadn't quite arranged a private little scheme of our own." Sinclair wondered what the scheme was, but refrained from asking. "He has a big depot somewhere up in the bush, this he runs with an assistant. I've never seen him: I'm not fond of inland traveling and, besides, it's not my palaver. My business is simply to cart goods to and from the steamers. Wentworth always sends his own nigger train down here with produce, a wild-looking set they are too! Now it strikes me if you got hold of his assistant you might get further details regarding various missing lots of ivory."

It struck Sinclair the "little scheme" referred to so casually was something fairly big to which "The Babe" alone held the key. For some reason he had fallen out with his one-time friend and ally and the German was anxious to retaliate.

After a few minutes' silence Sinclair said, "It would be a very good plan to get hold of Wentworth's assistant and hear what he has to say. It's no secret Schmutz & Co.'s reputation is far from the best. Any moment they may be given marching orders. All that's wanting is a direct proof of their being receivers of stolen goods and then—palaver set!"

"Yes, and out I go into the cold. They've done very well these last five years, in fact ever since Wentworth had charge of our up-country deals. Now if he's in any way connected with those raids it reflects on me. I bought the goods, unknowingly of course, but for all that there'll be the deuce to pay. I ought to have made more inquiries, etc., etc—ought not to have bought ivory from him without knowing where it came from. As if I had time to go into the history of every tusk that comes into the factory!"

"Where's Wentworth's place?"

"You're not the first to ask me that. I can't say exactly: somewhere about two hundred miles up country on the Nigerian side of the border. Last trip home I arranged to visit him concerning the little scheme I spoke of. He gave me a plan of the exact site; unfortunately I've mislaid it with—er—one or two other papers of which he alone has the duplicate."

Sinclair smiled to himself as he thought of "The Babe's" stealthy excursion the night of his sudden departure. He knew Langfeldt had only given his own version of the story and surmised he had tried to outwit his fellow-rogue and been found out. Personally he was just as anxious to find Claude Wentworth's headquarters as the German.

He took another sip of whisky and then said, "What do you propose doing?"

He guessed Langfeldt intended to take him up there, and then, if under threats "The Babe" did not return to their former arrangements, to give him into his, Sinclair's hands. He felt pretty certain the German knew enough of his late ally's dishonest dealings to effect his arrest.

Langfeldt examined the contents of his tumbler with great interest, finished the whisky at a gulp and then said, "We're both anxious to have our young friend once more in our midst."

Sinclair agreed it was so.

"Well, I happen to know it's not likely he'll be coming this way again; therefore I propose we pay him a surprise visit, and the sooner the better, before he moves too far inland."

"I thought you had mislaid the route leading to his place?"

"I can make a guess to within about thirty miles of the spot, and once there inquiries will soon lead us to his place; there are not so many Europeans in that part but what a description of our late young friend would soon find him. If he's not there, we'll follow him up—it's not the first time you've tracked people down in the wilds, I fancy, Major Sinclair. I alone know anything of Wentworth's up-country fixtures. He's not at all loquacious about family affairs. I promise you we shall be up there in a little more than a month. It will be rough traveling, but we can both stand that. I've lost the route; but the job he has done me out of will give me a keen scent for his trail."

Sinclair distrusted Langfeldt, but for the moment it was mutually beneficial to join forces. He knew that if the German and "The Babe" made up their differences they would shoot him with as much compunction as they would any bush fowl, but he would risk that for the pleasure of running the young villain to earth and finding out what he had done with his sister.

For a long time neither spoke. Langfeldt measured out another dose of whisky, watching his companion anxiously. If he went up there alone probably his late ally would shoot him, but threatening to unfold some of his transactions to Sinclair might bring him to reason. Single-handed he dared not move, not until he had those papers in his possession again; then he would carry out his frustrated designs. He pushed the whisky across to his neighbor. The latter helped himself with a lengthy care and precision which under the circumstances the German found trying.

"Well, Major Sinclair, do we take this little trip into the country together?"

"Considering we both want the same man it might prove a useful combination."

Of Langfeldt's approval of the decision there could be no doubt. Once Major Sinclair ceased to be useful he could easily be disposed of. But the other knew his man and it was not the first time he had joined forces with one rogue, at the risk of his own life, for the ultimate undoing of another.

The German fetched a map and marked on it, as well as he could remember, the supposed site of Wentworth's headquarters. Nine o'clock struck ere they parted company, both unaware that the dinner hour had long since passed.

With the next sunrise, Sinclair, accompanied by thirty porters, who when they got out of town fell at once into a swing that spoke of previous military training, and Carl Langfeldt, with an equal number of reliable-looking kroo-boys, went along a bush track heading to the north-east towards a spot, rather more than two hundred miles up country, marked in ink on their common map as X.

CHAPTER 8

"May heaven preserve thy guileless heart,
Sweet sister, fare thee well."

THE STORY GOES BACK a few days to the evening of the *Asabo's* arrival in Rio del Rey. The *soidisant* Claude Wentworth did not go below for the brush up he spoke of, instead he went along the lower deck, well out of the light of any lamp, and stood with anxious gaze still turned towards the spot, screened and shadowed by the dank mist and darkness, to the left of the German factory. There was a world of misery on the round, childish face and a glint of tears in the blue eyes that strained and watched for any shadow on the shrouded water. The little hands on the rail tightened when the faint splash of muffled paddles came out of the surrounding night. A moment or so later a tiny native "dug-out" crept stealthily along in the shadow of the vessel to the bottom of the gangway. He glanced along the deck, at that hour all but deserted, then went quickly down the steps and into the frail canoe with an agility betokening much practice. The echoing dinner gong sounded as they left the ship's side. "The Babe" looked back. A figure, tall and broad, moving at a languid crawl, was silhouetted for a moment against the round bright lamp that shone on the upper deck. A tear coursed down the youngster's face and fell with a splash on his hand. This seemed to bring him to himself; he squared his shoulders resolutely, looked no longer backwards, but forwards into the eerie, whispering gloom. There was no word spoken between him and the dusky oarsman. Captain Morton could have told at a glance that the negro was no native of that district. The wild-looking savage took as little interest in his passenger as would Charon at the end of a heavy, tiring day when he had carted more than the average number of unwilling explorers across the Styx.

"The Babe" sat lost in thought as they left the river and entered the gloomy waterway. The mangrove swamp, in the heat of the day so still and lifeless, at night was a buzz of strange and uncanny noises; the heavy splash of jumping fish resounded through the darkness with a startling suddenness; curious grunting sounds came from the adjacent mud banks combined with the peculiar scaly noise of crabs rushing and scrambling one over the other; out of the heavy, foul-smelling mist the twisted, gnarled trees loomed, assuming weird and fantastic shapes in the wreathing shadows. The canoe crept along, at times almost touching them, and the long aerial roots scraped its edge like ghostly skeleton hands stretched out from the darkness to grasp it. The swamp was full of creaking, groaning sounds as the branches rustled and played one against the other. Above all in eeriness was the strange whine and coughing sigh of crocodiles. Now and again a seeming log drifted past, but the strong smell of musk that impregnated the atmosphere denoted the close presence of one of those gentry.

For nearly an hour the canoe twisted in and out of a maze of ghostly passages, at every stroke of the paddle the waterway getting narrower and the matted vegetation more dense. A sharp corner was turned, barely wide enough for the canoe's length. A light shone out of the darkness and a few moments afterwards the craft ran on the soft sand of a small island. "The Babe" got out and went carefully over the bit of creeper-grown land towards the light that streamed out from the open door of a well-made two-roomed hut. It was evidently occupied, for when the small feet stumbled over an unnoticed root someone said: "Hello, Chrys; you got here at last? I'm tired to death of stewing in this beastly hole," and at the same time a girlish form in a serviceable, dark blue linen dress, with nether extremities encased in well-fitting, small brown boots and putties, and wearing a large, floppy, grey felt hat trimmed with a flowing, blue gauze veil, appeared in the doorway.

It was a young and unusually pretty girl to be found in the depths of a West African swamp at night, but as it leant against the door watching the figure proceeding towards it with even greater caution owing to the previous stumble, its hands sought that part of its anatomy which in a male would have been trousers' pockets and the professional manner it held a cigarette between its lips and talked at the same time rather detracted from the picture.

The person addressed as "Chrys," but who, hitherto, had been known as "Claude," made no reply, but pushed somewhat unceremoniously past the girlish figure and, seating itself in the only available chair, laid its head on the table and, despite its trousers, wept. The figure in petticoats whistled, looked at it in some dismay, then closing and bolting the door seated itself on a packing case opposite.

"What's the matter, old girl?"

Suppressed sobs were the only answer.

"Had a nervy time getting down here?"

"I can't do it any more. I can't! I can't!"

The petticoated one came and put a careless arm round the bowed shoulders.

"Didn't I promise this would be the last swop?"

The tear-stained face was laid against the blue dress and one small hand clutched another that was its twin and facsimile.

"You've promised before, Claude, and—and made me do it again. I thought I'd break down every minute this trip."

"You haven't ever had to do it for so long before, but we're on our last deal now. You've promised to see this through and I've promised to be a good boy for ever after and never give you another moment's anxiety. Lord! Chrys, I should have been in some awful holes if you hadn't backed me up like a brick. It's a pity the devil let your tender conscience leak into the family; you've got a deucedly one-sided way of looking at things that's not usual with our breed. We two have always stuck together though, haven't we? Ever since the old governor went below to fizzle and left us two curly-headed little piccaninnies to forage round for ourselves. Now we'll swop round; I guess you'll feel more comfortable-like in your own togs. Then you can tell me what Langfeldt's little game is and why you sent that cablegram to Gola and came out here a couple of weeks before you were due."

The weary little figure in trousers got up and went to the inner room. There was a handing out of garments one to the other, and a few minutes afterwards Chrysanthe Wentworth joined her brother attired in the clothes he had worn at her arrival and he in hers. Taken feature by feature they were exactly alike, but the expression was very different. The care that had previously lurked behind her eyes now spread over the whole of her face, and the air of reckless dissipation and devilment, which in him had been somewhat hidden by his feminine attire, was now doubly accentuated. There was no doubt which was the leading spirit and that the girl's one desire was to keep her brother from the result of his own lawless dealings. She watched him with patient anxiety as out of a "chop box" (luncheon hamper) he produced various comestibles, then, perching himself on the edge of the table, looked at her smilingly, lighted a small paraffin stove and proceeded to boil water for coffee.

"I guess you'd rather have coffee, Chrys, you haven't got the family palate for whisky. I've done my best to bring you up in the way you should go, but you've been a disappointment all round. It's enough to make all our lot turn on the grill to hear you talk at times. The old governor always said it was the devil's own mistake you were born a she. There hadn't been one in the litter for generations. But for that hopeless slip we could keep this little game going on for ever."

Chrysanthe said nothing. The reaction from the voyage, fear and anxiety for her brother, left her for the moment very numb. Her twin was used to these collapses after she had impersonated him for a time, and chattered on in his usual scoffing way until she had recovered somewhat. When the pan boiled he made the coffee; such a luxury as milk, tinned or otherwise, was not forth-coming, and dropping in a couple of lumps of sugar handed it across the table.

Then lighting another cigarette he said, "Now, Chrys, what's in the wind? What brought you back in such a deuce of a hurry?"

Chrysanthe revived as she drank the strong, hot coffee and plunged into her story.

"Langfeldt has some scheme on with Mungea"—her brother whistled—"I don't know what it is, but I'm certain of it. I dropped across them accidentally in Liverpool when I was supposed to be painting Paris red. I knew they wouldn't recognize me in veils and laces so I followed them. The whole time they were talking about you and the golden centipede. I dared not follow them very far for fear they should spot me, so I went back and told Krua. He found out where Langfeldt was staying and kept watch. The boots at the hotel was a friend of Krua's and told him they were as thick as thieves and Mungea was always up in Carl's rooms with maps and plans spread out as if they were trying to work out some route. I pretended to have sickened of Paris and got into your togs again. When I was out with Carl we passed Mungea, but they took not the least notice of each other. He was on the boat coming out too, and then they were entire strangers; Krua kept an eye on them the whole time. Mungea gave us one more chance and I refused it; I said I would have no sacrifice. He tried to kill a girl the third night out but I stopped that. Then he turned on me and I've got the mark still."—Here Chrysanthe pulled up her sleeve; the faint mark on the pretty white arm showed out in the flickering lamplight, and then went on—"I got an awful shock for he hailed me out of the darkness by name. I thought he had recognized me, and knew if he had all was up for me and Langfeldt would have hauled me off up country without giving me a chance of getting in touch with you again. I'm certain their idea was to go up home and get hold of me whilst you were supposed to be still in England; then lie in wait and shoot you unawares and get the map and document. Carl looked more than a trifle disappointed the day I told him I had decided to return with him. In spite of Mungea's threat I stuck to my job; but I nearly fainted when the brute crawled on me; it made the wild old story we found in the governor's safe so true. The thing seemed to know me! But I'll risk that, and a good deal more since you've promised to settle down afterwards."

Her hand touched his with a gentle caress. "The Babe" smiled.

"Lord! Chrys, your anxiety to keep me out of the clutches of our mutual godfather, the devil, is killing. But I'll be a bally monk once this deal's through, never fear. Go on with Mungea, and don't waste time pawing me over."

The small hand was hastily withdrawn as she went on. "The centipede crawled on to my arm; Mungea, who had previously thrown something at the girl and missed, sneaked round into the lifeboat near where I was standing and threw a bit of rope across it. It proved he thought I was you—he wouldn't have attempted to kill me just yet—and in a way it proved the old story all bunkum, because the brute went for me just as if I were an ordinary person. I thought I was due to join the old governor. It was one of the deadliest sort going, but—there was a sleepy-looking Josser on board, tall and broad, like the Danvers chap you warned me against"— her brother's eyes opened a little—"but the likeness ended there. With a red-hot fusee he persuaded the brute to come out, hurried me off to the doctor's cabin and pulled me round before the poison had time to spread. Mungea didn't play any more tricks after that and I gave the yellow-haired girl the sacred symbol, so he won't dare to touch her again. She's 'ju-ju' as far as all Mungea's lot are concerned."

"The Babe" sat in silent meditation for some minutes after his sister had finished speaking.

Presently he said angrily, "It would be far better to let Mungea have his little bit of the palaver—nothing pleases a nigger better than to dabble about in blood. You've made a mortal enemy of him by putting this spoke in his wheel. Lord! what does it matter? There are loads and to spare of yellow-haired girls. Every one of us has kept his part of the bargain down to the old governor, so why should you be so mighty particular? I'm sure it ain't like the rest of us!

Now you come along, the one we've wanted for the last few hundred years, according to that old scrawl; the conditions are given there square enough and you won't abide by them. I tell you you'll muddle the whole thing with your blasted conscience. Now look here, Chrys, be sensible. Do what Mungea wants. Let him have his innings. He's the high priest in the business. Let me tip him the wink when I get on board? If only you wouldn't be such a damned fool over a bit of blood-spilling, he'd be round on our side again like a shot, whereas, if he joins forces with Langfeldt, it will be a running battle the whole way up, and there'll be a. jolly sight more gore on the line than if you let things go on according to the old contract. I don't fancy him chopping you about, and he will if you don't do what he wants."

For a time nothing was said. Outside the wind moaned and whispered in the surrounding swamp. A loose creeper tapped impatiently on the tin roof of the hut. Attracted by the stillness a lizard crept out of its dwelling place in the rafters and looked at the two silent mortals with bright, inquiring eyes. Claude Wentworth watched his sister intently; so far he had always persuaded her round to his desires, but now, when the great venture of his life hung on it, she had turned stupid. There was a faint rustle outside, like the stealthy tread of bare feet, or it might only have been the breeze playing in the ground vegetation. Neither noticed it, both intent on their own thoughts. Chrysanthe's hands moved nervously. She studied them in the wavering light. They seemed to grow red, red with human blood, red with murder!

"Claude, I can't do it! I can't!"

There was a balked, angry look in the devil behind the watching eyes; a hard, short laugh that was more like a snarl, then a torrent of wild, mad abuse. She shivered and her small hands trembled pathetically. It had all been gone through before and she knew it would come again at her continued refusal. Then she hid her face against the chair and the slender shoulders heaved as the big, stifled sobs were lost in the cushions. Something seized her arm viciously, with a grip more like talons than hands, and hissed in her ear, "For the last time, you little fool, will you do it?"

"I'd rather he killed me."

As the low broken voice echoed through the hut the mad abuse died down suddenly. All was silent save for the quick-drawn, strained breath of someone fighting with a very demon of balked desire, and the impatient, ghostly tapping on the roof. Chrysanthe got up unsteadily and went to where her brother stood with clenched hands and working face. An arm was slipped round his neck and a soft cheek laid against his.

"I'd do anything for you but—that, dear."

The boy's throat moved convulsively: the passion-racked face was on her shoulder and as it lay there the wild rage died down.

"Chrys, why do you stick to me? Why don't you let me go to the devil headlong?" a husky, penitent voice whispered.

Her hands strayed lovingly over the bowed curly head.

"Because I know you can't help it, dear."

Two arms were round her in a hug that took all breath away and a voice said, "Why, Chrys, I don't believe you care a damn about the gold! You're only going up there to cry quits with the devil: to try and get the old curse broken and bring your one and only brother back to the steep and narrow way."

She took the boy's face between her hands and kissed him.

"It's no go, old girl, he's had his mark and seal on me from the beginning. As tiny piccaninnies I was the one who pulled the butterflies' wings off and you the one who fetched the gum and tried to stick them on again."

"The Babe" drew his sister back to the chair and perched at the side with an arm round her neck watching her for some time in silence.

"Now, Chrys, give an account of all happenings this voyage down, so that I can step into your shoes without exciting suspicion. Tell me some more about the chap you thought might be Danvers."

"That was what gave me the special jumps this trip. When I got on board at Liverpool expecting to book a lone crib like we always do, the boat was packed full of 'canaries.' I thought I should sink through the deck when the chief steward said there wasn't such a thing as an empty cabin going and he would have to put me in with a Major Sinclair. I tried for a lone second, but they were full up with a Dahomey Amazon show returning home. I had to get down here somehow so I risked it."

The youngster whistled softly and looked at her with admiration.

"You young demon! There's a good slice of the old leaven in you in spite of your one-sided notions regarding *meum et tuum*."

"That wasn't the worst, Claude. Major Sinclair turned out to be so like the Danvers chap you warned me about that I thought the end had come. I gave him all the cheek I could for the first day, but he took it like a lamb and looked at me in a sleepy, dozy way which was not exactly what the sharp-eyed cove in Blenka's land would have done, according to you."

"Lord! no, Chrys; he would have fixed you with his gimlets, taken you by the collar and hoofed you out of his sight."

"So I thought, and as he didn't I breathed again. But it was wearing work those first seven days on board. He wasn't a bad sort though, sleepy and slow-like. Langfeldt had him all sides up and rooked him no end. His sister was the girl Mungea went for and afterwards we got quite friendly. I felt sorry for him; he's not the kind that ought to go out alone, gets done all round. Old Morton was fearfully riled; he'd nabbed Sinclair for his own—two slow old duffers together—and wasn't a bit pleased when I began to take an interest in him."

"The Babe" laughed. For the next hour they went over the details of the voyage. Then he gave a brief account of his doings since they had parted, but omitted to mention his excursion to Fernando Po. Afterwards conversation drifted round to Langfeldt. No mention was made of their late disagreement on this subject. Claude, who now was sitting on the table, rubbed his chin with an air of great perplexity.

"Chrys, I was a fool ever to give him a plan of the home route. No one could find our little crib without it. I promised him a goodly share too, but he's greedy and evidently wants the lot. Mungea don't know the whole way up to beyond, that's one good thing, only as far as the family chapel. Afterwards he can only go by guesswork and he'll be a long time guessing his way up there. But it will be deuced uncomfortable having them hopping round our little nest when we start out, and, noses down, red hot on our trail afterwards. I bet Langfeldt wouldn't let that plan go far from his juicy person, or our little signed and sealed arrangement either. You always said he would sell me for the price of a drink if he heard of a better job. Lord! I thought I had his head held in too much for him to attempt a bolt. It's a deceitful world and when we've got this deal through I'll go and found a monastery somewhere—see if I don't. Then there's Mungea to be considered."

The consideration of this point kept "The Babe" quiet for some time.

"It's just possible he may slip off here and try and get up home by the short cut, with the idea of nabbing you before I get there. He'll have some difficulty either way; he's not over sure of the route, but he knows this one better. Langfeldt daren't attempt this way; that would arouse my suspicions at once. Probably his idea is to go on leisurely with me seeing as how I have partially stopped his little game by returning sooner than he expected. He will pretend to be entirely unaware of your existence, will evince no surprise when we fall on an empty crib and be deeply grieved, alarmed and condolent when I apprise him of your disappearance. I never mentioned you when I asked his assistance in this deal and he's not the sort entirely to trust a nigger, and he will allow me to live until he has satisfied himself of the existence of my sister. Afterwards the main idea of our mutual friend will be to let daylight through my curly head and relieve me of the old map and document. If I can get the home route from him it will take him some time to grope his way up there in the dark. If they both go on to Dwala, Mungea wouldn't dare show his nose within a mile of Langfeldt lest I should suspect, neither would our dear Carl shoot me until he was sure of you. If it were not for that Sinclair chap you spoke of I'd chuck my excursion on the *Asabo* and start off up country 'one time' (at once) with you. But I must have a look at him; I've seen him though he hasn't seen me—that time I told you about when Gola dressed up as a Mohammedan trader and I was his favorite wife. He was fearfully anxious to connect me with certain gas-pipes of the latest improved pattern imported into Northern Nigeria, ordered and paid for by the Improvements Committee of a certain tribe whose favorite occupation is pulling the lion's tail. He nearly had me that time. Lord! I never hopped as quick in all my life, and before I got paid in advance for the fifth dose, too! Now if this Sinclair chap should turn out to be Danvers, which ain't likely, but it's suspicious him coming down here for pure fun—besides he was after birds last time—we shall have to be more than ever wary, my child. He swore he'd have me, alive or dead, and he's an awful one for keeping his word. Moreover at the present moment there's a lot of rubbish up home that I shouldn't care for him to see."

Chrysanthe looked at her brother anxiously.

"What have you been doing whilst I was away?"

"Sitting up home playing patience and ticking the days off the calendar till your return"—laughingly.

"Why did you make me go to England in your place?"

"So that I could complete arrangements out here without exciting suspicion. We'd have every white in West Africa on our trail if they'd an inkling of what's in the wind."

"Then why did you tell Langfeldt?"

"Because I got all the kit through him and he'd have smelt a rat in any case, and so that things could be shipped off to England without any questions being asked."

"You can't do that now."

"No; but once we get hold of the stuff I'll soon find a way out of that difficulty!"

"There may be nothing to get hold of."

"That ain't likely. There'll be about enough in that brew to see me through my little span. You're losing your nerve to such an extent that most of my wind-raising schemes will be settled and my tastes are so deucedly expensive. I've had six months of His Majesty's hospitality and I ain't craving for any more."

"The Babe" pulled out his watch and glanced at it.

"It's about time I made tracks for the old tub. Krua will be hopping round in a fever until he has got you once more under his dusky wing. I'll send him off the moment I get on board. He knows the way better than I do and will have you up home in less than no time. You haven't traveled this way before. In three days you'll be out of the swamp and there Mammy is waiting for you with a hammock and a whole string of 'boys.' The old girl nearly cried her eyes out when I landed up home in your togs. She and Krua are the only ones who can spot the difference, but they'd have their black hides taken off inch by inch rather than give us away. They're not as fond of me as they are of you though! Mammy hugged me, the first time for the last twelve years, when I told her she might come down here to meet you—spoilt your best pink dress with her tears, wept as much as she did the day I cut your curls off so that you might take a trip up the coast in my name whilst I went out foraging. She has spent all her time since you went away in making frillies for you. Brought a whole pile down! I wanted to air some of them but she wouldn't let me—made me wear out all your old togs whilst you were away. Deuced shame, I call it! I sneaked that pink dress when she wasn't looking."

There was a much happier look on the girl's face as her brother rattled on about their foster-mother and Krua, her son, their elder by eight years, the devoted slave of both and special bodyguard of Chrysanthe since babyhood. Always when she traveled as "Claude" Wentworth, in the second class would be a big brawny negro, something like six foot three in height and proportionately broad, who lounged in the sun all day or huddled round the engines in the cold and took not the least notice of "The Babe" but got off and on when he did, stayed in the immediate vicinity of his hotel but never spoke unless by given signal, and was always there when wanted.

"The Babe" slipped off the table, and picking up a revolver examined it carefully and laid it by his sister's elbow. He went through into the second room: there was not much in it beyond a string hammock, a traveling rug, a well-used Madeira chair and an inverted packing case for a washstand. This he turned up to assure himself of its complete emptiness, then he drew and care-fully barred the heavy shutter over the window. Coming back into the sitting-room he examined the bolts of that shutter. Chrysanthe watched him with rather scared eyes; four hours' lone wait in the depths of a mangrove swamp with the possibility of Mungea rov-ing round was not exactly cheering.

"It ain't lively for you to be left here alone, Chrys, but I must have a look at that Sinclair chap and have a shot for Langfeldt's papers. I'll slip off in Cameroon river. Gola has orders to prowl round there till the *Asabo* turns up. I'll come on home by the front way. Don't worry if I'm a bit late. It may suit me to keep an eye on Carl for a time. Now, so long, Chrys, I'll wait outside till you've got the door properly barred and give you a hail when I'm in the boat. There are several books in the box, lots of chocolates and a tinned cake for you to amuse yourself with until Krua turns up. When you get home see the rubbish in No. 3 shed is put out of sight, it might give offence if Sinclair turned out to be Danvers."

There was an echo of sadness in Chrysanthe's voice and a slim finger rubbed up and down the table edge as she said, "No fear of that, Claude. You—you won't let Langfeldt rook him too much, will you? He's such a sleepy innocent kind that I—sort of looked after him on the way down."

"The Babe" glanced at her sharply.

"Don't you worry; I'll take your place entirely—be a mother to him! Now, good-bye." The boy's hands were on her shoulders as he watched her anxiously. "There ain't anyone you'd swop for your reprobate brother, is there, Chrys?"

Two arms were round his neck in a hug that was sufficient answer.

"We're the only two left now, ain't we, old girl? The last of a bad lot! And we'll stick together to the finish. Now, good-bye again. Don't eat too many chocolates. The book with the red cover is a ripping yarn and will keep you going till Krua turns up. Don't for-get to bolt the door after me."

"The Babe's" hand went to his cummerbund as he slipped quickly out and waited until the bolts were in position again. Then he went rapidly to where Charon slept in the tiny canoe. A farewell hail apprised Chrysanthe of his departure.

She sat down again and picking up a book tried to lose herself in its contents. How quiet it all was, yet full of strange, whispering voices! What funny shadows the lamp cast, like gaunt black hands creeping towards her! If anything happened to Claude on the way down! What if Krua did not get up all right? Four hours before he came, four hours alone in this awful, haunted swamp! How the wind moaned and sighed, rustled and crept along for all the world like stealthy naked feet. It was silly to be afraid.

A heavy startling splash in the swamp close by cut through the eerie, whispering silence. Her hand clutched the revolver. It was nothing, only a fish. Mammy said there were devil-men who came to the earth at night—awful ravening creatures with long, pointed leopard teeth, claws for hands, that walked on all fours, and had eyes that could see through anything. Perhaps they were looking at her now! A huge beetle scuttling along the rafters missed its hold and fell with a heavy plump on her book. A little gasping scream, a hysterical sob and a frightened face was hidden in the cushions. She lay there with closed eyes and beating heart, with hands over her ears trying not to listen to the hundred uncanny voices calling and moaning around the hut.

Presently she came out of the cushions and peered round furtively, half-expecting to see some fearful shape beside her. Every weird old native story, every uncanny negro superstition told by her foster-mother, came back with startling recollection. Childhood's stories long since forgotten ran through her mind like a sudden flood. She got up and walked round to the box, humming as she went, but it echoed so that she soon stopped. She picked out a packet of chocolates and shut the lid with a resounding slam to show courage. Then she wished she had not. The sound would never die away! It seemed to go all through the swamp. They would hear it on the *Asabo!* She looked at her watch. Only half-an-hour since Claude went! The sudden creak of the chair made her start up again. Why is it at night empty wicker chairs make those funny long creaks, just as if someone were sitting down in them? She watched the seat, half expecting to see something take shape therein. Then picking up another book she tiptoed back to her place. Claude was quite right: she was getting as nervous as a cat.

For nearly two hours she sat quite still trying to persuade herself she was reading but omitting to turn any page during the time. The sudden click of the latch made her clutch the revolver in an agony of fear. She stayed white and still watching the door with dilated eyes. How foolish she was! Latches often jump like that. It had not been properly down at first. She ought to make herself undo the door, walk three times round the hut, then sit inside with it wide open and her back to it. She was such a coward now!

The latch clicked again! The book dropped to the floor. There was no mistake this time. Something was there, pushing and trying the door! What if it were Mungea? The thought chilled her to the marrow and her hands trembled so she could hardly hold the revolver. A rustling outside! Hands stealthily pawing over the shutters! The thing crept all round and once there was a sound of a toe-nail scraping along the corrugated-iron exterior. It crept right round back to the door, then knelt there and snuffed like a dog to get the scent of the person inside. Chrysanthe sat frozen. Those stiff, frightened little hands could never use the firearm. The thing got up and a heavy weight was hurled against the door. Three times! But the bolts withstood it. A scratching of bare toes on tin and something climbed up on the roof. Wide, frightened eyes looked up. It was an extra strong iron roof, heavily riveted into solid rafters. Whatever it was it scraped along on all fours, stopping at each separate length. For a time all was still. Then came a steady noise. The thing was filing the rivets! Chrysanthe counted them. Four on each side. When it cut through half of those it would be able to get in! She watched the roof fascinated. Two lizards who had a lodging immediately underneath scuttled off in alarm. How long before the screw was cut through? A sudden long grating noise of a file against tin! Something grunted. The first bolt was done. The second started. How long would that take?

To the white-faced listener underneath there was nothing but the scraping, filing noise and her own thumping heart-beats. What

would he do when he got in? Another grunt. Fingers were scratching and trying to get a hold under the tin—pulling and wrenching.
A huge black paw with half the fourth finger gone appeared.
Chrysanthe got up, one hand at her throat, the other groping round
for the revolver it could not hold. The fellow hand came wrenching and twisting at the tin. It refused to be raised beyond a couple
of inches. The thing on the roof grunted again, moved higher up
and commenced on the third screw. As it filed it crooned a low
song in the Blenguta tongue. Chrysanthe had not heard it before,
but she knew it and her strained white little face went even more
ghastly. The file ran into the heart of the rivet and the thing called
her by name. Called and mocked and laughed. The wind howled
through the swamp, moaned and sighed and rustled. On its eerie
whispering came the wail of a distant tree-devil, sobbing, tortured
and weird. The third screw was through! The roof raised six inches.
A black face looked at her with rolling eyes and slobbering lips.

"Arru, Golden Flower! But one more and we are together!"

Chrysanthe stood with her hand on her throat waiting. The
thing went back and as it filed it sang, loud and triumphant. The
swamp echoed and reechoed with the sound. The wind soughed
round the hut, sighed and crept and rustled; stirred the creeper on
the roof and it tapped patiently—a steady, waiting death watch!

A whirr like a bird through the air, a whine from the thing on
the roof, the sharp metallic click of steel against iron, a dull heavy
thud of some weight falling to earth and plunging through the bush.
Then a shower of blows on the door.

"My flower, my little golden flower! It's I, thy brother Krua."

There was no reply but the noise of something falling.

The sound of footsteps retreating, a sudden rush, a crash and
the bolts gave way. The figure that entered in this unceremonious
manner was not a sight calculated to soothe a frightened girl. Krua,
on principle, avoided European dress except when in Europe, and
became essentially African the moment he arrived in Africa. The
hut seemed to shrink as he entered, an ebony giant clad in the na-
tional dress of his country—a loin-cloth, three leopard's claws
twisted in his woolly hair, and, the dearest treasure of his heart, a
many-rowed necklace of buttons, each one pilfered from some

dress of his foster-sister's. He picked up the limp heap from the floor, carried it carefully into the inner room and laid it in the hammock. Then he went outside and on the roof. There was a dark patch on the tin, or it might have been only a shadow. Krua put his finger into it to convince himself on the point. It was wet. He tasted it, smiled with some satisfaction, then spat it out again. The first blood on the trail! Picking up the knife lying there he went back into the hut. There was a look about him, as he watched the unconscious face and chafed the cold small hands, which boded ill for someone. Presently the blue eyes opened with a strained look in them as from some hideous nightmare. A smile that for the moment occupied the whole of his face greeted the opening of those eyes.

"Why it's you!" a small voice gasped unbelievingly.

The smile if possible broadened and the black paws patted the little white ones reassuringly.

"Was . . . was it Mungea up there?"

"There was something, my flower, and it sat and sang loud and long. Then it changed its tune all at once and slunk off with a whine."

"He sang the doom. I heard it. I felt it! Oh, it was awful!" and Chrysanthe's hands covered her face as shudder after shudder ran through her.

A black paw patted her shoulder.

"My flower, there is a doom even for the doom-tellers."

Krua's face was turned away as he smiled. It was not good for the flower to see that smile. "Now my flower must sleep and I will sit outside and watch. There is nothing more to fear. In but a few hours we start our journey."

After straightening the cushion and readjusting the rug he went outside and squatted by the closed door crooning a soft lullaby that had often hushed his foster-sister to sleep in the days of babyhood. From his loin-cloth he drew three knives, one still had traces of congealed red matter on it, and a stone. This he spat on and sharpened those three knives to the tune of the slumber song, then laid them in a row in front of him and smiled at them. After a time he returned them to their place one by one. The third and sharpest he lingered over, handling it lovingly. For a moment the lullaby ceased.

"This, O Mungea, will reach thy heart!" and the simple baby song went on again.

Dawn was well over and Krua still sang outside the bedroom door. Then he got up. The revolver he put into that seemingly bottomless well, his loin-cloth. Usually he looked askance on firearms, preferring his own weapon, a well-aimed knife that hits and leaves no sound. But it was just as well to be prepared. Going outside he picked up a tin box he had dropped in his haste some hours previously, and re-entering tapped at the inner door. A small sleepy voice answered.

When Chrysanthe appeared breakfast was waiting and a smiling black footman in attendance. There was coffee, milk in a tin, eggs cooked to a turn, rolls and butter, and honey in a jar. She looked at all this with some surprise. Her brother's "chop box" boasted only tinned beef, ship's biscuits, chocolates and a cake. "The Babe's" idea of catering for his sister's wants never got beyond the two latter: he could live and thrive on anything and after months of the former came out bright and cheerful.

"Where did you get all these things from, Krua?"

There was a broad grin on the ebony face.

"My flower, am I not a descendant of thieves?"

"Indeed you are; but what will the chief steward say when he misses them?" glancing towards the open box which gave signs of further stores.

"I am too far away to hear. My flower cannot live three days in the swamps on chocolates and cake alone. Tinned beef and biscuit are but for the teeth of a man."

There was a certain amount of truth in the latter.

Whilst Chrysanthe finished her breakfast her bodyguard went outside to prepare the canoe for the journey. Charon had in the night retired to the swamp village, where he dwelt, until such times as his services would be required again. The canoe for the journey was a much bigger affair than the one that had been used to and from the *Asabo*, and lay well hidden behind a screen of matted creepers on the far side of the island. As Krua went along he looked for any traces of the night visitor. There was nothing beyond the filed roof to tell of him. The red patch had been cleared away by the ants. He paddled the canoe round to the more accessible side of the island, where Chrysanthe now stood waiting. The tin "chop box" stored at the *Asabo's* expense, the hammock, cushions and rug were put in and presently Krua and his "Golden Flower" started their voyage. All day they paddled through the hot, oppressive swamp, gliding in and out of an intricate maze of dim shrouded passages, with here and there a glint of sunshine to break the green gloom. Not a sound broke the stillness, except the droning buzz of flies and the occasional screeching of parrots flying out of sight beyond the dense tangled mass of vegetation.

Night brought them to a native hut built on a strip of land in a mangrove-surrounded lake.

After dinner Chrysanthe stood watching the moon as it rose through a cloud of yellow mist, a ball of fiery red in the reflection of the sun that had just gone down leaving a flood of amethyst, gold and carmine that spread and mingled and died away in the clear indigo sky as the moon gained undisputed possession. A silver beauty then spread over the surrounding scene and the still, lifeless swamp again became a world of strange and curious voices calling. All around could be heard the not unmusical croaking of frogs, the whir and buzz of night insects and from a little way off, in the darkened creeks, the splash and bellow of crocodiles. Anon came the flesh-creeping cry of the tree-sloth, and over all the gentle murmur of the silvered water.

It was a sad small face that watched. Everything was black or white, there was no other colour. When the sun shone all was different. What looked dark one minute was light the next and you never knew where you were! But when the moon came out there was no mistake!

She sighed and went and talked to Krua.

CHAPTER 9

"Whence does she come?"

SOME SIX WEEKS AFTER LEAVING DWALA, Major Sinclair and Carl Langfeldt were still looking for Claude Wentworth's country seat. The arduous journey into the wilds had greatly altered the appearance of both. There was an alert, wide-awake look about the former which had not been noticeable on the *Asabo*; a keenness about the eye and a hardness about the mouth that grew as the days and weeks passed. Major the Hon. Tracy Sinclair on the warpath was very different from that same individual standing at ease. The manifold trials and tribulations of the past few weeks, combined with the heavy marching days, had robbed the German of his overfed look, one or two attacks of fever had toned down his colour considerably and his smile was not so frequent. On the whole their little jaunt into the country had improved both. They had waded waist deep in swamps, hacked their way slowly through dark, tangled forests, traveled all day on native tracks and come out exactly on the spot they had camped the evening before, and finally, after many grievous disappointments, had reached the place marked X on their common map. It was not a populous part. During the last week they had seen one man and he a negro. On him they pounced clamoring for information as to the whereabouts of a person called Wentworth. The native looked puzzled, scratched his woolly head and assured them there was no one of the name living in the neighborhood, or had been within his memory. It was extremely damping but still they did not give up hope.

Three days ago they had reached X. There they camped, radiating into the surrounding district in small detachments. The tents were pitched in a natural clearing. All around was a dense green wall, a forest of giant trees, some of them over two hundred feet high, festooned and girt about with thorny creepers; these made traveling difficult and depressing. It was impossible to get a view of the surrounding country owing to the height and density of the vegetation. Now and then a track was found, but it branched and forked and split up and invariably led back to headquarters. It was possible they were fifty miles away from "The Babe's" residence, or perhaps only five, yet they might stay for weeks in its vicinity and not find it because of the baffling tangle. Their camping place was an open patch with a few palm-trees. Close at hand was a lake fed by a small stream. On the morning of the fourth day Sinclair sat at a *tête-à-tête* breakfast with Langfeldt. There was not much conversation between them. "The Babe" was the link that joined them, but for him they would have been divorced long since. As Sinclair was consuming what, according to the label on the tin, was haddock, and decidedly dingy-looking slices of bread spread with butter of a pronounced metallic flavor, washed down by thick coffee out of which he often paused to abstract a too adventurous insect, his gaze wandered towards the lake. To-day he intended to try and follow the stream feeding it. All the previous day had been spent hacking away at the undergrowth about it, and they had progressed not more than a quarter of a mile. Wherever Wentworth's place was there was sure to be a stream close by. It might not be that one any more than a dozen others they had passed during the last week, but this was the biggest tangle they had got into so far, and a very likely place to be chosen for "The Babe's" nest.

Shortly after breakfast Sinclair and Langfeldt, accompanied by a detachment of the Hausas, reattacked the stream. It struck the former the farther they got up the gully the less dense became the tangle. Traveling was very slow. The close and undesired embrace of the thorny "bush-ropes," as the spiked creepers so prevalent in

West Africa are called, impeded progress considerably. They worked their way up slowly, slipping and floundering along in two feet of water, over sharp stones and occasionally into deep mud holes. The towering vegetation at the sides made the little ravine dim and cool. Here and there, where the sunshine trickled through, the dense creepers burst into a profusion of blossoms and now and again, in the less screened parts, a cascade of brilliant flowers and many-colored mosses covered the rocky sides. After an hour's traveling Sinclair calculated they had gone a quarter of a mile, which was a decided improvement on the day before. A halt was called for breathing, then on again. The struggle became less laborious and in the next hour they covered a good mile. The gully widened and was now about six feet across. By walking through an average foot of water they made fair progress. The brook babbled along between moss-grown boulders, down a series of long shallow rock steps in miniature waterfalls and an occasional deep, silent pool. The crevices were grown with tiny plants and the rough rock sides of the ravine were curtained with maiden-hair and hart's-tongue ferns. The trees around were a mass of many-hued orchids. A couple of hours through this brought them to a plateau on the hillside. A veritable little garden of Eden! Feathery palms grew by the water's edge with here and there a glowing red acacia. Banana plants fluttered their long graceful pale green leaves in the light breeze. There were banks of flowering shrubs and little starlike creepers on the ground; the whole festooned and wreathed with a mass of rainbow-hued blossoms as for a gala day. A gaunt leafless baobab stood at the foot of a twisted glen—the only blot on the landscape—and its weird gnarled branches were hung with huge hard pods whispering and talking together like so many moldy green skulls as the light wind rattled them. There was a subtle air of cultivation about the whole that is occasionally met with in the depths of a West African wilderness.

A halt was called for lunch. The Hausas lay down beneath a dense bush out of the sun. Sinclair and Langfeldt seated themselves on a couple of big boulders under a group of palms. It was not a very luxurious repast; slices of tinned beef sandwiched between hard biscuits and washed down by a mixture of whisky and water. As the former munched he studied the glen; the meal completed he intended to lead his little band up there. Suddenly there burst into view a sight that made his hand go quickly to his gun. Tearing round the corner came a huge tawny beast, which, for the moment, he took for a lion, though he knew full well such an animal was not known in that part of Africa. In its mouth was something white and limp, which afterwards proved to be a hat. Then after it, full steam ahead, came a figure in pink, which as it ran held its fluffy skirts amazingly high, displaying a quantity of remarkably pretty brown-clad leg. Owing to the position of his seat Sinclair alone was privileged to see this sight. It held him breathless. The beast, which he now saw was a dog, slowed up somewhat. The flying figure over-took it, made a grab at what was in its mouth, missed and grabbed again. A tug of war ensued. The hat, a large soft felt trimmed with a quantity of pink, and ribbon strings to match, refused to become the sole property of either. Little brown feet kicked at the yellow animal with some viciousness; it bared its teeth in apparent anger and its tail wagged with greater vigor than before. Renewed tugs. The pink one became coaxing, gentle and persuasive. This had the desired effect and the property was returned to its owner. Then swinging the hat in one hand, two fingers of the other holding the dog by one ear, the figure advanced slowly towards the clump of flowering shrubs, some hundred yards away, that hid the luncheon party. Sinclair's eyes were glued on it. Its hair had grown some-what since the days he knew it, and coiled and twisted in a most delicious manner round and about a band of pink ribbon that was threaded through its curls and tied in a big bow over the left ear. The dress was a very pretty one, all frills and softness. As he watched he thought it was the most bewitching little creature he had ever seen and wondered how it could find it in its foolish little heart to put itself into straight and untrimmed trousers. The dog stiffened and growled. The party, who so far was entirely unaware of the tableau that had fallen to Sinclair's lot, started up suddenly. The forest nymph stopped abruptly, hooked a finger into the dog's heavily spiked collar and looked at them with wide, startled eyes.

Sinclair forgot he was not supposed to know this little girl and advanced quickly with outstretched hand and reassuring smile. Langfeldt stared in open admiration. The Hausas stood with broad grins and covert whispers. The beast growled more savagely than before, impatiently awaiting permission to attack the strangers.

For a moment Chrysanthe did not recognize the figure coming towards her. Major the Hon. Tracy Sinclair clad in khaki linen nethers, a rough grey flannel shirt, heavy mud-splashed boots and putties, and a battered slouch hat, was very different from the person who, in immaculate flannels, a well-chosen tie and a flawless panama, crawled languidly about the *Asabo*. When she did her thoughts flew at once to Claude, who, three miles away, on the back veranda of their residence, was leisurely superintending the casing up of certain gas-pipes surreptitiously removed by him and his following from the Hausa regiment at Calabar, and awaiting the buyer's arrival the next or following day. Sinclair, during his visit ashore there, had been apprised of this removal, but at his request the fact was suppressed and he lived in hope of finding the missing property on "The Babe's" premises, thereby bringing home to the young villain that most heinous of crimes—gunrunning.

That the "sleepy-looking josser" was his arch-enemy Danvers had been her brother's first remark when he arrived home by the front way, rather more than a fortnight ago. She had been twitted somewhat on her lack of perception. This and the fact that the gimlet-eyed, stern-faced personage advancing towards her had sworn to catch her brother, alive or dead, at his favorite occupations, stifled any former liking. The unfriendly look in her eyes reminded Sinclair they were not acquainted. Joy at having found his babe alive and well had for the moment drowned all thought; then his native discreetness returned. Chrysanthe stood and waited. Sinclair was forcibly reminded of a daring young robin that had hopped in at an open window and then found all retreat cut off. Afraid? Certainly not! But wondering seriously what was going to happen next. Hat in hand he accosted her and made the following inquiry:

"Excuse me, but can you tell me if anyone named Wentworth lives in this part?"

Chrysanthe looked from him to Langfeldt and then back again. Sinclair knew he was judged by the company he had adopted.

"That's my name. Why?"

"We"—introducing Langfeldt who received the smallest and coldest of bows—"wish to see your brother on a matter of some importance."

Here the German determined to have his innings.

"I know your brother very well, Miss Wentworth. I've been his greatest friend for the last six years."

"Have you? I thought I'd heard your name before. My brother once mentioned you might be coming up here"—then looking again at Sinclair—"Are you a special friend of my brother's, too?"

"Well, hardly that, but we got rather friendly during the voyage down."

"Really!"—a dimple lurked in the corner of her mouth but it quickly died away, chased off by an anxious look.

"Will you take us to the house?" Sinclair asked, watching the site of the dimple.

Chrysanthe's brain was working quickly. At all costs this undesirable visitor must be kept off the premises until those dreadful guns were out of the way.

"I—I'm sorry I can't because—" Some really adequate reason must be given, something that would satisfy this sharp-eyed cove without exciting suspicion.

Small nervous hands tied and untied the ribbon strings as she awaited an inspiration. It came at last.

"Because I've lost my way."

Sinclair had difficulty in suppressing a smile. "Have you been lost for long?"

One fib invariably begets another.

"Since—early this morning."

He was gravely sympathetic: the situation pleased him. His babe said she was lost therefore it was his bounden duty to look after and care for her until a responsible person came and claimed her.

"Then you must be very tired and hungry."

"Yes, I am"—plaintively.

"Let me offer you some lunch. It's rather a scratch meal but better than nothing under the circumstances."

Chrysanthe walked thoughtfully by his side to where the meal was spread. The next thing was to escape and give warning. If that proved impracticable—she studied Sinclair's profile covertly and sighed—then the only thing would be to lead them as far away from the homestead as possible. There was no telling what these two would do if they got Claude unawares.

The two men vied with each other in pointing out the most comfortable boulder. The contents of the "chop box" were laid at her disposal. She glanced into it hungrily and picked out a hard biscuit. (The choice lay between that and slabs of stringy beef.) Sinclair washed the cup of his spirit flask in the adjacent stream and half-filling it with whisky and water set it at her side. Both he and the German were too much excited at the advent of their guest to continue their repast. That his late friend's sister should have turned out to be such a little beauty bid fair to alter the latter's tactics somewhat.

Chrysanthe broke the biscuit by hammering it on a sharp point of rock; in doing so fully a quarter of it fell unheeded to the ground. Then she ate a small piece with simulated hunger. (She had to live up to her statements.)

"In which part are you staying?" she asked.

Whilst they were both fully occupied explaining in which direction their camp lay she surreptitiously poked another piece into a crevice in the rock. Sinclair glanced at her in time to see one small finger hurriedly pushing the undesired morsel out of sight.

"Is it far from here?"

He kept his eyes dutifully turned away as he replied, "About six miles."

When he looked again the dog appeared to be eating something under protest and only half the biscuit remained. She ate another scrap taking care that he should see. The dog retired beyond reach, which to say the least of it was rather mean.

"I think I'm past eating"—a small voice said presently rather plaintively—"I've had a very tiring morning. It's worrying work being bushed and I don't know what I should have done if I hadn't met you."

Immediately Sinclair was all sympathy.

"Try and drink this"—coaxingly, offering the whisky—"then you may feel better and be able to finish the biscuit."

Chrysanthe took one sip, made a wry face and put the cup down.

"I can't drink it, thank you. I don't often have whisky. I don't like it; it burns my tongue so and makes me more thirsty than ever. This biscuit is so hard and I'm too tired to eat it."

"I'll try and find something nicer for you when we get to the camp—if we don't succeed in finding your brother's place."

Chrysanthe sat lost in thought. How could she possibly escape? If they went up the glen (the thought made her shiver) there was Krua and an empty luncheon basket! Direct evidence of her having tried to mislead them. This horrid, sharp-eyed man would immediately suspect, follow and catch Claude in the very act. The best thing would be to go quietly back with them to their camp, then try and get a penciled message through by the dog, telling Claude what had happened. But it was very trying work.

She glanced at Langfeldt. Sinclair noticed the look and also that the hand picking nervously at the moss-grown rock trembled a little. Then he became aware that from under the shadow of the wide-brimmed hat she was studying him. He knew the company he had adopted and the knowledge of his previous deceit would not have a very reassuring effect. He wondered if there was any risk this small girl would stop at for the sake of her reprobate twin. A lot of his animosity towards "The Babe" had died down now that he had found the feminine duplicate safe and sound.

"When you are sufficiently rested, Miss Wentworth, shall we try and find the way back to your place?"

This was just what Chrysanthe did not want.

"I . . . I haven't the faintest idea which way to go. Grip and I have been walking round all morning and muddled ourselves entirely, haven't we, old boy?"

Grip who was standing with his head on Sinclair's knee (the fact had reassured Chrysanthe somewhat; the German he growled at and refused all offers of friendship), said nothing, but wagged his tail and winked so barefacedly that Sinclair bent his head over the animal to hide a smile that escaped him in spite of himself. It was just possible this little babe of his was lost. Had she not said so? But she was not nearly as lost as she pretended.

"In which direction does your brother's place lie, if you had to make a guess?"

She glanced calculating towards the sun, now well past midday.

"Westward, I think."

"Shall we have a shot and see?"

"If . . . if you like, but—I'm very tired."

It was such a worried, anxious small face that Sinclair's heart smote him and he decided to take her back with him at once and not tease her any more.

"Then shall we make tracks for my camp? Your brother may be there now making inquiries for you. If no one turns up by the evening I'll try and fix you up comfortably. To-morrow if you are rested we'll have a proper search; we are bound to drop across your place in a day or two. Until then you'll have to let me be your brother and I'll do my best to fill his place."

"How long will it take to get to your camp?"

"It took us five hours to get up here, but we had a lot of hacking to do. Probably we shall get down in two and be there just in nice time for tea."

There was no escape. It was either going with them or them coming with her, and the sooner they went the less likelihood would there be of Krua appearing. At all cost this sharp-eyed chap must be kept off the trail for a couple of days at least.

"Yes, I think that would be the best thing to do; my brother may be there. In any case I shall be ready for some tea. Hard biscuits are not nice even if you're hungry and I don't like whisky. Claude makes me have it sometimes though, he says it keeps off fever. Your track may be the one I've been looking for all morning. I shouldn't be surprised if we picked up the home route that way. It leads westward doesn't it?"

She got up and her hands shook as she tied the ribbon strings—this small girl seemed afraid in spite of the nonchalant, careless air she adopted. She talked away at a great rate as they crossed the plateau, for much the same reason as she slammed the lid of the swamp hut rather more than seven weeks ago.

When they reached the edge of the plateau another problem confronted her. The way down to her new friends' camp appeared to be through a stream of water varying in depth from six inches to two feet. More than ever she regretted having come this picnic to her favorite resort. There was no possible way of crawling along at the side; the uncovered rocks were too far apart to serve as stepping stones, and the bottom was strewn with a lot of sharp, rough pebbles. She had not come out prepared for that sort of walking, and thought ruefully of her thin shoes, wishing she had put on workmanlike boots and putties. Sinclair was thinking also. In his anxiety to get her back where she could be properly fed and rested he had forgotten the extremely crude route by which they had gained their present position. It would be impossible for her to walk down in those slipper things; her feet would be bleeding before they had gone a mile. She would have to be carried. The prospect did not dismay him in the least, but it might have a very different effect on his small companion.

Chrysanthe paused on the edge of the little rock gully.

"Is this the only way down to your place?" nervously.

"I'm sorry to say it is"—Sinclair's sorrow seemed forced.

"But I can't go down there in these shoes"—displaying a toe— "I—I think you'd better go on and leave me to my fate. I've been bushed before and always found my way back all right."

The two agreed such a thing could not be thought of, and Sinclair added a rider to the effect that if she wished he would send the Hausas on with instructions to bring up the tents and baggage. They would just about manage it by nightfall.

It was just what Chrysanthe did not wish. Long before that hour Claude would be coming to the plateau for his daily walk. Her only desire was to get these terrible people out of the way before he appeared.

"I shouldn't think of putting you to so much trouble. I'll try wading. I've done worse than this many a time."

"But not in that kind of shoes,"—Sinclair added, then seriously—"The most sensible thing would be for you to let me carry you. By-and-by the path is not so rough and you can walk again."

"Will it be very far?"

"Oh no, no distance at all"—measuring from his point.

"Very well"—rather shakily—"but I'm bothering you a lot."

As Sinclair lifted her he tried to keep all personal feeling out of the matter. But it was his own babe he was carrying for the first time and the situation had a rare charm. It was not until he had her in his arms that he knew exactly how frightened she was; the poor little heart was thumping to such an extent it made her shake from head to foot; he had often caught and held small wild birds and it always had this same effect. She was not heavy in spite of her five feet four, just a nice weight that he could have carried for ever. The pink bow tickled his cheek as she lay against his shoulder. He wanted to have a peep at her, to see how she looked there; however, he sternly repressed this inclination, kept his face religiously turned away and appeared to take a deep and abiding interest in the path. After a while the trembling subsided and the heart got back to almost normal. Sinclair became aware someone was studying his profile at length and in detail.

"Is it much farther now?" a voice asked presently.

"No distance at all"—still taking his own view of the case. A pause.

"I'm afraid I'm tiring you."

"Not a bit. I've often carried your weight all day."

"Once when I sprained my ankle Claude carried me back; he grumbled the whole way and said I was an awful lump."

"I'm a size or two bigger than your brother and that makes a lot of difference."

"Claude is my twin, he's an inch taller than I am. Do you think we're much alike?"

Sinclair smiled to himself. This babe was fishing. "Yes, you're very much alike, but yet there's a difference."

"Would you have known I was his sister if I hadn't told you my name?"

"Certainly I should have taken you for a relation of his."

The answer appeared to satisfy. Conversation languished after this. Sinclair picked his way lightheartedly down the stream with apparently as little interest in his burden as if he were carrying a bag of flour. Chrysanthe studied him in a much kindlier light. On the *Asabo* she had rather liked him. Now every step took them farther away from the beloved but sinful Claude, and there was every possibility of those guns getting off without anyone knowing anything about them, some of the old liking returned. To-morrow she would say she was tired, that would postpone the search for one day, the next she would take them in the wrong direction and on the third suddenly drop on the home route. There was a very safe feeling about this shoulder too, as if it would not give way behind her like most things had done in her short and wild life. It was funny he should be with Langfeldt. He was not a bit like him—did not swear, or drink more than he ought, tell horrible tales, cheat at cards, take things that did not belong to him or do any of the things she had hitherto connected with men. Perhaps that beauty had decided to sell Claude for a good round sum, knew about those guns, and had brought Major Sinclair up purposely! If so, she had settled his little game much in the same way as she had settled his last big cheat. Once those awful guns were out of the way she would ask this sharp-eyed cove to come and stay with them. It would be no end of a lark to see him smelling round all day and finding nothing. He would think he had mistaken his man entirely and go back to England again. Claude was going to be quite good when the centipede deal was through; then they would go and live somewhere else—Monte Carlo he said—and there would be no need to take things which did not belong to them for the sake of raising the wind. The centipede was theirs; it had been found by one of their people hundreds of years ago. What would Major Sinclair think if he read that old scrawl? It was nervy work going up there and—! Chrysanthe shivered.

The shiver made Sinclair glance at her sharply. She appeared to be lost in a maze of worrying thought. The sight made his mouth harden. What villainous scheme had that young devil on now?

Then she came back to the present moment. Again Sinclair became aware he was the object under inspection. What a very hard mouth he had! He used not to look like that before. Perhaps he objected to females and was cross at having to carry her. On the *Asabo* he took very little notice of the women, there were some not bad-looking girls on board too, and preferred to talk to her. It was strange that after being so chummy he should come and want to nail his late friend—probably he had made up to him, or rather her, with the idea of trying to find out more. He had been taken in nicely! He was sharp, but not as sharp as they were! His was a different kind of sharpness—his sort had hunted out her sort from the beginning of things. It would be funny to see him sitting up on the front veranda where his kind had died painful deaths more than once, according to family tradition. The last, in the old great-grandfather's time—a fearfully cute chap, something like him, had made up to them, pretending to be one of them and had been found out! There was a horrible stain on the front balcony still, all that remained of him half-an-hour after they spotted his little game. Grip's ancestors knew what happened to him!

She looked at the dog wading solemnly by Sinclair's side. In appearance it might have been a cross between a bloodhound and a mastiff and was about the size of a small donkey. Grip was the last of his race too—like Claude and she were. They had started just two of them; flourished and prospered, become quite a colony, drifted down to two again, and now the time was up. Palaver set!

She studied Sinclair afresh. On the *Asabo* he never did things like other men she met when she took Claude's place. There was a very safe feeling about him always. But for him thinking she was Claude she would never have known him, they were always rank outsiders. She sighed. Sinclair's mouth hardened. She watched it contemplatively. What effect would it have if she suddenly put one finger on the hard stern line at the corner? She wanted to rub it out and make him look like he used to sometimes, especially the last evening in Rio del Rey. She had nearly given the show away then! Now her arm had gone to sleep and had got pins and needles.

She wriggled a little. The first time she had dared to move since Sinclair lifted her. He looked at her—the hard, stern line she had been contemplating vanished completely—and he smiled as he used to on the *Asabo* when she had been talking extra "rot."

"Are you quite comfortable?"

The smile swept away all lurking doubts. At that moment Chrysanthe felt safer than she ever had done in the whole of her daring little life. Also it said he did not object to carrying her, in fact rather liked it. Thereupon it dawned on her it would be "no end of a lark" to tease this sharp-eyed cove. As if she could be "quite comfortable" carried by a man she had known barely an hour? This bird-hunter must be taught a lesson.

"No, I'm not at all comfortable. It's very hard and scrubby here. I shall be glad when I can walk again."

This was the opportunity Langfeldt had been waiting for. It appeared to him he was being cheated out of his fair share of the spoil.

"Let me give you a lift, Miss Wentworth," he said, "I'm certain I could make a better job of it than Sinclair."

Chrysanthe had not counted on him when she decided to tease her bearer. Sinclair felt her heart start its wild beating again and two small hands clutched the objectionable scrubby shirt in the way babes have if they think they are going to be given to someone they do not like. Only for an instant and they dropped again, but quite long enough to make Sinclair's heart beat nearly as wildly as her own.

"No! no, thank you. I—I've got used to being here."

Langfeldt looked disappointed but persisted, adding a clause to the effect his friend might be tired.

Sinclair's arms tightened round his babe as he said, "You'd better go and hurry up those Hausas, they seem an unconscionably long way behind."

The German was inclined to demur, but he had had one trifling disagreement with his companion during their weeks together and was not anxious for another, and then went with obvious reluctance.

The teasing of this "sharp-eyed cove" had proved somewhat of a fiasco.

Presently a shaky voice asked concernedly, "Are you tired, Major Sinclair?"

"Not at all."

For the next hour nothing was said. Chrysanthe lay uncomplainingly against the hard shoulder and felt sorry Major Sinclair should have turned out to be the man who had sworn to have her brother. She could never really like him again because of that.

"How long before we get to the part where I can walk?" she asked at length.

"We've hardly gone any distance yet."

"It seems a long way."

"That's because you're tired and hungry and I'm afraid not very comfortable. I'm not used to carrying people and perhaps make rather a poor business of it."

"I've never been carried by anyone except Claude and Krua and you do quite as well as they"—graciously.

Sinclair was enjoying himself. His wild bird was getting over its fright and beginning to talk.

"May I ask who Krua is?"

"He's my brother."

"Then you've two brothers"—surprisedly. "Is Krua like you, too?"

"He's different altogether. You would hardly take me for his sister. He's dark, very dark and very tall; taller than you are by two inches. You're sure to see him though. When we pick up the home route you must come and stay with us. Claude will be delighted. His friends don't often come up here to see him; it's too far and very rough traveling."

Sinclair expressed his delight at the prospect of staying with Claude.

As he went along he held his precious bundle just a trifle closer. It was such a brave, foolish little girl, and did its best to screen that young villain of a brother, that he hoped he would find no damning evidence on "The Babe's" premises. Then, as the path narrowed considerably, he was too busily employed in picking his way and preventing the barbed, thorny creepers from damaging his charge for further conversation. When he emerged from the gully and put his babe on her feet there was not one scratch on her, neither had the tiniest scrap of the fluffy pink dress been left in the thorny tangle.

"Why, we're at your camp!" Chrysanthe said as a few minutes' walk brought them to the tents.

"Yes, and I expect you would like a wash and brush up after your day's wandering. This"—pausing outside of a faded green tent—"is the very rough accommodation I must apologise for. It's not stocked in exactly the way I should wish for you. Look upon it as your brother's and if you can't find all you want there, don't be afraid to ask. In a few minutes tea will be ready."

As the pink figure vanished through the green curtain Sinclair called his orderly and they went to the store tent. During the day in Grand Canary, when he had seen this small bird of his more or less "off-duty," he had made a fair estimate of what it liked and did not like. Afterwards he had telephoned to a shop in Les Palmas for a case of special bird food to be sent on board the *Asabo*. Why he should have done such an extraordinary thing he did not know; but it pleased him to do so. This same case of dainties had made his heart ache in an unaccountable manner when he saw it hauled out of the vessel's hold at Dwala. His little bird had flown! Nevertheless he stuck to the box and kept an eye on it during the whole of the journey up country; and now, it seemed too good to be true, he had caught the same small bird again and would be able to feed it on just what it liked.

The black orderly watched in round-eyed astonishment as his master opened the box of bird mixture whistling a merry tune meanwhile. Then he hung over it for some minutes in a happy state of indecision and finally abstracted four tins. Afterwards he went round to the kitchen department and the negro cook had the time of his life. Many uncomplimentary things were said regarding the state of his crockery and his skill as a maker of tea. Three lots were made before the brew was considered fit to appear before a lady.

Meanwhile Chrysanthe fluttered round the tent portioned out to her in a state of great curiosity. It was Major Sinclair's tent, she knew. There were two black japanned cabin trunks with his name in big, white letters. The shabby brown leather dressing-case with T. S. on it in little black letters she had become acquainted with on the *Asabo*. There were several other things she knew and all were looked at with an equal amount of interest. She could never have done that dreadful week had she known who he really was. It was awful enough as it was, but to have known those gimlet eyes were watching her every movement would have settled her entirely!

She washed her face and hands and sat on the flat tin box and dried them ruminatingly. Her hair was much longer than Claude's now. What a good thing she had given him a prison crop only the day before yesterday. It made them look very different. Major Sinclair was sharp to spot a swop would be possible! Now she would use his comb. Small fingers poked round the rather stiff catch of the dressing-case and eventually succeeded in opening it. Why did he keep chocolates there? Only one, in silver paper that looked as if it had traveled. A thumb and finger pinched it to ascertain if possible what lay within. In shape and feel it might be an almond. How funny! They were the kind she liked the best! She did not remember seeing him eat those kind of things on the *Asabo*.

Standing the little square mirror up on the case she combed out the chestnut curls, but with one eye on the chocolate. Perhaps it belonged to some girl he liked and had been given to him just before he left England. What sort of a girl would he like?

The combing operations ceased as she tried to form a mental picture of the former owner of the chocolate. Someone something like Marjorie, little and clinging, who had never been off her own doorstep alone, who did not know whisky from gin, would be shocked at the idea of smoking and had never heard a swear word in her life. The curls were raked at again with some viciousness, then the pink ribbon threaded through and coaxed and twisted into a most becoming bow.

A voice announced tea was ready. She put on her hat and went out. Under the shade of a mango-tree the feast was spread on a folding table. Sinclair soon had her installed in the only chair the camp boasted of, and seated himself on a case that had once contained whisky. Opposite sat Langfeldt on a wooden box hastily requisitioned from the stores department and marked "Milk."

It was really rather a nice tea Chrysanthe thought as she poured out and made inquiries regarding sugar. She knew Sinclair never had sugar and Langfeldt never had tea. Why had the latter suddenly taken to it? He always called it by a very inelegant name and had a whisky instead. She glanced over the table. There were chocolates—just like the one she had seen in the dressing-case, evidently that girl had given him a good supply—coloured marzipans in heart, diamond, club, and spade designs, shortbread biscuits, and a fruity cake with almonds on the top—nicely browned ones that can be picked off and eaten separately when nobody is looking. The bread was obviously bush-made and the slices cut and buttered by the hand of a man. (Sinclair had prided himself on the waferlike thinness of those slices.) Altogether not at all the sort of things men usually have with them when they camp out in the wilds!

Sinclair watched the slim fingers that hovered over the teacups, with as much interest as he watched them pick a cigarette from his case on the occasion of their first drink together, almost three months ago. They had had a good many drinks at each other's expense since then; the last in Rio del Rey river. It was a long time since they had had that and he would not like to live those separating weeks over again. He was standing treat this time, which was even as it should be, because the next drink was to him. When this daring small bird was really his and wore a ring with its owner's name and address he would tell it all these things. Some day perhaps when it perched on his knee and smoked a cigarette turn about with him. The thought made him smile.

"What's amusing you, Major Sinclair?" a voice asked rather sharply.

The smile died a swift and sudden death. Two blue eyes were looking at him suspiciously. Unintentionally Langfeldt came to the rescue.

"I expect Sinclair is thinking to-day's hunting has ended in the capture of quite a different bird from usual. Every day after dinner he messes about identifying and classifying the day's bag and then writes about them. To-day's entry will be—Caught Lat. so-and-so, Long. something else, a specimen never before known to exist in these parts. Plumage, soft fluffy pink. Eyes, a deep dark blue, big and a way of opening wide when startled. Chestnut crest with a band of pink. Habits but little known; appears to be rather shy and does not make friends easily. Nest, built in the most out-of-the-way inaccessible part and not yet found. Altogether quite the most remarkable bird ever caught in the depths of a West African forest."

"Was that what you were thinking?"

For his own sake Sinclair said it was, and felt grateful to Langfeldt. It would never do for this small girl to learn the truth!

"Have you caught many birds on the way up here?"

As the question was asked those slim fingers that interested him so much poised over the marzipan mixtures. He watched them covertly. Would it be the pink heart or the green spade? They seemed undecided.

"More than I expected," he replied.

The fingers swooped down on the pink heart.

"Did you come with the idea of hunting for any special specimen, Major Sinclair?"

The German laughed.

"Why are you laughing, Mr. Langfeldt?"—looking at him in wide-eyed innocence.

Mr. Langfeldt's mirth was such that he could not reply.

As Sinclair answered he watched the pink heart. It seemed to him the most desirable morsel on earth. He wanted it and the one daring small babe who held it.

"Yes, there is one special bird I hope to catch. I want it for my aviary in England. I've a good many rare kinds but not that one."

The heart was bitten clean and straight through the middle, and eaten with gusto. "Have you seen anything of it yet?" she asked.

"Yes, I've almost, as you might say, had it in my hands. But I hadn't a very firm hold and it slipped out."

The remaining portion of the pink heart disappeared and Chrysanthe asked interestedly, "What sort of a bird is it?"

"I know very little about it beyond the fact that it's very wild and difficult to catch. I've read a bit about it, looked for it in several parts of the world, but this was the last place in which I should have said it could be found."

"What is it called?"

"I shall give it a name when I catch it."

"Has anyone ever caught it?"—with deep interest.

"Not one exactly like the specimen I want."

Langfeldt thought it was time Chrysanthe devoted a little of her attention to him therefore he passed the fruity cake. She took a piece, refusing Sinclair's proffered shortbread. Then something suddenly took her attention, she was up and flying along to where a couple of Hausas appeared to be holding an argument with a wild and savage figure that had just emerged from the bush. The soldiers, who seemed inclined to dispute the right of way, fell back with considerable force—in fact they fell one on the other in an undignified heap. Sinclair and Langfeldt rose hastily. Chrysanthe flew on to meet the advancing black giant. She spoke breathlessly, with amazing rapidity, and small fists pummeled him with emphatic vigor. Evidently he was to be made to understand something and quickly. A grin spread over his ebony face, one huge hand pulled the broad white hat, that had slipped down her back owing to hurried flight, into position. Then, with an arm slipped through his and clasped hands on the muscular limb, she advanced at a half dance, still talking at a great rate, to where the two men stood in natural astonishment.

"Major Sinclair, this is my brother Krua."

He acknowledged the introduction gravely, conscious this brawny giant was watching him in the manner Grip had on first acquaintance, and smiled to himself as he remembered this small girl, the last evening in Rio del Rey, had spoken of her negro foster-mother. This "very dark" brother she had led him to suppose she possessed was evidently the son of that woman. The man seemed vaguely familiar. It was not the deck-hand he had remarked the first day on the *Asabo*, he was an older negro and had not the physique of this. As regards features one black is very much the same as the next. Then he remembered. The time in Grand Canary, when he and "Claude" Wentworth returned to the boat in the small hours of the morning, loafing on the quay was a huge negro. He had noticed the man followed them and had kept a watch on him, wondering what his intentions were. His companion did not appear to him, but he was pretty certain this was the same negro in spite of his present barbarous attire. Evidently "The Babe's" double did not travel entirely alone!

"All day Krua has been looking for me," Chrysanthe went on, "walking up and down forest tracks until he's almost as lost as I am and at last dropped on your camp and found me here. Are we far from home? Shall we be able to get back to-night?"

"As the bird flies, my flower, it is good twelve miles, but the track leads with many a twist and turn. There will be no returning to-day, nor perhaps to-morrow. Even I am uncertain of the way. When the breakfast hour passed and the flower did not appear we started, my brother and I, to hunt in the forest for the lost one—he to the east and I to the west, others to the northward and southward."

"And you found me like you always do, Krua."

"Am I not the flower's great thorn, ay, from the time it was but a pink bud in my mother's arms. There are hands stretched out to pluck it, black and white. But they who would have the flower must first pass the thorn. There was one who would have it; for these long weeks he has licked his scratch. There is another who desires it, he works by stealth, is with this one, then with that and again with another. There is a third I must watch for I know not what he means. But there is no way to the flower except through much blood. It was so with the first in the days of my father's fathers, when my people were as a great army. It is so with the last when I alone am left of the flower's thorns. Ayati! Golden Flower! in the days that are lost in the mist thou wert our queen! Ayati! Golden Flower! in the day that is, I alone am left of thy subjects!"

Chrysanthe laughed but at the back of her eyes Sinclair noticed the strained, listening look that had been there the night of her delirium. More than ever the feeling grew on him that there was some wild old Mystery behind it all. Something that hung and evolved round this little girl.

"In the day that is, O Krua, I had but half-finished my tea when you appeared. Therefore, last of my subjects, I will return unto it now."

Krua dropped two paces behind as she went back to her seat.

Chrysanthe reattacked the piece of fruity cake, and a most provoking dimple lurked in the corner of her mouth as she said, "How do you like my brother, Major Sinclair?"

"I've taken a great fancy to him, Miss Wentworth. Don't you think he will be hungry after his day's wanderings? Let my orderly take him round to the kitchen department and give him a free range."

"Are you hungry, Krua?"

"No, my flower, we of the bush pick up many things as we go along."

"What did you pick up?"

"The trail of the maimed paw!"—in the Blenguta tongue.

Chrysanthe's hands shook to such an extent she could hardly hold her cup.

"That is why I at once searched for my flower"—continuing in the same dialect—"and rejoiced to find it. The maimed paw is in touch with those who sit here. I know it. It is not safe that the flower goes one little step alone. It will be well when this thing is finished. I like it not. Of the two men here, one would kill our brother and take the flower by force. The other, I know not what he desires, but he is with one whom we have proved a traitor. But say the word and I will kill these two men as they sit. Two knives, and each hand throws with equal aim! I will have my flower away in the bush before their servants know it."

Sinclair, who was well versed in obsolete negro dialects, listened to all this and awaited Chrysanthe's reply with the deepest interest. The position of the table was screened from the rest of the camp, and Krua could have carried out his design successfully.

"There is to be no bloodshed, Krua, that is why the maimed paw thirsts for mine. He sang the doom that night! There is a lake of blood to cross before the end is reached. Blood of three hundred years! Each drop spilt by the hands of my people! But I will have no more. Our race is finished and I go back whence I came. It is well for I am tired."

She lay back listlessly with brooding, clouded eyes, like one who looks back a long distance. Sinclair watched her wondering what lay behind all this.

"I'm afraid Krua has been the bearer of bad news," he said presently.

Chrysanthe pulled herself together with an effort.

"No, only I was reminded of something that—that I try to forget," then lapsing again into the Blenguta tongue, "Does our brother know this beast is on the trail?"

"It will not touch him until it has thee."

"It's all my fault, Krua."

A big hand patted her shoulder.

"My flower, the fault is with those who have gone before."

"What gibberish is your black spaniel talking, Miss Wentworth?" Langfeldt asked. What had been fairly intelligible to Sinclair was so much Hebrew to the German.

"It's Krua's own language."

"But it's not the ordinary lingo."

"He's not a native of this part."

She got up wearily. Sinclair wondered what fresh weight had been laid on those slim shoulders.

"I guess I'll go and lie down for a bit, I'm rather tired. Wandering about so long this morning has given me a headache."

He watched her as she crossed to the tent, Krua and the dog following. Would he ever get this little girl out of the weird, barbarous tangle that seemed to grow ever thicker around her?

CHAPTER 10

"Where has she gone? And who is she?"

THE CAMP SAW NOTHING MORE of its visitor that evening. When dinnertime arrived Krua brought a message to Sinclair that the headache had increased, together with an apology. The hard, stern line Chrysanthe had contemplated deepened, and the best provender the camp boasted of was sent along to the invalid. Outside of the faded green tent Krua engaged in his favorite occupation of "thorn" sharpening. To his armory had been added a huge, double-edged knife, about two feet long, with a heavy, brass-studded handle and carried in a leather sheath. This was not for throwing purposes but for close quarters, and its sharpness was such that it almost cut on sight. With nightfall Sinclair set a double guard round his little bird's cage, at a distance sufficiently far away not to arouse suspicion. As he went his round later on he noticed the dog was no longer with the negro and supposed it to be with its mistress. Afterwards he sat outside of an extempore tent lost in a cloud of tobacco and thought. What he had seen and heard during Chrysanthe's brief delirium, "The Babe's" midnight excursion to Langfeldt's person and cabin, the little scheme the German had spoken of and the tea-time conversation, worked out and put together gave him a fair idea of what was on foot. A man of Langfeldt's stamp would not take a perilous journey into the wilds unless he was going to be paid for it and at a high rate. He felt absolutely certain "The Babe" had some treasure-hunting scheme on that could not be worked out without his sister, owing to ancient superstition. He was equally sure the German knew this and intended to get possession of this small girl and take the lot himself. He had a fair idea the "maimed paw" was the "Mungea" mentioned the night he discovered the secret of Claude Wentworth's successful "alibis," and also this same Mungea was the man he had marked the first day on the *Asabo* and who was responsible for the centipede on his sister. No doubt this was the deck-hand who had deserted at Rio del Rey and the recipient of the scratch referred to by Krua. He was perfectly aware the latter suspected him because of his present connection with Langfeldt. Probably those same eyes had watched him many a time when he had been strolling up and down the deck with his babe. He would like to gain the man's confidence—the heathen savage took better care of her than her own brother. Heaven alone knew what fearful place the young devil was going to lead her into now! If he found an ounce of evidence on their premises he would arrest him straight away and so stop his latest game. It would kill whatever liking that child had for him but it would keep her out of harm. Whatever happened he would not lose sight of her again. If the worst came to the worst he would arrest them both; he would not use what he had learnt accidentally except as a last resource, but he would be sure of getting her safely back to England that way; he had sufficient influence to get her off afterwards and, whether she liked it or not, he would watch over her and see no harm happened to her. At least he would know she was alive, which was probably more than she would be if this thing went on. In any case if this one small wild bird ever became his he would have to throw up his present position.

He got up for a final round before turning in. The camp lay like a pool of moonlight in a setting of black trees. Out of the bush came the snarl of a leopard prowling close at hand; away in the distance the howl of another, together with the shrill, high wail, of the bush-cat. The forest was full of subdued whisperings, and now and again there was an echoing crash of a heavy weight plunging through the undergrowth. He approached the faded green tent where the white light glinted on four knives spread out for his inspection. He paused, conscious of being closely watched.

"It's a sharp thorn that guards the flower, O Krua."

"It is, and as swift to prick, hunter of birds."

"The flower sleeps secure in my camp, thou black watch-dog."

"There is no safe sleep for the flower, thou friend of traitors."

"The leopard and the bush-dog drink at the same pool."

"But not at the same hour, or it goes ill with the bush-dog, speaker of parables."

Sinclair laughed and seated himself on an empty box close to where Krua squatted at a distance from the tent that gave him a view all around it. He was anxious to hear more of what this negro had to say.

"There is a way and yet another way, Krua, and each leads to the same spot."

"There is but one way to the flower and that red."

"I desire only to protect the flower."

"In the days that are as yesterday, that are now grown over with the moss of time, green bones from which all form has gone, whose shape remains only the sight of a few, there was one who spake even as thee, one of thy colour! In the days of my father's fathers a flower grew in an evil land. No one knew whence it came; it was found a small pink bud. As it grew many thorns were set about it. There was a temple wherein dwelt the Evil One who had ruled this land from the beginning. And he loved blood and gold, but beyond all the Golden Flower! As a child the flower strayed in. No one had entered there and lived. My dead brothers, the thorns, searched high and low, and at the temple gates found one small shoe of soft hide worked with gold which had been on the foot of the flower. A wail went up reaching to the town. Even as they wept there came a child's laugh and at the gate stood the lost one leading our father the devil by one horn! Arru! but it was so! Always afterwards the Evil One waited at the gate for the Golden Flower, and caused many things to be made that she might stay and play and laugh around him. There were soft-voiced golden bells, even now at times I hear them with the ear of ages; and curious little glittering toys. Sometimes from the temple she brought shining pebbles that flashed and sparkled in the sun. The bud blossomed into a flower, even as now. And there came one unto the land who found the flower seated among the thorns, decked in the gifts of that which dwelt in the cave. It would have been well had they slain him then! But even as now the thorns pricked only at the flower's desire. For a time he dwelt in the land. But he was brave and feared neither god nor devil. He loved the shining pebbles that had been the flower's toys and desired to enter the cave wherein they were found. The flower laughed and held the Evil One by one horn that this stranger might enter and see what lay within. What passed between those three I know not. But the stranger would have plucked the flower by stealth and taken it whence he came. It awoke and cried; the thorns heard and would have slain him but he had a poison we knew not in those days; the thorns fell before its loud voice and the thief escaped. For a time the land saw him not. Then he returned with others of his own colour and many of a strange tribe. A cloud was over the land, black and red. The thorns fell one by one till but a handful remained. Then the flower came and knelt at his feet, begging that just these few be spared. He was a great man this robber, even as thou or I or the traitor who sleeps yonder. It was a limp flower he tossed on to his shoulder as he bade the poison sticks cease their calling. There were those with him of his colour who clamored for the pebbles of gold and red. He laughed and took them to the hill wherein lay the temple. Laughed as they went in one by one! Laughed as he stood at the rocky gates with that limp white flower on his shoulder! No one has laughed in the land since that day! In a place that is far, there waits one for the stolen flower and the stealer. Arru! I speak with the words that come out of the mist, even as the mist twists and curls and takes shapes that mean nothing, so may they! I tell this because of another who said, 'I desire only to protect the flower.'"

For a time Sinclair said nothing. Krua rearranged his knives and smiled at them.

"When did this happen?" the former asked at length.

"The scent of the crushed flower wafts down on the wind that blows cold from long dead years. I am but the mouth of those who whisper out of the mist. Maybe I hear awrong! The voices speak from afar off and but faintly."

"And the crushed flower and the stealer! What of them?"

"A thief tells not his comings and goings. Even that other was over curious and desired to know much of the flower. There is a day far off and lost, but since that day only the splash of blood has sounded in the ears of my people. There was a time when the mists were not and one saw even unto the blue whence came the eyes of the flower. There is a time when the mists are thick and one sees no farther than the throwing of this knife."

Here Krua picked up the longest and most vicious-looking of his weapons. Sinclair took it as a hint that for the present the subject was closed. He went back musingly to his tent, and that night dreamt of a little girl in a pink dress who lay crushed and hurt beneath a heap of red and yellow pebbles. On the top sat another, her twin and facsimile, who laughed and mocked him as he tried to break through a bristling barrier of red dripping knives and reach her.

In the morning the headache was better. In spite of this Sinclair noticed there were deep dark rings under Chrysanthe's eyes that spoke of a wakeful night. There was a look about Grip too as if he had not slept. As a matter of fact, during the hours when the camp lay wrapped in slumber, he had gone some twenty miles, the bearer of an important message. This was rather trying to dog nerves in a forest over-productive in leopards. Also there had been some difficulty both on the outward and homeward journey in sneaking through those watching Hausas. But more than one of his forebears had acted postman under equally arduous circumstances. The time had been almost as trying for his mistress lying sleepless and anxiously awaiting his return so as to know whether the note had reached its destination safely.

In spite of the dark rings under her eyes Chrysanthe had recovered her spirits. Claude, the beloved, knew exactly how things stood and would be able to make his arrangements accordingly. The Sinclair, Langfeldt and Mungea combination, viewed in the light of early morning, with the knowledge that the clever but unscrupulous one had been made aware of its nearness, did not look so appalling as when seen at the end of a tiring afternoon when the saving of the whole thing fell on a pair of weary girlish shoulders.

Chrysanthe poured out coffee with a meditating air. It was hard lines when Claude had a deal on that was really legal and no one else's business Major Sinclair should come hopping round. Many a time she had sat in fear and trembling on the front balcony dreading a similar visitor because of things in those back sheds which should not be there. It would be a fortnight yet before they would be ready to start on their last great deal. Meanwhile it would be sport to have this sharp old bird staying with them. It would be better to have him there than hopping round the district not knowing exactly where he was. And Langfeldt too! There was nothing like keeping a close eye on the enemy. Everything would be so open and aboveboard that this sharp-eyed cove would suspect nothing. Then when the time came for starting they would slip off in the middle of the night, leaving their guests in possession of the homestead with a note bidding them adieu and a P.S. to say they might use the place as long as they wished. She would like to see Major Sinclair's face when he read it; he was not a bad sort, a bit too sharp for everyday use though. Cute as he was he would only be able to do one step to their three on the way up there. She would be glad when it was all finished and they were safely settled down in Monte Carlo. It always gave her the creeps when Krua started on the "voice of ancient days" tack. There was quite enough of it in that old scrawl to settle the average nerve. Claude said that part was all bunkum and only to scare off trespassers. She was not so sure; sometimes it seemed as if voices were whispering to her from a long way off. Probably most people felt like that at times. Did Major Sinclair ever feel like that?

Over the top of a coffee cup two blue eyes looked at him speculatively.

Sinclair thought she had been silent quite long enough. Before breakfast he had made another dive into his box of bird mixture. This he proffered now with the idea of making her talk again.

"May I pass you some honey, Miss Wentworth?"

"Yes, I will have some, I've not had any since"—she stopped abruptly and the small round face went the colour of the pink bow in her hair—"since I don't know when"—finishing with a visible effort.

"Talking of honey," Langfeldt remarked, "reminds me it was a favorite dish of your brother's this trip down. At Rio del Rey a nigger deck-hand bolted in the night. Before departing he broke into the chief steward's store of special dainties and absconded with the lot. I remember the row your brother made at breakfast when none appeared—the first really healthy row he had made since leaving Liverpool. He's like that though; one time as quiet as a lamb, the next a perfect young d— terror."

"Yes, Claude varies. He—he has fits and starts of—of—" One slim finger rubbed up and down the table edge nervously.

"Devilment!" Sinclair suggested, anxious to assist and knowing the slip had somewhat shattered this small babe's nerve. Probably she had never, when wearing a fluffy pink dress, been called upon to discuss her brother's peculiarities in the presence of two whom she had known when taking his place.

"He—he's a little wild at times. It's in the family. Oh!" with an unbelieving gasp, "oh! here he is!"

Sauntering out of a tiny bush track came "The Babe"—white drill suit, blue cummerbund, grey felt hat and cigarette complete, with the air of having just stepped out of a band-box, the figure Sinclair had so often looked for on the *Asabo*.

Chrysanthe got up, one hand went to her throat as she looked first at Sinclair, then at Langfeldt, then went quickly across to the approaching jaunty figure. The two men rose also, the German somewhat undecided in what spirit to meet his late friend. One thing, the girl's presence would prevent any immediate outbreak of hostilities. If Claude was perfectly content to let bygones be bygones, and proceed as before his private deal with Mungea, he was perfectly willing it should be so. He had not seen this small personage in pink when he made his agreement with the nigger.

Sinclair likewise employed the interval in thinking. He must meet this smiling young devil with the air of one who had known and liked him for a full month, moreover, of one whose acquaintance with his sister did not run into twenty-four hours, knowing quite well two pairs of eyes would be waiting and looking for the least slip. He watched the slim figure in pink as it went swiftly towards the approaching white one. "The Babe" threw away his cigarette. Chrysanthe's arms were round his neck as she spoke to him quickly. He laughed and kissed her in a careless, matter-of-fact way that annoyed Sinclair, and left him with a desire to show how it should be done. Then, with his arm round her waist, the youngster came towards the table.

"Lord! Chrys, what have you been doing with yourself these twenty-four hours? I had the shock of my life yesterday when you didn't turn up for breakfast. Who are your friends? Well, of all the—!" with the air of one doubtful regarding his own eyesight. "How do, Carl? How do, Major Sinclair? Who'd have thought of seeing you two here! What do you mean by stealing my sister? The whole show has been out looking for her since this time yesterday. I never had such an awful night as last—was out till long past midnight, prowling round trying to find her. Went back to see if anyone had found her. Grabbed a whisky and a sandwich, and was starting out again when a nigger came and said he'd heard there were two whites camping in 'Palm Hollow.' Came along 'one-time' to see if by any chance they'd dropped across you, Chrys. I spotted the tail of your dress long before you spotted me"—then looking again at the men—"So you're the butterfly-hunters camping out here—pleased and delighted to see you both I'm sure. You must have hooked Chrys out of an almighty hole. She hasn't the air of having wandered about all night. Where did you find her? Ain't surprised to see you, Krua! You'd nose round into the hottest corner of hell if you thought there was a chance of 'your flower' being there. There ain't much fear of that though! That spot's being reserved for me—a warm and comfy seat after a cold and unappreciative world! I'm jolly glad you chaps found her; the bush at night ain't the place for a girl—too many big pussies on the prowl!"

It was noticeable "The Babe's" hand never left his cummerbund during the whole of his chaffing explanation and rejoicing, likewise Krua's fist grasped the handle of his great knife. Chrysanthe stood between her brother and the two men. Small hands straightened his long loose tie, pulled out the pin and stuck it in again in exactly the same place, took his hat that he swung to and fro in the manner Sinclair knew so well, put it on his closely cropped head and held it down over each ear with one finger so as to form a bonnet, patted and poked and smoothed him.

"Lord! Chrys, anyone would think I was the lost sheep, not you. Your sister don't paw you over like this when she hasn't seen you for half-an-hour, does she, Major Sinclair?"

"My sister has half-a-dozen brothers, so I'm not as appreciated as I should like to be. Now Wentworth, I expect you're ready for some 'chop' after your long walk. Have my seat, I'll send along for another."

"You sit down, old chap, I'll perch up here on the milk cans with Carl. Grub's a good sight after a twelve-mile walk on one lone whisky and a sandwich. You two seem to be living high for a couple of raw hands in the wilderness! Is this the everyday menu or have you been sacrificing at the altar of the lost? Chrys, I expect you're the unconscious cause of all this willful, wild extravagance. Let me tell you chaps that's not the way to Chrys's heart. It's the one thing she don't approve of. I'm a bit inclined that way myself, but I ain't allowed to hop too far. I'm a good boy, I am, when I'm home. I'm on an allowance now, one whisky at lunch, one at dinner and another before I go to bed. If that ain't enough to drive a saint to the devil, what is? You two must pack your little trunks after breakfast and come along and stay with us. Chrys won't dare to hide the wets when there are visitors in the house. Carl here once promised to come and pay me a visit. I gave him the route and nicked it again for a lark the last night on board when I was half seas over. Message came on board at Victoria to say an old friend of mine was dying ashore there. Hopped off 'one-time' and just got his last blessing. It wasn't until I landed home and unpacked my bag and found it there, that I remembered what I'd done. Chrys was wondering why the visitor didn't arrive. I daren't explain because I'd promised to be good this trip and always, always go below in the upright attitude that becomes a man. Now you big chaps have come along I ain't afraid any more. I'll have a whisky every day directly after breakfast now—see if I don't—if I have to stand behind you two and drink it! You'll come and protect me, won't you, Major Sinclair?"

"Major Sinclair and Mr. Langfeldt have already promised to come and stay with us," Chrysanthe said as he finished.

They heartily agreed they had. Claude expressed his delight, and then started talking about the incidents of the late voyage with a correctness of place and time that surprised Sinclair. But these two babes kept detailed diaries which they found of considerable value as works of reference.

There was a relieved look about Langfeldt as "The Babe" rattled on. Evidently bygones were to be bygones. It was just possible the whole thing had been a drunken spree. He had known Claude do similar things to others, but not to him, Carl, his bosom and trusted friend! But it was more probable Sinclair's presence had had the desired effect and brought him to his senses. When he got Claude to himself he would talk the whole business over quietly. He would not trust him until he had those papers once more in his possession. His share would have to be considerably increased too. According to the nigger there was a lot more in it than his very dear young friend led him to understand. But for the sister he would stick to his original plan. She was the smartest little filly he had seen for a long time and took his fancy more than any he had come across. She was shy and inclined to be stand-offish, but he liked her all the better for it. If Claude cut up rusty and refused to fall in with his idea he would acquaint Sinclair with a few of his deals and stick to his arrangement with the nigger.

As Langfeldt went over the various irons in his fire Sinclair watched Chrysanthe, who was pouring out coffee for her brother with a care and attention regarding the size of sugar and proportion of milk that roused his envy. She passed it to him and then became really agitated over which dish he would like.

"Lord! Chrys, any old thing will do for me," he said laughingly as she fluttered round him, buttered his toast and had eyes for nobody else, big, soft eyes that overflowed with mother-love and made Sinclair realize just what chance he had if he laid a finger on the young reprobate. There was a cold, hopeless feeling about him as he watched them.

Breakfast completed, "The Babe" took over the care and arrangement of everything connected with his friends' camp. The best thing, he said, would be for the four of them to go on first with some lunch. It was a good walk to the homestead, they would have to travel slowly because of his sister, and would not get there much before tea. Krua could stay behind and bring up the porters and kit; he could follow their trail all right. Presently Krua having been instructed in his part of the palaver, and Sinclair having given one or two orders to his headman, erstwhile sergeant of the smartest Hausa corps on the coast, the quartette set out.

It was getting on for five in the afternoon when they reached "The Babe's" premises. The whole way there had led through a maze of tangled, twisted tracks up a slight incline, and finally they came out on a plateau similar to the one where Chrysanthe had been found, but larger, surrounded by the usual dense forest. In the middle, crumbling and decayed, grown over by a score of creepers, stood what Sinclair knew at a glance to have been a rock-built fort. A strong old place it must have been once upon a time; but things neglected soon decay in West Africa. He wondered what its history was. There was a grim look about it still in spite of its roofless condition and the great gaping cracks in the thick old walls. Palms nodded their graceful heads in the shadow of its battlements; ferns and flowers grew in the slit holes in the crumbling sides that had been made for heavy, old-fashioned guns; great cuplike blossoms in blue, yellow and white crept and twisted round ancient cannon that lay red with deep, flaky rust on shattered heaps of masonry. There was no sign of life about it; nothing moved except the leaves as the wind crept in and out of the cracks and crevices.

"The old place looks a bit out of repair, don't it?" "The Babe" remarked as the fort came into sight, "but we ain't as well off as we used to be. Once we did a tremendous export business with America and the West Indies, but like most of our little moneymaking schemes it went smash. Now we live in a corner you can't see yet, and I draw teeth for Schmutz & Co., at a small commission, and Chrys ekes out the family income by making blinds for a firm in England. It's a bit of a come-down but there are other ancient and decayed families much the same."

A little more walking brought the habitable portion into view. A rough trunk of a tree thrown across a broad stream led on to a smooth green lawn—the first Sinclair had seen since he left Grand Canary, and he marveled at it, for such a sight is a rarity in West Africa. A grove of thick mangoes, studded with deep golden fruit, shaded one corner. Splashing over a six-foot high shelf at the back was a waterfall which gave a welcome cooling sound to the scene, and then babbled on sheltered by fluttering bamboos, through fern-grown nooks, round moss-covered rocks, and on between groups of orange-trees, magnolias and oleanders, until it reached the main stream skirting the garden. A wide, white-painted balcony draped with roses, and with hanging baskets of flowering plants suspended from the green roof, ran round the habitable portion of the fort. One end led to an old stone terrace and finished with a gaping crack and a heap of shattered blocks; the other disappeared round the corner evidently to the back premises. Broad steps led up to the balcony which, after the manner of the country, was dining, sitting, smoke room and lounge combined. In the widest part a fountain splashed from the middle of a large basket of ferns held by a marble water nymph, who stood in a huge shell with gold fish swimming about her feet; around were inviting-looking cane lounges and small tables strewn with books, boxes of cigarettes, syphons, packets of chocolates and plates of fruit; big palms in green, brass-bound tubs added to the coolness of the scene, and an aeolian harp sighed and murmured in the wind that wafted lightly through the balcony. Green reed blinds screened the doors and windows of the rooms behind this delightful lounge. There was a dead quiet calm

over it all, an indescribable air of unreality. To Sinclair it seemed
as if at a touch the whole thing would fade away, and he would
find himself again in Liverpool on the *Asabo's* bridge watching the
tender coming from the landing-stage. He would wake and find
the last months a bitter-sweet dream that would leave him with a
heartache for ever! It was no girl-babe he had found in his cabin
that night! No daring little sprite who had coiled round his heart
as the curl had round his finger! No pink flower he had found—
was it only yesterday—and carried in his arms and felt its heart
beating against his! It was all a vision, a picture out of the mist,
even as Krua said! Something that would fade and vanish the moment he tried to make it his. There was no girl-babe at all! Only
the sunlight dancing on the Mersey, and Morton droning in his
ear about the young villain whose track he had been on since a big
gun-running into Northern Nigeria.

A figure attired in a voluminous heliotrope print overall with a
striking design in pale pink and green, wearing on her head a handkerchief of a brilliant red and yellow pattern, and round her plump
brown throat a string of gold-colored beads, that came as quickly
round the corner as circumference and flowing garments would
allow, gave a touch of solidity to the scene. She seized Chrysanthe
in such a big motherly hug that she was almost lost in the ample
bosom and equally ample skirts.

"Mammy, won't you give this other little piccaninny a kiss too?"
"The Babe" asked plaintively.

"What did you go and do wi' your sister all yes'day, Claude?"

"I didn't do anything"—in a deeply injured tone. "She went and
lost her little self."

"Yes, Mammy, I did. It ain't Claude's fault at all this time.
This"—drawing the weighty but handsome lady to where Sinclair
stood—"is Major Sinclair who found me and this"—looking at
Langfeldt—"is his friend Mr. Langfeldt." Two identical dimples
appeared in the left corners of two similar mouths as Chrysanthe
united Sinclair and Langfeldt in the bonds of friendship, then looking at the former again—"This is Krua's mother, our mother too,
ain't you, Mammy?"

"Mammy don't own me, I'm the black sheep of the family," "The Babe" said sorrowfully as he pulled two lounges into position and bade his guests make themselves at home.

Chrysanthe laughed and turned away with her foster-mother to make arrangements for the housing of the visitors. Sinclair's gaze followed them as they went along the veranda. The whole time he had noticed the woman watched them, "The Babe" included, like a hen with one chick when there are several hungry cats prowling round, and he felt the stout, motherly person had about as much love for that little girl's double as he had.

The week that followed was the happiest of Sinclair's life. Claude and Carl had apparently made up all differences and were so devoted to each other that the burden of entertaining him fell on Chrysanthe's shoulders. He was made acquainted with the ins and outs of the old place, taken into the sheds beneath the balcony and round to the back premises. Every nook and corner was open for his inspection, even the old cellars under the ruins he was shown into. There he found some well-rusted chains and shackles, out of use long before "The Babe's" time, but which showed quite plainly what the large export trade with America and the West Indies referred to had been. But for his own secret store of knowledge he would certainly have thought he had mistaken his man.

Every day passed very much the same as the last: breakfast on the veranda in the cool hours of early morning, presided over by a small personage sometimes in pink, now in green, again in white, perhaps pale blue or a delicate shade of mauve, but equally charming and desirable in whatever colored plumage. After this repast very little was seen of her until lunch; her time appeared to be spent with Mammy superintending the arrangement of things in the back premises. The morning Claude devoted to his guests, played bridge with them, had a knock round at billiards, took them out shooting and drank more whiskies than he declared he would have dared to do but for their saving presence. Lunch, as is customary on the Coast, was at eleven, then two small saucy people, who did not look so exactly alike owing to length of hair, difference of expression and dissimilar garments, kept up a running fire of chaff at Major

Sinclair's expense and, but for the laughing devil at the back of
"The Babe's" eyes, that individual would have been inclined to
doubt the tales he had heard and the things he knew concerning
this innocent-looking youngster.

After this meal the custom of the land was to retire to one's
own room and sleep during the intense heat of the midday hours.
This Sinclair did once, but the next day he happened to want something he had left on the balcony, and there found his babe sitting
on the edge of the marble shell playing with the goldfish and talking to Mammy who sat sewing in a capacious wicker-chair; thereupon he refused to go to bed in the afternoon and stayed and talked
too, and this comely brown lady, whom he liked, began to look upon
him with less suspicion. At the ringing of the tea-bell Claude and
Carl appeared and Mammy packed up her things and retired unto
the back balcony. Carl by now was a confirmed tea-drinker. "The
Babe" looked on with wicked, twinkling eyes. These two who had
come up to catch him were fairly caught in the skirts of his sister!
He smiled to himself as he thought how much the world judges
one by one's clothes!

When the cool of the afternoon came on, the brief hours between tea and sunset, the only time after nine in the morning possible for anything approaching violent exercise, the four assembled
on the lawn for tennis. "The Babe" and his sister nearly always
played together and they invariably won. Once or twice Sinclair
persuaded Chrysanthe to take his side, but her brother and
Langfeldt lost so hopelessly that after a few times she refused to
play with him any more. She played with Langfeldt and won too;
then she returned to her brother and nothing would make her leave
him.

Often in the days to come Sinclair thought of the evenings on
the little fairyland of a veranda, lit with lamps in fantastic Chinese
lanterns—of the gay dinners when the tiny red-shaded lights glowed
in a bower of flowers and flashed and sparkled on old-fashioned
cut glass and quaint heavy silver, all of which curiously enough
were marked with a big and clearly defined D. The fact did not
surprise him; he had long since connected these two children with

the "Devereux" mentioned by Captain Morton. At this meal the small bird he wanted for his own aviary appeared in a soft silky dress of pale cream, or a delicate shade of shell-pink, or a green so faint as to be hardly noticeable, that billowed and clung round her like a cloud of mist; but although the neck was low the sleeves never got higher up than the elbow. Afterwards coffee was served round the fountain, and she in the misty dress, who got rather in his head and robbed him of some of his native discreetness, perched on the side of her brother's chair with an arm round his neck; then Sinclair felt he was nobody and became conscious of a chill not usual in the climate. Sometimes when the fountain splashed and murmured into its marble basin and the sweet, soft notes of the harp came sighing down the balcony, this mist-wreathed maiden would condescend to come and sit against him. Then he became so interested in talking to and watching her that he forgot "The Babe" was watching him. There came a time when the combination of gentle splashing water, whispering music and mystic, mist-wreathed maiden mounted into his head more than usual, and he all but connected something with her which ought to have been mentioned only in connection with her brother. He stopped himself quickly and switched the incident on to the right line. Chrysanthe did not notice the sharp change, but Claude, who sat close by instructing Langfeldt in the latest card trick invented by himself, did. Apparently so engrossed was he that, when Sinclair spoke to him a moment or so afterwards, to ascertain whether the error had passed unnoticed, he did not answer until the second hailing. There was a greater look of innocence than ever on his face as he replied to the trifling query, and quickly returned to his card trick with the air of one suddenly disturbed from a deeply interesting and absorbing occupation.

That night after the guests retired, "The Babe" sat up and did a little serious thinking. Sinclair's slip had not been sufficient to condemn him entirely, but it was enough to be suspicious—"damned suspicious"—thought he as he sat up into the small hours of the morning trying to think of a plan whereby to confirm the subject one way or the other. He knew Sinclair kept a watch on his premises. Those lynx-eyed porters of his visitor's he had seen before in Calabar dressed in the uniform of their regiment. He made no bones to himself regarding the object of this visit, and knew there was nothing on the premises or in the district that could be brought forward as sufficient evidence to permit of his arrest. There was no fear of Langfeldt giving him away just yet! But if this damned Sinclair, alias Danvers, had spotted his double game and was merely biding his time and connecting his links, then—("The Babe's" finger ran round his collar as if it suddenly choked him) then there would soon be a hempen rope round his neck; he would be footing it lightly in mid air with a black flag waving over him such as had often flown at the mastheads of his ancestors, but bar the skull and crossbones.

Claude Devereux, alias Claude Wentworth, poured himself out a good stiff whisky as he sat thoughtfully on the remaining whole corner of the family domains that had once been the stronghold of a nest of pirates, buccaneers, slave-dealers, rogues and vagabonds of the first water, whose only qualifications had to be gentle birth and total lack of scruples. He felt it would be an unworthy end for the last male member of an ancient and all-but-forgotten family. According to family annals not one of them had died in their beds, but again not one of them had put any government to the expense and trouble of hanging them. Such a record must be kept unsullied.

He sat gazing out into the darkness. Did or did not Major Sinclair know? If he did, the thing would be to clear out "one-time" before he got his chain of evidence completed, get this deal through as best he could and then to some nice little haven in South America. If he did not, it would be foolish to start up country before everything was in working order and so lead his sister into a lot of unnecessary privations. At a spot some twenty miles away a trusted retainer was getting things ship-shape, but it would be a week yet before all was ready. The thing was to find out without letting Chrys know. If she thought there was any chance of Sinclair having spotted their little game she might get a bad attack of the jumps and give the show away in less than half-an-hour. He must get this gimlet-eyed josser on a tender spot and see how he acted then. See if he gave himself away any more. If he did—! Well, they would clear out the very same night and in a way that would give them a good start. If he did not, they would stay on until everything was quite ready, and go up there as comfortably as circumstances would allow. Day was breaking when "The Babe" got up from his musings. The devil behind his eyes smiled broadly as he strolled round for his morning dip. He had thought of an excellent test for Major Sinclair!

The next day Sinclair kept a watch on "The Babe." In spite of the absorbing interest in the card trick, and the look of innocence on the youngster's face when he responded to the query, he was not at all sure but what the young demon had heard and guessed; however as the day wore on, and his host met him always with the same kindly, unsuspicious air of the preceding week, he began to think the slip had passed unnoticed.

At tea the conversation drifted round, as it often did, to the various superstitions and fantasies of the land. "The Babe" quoted at length all the wonderful and seemingly impossible things which could or could not be done by "ju-ju." For example, said he, a man might possess a "ju-ju" charm against snakes; this same man would be able to pick up any reptile, no matter how poisonous, do what he liked with it and it would not touch him. You might be "ju-ju" with leopards, go to sleep in a cage full of them and they would no more dream of attacking you than so many domestic cats. You might be "ju-ju" against drowning, no matter how you tried you could not end your life that way, not if you stood on your head in water all day. You might leave a thousand pounds in gold in the middle of a native market square but if a "ju-ju" was on it no God-fearing, or more correctly devil-fearing, negro would dare touch it; yet you could not leave an "unjujued" shirt hanging out in the backyard at night but someone would come and steal it. Again you might have a "ju-ju" against poison and if you drank prussic acid all day it would do you no more harm than water.

Langfeldt laughed scornfully. Sinclair's air was obviously that of an unbeliever. "The Babe" said he could not vouch for the truth of all of them, but he could for some because he had seen them done.

"It's the truth, ain't it, Chrys?" appealing to his sister. "Can't one person under 'ju-ju' do things that would kill the next."

She agreed it was so, taking his side as she always did.

Langfeldt's laugh was louder and more scornful. Sinclair's face showed he needed proof before being converted.

"These two think I'm an out-and-out liar, Chrys. Shall we give them a private séance to-night just to prove I speak the truth occasionally?"

Chrysanthe put her cup down suddenly and gazed across at her brother with wide, startled eyes. He watched her intently.

"Will you, Chrys, just to prove you're on my side, and so that Sinclair won't believe all the tales told to him regarding my reputation?"

Sinclair glanced from one to the other quickly.

"The Babe" caught the glance, smiled at him sweetly and looked again at his sister.

"You always stick up for me, don't you, Chrys? Don't let 'em run away with the idea I lie on any and every subject. Let 'em see sometimes my statements are to be believed, wild as they may sound."

She took up her cup with a nervous laugh, looked at Sinclair and then back to her brother.

"Very well, Claude."

Claude came round to his sister's side and stood with his arms round her neck and his chin resting against the bow in her hair. There was a vicious look in his eyes as he glanced across at Sinclair. The cup was put back on the table and two small shaking hands fluttered up and held the ones, just a size bigger, that lay on her breast.

"Chrys, we'll show these chaps something I wager any amount they've never seen before. Something that'll make their eyes stick out. We'll let them see there's more truth in some of my statements than the world at large is inclined to believe. Something that ain't seen every day! Something you're going to do to prove your one and only brother ain't a liar always."

As Sinclair watched the two faces an icy chill pierced his heart. What was that young devil going to do now? Did he suspect? Was he preparing some diabolical test? He knew exactly the right spot to hit and hurt him—the one thing that would throw him off his balance and make him show his hand.

It was in Sinclair's mind to arrest him on the spot. He looked round and calculated his chances. A little way off stood Krua and a couple of brawny negro attendants. Langfeldt was hand-in-glove with "The Babe" again. Five to one and he was unarmed! He would be given no chance of getting in touch with his men if this young fiend suspected. It would be sheer madness to attempt it! The little girl's eyes watching the mocking face had stayed his hand. He would put it off no longer. To-morrow he would arrest them both, there was nothing else for it. To-night he needed all his nerve to stand whatever test the arch-villain had in his mind. Any slip would probably mean a bullet through his head and there would be no one to save that child from her brother's devilish devices.

After tea Chrysanthe did not join in the usual game of tennis, neither did Claude desert his guest for one moment. The whole time Krua hung round within hailing distance. Sinclair knew "The Babe" suspected, but not a word of it drifted into the latter's conversation as he rattled on in his usual chaffing manner and looked at his guest with eyes that danced and sparkled in an ecstasy of wickedness. When Sinclair went to dress for dinner Krua loafed on the balcony outside of his bedroom door, and there seemed to be more black servants about than usual. When "The Babe" appeared, bland and charming in manner, innocent and cherublike in appearance, Krua departed. Once Sinclair thought he heard sounds of suppressed weeping, or it might have been only the wind sobbing on the strings of the harp. As Langfeldt came along he left the two together and went to the side of the veranda. It was an eerie, whispering, tropical night, dark and moonless. Great silver stars hung in a sky of deep purple velvet. Fireflies flashed and sparkled in the shrouded garden. The breeze moaned and sighed round the tree-tops, and the murmur of the fountain came like the heavy splash of tears. Sinclair's face was very drawn as he gazed out on the faint starlight scene. To-morrow his dream would have vanished! His little girl-babe would never come to his side again.

He would be the man she hated!—the man who had come to take her brother to his hanging!

The faint clash of soft-voiced, golden bells made him turn suddenly; he stayed with one hand on the rail staring at the figure coming slowly towards where "The Babe" stood by Langfeldt's side. As he watched, a sentence of Krua's rang in his ears. "And there came one unto the land who found the flower seated among the thorns, decked in the gifts of that which dwelt in the cave." It was a floating, misty little thing that drifted towards them in a cloud of red and gold. Sometimes the red drowned the gold, sometimes the gold smothered the red—a gauzy mingling veil of blood and gold that foamed and billowed round her like a sea, yet barely hid the outline of the delicate limbs. Circling the slim waist and coiled round the slender body, with its awesome head resting on her breast just above the heart, was a huge golden centipede. Two great spots of red flashed on the poison jaws as if they were really embedded in the delicate white flesh. A cascade of rubies showered down the misty covering, for all the world like blood dripping from the wound. The slim arms were bare, but on the left, twisted and coiled round till the uncanny birthmark was all but hidden, was another weird, glistening insect. A wreath of golden flowers in shape and form like marsh lilies, yet each one in itself a tiny, soft-voiced bell, was threaded in and out of the chestnut curls. There was a bunch of bell flowers on one shoulder holding the cloudy robe in position, and the other was fastened by a small glittering centipede. Flowers tinkled on the right wrist, and on the third finger of the left hand was a ring like a big splash of blood.

It was a dreamy, wistful little face, with eyes that looked back a long way and watched and waited—strained and listened and seemed unconscious of the present. As Sinclair gazed at her, hardly daring to breathe lest she should slip away into the mist she so resembled, he felt a keen sympathy with the long-dead robber. Who was she? What did it all mean? He had often tried to bring Krua round to the subject again, but he refused to be drawn.

The soft-voiced little bells ceased their whispering as Chrysanthe stopped in front of her brother. There was no sound save the plaintive sighing notes of the harp and the splash of the weeping fountain. To Sinclair it seemed like some old mystery play that had drifted down from forgotten times. These two were actors from a long-dead stage—a tragedy once played yet not completed; laid aside, and brought out again from the mist of ages. Other whisperings wafted through the balcony as the two faced each other—the wild clash of distant arms and the sound of a girl's voice sobbing. "The Babe" stood with a hand on his hip watching his sister with mocking, teasing eyes. One of the lanterns swayed in the light breeze and threw a shadow over him. For a moment he seemed to grow, tall as Langfeldt or taller. Chrysanthe watched him with frightened eyes. He lifted his hand as Krua had done when he saluted her, but with mock deference, and a teasing, bantering echo ran through his voice.

"Ayati! Golden Flower!"

The lantern swayed back. Chrysanthe laughed nervously and the little golden bells started whispering again.

"Why, Claude, it's you! I thought—I—I don't know what I thought."

"The Babe's" hands were on her shoulders. There was a wild hungry look in his eyes.

"Who else could it be, Chrys, but your one and only brother whom you'd follow to hell if necessary?"

She bent forward and kissed him and then became conscious of the two men who were watching her.

The small round face flushed as she said, "I'd forgotten there was anybody else here. Claude wanted me to wear this silly dress to-night because of the séance. It makes me forget like that. I don't know there are other people about unless they move or speak. It seems just as if it were watching and waiting for someone or something I don't want to see"—ending with a shaky, nervous laugh.

Then she went to where Sinclair stood watching her with drawn face and hard, stern mouth. A hand was laid timidly on his arm.

"What is the matter, Major Sinclair? You look very tired and"—with a wavering smile—"rather cross."

He drew the cold little hand on to his arm. The "cross" look vanished but the tired, pained look deepened.

"The Babe" laughed.

"I guess Sinclair is tired of waiting for his dinner and cross at you for being so confoundedly late. I know I am. Ain't you, Carl?"

For once Carl refused to agree with his dearest friend.

To Sinclair during the repast there was nothing but a little girl in a red-gold dress who sat listlessly, without appetite, watching with wide, weary eyes the evil, laughing face opposite her. "The Babe's" spirits were running at their highest. Over a brimming glass of champagne he looked at his victim mockingly.

"I guess you recognize part of Chrys's get up, don't you, old chap? The tricky little beast there on the left shoulder! It's the twin to the one I gave your sister. Chrys once bet me I couldn't persuade any girl to wear an awesome animal like that. I swore to win if I had to wade to it up to the neck in lies. She wouldn't believe me when I said I'd done it. Chrys, ask Sinclair if I ain't speaking the truth."

Sinclair did not give Chrysanthe time to put the question. He looked at her smilingly, corroborated his host's statements, adding he had recognized the ornament under discussion at once and was wondering why her brother had disclaimed all knowledge of it.

It was cut-and-thrust the whole dinner-time, still "The Babe" remained undecided. He hummed gaily as they sat round the fountain for coffee. He had not nearly finished with Major Sinclair! He smiled to himself as he watched the strong face. There was one tune he could make this damned Sinclair dance to or his name was not Claude Devereux! One card in the pack this sharp-eyed cove wotted not of when he came up on his bird-hunting expedition. One small bird that bid fair to be the undoing of this hitherto successful catcher of all ill-omened species. He smiled at his sister, who was sitting by Sinclair's side. Thus does the devil arrange things!

Coffee finished, "The Babe" got up briskly. Hailing one of the servants he bade him clear away the things "one-time" and set the table well under a lamp hanging to the left of the fountain, between it and the steps leading into the garden, and then put out all the lights but that. Chrysanthe got up also, so did the two men. Her hand went to her throat and then to the hideous head resting on her heart; the antenna waved backwards and forwards at her touch; the glittering, flexible ornament seemed to take a firmer grip of her body and the streaming cascade of rubies glistened and sparkled at the movement.

The lamps went out one by one till only the red light from the great round eyes of a fearsome-looking Chinese dragon remained. One made a lurid circle round the table and cast an awesome glow on "The Babe," who was busily engaged in unwrapping what appeared to be an ordinary three-pound jam jar. The other winked and twinkled on Chrysanthe, who stood by Sinclair's side dreading and knowing what lay within the innocent-looking parcel. Sinclair's breath came hard and drawn whilst he watched the young devil by the table, waiting for what was in the jar. Little golden bells whispered as a slim white arm crept timidly through his and a hand lay trembling on his coat sleeve as if afraid of its own boldness. It quivered and shook so that a much bigger one came and held it. The cold morsel would have slipped away, scared for what it had done, but he held it firmly; by-and-by it stopped trembling and got quite warm again.

"Now, you chaps, come and look at these pretty little creatures," "Babe" called as the wrappings were removed. "Sinclair,—you know a bit about these gentry, ain't they quite the nicest of their sort you've ever seen?"

Sinclair started. In a vicious, squirming heap at the bottom of the jar were three of the biggest and deadliest centipedes he had ever seen! One he calculated was nearly a foot long.

"The Babe" looked at them lovingly and then went on, "Now, you chaps seemed inclined to doubt some of the 'ju-ju' yarns I was telling you at tea. Well, Chrys here is 'ju-ju' against centipedes, and to prove I don't always lie she's going to take these lively-looking coves out and show you just what she can do with them. My boys, you'll see a sight that couldn't be got for ten guineas at the best London music hall."

Sinclair' hands clenched and his face whitened under its tan.

"Good God! Wentworth, you're not going to make your sister do a thing like that because of a silly, trivial conversation. There's enough poison in those brutes to kill her three times over!" he said hoarsely.

"I ain't making her"—in mock astonishment. "She's doing it to show you I'm right sometimes."

Langfeldt's face went ghastly as he gazed at the wriggling heap.

"Don't let her do it, Claude. I'll take every word you say as gospel rather than she should touch those vile things."

"The Babe" laughed and turned the jar up and down again.

"Lord! What a fuss you chaps make! Chrys could play with 'em all day and they'd do her no more harm than three straws."

"Then why—er—do they touch you?"

Sinclair's break was hardly noticeable but it was what "The Babe" was listening for. He shook the jar up again and watched the insects wriggle with obvious delight.

"I ain't 'ju-ju' on my little own. That beast on the *Asabo* wouldn't have touched me had Chrys been there. That's another trick she's going to show you. See that big beast there," putting a finger on the side of the jar and laughing when the insect made vicious frantic dabs at him, "she's going to take him out and tame him down and make him walk up and down my arm with no more vice and temper in him than an angel. She'll make him crawl up and down you too, Carl, if you wish"—smiling when the German's face whitened at the suggestion—"and you as well, Sinclair, if you'd like to see how it feels," looking with mocking eyes at his white, drawn face.

"The Babe" had heard enough to satisfy himself, but it was not his intention to let his victim off lightly; Major Sinclair should dance until he was tired of piping.

"Now I'll shake 'em up well," said he, acting on his words. "Get 'em nice and lively, then Chrys can pop her little hand in and get out that big chap and put him through his paces."

Sinclair's hand was on "The Babe's" shoulder. The youngster's went to his cummerbund.

"Don't be a fool, Wentworth. We don't want to see your sister killed"—the hoarse, strained voice would have satisfied any ordinary mortal.

"She ain't going to be killed. Chrys ain't afraid of 'em. She's dying to have 'em out and play with 'em. Why, I have to hide 'em away or they'd be all over the place running after her like so many little bow-wows."

"Don't let her touch those devil's messengers, Claude, you fool!" the German broke in.

"The Babe" kept a firm hold on the jar and watched the two men carefully, then glanced across to where his sister stood on the opposite side of the table.

"Why, they're dying to get out and play with her! Can't you see 'em scratching at the glass and looking at her?—asking with all their eyes to be let out for a run?"—then giving the contents an extra strong shake—"Here you are, Chrys," and put the jar quickly in front of her.

Two shaking hand fluttered round the glass stopper, but, before she had time to open it, Sinclair leant over the table, seized the jar, threw it across the garden and it smashed against the rocky side of the waterfall.

"You young devil, I believe you would make her do it!"

"The Babe" looked at him in good-humored surprise, laughed and lighted a cigarette.

"Lord! Why not? Chrys is 'ju-ju' against them. When I can prove I ain't a liar they won't give me a chance, will they, old girl?"—appealing to his sister, who stood looking from him to Sinclair with wide, startled eyes.

The tiny bells whispered as her hand went slowly to her head.

"Claude is quite right. They would not hurt me provided I wore this ring and jewels. There's a tradition in the family that it's a gift of the first daughter with blue eyes, through an ancestress who lived more than three hundred years ago. There have only been two girls since then; they were both dark and tall like my father, like all the men but Claude. We had a—séance just a day or so before you came. He—I wanted to see if there was any truth in it. All

these jewels were hers and the dress was copied from a little painting of her. Claude and I are supposed to be just like her. I don't
think so though! She looks so sad and lonely. We don't look like
that. The old governor always said we were as big a pair of demons
as the first two, only they were twin boys. One married the little
girl these things belonged to. It's said she didn't like him a bit because of—of something he had done. But tradition drifts down very
funnily, and all our people draw the long bow—that's why we've
got such an awful way of fibbing. Claude hasn't done any of the
wicked things he pretends he has, but he likes to keep people lively
and talking."

"The Babe" laughed, and going to the side of the balcony, threw
his cigarette into the garden.

"There ain't much life without lies, Chrys," he said as he came
back and perched on the table beside her; then he touched and
played with the horns of the great centipede coiled about her until
the thing seemed to live and crawl round her, and the streaming
cascade of wet-looking stones joined and mingled with the lurid
red glare cast by the lantern.

Sinclair shivered as he watched them. The two seemed to stand
in a great round pool of blood that dripped and oozed from the
girl's breast.

"The Babe" glanced across to where he stood just beyond the
awesome circle.

"Don't stand out there in the cold, old chap. Come here in the
firelight with Chrys and me. Move up a bit, Carl, then Sinclair can
come by my side," smiling at him with sweet friendliness as he
joined them. "Chrys hasn't forgiven you yet for throwing away her
little pets; she'll be hunting in the garden for 'em all to-morrow
morning. I'll put a word in for you though. She's kind-hearted is
Chrys, fearfully forgiving-like. Forgives me all my backslidings, and
I'm a bit of a handful at times. Mammy gave me the go-by long
before I was ten. Governor washed his hands of me when I was
fourteen. The old boy got pious in his declining years. Sent Chrys
here to a convent for nearly five years. The devil hooked him
under a bit sooner for that. Such a thing was against rules! Chrys
never knew him in his virtuous end, she only remembers him as

an old terror who spanked her thinking she was me. We used to swop our little overalls as kiddies. He'd chase round looking for me in a red pinny, pass me sitting good and innocent-like on the steps quietly threading beads in a blue pinny, find Chrys in the garden flying my flag and the storm broke and was over before he spotted he'd got the wrong one. The old boy died a few months before Chrys got back from school. We were elephant shooting up country. A big beast knelt on his chest and all but settled him before I settled it. He died about half-an-hour afterwards, raving the whole time for Chrys. He would have sacrificed me, his one and only son, for a sight of her. Lord! I can hear him now yelping 'Chrysanthe!' The old boy left us threepence apiece in one good solid silver sixpence; it seemed a shame to break it so I tossed Chrys for it and won. Banged the whole lot in one inferior whisky, and then we were two lone, penniless little orphans with no one to take care of us—same as now. So we put our curly heads together and did the best for one another. I looked after Chrys, Chrys looked after me, and we stick together to the finish. No one ever cared a twopenny dawn for me except Chrys and—" "The Babe's" arm was round his sister jealously—"Chrys don't care a damn for anyone except me."

Chrysanthe patted the hand on her waist, felt in his pocket for his cigarette-case, took one out, put it in his mouth and lighted it, then she handed the case to Langfeldt who stood against her, and afterwards leant across to Sinclair, who was on the other side of her brother.

The youngster watched her anxiously, then laughed and gave Sinclair a light from his own cigarette saying, "I say, old chap, would you like to see the painting of the three-hundred-years-old little girl Chrys and I are supposed to be like?"

Sinclair agreed he would. He had to play his part to the end, still doubtful whether "The Babe" had guessed or not, and knowing that to-morrow with his own hand he would sweep away all that now made life worth living.

"She was the first Chrysanthe," "The Babe" went on, "Chrys here is the second. There's a big gap between 'em. Chrys looks like her though at times, especially when I've been an extra bad boy and worried her more than enough. I've promised to turn over a new leaf henceforth and for ever!—to be no end proper and virtuous! Wasn't I a marvel last trip, Carl? Only one real drunk! A bit rocky the first night perhaps, but I managed to walk down on my little own. I bet Sinclair here fancied he was let in for a high old time when he found me in his crib. My reputation ain't exactly savory and old Morton piles the agony on. He can't say my name three times without a cuss," with a deeply grieved air.

Chrysanthe toyed nervously with her brother's tie during the latter part of this speech. Sinclair watched her with the same drawn look that had been on his face all evening. The little trusting hand that had lain in his for those few minutes had hurt him more than all "The Babe's" ingenious modes of torture.

There was silence for a few moments. The distant singing harp's voice came sighing along the darkened veranda. The youngster jumped off the table suddenly. The noise echoed out and through the night.

"Lord! what a quiet lot we are all at once! Chrys, hop along to your room and fetch the old painting and get Sinclair's opinion. Carl, old man, give me a pack of cards and I'll show you another way of working out that trick. Kept awake all last night thinking it out."

Chrysanthe paused by Sinclair's side. One slim finger rubbed up and down the table edge nervously. It was a wistful, dreamy face that looked up at him from beneath the wreath of golden flowers.

"Would you really like to see it? Things that interest Claude and me don't often interest others."

There was a curl hanging on her left temple. It always hung and danced there, the same one, but a trifle longer, that had coiled round his finger the night he found her. How often since then it had tempted him and dared him to touch it! He took it now with gentle reverent fingers and put it back among its less wayward neighbors; why he did not know, because it was out again at once.

"Yes, little girl, I should like to see it very much."

He watched as the darkness swallowed up the little floating, red-gold cloud, and stood with eyes on the same spot, waiting until she appeared again. A ray of light like a sharp, keen knife came suddenly out of a room a little way down on the other side of the steps. Just for a moment and it was out. Whispering bells came faintly tinkling back again. She drifted out of the shadow like a misty cloud of red. Something crouching in the darkness sprang on her as she passed the balcony steps. There was a scream of girl-ish terror, a hideous laugh as a weird, naked figure with a great red centipede painted on its chest, a girdle of dried reptiles about its waist, and its wild, mad face striped black and red, tossed Chrysanthe lightly on to its shoulder.

At the scream Sinclair sprang forward, but quick as he was "The Babe" was quicker. Twice the youngster's revolver rang out. Twice he fired at the ghastly figure flying down the steps; but haste, dark-ness and fear of injuring his sister spoilt his aim. Before the three reached the bottom of the flight the hideous black shape had gone, swallowed up in the night.

"My God, it's Mungea!" the German gasped.

"The Babe" put up his hand for silence, leant forward with strained eyes, listening for any sound. He fired again. The same fearsome laugh echoed across the lawn. From the back came the rattle of a heavy chain and the melancholy baying of a hound with an anxious note in it.

"Grip knows," "The Babe" said hoarsely. "Loose the dog!" he called to the group of scared servants who rushed along the veran-da, and then he was tearing across the lawn in the direction of the laugh, Sinclair and Langfeldt at his heels.

A crashing noise! The sound of feet splashing through water! Another shot! A diabolical laugh and all was quiet. The three rushed on, halted at the edge of the stream, listening and waiting for any sound. Not a rustle from the dense bush beyond! Not a sign of the awful, laughing figure. Nothing moved in the deep, shrouded gloom, only the silver stars mocked and twinkled in a sky of deep purple velvet.

Presently, across the lawn, came perhaps the most flesh-creep-ing sound possible to hear on a dead-quiet tropical night—the hoarse, wild bay of a hound on the blood trail. Nose down, flying over the garden, was Grip, but heading towards a spot opposite to where the last sound appeared to have come from. "The Babe" started, looked at Sinclair and Langfeldt sharply as he reloaded his revolver.

"Have you got your shooting irons?" he asked quickly.

In their haste they admitted these very necessary tools had been forgotten.

"Carl, get back to my room 'one-time.' You'll find a couple there loaded. Sinclair, mark the trail Grip and I take and then both of you follow on like the devil. There's more than one black beast on the prowl to-night."

As the German dashed back to the house, Sinclair and the youngster headed across the lawn to where the dog snarled and growled like a veritable demon as it nosed round for the scent it had lost when the thing it wanted crossed the main stream. A mad, wild bay echoed and rang through the forest as it set off again.

"Wait here till Carl brings you a shooter, old man, you'll be less than no use without, then follow on like hell," and "The Babe" was flying along in the dog's wake at an almost incredible pace.

To Sinclair the moments he waited until Langfeldt came back seemed a century. He snatched the weapon and was on again, quickly outdistancing the German, whose build was not that of a racer. Farther and farther away grew the sounds of the two ahead of him. The youngster had the advantage of knowing his ground. Presently the dog's voice ceased, after the manner of its kind when the scent runs hot and strong. Fainter and fainter grew the distant noises until finally they died away. Sinclair stopped, every nerve alert. Not a sound in front or behind him! Not a breath or whispering rustle in the dense tangle that edged the narrow track! He went on at a quick, noiseless walk, ears and eyes strained for the least noise or shadow that drifted through the bush. For good ten minutes he followed the path. Not a rustle except of his own making! Then came an echo that made him set off at a frantic, tearing run. Ahead, quick and sharp, but some distance away, was the sound of rapid shooting. Five times it rang out! A pause. Wafted down on the sighing night wind came the snarling sound of a dog engaged in a death scrimmage. Sinclair ran as he had never done before. A shot—a lone one that told its own tale! He dashed on. Another shot—from his own revolver this time. In the quick sharp flash he saw, in a clearing ahead of him, a slim, boyish figure, limp and prostrate, with a widening red patch on the white coat. Over it, fighting like a hell hound, was the tawny dog, snarling, snapping and tearing with foaming jaws at a trio of negroes who were circling round with long knives. Two lay dead by "The Babe's" side. Another was huddled up in Sinclair's path, and one, with torn bleeding throat, gasped his life out on the far side of the clearing. But of Chrysanthe there was no sign! He stopped, took careful aim and fired again at one of the three shadows flitting in the shrouded gloom. A yell as the shot went home and the man fell dead. The remaining two took to their heels, three shots followed them: there was a double yelp of pain but they kept on.

Grip moaned and whimpered as he crouched at the boy's side, and licked his limp hands in an agony of dog broken-heartedness. Sinclair was not fond of "The Babe" but he freely forgave him all his sins as he came rapidly to where he lay with closed eyes and still pale face. Kneeling beside him he laid his hand on his heart and heaved a sigh of relief. He examined the wound on his shoulder; it was a fairish gash, but nothing serious. He looked the youngster over carefully and found a little oozing wound on his head which showed he had been struck down from the back and stunned. Grip watched him and seemed relieved. He laid him down again and searched round for any sign of Chrysanthe. Not a trace of her could be found! Calling Grip he tried to get him on the trail, but the dog only whined and went from the unconscious youngster to the homeward track. For some time he stood in the clearing waiting for any sound out of the surrounding forest. Not a breath or whisper reached him from the gloomy, tangled waste. Grip came to him, licked his hand, ran to the boy and then to the homeward trail. There was nothing for it! He must go back. The black African night had swallowed up his little girl. To the end of his life he would

hear whispering golden bells, a scream of girlish terror and a hideous, mocking laugh—always see her a little red cloud floating out
of the darkness, that had gone before he could save her!

Going to "The Babe" he lifted him carefully. Sinclair studied
the face as he went along. He looked just like his sister as he lay
there white and unconscious, so much so it was difficult to imagine it was not. It was just one of Fate's tricks to take her and leave
him with the brother—leave him with the arch-villain he had sworn
to have at any price. He had no idea what the price would be then.
Now he had got the man he had been after for nearly two years.
Got him here—in his very arms! A hoarse laugh echoed through
the silence. Grip looked up at him, whined and licked his hand.
The action steadied him. Villain as he was, the young devil had
fought for her seven to one. To-morrow he would have the whole
place out scouring the country. To-morrow he was going to arrest
them both—arrest his little girl and take her back to safety! Now
she had gone beyond his reach forever! Heaven alone knew what
fate would be hers! Would this youngster know where to find that
fiend Mungea? He would let him go free to do what devilment he
pleased for a clue to the whereabouts of that black fiend, for a
chance of killing him with his own hand! That was the only joy the
world held now!

A moan stopped his thoughts.

"Chrys! Did they get Chrys? Those villains!"

"She wasn't in the clearing when I got there, youngster."

"The Babe's" eyes opened quickly as Sinclair spoke. One hand
went to his head in a half-dazed way.

"Hello, old chap, I thought they'd settled me. I killed three of
them. Grip mauled another so that he won't recover. How many
were there when you came?"

"Three, and they would have settled you but for the dog."

"Three were there! That makes seven, don't it? How many did
you account for?"

"Only one, the other two slipped down a side track. I winged
one or both of them though."

"Didn't you get a glimpse of Chrys? That villain still had her but I couldn't get through for those black devils. Didn't you see anything of her and that thief? Nothing at all?"—big anxious eyes looked up at Sinclair.

"No, youngster, not a trace or sound!"—brokenly.

"Stick me on my feet again. I'm all right now. I can't think when I'm carried like a blooming baby."

Sinclair put him down but kept an arm round him he looked so white and shaky.

"I'm a bit rocky on my pins, ain't I? One of those devils got me round at the back before I spotted him. Knocked me silly before I knew it or I'd have killed the whole blasted lot. I'll root 'em out neck and crop! Let 'em know whose boss this deal!"—with ever-increasing passion—"I'll catch that damned Mungea and roast him! By hell, I will!"

Sinclair stood aghast as "The Babe" went off into one of the wild mad passions that had fallen to Chrysanthe's lot in the swamp hut. It was very short-lived. Half-stunned and weak with loss of blood, the tearing mad rage took what little strength was left in him, and he fell back, limp and white, against his companion's arm. As Sinclair lifted him and continued the homeward journey, he felt a real affection for the youngster. He would like to be in at that roasting too!

CHAPTER 11

"I must gallop fast and straight, for my errand will not wait,
Fear naught, I shall return at eventide."

IT WAS NEARLY MIDNIGHT when the three got back to the plateau. Half-way down the homeward track Sinclair came across Langfeldt limping along towards the clearing where the fight had taken place. Early in the running he had slipped and sprained his ankle; hence his tardy progress. "The Babe" was still unconscious when they met, but a dose from the German's flask soon brought him round. A few minutes afterwards, white and shaky-looking, but alert and wide-awake, he was able to continue the journey without assistance. The place was a buzz of scared, anxious servants. Flitting lanterns showed up at all points of the garden and little plain. The whole thing had happened so suddenly no one seemed to have grasped what really had occurred. The garbled news had reached the cluster of huts at the farthermost end of the plateau, where the native quarters were situated and the visitors' porters housed, and at once the Hausa headman had organised a hasty search of the immediate surroundings. The result had been no better than his master's except, that by the side of the steps had been found a little painting on ivory in a quaint oval gold-case—the picture dropped by Chrysanthe as the black made off with her. Sinclair's face was very tense and drawn as he took it without a word and slipped it into his pocket.

146

Until the small hours of the morning the three sat up talking, trying to arrange what would be the next best move. At first Langfeldt watched "The Babe" with nervous anxiety. The sudden apparition on the balcony had robbed him of his natural cunning, and he had mentioned a name he was not supposed to know. In the excitement of the next few minutes he had forgotten this slip. It was not until he was alone and following on Sinclair's heels along the forest track that it occurred to him what he had said. A few other things occurred to him likewise, so many in fact that he sat down and thought and did not hurry at all, but developed a sprained ankle during the course of those quiet musings. He had not spoken a word to Mungea since they parted in Liverpool, as strangers, each to go their separate ways, and work out the little bits of the same plan until the grand whole was completed and they met again, as friends, at a certain given spot known only to themselves. Mungea's sole business was to get possession of the girl. This he appeared to have done. His, to obtain an old map together with an ancient document of which "The Babe" had once shown him a glimpse and nothing more, and that he knew reposed always on the person of his young friend.

As Langfeldt sat on the veranda, listening to the arrangements and putting in suggestions, he found it in his heart to be sorry Sinclair had reached the clearing in time to rescue Claude from the clutches of Mungea's minions, or perhaps, more correctly, that this same Sinclair, and not he, had had sole possession of the youngster's unconscious body for a time. Once having got the girl and the papers he could snap his fingers at Claude and carry out the thing his own way.

He would let the nigger go on thinking he was to have the bit of blood-spilling he was so raging for when that pretty little filly ceased to be useful, and, after the deal was through and the gold really his, he would shoot the black beast before he had time to work his fancy design on her; alone with him up there, entirely in his power, that fascinating little bit of femininity would have no choice but to fall in with his wishes. She had not the liking for him she had for Sinclair, but she would have to do just what he wanted or he would very soon find a way of bringing her to reason.

Langfeldt looked at "The Babe" speculatively. Mungea had stuck to his part of the Liverpool contract. Got the girl right enough! Without her nothing could be done—no nigger would dare to go within fifty miles of the place. Therefore it behooved him, Carl, to complete his, and stick to that arrangement, not the latest one with his young friend. Had or had not Claude heard his remark? If he had not, well and good. If he had—! The German's eyes went to that part of the youngster's cummerbund from which protruded his revolver. The name of Mungea had not passed between them. The existence of that party should be unknown to him, Carl. What explanation could he give if called upon to do so? He breathed more freely as the time went on and neither by look nor sign did Claude give any hint of having heard his exclamatory remark.

Sinclair was the first to mention the name that caused Langfeldt so much deep and serious thinking. The latter in his efforts to work all things round to his own liking had somewhat entangled himself.

"Who is Mungea?" Sinclair asked presently. He knew a little about this party, but was anxious to hear what the youngster had to say.

"The Babe" swore with a gusto out of keeping with his shaky appearance.

"He's a 'ju-ju' priest, sort of chaplain to the family. His people have had charge of our morals for generations. He came howling round here one day wanting Chrys to do something she didn't want to do. She's a bit of break-off from the rest of us, is Chrys, and she refused point blank. These chaps make such an awful fuss if things are not done according to routine. He came and raved here a few times and finally I kicked him out. Threatened to shoot him if he ventured within ten miles of the place. He swore to be revenged. That was more than a year ago. I never saw a sign of him until this last voyage down when I spotted him on the *Asabo* disguised as a deck hand. I wondered what his little game was and kept a sharp watch on him, but found out nothing"—Langfeldt had a sensation of great relief.—"Hadn't seen him since Rio del Rey until to-night. Next time I see him he'll roast on a spit to my turning—he and all connected with him"—with grim significance.

The German glanced at him covertly, but "The Babe's" attention was fixed on a detailed map of the surrounding country; he was pointing out to Sinclair the clearing where the fight took place and the tracks branching from it. Each of these, he went on to say, led to some village of which Mungea was the high priest; any one of his curates might, with a little persuasion not too gentle, be pressed to give information as to his whereabouts. The best thing they could do would be to visit these three villages with a sufficiently impressive number of retainers and find out what they could. A little display of firearms will draw more truth from a nigger's tongue than preaching at him for a year. If the choice lay between giving the site of Mungea's headquarters or the immediate despatch of them, the underlings, to a better and less sinful world, probably the high priest would have to go to the wall. In the evening they could all meet again here, compare notes and act on information received. It meant a day's delay this end, but it might save them many a day afterwards. He felt sure Mungea would not harm his sister until he got her to the chief temple. The place was some two hundred miles up country, exactly where he did not know, not near enough to start out without endeavoring to get a few more details. The best thing would be to nab the most reliable of the nigger priests and make him act as guide under pain of death. He, personally, would know enough to tell if they were being led in the right direction, but without outside aid they might get off the track and be bushed for a week.

Here "The Babe" brought another and much less detailed map and made a round O in pencil where he thought the temple was, but he could not swear to twenty miles. Mungea would probably be traveling short-handed up there owing to those devils they had killed and winged. There was a chance they might get there in time to save his sister. This was his idea. Provided of course that Major Sinclair had no better plan to suggest.

Major Sinclair had no better plan to suggest, and he loved the anxious-looking, white-faced youngster with a depth of affection he had once deemed impossible.

Langfeldt agreed the arrangement was a good one. He knew full well Mungea would not be found in that direction. Moreover the scheme might give him many excellent opportunities of relieving his young friend of those papers. When this came to pass he, with his thirty kroo-boys, would join Mungea and proceed as per Liverpool arrangement, but bar the nigger's grand finale.

Thereupon three people retired to their separate couches, each too full of anxious thoughts to sleep.

At the first glimpse of day Major Sinclair with his Hausa porters, who suddenly developed an amazing display of arms, which they carried in a strangely professional manner, Carl Langfeldt with his kroo-boys, who shouldered guns as if it was not the first time they had held them, Claude Wentworth and Grip with a train of eighteen wild-looking savages beaten up from round and about the premises in frantic haste, with firearms that half of them carried as if they did not know one end from the other, and these for the most part requisitioned from Sinclair's spare supply because "The Babe" had not more than half-a-dozen guns on the premises, went along the track leading to the clearing where the latter had so nearly met his death the previous evening.

There they parted, each train of niggers led by a white taking a path that went to one of the villages under Mungea's sway, to meet again at the fort and compare notes during the coming evening.

Major the Hon. Tracy Sinclair insisted on "The Babe," owing to wounds and weakness, taking the nearest village. The youngster demurred but eventually was overcome. Because of his limp he said Langfeldt must be given the middle one and he, being the only whole man of the party, took unto himself the most remote. Also he wanted to reinforce "The Babe's" scratch team with half of his Hausas, but the youngster said the village, he, Sinclair, had taken unto himself was the biggest and might prove unfriendly and he would need all his display of arms, whereas the one he was taking

was little more than a bunch of huts and the people mostly relations of his own servants.

At eight that same evening Carl Langfeldt returned, footsore
and weary, to the plateau with his supply of information. He was
the first back. At nine Sinclair came in, looking fairly fit considering he had done nearly thirty miles in the day. He was the second
back. They compared notes and the store of news accumulated
showed the villagers had not lied beyond the elastic limit of the
country. They awaited "The Babe." Ten o'clock struck and he was
not with them. They got anxious about him and both agreed he
looked very white and shaky. Probably the eighteen-mile walk had
been rather a strain on him, and he was taking the last laps very
slowly. Midnight came, their, anxiety increased apace. Had he
fallen in with Mungea? Found his trail and followed on? What had
happened? The hours passed and the next day dawned, in fact the
morning came, but without Claude Wentworth. Two men sat on
the veranda of his residence and looked at one another. Neither he
nor one of his eighteen niggers turned up with explanation or apology. Neither did Major Sinclair's spare guns!

Then two men made a bee-line to the village, some nine miles
away, which had been the missing one's destination.

"Had a person answering to the name of Wentworth visited
them the previous day?" they inquired of the startled inhabitants.

"No, Mr. Wentworth had not, and it was fully a week since they
had seen anything of him; then he had been round buying up their
strongest men for an expedition up country. He had come at a very
unusual hour, at midnight in fact, when they were all in bed, hauled
a dozen of their best men off, paid their wives six month's wages
in advance and departed into the night whence he came."

"Could they tell Major Sinclair what night it was?"

"Yes, they could. It was just the fingers of two hands ago."

Ten nights! The night Chrysanthe had slept so safely guarded
in his tent! Sinclair sat down thoughtfully on a carved wooden stool.
The village pastor squatted on his haunches and watched him with
some slight qualms.

"Did this village priest know anything of a certain Mungea?" the one on the carved stool asked after a trying pause.

"Yes, he was even now in the hut of the speaker's brother-in-law, sick of a fever that had laid him prostrate some days, the fingers of one hand ago."

"Where was this same brother-in-law's residence?"

"It was not in this village but one laying to the south-west, some three days' march away."

This information more or less tallied with that received at the other villages.

Further inquisitive and peremptory questions were asked and then two thoughtful-looking people returned to "The Babe's" residence. As they went along sorrowfully, it dawned on Major Sinclair and Carl Langfeldt that it had all been part of their host's little plan to get a good start up country. Chrysanthe's sudden disappearance also had been part of the plot. They were certain she knew nothing of it, her terrorized scream was not forced. The fight at the clearing puzzled Sinclair; that likewise was no acting. During his previous morning's march to the most remote village it struck him he had seen nothing of Krua since the time he hung outside of his bedroom door. It had been his intention to inquire further into this matter when the triple expeditions met again. The loss Sinclair had suffered had knocked him off his balance a little, and his sharp, active brain did not work in the manner it used to before his heart became so seriously affected.

It was evening before they got back to the bungalow. When Sinclair reached the balcony, a note, addressed to him, lying on a table near the splashing fountain where he had dreamt so many dreams as he watched a slim little girl playing with the goldfish, took his immediate attention. He opened and read it. It was rather lengthy and took some time. He sat down, read it again, and then Langfeldt became acquainted with a few swear words, forcible and vigorous, hitherto not in his vocabulary. He looked at Major the Hon. Tracy Sinclair in pained surprise. He had never known him to do such a thing before!

The following is the epistle which roused all this unseemly wrath:

DEAR OLD CHAP,—I must apologise for leaving you so hastily, but urgent and important business up country, about which Carl will probably be able to give you further details, demands my immediate and close attention. For reasons you will quite understand I was unable to make my adieux in person. It is perhaps a trifle indiscreet of me to apprise you of my departure, but I fancy before this the fact will have presented itself to you, moreover I could not deprive myself of the pleasure of sending you this little farewell note. It would be unkind, considering our close friendship, both on the *Asabo* and during your very pleasurable visit, not to let you have some idea of my future movements and intentions. Let me pause here for a moment to say I wish you to look upon the bungalow and its contents as your own. Please use it as long as you like and do not hurry away because of my sudden and pressing engagement in the remote interior. By the time you get this note I shall be some fifty miles away and I cannot, for reasons it is unnecessary to go into, forward you my future address.

Perhaps you would like to have some really reliable information concerning the happenings of the last few days. I repeat myself, I am indiscreet, but I doubt if you can fully understand the thrill of really exquisite pleasure it gives me to think I have successfully outwitted the sharpest man on his Majesty's staff of private detectives; not only that, but made him the direct means of saving my life, thereby causing him to lose that which has become perhaps dearer to him than his hitherto successful career, to

wit, my sister. But for her quite absurd dislike to
bloodshed, I should have had no qualms about putting a bullet through your head as a souvenir of my
little self—I may add that if you insist on pressing
your amiable society on me again this will come to
pass. If you take the advice of one who has your welfare at heart let bygones be bygones, return quietly
to England and cease troubling about me any more.
The deal I am on now is perfectly legitimate and no
one's concern but my own.

Exactly when and where you found out that occasionally I substituted my sister for myself I cannot say. Let me say here she has no idea you have
made this intensely embarrassing discovery. Considering the interest you take in her perhaps a slight
sketch of our dual career may be entertaining. My
sister, as you may have noticed, is under my sway
and fond of me more than is usually the lot of a
brother. Added to this she is, or was, a remarkably
daring little customer. Unfortunately she has, during the past twelve months, developed nerves to such
an alarming extent as to necessitate this prolonged
sojourn in the country. About five years ago I dared
her to take a trip up the coast in my name, my mo-
tives for doing so I did not explain. This passed off
successfully all round as you know. It was some time
before she discovered my reasons for this same journey and, believe me, she was considerably cut up.
Afterwards, admittedly with some persuasion, she
took several other trips in my name and place, and
knowing how much hung on them made her play the
part excellently. You may say it is her misfortune to
be so remarkably fond of me. There I agree with you.
She would sacrifice her life to keep me from the fate
which doubtless you think I deserve.

Now without any further preamble I will give you a brief summary of the events leading up to my abrupt departure.

Perhaps you remember some few nights ago making a slight slip when converging with my sister. Nothing much, and you corrected yourself in a manner that roused my admiration. But that small error, combined with what she had said concerning your unusual bush commissariat, set me thinking. I resolved to probe deeper and on a tender spot. This resulted in a further slip. I had it in my mind to shoot you at the time, but my sister's presence and regard for her wishes stayed my hand. Previous to my ingenious little test I had made arrangements with Krua as to what his course was to be if my worst fears were verified. By a private code of signals between us he knew whether or not his part had to be played. My sister did not know anything of this scheme and was as alarmed as yourself or Carl when Krua, in Mungea's gala garb, suddenly swooped on to her. I need hardly say my revolver was purposely aimed wide. I am a much better shot than that evening's proceedings would lead you to believe, as you will find if you insist on following me. I pride myself on the extremely dramatic way in which I played my part. There was no magic about Krua's disappearance. If you care to risk a shower bath you will find a passage screened by the waterfall, leading up to just near the clearing where you found me. Now there was an unexpected sequel to all this for which I owe you thanks forever.

It appears there was a counterplot on foot that same night. This I had no notion of until Grip got on the trail. There is only one nigger in the whole of Africa who can make him howl in the manner he did.

That is Mungea. Imagine my surprise and alarm
when the dog came heading across the lawn, full tilt
towards the track leading to the clearing where my
sister and Krua would eventually appear, nose down
and red hot on the late family chaplain's trail. I am
sufficiently acquainted with my man to know he
would not venture on my premises without a considerable staff close in hand. Also, the one thing he
lives for is my sister's life and taken in a way that
makes even me shudder. She has had the misfortune
to step heavily on his pet religious corn—all because
of this antipathy of hers regarding bloodshed. I have
reasoned with her but to no avail. I knew if Mungea
obtained possession of her it was extremely doubtful if I should see her alive again. Left to himself he
would not have killed her within a two-hundred-mile
radius of my place, but interference on my part, had
it seemed likely to result in victory for my side, would
have led to her immediate despatch. I desired to
frustrate his designs for two reasons. Firstly, I am
very fond of my sister; secondly, the little scheme I
have on hand cannot very well be worked out without her assistance. It is extremely probable you will
scoff at my premier reason. Let me say you do me an
injustice. You may have noticed that I headed along
that track at a fair pace leaving you with instructions
to follow on as soon as possible. I reached the clearing in time to find six of Mungea's staff, headed by
himself, going in the direction Krua must have taken
only a minute or so before entirely unaware of their
presence. The appearance of Grip and myself they
had not reckoned on, and you can imagine their surprise when we suddenly barred the way. The result
you know. But the point I wish to impress on you is,
but for your timely appearance and rescue of my
unworthy self my sister, who is now here with me,

would have returned home within the next day or two wondering what had happened to the writer, who would be lying up in that clearing a stiff, cold little corpse. The three villains, including Mungea, who it was knocked me silly, would not have left until they had settled me. By that time Krua would be far enough away and would have joined a considerable reinforcement of my people who were waiting farther along the line. Naturally when I recovered consciousness and found myself with you, knowing what little secret of mine lay in your possession, I was anxious to know whether Krua had heard the shooting and returned to see what the matter was—his reappearance with my sister would have given me away entirely. However, you quickly soothed my fears. As a matter of fact he had heard it, but knowing nothing of the counterplot concluded it was all part of my evening's entertainment and continued his journey according to our arrangement. My original plan was to leave that same night in the confusion caused by my sister's sudden departure, but as you see the counterplot prevented me. By the rescue of my humble self, for which I am eternally grateful, I am enabled to carry out this jaunt into the interior. And it will be pleasant for you to reflect that but for your promptitude in following me and courageous behavior in the clearing, my sister, for whom I believe I may safely say you cherish some regard, would be sitting now on the balcony of our late home lamenting my decease, and it would be your privilege and pleasure to be a stay and comfort to her during this dire tribulation; in fact, freed from the incubus of her twin, she might, after a season of mourning, have been persuaded to look upon you in the light of something more than an agreeable acquaintance.

"She is sitting in front of me now and she asks me why I laugh. I tell her the joke is a private one between myself and you. You did me out of an excellent deal once up in Blenka's land—caused me some of the most anxious minutes of my life. I swore to be revenged and have succeeded beyond my wildest hopes. My sister wants to read this letter, but I tell her it is a confidential and somewhat indiscreet missive for your perusal only. I understand you well enough to know the secret of my successful alibis will not reach the ears of the world. Our mutual liking for my sister will keep this from going further. You will be pleased to hear she has almost recovered from the shock of that evening. I extremely regretted having been compelled to give her such a severe fright, but I think the fault was as much yours as mine. However, when I explained my reasons for doing so, she forgave me freely. I did not mention you had discovered our double game; it would have alarmed her too much in her present state of health and she would worry on my account more than the occasion demands. I merely said circumstances had arisen which behooved us to start our jaunt a few days sooner than we had originally intended. That excellent little scheme of mine for finding Mungea's headquarters has given us a good two days' start. You will have some difficulty in getting up here. By the time you do we shall probably be some hundred miles farther inland. I doubt if you will take my advice and remain where you are in spite of the heavy risks you run in following me. For your future guidance let me say that after leaving this spot it is extremely difficult traveling. I have a very detailed and reliable map of the route I intend to take; this will enable us to proceed at easily treble the rate of the ordinary tourist.

Now, old chap, I will conclude with apologies for trespassing on your valuable time and kindest regards from my sister and myself, trusting you will forgive our abrupt departure, which I think I have fully explained.

Thanking you for the loan of those guns, which, believe me, I shall find most useful—Ever yours gratefully,

Claude.

P.S.—Give my love to Carl. It pained me to leave him in the lurch, but I think he will quite understand why. It may save him some moments' anxious thinking if I mention here that the new plan I gave him, although so closely resembling the one of which I relieved him on the *Asabo*, is of no use whatsoever.

—C.D.

In a very few words Sinclair gave Langfeldt the main points of the letter and its messages. When the departure of his young friend dawned on the German in all its full significance, he straightway opened his heart to Sinclair and told him as much as he knew of the youngster's future movements. This, with one important exception, was very little more than what that individual had already culled for himself. The exception was that "The Babe's" destination was a mountain peak some seven hundred miles farther inland. He, Langfeldt, had seen the route, full of strange signs and symbols, that led in a twisted red line from the fort to the forest surrounding the peak. The peculiar handlike shape of it, as given on the old map, had taken his attention. With a pencil he made a sketch of it for Sinclair's inspection as follows:—

Likewise he had had an ancient document in his hands telling more about it. Owing to the fact that it was written in Greek he had not had it long enough to make anything out of it. The treasure, which was supposed to be in a buried temple there, had been discovered by a remote ancestor of "The Babe's," who had either mislaid or purposely hidden the map and manuscript. For generations the legend was handed down, but the clue to its whereabouts remained a mystery. Three hundred years afterwards, a fresh crack in the wall had brought to light a secret chamber, and in an old iron box there, by a pile of bones, "The Babe's" father had found the missing documents; these had come into the youngster's possession on the decease of his parent.

Sinclair gazed at the sketch, listened to all this and said nothing, but the grim look on his face deepened. When the German retired, he sat up with maps and compasses regretting a certain diary of his in England, which gave the exact site of the mysterious peak he had seen when traveling to Blenka's country via Mombassa; the legend he had heard when in that district, the sketch Langfeldt had drawn, the ancestress of three hundred years ago "The Babe" and his sister had spoken of, and Krua's story of the "Golden Flower," all pointed to it being the scene of the treasure hunt. If it were so, there was every possibility of his getting there considerably sooner than "The Babe" reckoned on. Once having found the starting point this end, and knowing in what direction the ultimate destination lay, the task of following would not present so many serious difficulties. That young devil, in spite of his detailed route, would hardly be able to travel three steps to his one. There was a chance he might get there in time to save his little girl from whatever fate awaited her in that ghastly peak.

Sinclair folded up the map, then, taking a quaint oval gold case from his pocket, opened it. Two faces looked back at him. One was Chrysanthe's, dreamy and wistful, gazing at him with sad, frightened eyes—. Chrysanthe as he had last seen her in the red-gold dress and awesome jewels! The grim look that had been on his face since reading the letter softened. There was a curl just there on her left temple too; but heavy masses of chestnut hair rippled and coiled far below this long-dead girl's waist. Who was she? Where did she come from? Then his gaze went to the man who stood behind her, with his hands laid lightly on her waist, towering over her head and shoulders—a handsome, dark-haired villain in the picturesque dress of the period. For a long time Sinclair studied that face. In the eyes watching him from over the little girl's head was the laughing devil that still lived at the back of "The Babe's." He looked at the case, then closed it thoughtfully. Picked out in rubies on the inner side of the cover were the names—"Claude and Chrysanthe Devereux."

What old tragedy was to be played out and finished in the present two?

CHAPTER 12

"On the sands of yon arena,
I shall yet my vengeance see."

THREE DAYS AFTER RECEIVING "The Babe's" epistle Sinclair found the
spot, some twenty miles away, that had been the scene of the
former's preparations for this trip into the interior. In small detachments they had scoured the forest, blazing each track as they
went along, so as to avoid all possibilities of going over the same
ground twice, and, finally, a band of twelve, led by Sinclair in person, had, just before sunset on the third day, dropped across a little
rock gully, hemmed in by the usual bush tangle, that gave signs of
recent occupation. Probably the very place where the note had been
written! That the departure had been somewhat hurried was obvious from the litter lying about. A quantity of stores had been left
behind, owing either to insufficient porters or a desire to travel as
quickly and lightly burdened as possible. The tense, grim look that
had been on Sinclair's face since reading the missive deepened as
he went over the cases. Fully half of them contained supplies doubtless got for Chrysanthe, and these, being of the nature of luxuries,
had been thrown out so as to make the running more easy. All the
spare kit, such as extra tents, hammocks, etc., also reposed in the
gully. Evidently "The Babe" was traveling with the barest necessi-
ties, his one object being speed.

Sinclair left the gully and searched round for the track taken.
Three trails each leading in an entirely different direction showed

the party had left in separate bodies. The fact, though a trifle baffling at first observation, did not trouble Sinclair—he was too old
a hand at his game to be confused by a child's trick like that, and
knew "The Babe" was not likely to keep his retinue broken up for
long; without doubt these same three parties would meet again at
a given spot farther inland.

As it was too late to return to the fort that evening, he decided
to spend the night in one of his late host's tents, instead of under
the stars as he had expected. Likewise he supplemented his mea-
ger supply of rations from the cases strewn about. All this gave
him a feeling of grim satisfaction. He was pretty well convinced
"The Babe" had not counted on him finding this spot for a full week.
At the outside the young devil could not be more than fifty miles
away. He would have had to travel at an abnormal rate to be that.
Twelve miles a day was good average bush traveling when encum-
bered by a train of porters and heavy baggage. Sinclair knew quite
well the youngster would spare neither himself nor his sister nor
any man of his team during the early days of his flight; afterwards,
when he fancied something like two hundred miles lay between
him and his undesired guest, he might slow off a little. There was
an unpleasant look on Sinclair's face as he laid him down to rest in
the accommodation unknowingly provided by his late host. The
young devil was wholly unaware of his acquaintance with the mystic peak to the northeast of Blenka's land. He slept soundly that
night, not with the fitful dozes and interludes of weary, anxious
musing that had been his lot since Chrysanthe disappeared.

Before the next dawn Sinclair rose. By lunch he was back at the
fort with news of his discovery. In a few hours everything was in
working order, and early the next morning he and Langfeldt with
a train of sixty porters set out for the little gully. The night was
spent there. Claude's brand-new tents, hammocks and some of his
stores were requisitioned for their future use, and Sinclair felt he
was getting the price of those guns back.

One evening, a week later, they again camped on a spot use by
the man they sought, or one of his detachments, nearly sixty miles
farther inland to the eastward. They had not progressed quite at

the rate they would have liked, and "The Babe" had been truthful when he said it was extremely difficult traveling; one whole day had been lost by taking a track which ultimately landed them at a bush village. There they made inquiries for the missing ones. Nothing had been seen or heard of them, but a man now visiting there, from a village some four days' march away, on his way had seen a train of twelve, headed by one of their own color, not a white man. These had no stores or anything, but went along at a quick, quiet walk as of those who smell the scent but from a long distance. The natives put them on the track of this mysterious party, and two days afterwards they camped at a spot showing signs of recent occupation, but by a larger force than the twelve the villagers referred to. It lay at the edge of the first forest belt and the character of the country underwent a sudden and radical change. Hills appeared parched and desolate, radiating heat and strewn with huge rocks and boulders; here and there were clumps of stiff grotesque cacti and an occasional half-dead baobab—an arid barren place where the shifting sand would soon wipe out all trace and trail—a lifeless, volcanic patch in a desert of tangled matted forest.

After dinner Sinclair sat in front of his tent. It was a dark, starless night, breathless and stifling. Occasionally a lurid streak of lightning flickered and played across the sky and spoke of a rapidly approaching tornado. As he smoked thoughtfully he went over the situation. This patch of desert bid fair to retard progress. As far as he could estimate from what he had seen before darkness fell, it appeared to stretch as far as the eye could reach on either side; ahead the range of low rocky hills screened the view. Would it be better to make as straight as he could for the remote inland peak, or spend some valuable days in endeavoring to get on "The Babe's" trail again, and perhaps be unsuccessful? This desert did not stretch far he was sure—a matter of thirty miles each way at the most—quite enough for that young devil to double and turn, and put him off the scent altogether. To make his way straight to the peak, without the occasional assistance he had had so far, would mean an extremely difficult task. Heaven alone knew what obstacles lay in the forest depths and beyond!

As he sat there musing a light, suddenly flashing in and out on a shelf of the hill ahead, made him start up. It was there and gone so quickly he almost doubted his eyes. He appealed to Langfeldt, who, however, had noticed nothing. Stationed about a hundred yards away was one of the Hausas on duty. Sinclair went to him. Even as his master, the man thought he had seen a light, but so sharp and sudden as to make him uncertain without further evidence. They compared notes, and the point of the mysterious flash tallied. Then with a deafening crash the tornado broke. Sinclair went back heavy-hearted. It would be impossible to make any search whilst this storm and deluge lasted. He studied the spot as the blinding flashes lit up the country. To-morrow he would find out more about that light!

He joined Langfeldt in the latter's tent. The pouring torrent hissed and streamed round, thundered down on the stout canvas and ran like a young river through one side and out at the other. In the stifling, steaming heat they sipped their after-dinner whisky. Their renewed mutual interest in "The Babe" had drawn them closer together than before, and Sinclair now knew enough of his dealings to effect his arrest without compromising his sister in the least. He knew he could trust the German until the desired map and document lay in their possession; afterwards he would have to walk very warily, keep a sharp eye on his present companion and a double guard round that small wild bird of his, if he ever got it into his safe keeping. However, he could back his Hausas against the kroo-boys, but there was just a possibility of his German friend being in touch with Mungea and considerable of his kind. Although he had never been told anything to confirm his belief he fancied "The Babe" and his one-time bosom companion had parted through some underhand connection of the latter's with that black fiend.

He sat thinking over the days and all that had happened since the time he saw this shifty-looking German on the *Asabo's* deck, when the splash of feet through the flood outside roused him. Over the thundering downpour his orderly announced that a man, apparently a native of the district, wished to see him. Sinclair straightened himself a little, sat with his face in the shadow and bade him bring the man in. Langfeldt looked up with as much interest as the occasion demanded.

An almost naked savage entered—a man of rather more than forty, tall and powerfully built, though hardly of Krua's physique. His expression was intelligent beyond the average negro, the glint of the fanatic was in his eyes and a look of intense cruelty predominated his whole countenance. He faced the two Europeans without the least salutation or sign of fear. The flickering lamp played on his steaming wet skin and dripping woolly hair. Sinclair glanced over him sharply, then gave an almost imperceptible start. Half the little finger was missing! The maimed paw! He felt certain it was Mungea. In height and build he resembled the deck hand he had remarked on the *Asabo*, but his inspection on that occasion had been so casual that he could not swear to the face. What was this arch-fiend's motive in coming to him? He sat waiting for the negro to speak. Langfeldt gazed at the newcomer curiously but claimed no acquaintance.

The orderly retired. There was silence in the tent except for the hiss and whish of the pouring tropical rain. For a few moments the two eyed each other. Sinclair felt he was dealing with no ordinary savage, but one who came from a stock of rulers, who had been the leading spirit of his kind from the earliest days. The newcomer raised his hand and saluted with markedly forced deference, then spoke in the dialect of the country, but with the tone of one accustomed to command, and as if it would go hard with all who went contrary to his will.

"There is one whom you seek. One who has crossed the laws of his country. One who flies before you into the forests beyond."

Sinclair played lightly with a book on the table and watched the visitor with an air of careless indifference.

"For one of the wilds you are well informed?"

"They who dwell in the bush are keen of hearing. Whispered news is wafted on the wind and reaches the ear of those who listen from afar."

"It needs a loud whisper and a strong wind to reach here."

"There is a wind called vengeance. It calls and moans through the forest and dies not down until it reaches what it desires. It is a wind that has blown from the beginning and whispers alike into all ears, be they black or white."

"It is not that wind that whispers into my ears, but one called justice. I seek this man as I have sought others—because he has broken the laws of his country."

"The winds of vengeance and justice blow keen on the same track. Even as this one has broken the laws of his country, so he has crossed the laws of mine. The wind of vengeance has moaned in my ears this long year. But I was alone and could do nothing. Now justice comes! What better vengeance than to give him into your hands?"

Sinclair looked at the negro intently, the man returned his gaze unflinchingly.

"And for this, what price?"

"I want no price. Only this law-breaker taken. I am but the mouth of one who now dwells beyond the shades. On me has he put the burden of his vengeance. I am but one finger of a once-powerful hand now broken and distorted by the heavy seal of time. There is one who mocked and laughed! But the old blood stirred! There is yet strength to strike the mocker! Time was when the shadow of this hand spread throughout the country. Even in those days there were they who laughed! But not for long! The hand grew red with the blood of the scoffers, and crushed their land till but few knew its shape or where it lay. This one travels now for the frozen blood and yellow bones of that people. On his way he passes a once-great temple, where he who whispers in my ear ruled until a flower grew in a far country. This whisperer was cunning and joined with those of thy color, and went forth and crushed the flower. But there was a poison in that flower and the hand weakened and withered and now but one finger remains. Many crops grow on the same land, are sown, tended, then gathered and pass away forgotten. No one knows what comes after save the sower. Others flourish, have their season, and are gathered into the Barn of Time. The land remains and the Barn is not full! Yet the same crop may come again! Many harvests have been since the hand helped at the plucking of a flower, since one took it limp and crushed and wore it on his heart until it faded—wore it at a price this one refused to pay. I would this scoffer were taken from the land. Is that not also your desire? You seek but this one who flies before you into the forest yonder. If I lead you to the temple that lies three weeks' march beyond, and deliver him into your hands, is not your mission ended? The thief who has crossed the laws of both our countries is run to earth."

For some time Sinclair sat in thoughtful silence. He knew quite well that this man's object was not to bring the brother to justice, but to get the sister into his power. He was equally sure he was to be made the cat's paw of these two now with him in the tent. They must both know he would not take "The Babe" and leave Chrysanthe unprotected! What was their idea?

The rain thundered down on the tent and the little hanging lamp swayed, casting flickering shadows on the three faces; one wrapped in thought, another watching covertly and a third that looked at the two white ones with veiled contempt.

Sinclair went quickly over the main points of the case. Once "The Babe" was his prisoner it meant the breaking up of that young devil's force. Chrysanthe with her brother, who knew their desires, presented a much more difficult object to attain than with him (Sinclair), who, as far as they were aware, knew nothing of their intentions. It was more than probable this negro was only using Langfeldt as a means to his end. Also Mungea was not as alone as he pretended. Those same twelve the villagers had spoken of were without a doubt part of his troop, and the nearer this fanatic got to headquarters the more of his kind would join him. If this black fiend knew the route to the temple he spoke of as being one of "The Babe's" landmarks, it would be a considerable saving of time to get up there under his guidance. If he succeeded in catching his man there, some very careful sailing would have to be done afterwards. But he had been in tighter holes than this might prove and come out all right. Once he had his little girl again it would have to be a stronger combination than the present that took her from him.

Sinclair knew his man, but it was not his intention either the German or Mungea should have the least inkling he suspected them of being in concert. Turning to Langfeldt he said in English, knowing the negro would understand, "Could you follow our new friend's palaver?"

Considering it was the ordinary language of the country the German agreed he could.

"What should you say? Does it strike you the whole thing is a hoax on the part of Wentworth? Probably this man is in his pay and sent here to offer himself as a guide for the sole purpose of leading us astray. Personally I think we had better put him out into the rain again. I fancy it will be a considerable saving of time in the long run. That young demon is hand-in-glove with all the niggers in this part."

The German looked at the new-comer speculatively. "These black devils will do a lot for nothing when vengeance is their game."

"Wentworth would know that and send him here with this pretty little yarn."

"Yes, it might be so, but still this nigger would know he was running a fairish risk by putting us on the wrong scent. We'd neither of us have much compunction about letting daylight through his head if he tried on that trick. What he says about the temple sounds a bit truthful. His mentioning it brought back to my mind a sort of broken ring marked on that old map I saw, and, as far as I remember, from the glimpse I had, it would be about a third of the way up from the fort—pretty much the distance he says from here, though the sign I saw may have had nothing to do with any temple, the position is all I go by. You're boss of this expedition, not me, but, since you want my opinion, I should say, try him a couple of days or so and if we don't drop across the trail within the time, well, shoot him! Let him know exactly what your intentions are. If he's a fraud he'll probably take the opportunity of departing before daylight. If he doesn't there may be some truth in that he says."

Sinclair appeared to give his companion's advice serious attention. The reply confirmed his opinion that the two were in league. He had not for a moment doubted the man's ability to lead them to the spot mentioned; the negro had only lied as regards his motive for doing so. After a few minutes of apparent deep and serious thinking he told the waiting negro he would take him on as guide, apprising him in detail what would happen if he played them false; knowing quite well there would be no fear of that until these two villains had made him serve their purpose.

The negro laughed and looked at Sinclair boldly.

"I am no servant of him you seek. In three weeks we shall be at the temple. If he is not there all reward I ask is to serve you until with my own eyes I see this scoffer in the grip of justice. Up to the temple I know my way; I have trodden it in the days of my father and his. Beyond is darkness! The path lost to all but one!"

With a curt nod Sinclair dismissed him, and shortly after the negro left he rose with the intention of going to his own quarters. A tearing flash of lightning lit up the low range of hills as he stepped out of the tent. The mysterious light he had seen there no longer gave him food for reflection—considering the events of the evening it was more that probable it had been a signal to Langfeldt apprising him of the coming visit. He wondered why the two had not come into union sooner. Probably they relied on him finding his way up to this spot without assistance, and agreed to meet here so as not to arouse suspicion, knowing the first real obstacle lay in this desert patch. There was a very keen, hard look about his eyes as he went musingly towards his quarters. Once there he sent for his Hausa headman. For considerably more than an hour they sat in close confabulation and the erstwhile sergeant learned one or two things, not altogether surprising, but which hitherto he had only suspected. When they parted there was one who knew exactly what to do in case any unforeseen accident happened to Major Sinclair.

With the passing of the night the storm abated, and the early morning sun flashed and sparkled on large pools of water and little rushing streams, all that remained of the previous evening's deluge. During breakfast Sinclair inquired for the guide and evinced mild surprise when the man presented himself. That same night the combined forces camped some eighteen miles away on the far side of the desert patch. A track lying just close at hand, twisting and turning into the dim depths of the forest, was pointed out to him as the direct route to the old temple which lay rather less than two hundred miles away. Along the path, he was assured, the man he sought had traveled only a week ago. It certainly gave no sign of recent use, but quickly growing vegetation and the recent pouring deluge would have successfully wiped out all traces of those ahead, and "The Babe" was not likely to leave much evidence of his presence lying about.

Sinclair went to sleep that night wondering if he could possibly get twenty miles a day out of his men for the next fortnight; if so they would land up at the temple pretty much the same day as his late host.

CHAPTER 13

"We may stand in the pale of the outer ring,
But forbear to trespass within the inner,
Lest the sins of the past should find out the sinner."

THE FULL AFRICAN MOON hung like a giant ball of glowing silver in the soft indigo sky, and its brilliant white rays almost obliterated a tiny pale yellow light that flickered and danced in an open patch in the dark forest beneath. Its streaming flood of silver washed round great uncouth stones standing in a broken circle in the middle of this break in the tangled waste, and they cast long, pointed, black shadows that crept out and were lost in the dim aisle of towering trees. It played round an ancient stone altar, where a hideous carved image lay coiled with hungry vicious jaws poised over an old worn slab marked with curious patches that made the pale brown rock a deeper color than its neighbors. In the white light they showed up clearly, like dark pools in the hollowed surface, but what had once been wet and warm, long since had oozed and mingled into the stone, and now nothing remained but the suggestive patches the growing creepers tried to hide.

Gaunt leathery-leaved weeds, rank and noisome, pushed through the flagged platform where the altar stood, and flourished on the broken steps leading to it. A passion plant, with pure white flowers challenging the moonlight, coiled and crept round the hideous body hanging over the patched stone. A soft breeze whispered and sighed round the temple and played gently with the long, bleached, hair-like substance that fluttered and coiled about the legs of the waiting monster. Fifteen golden circles marked the site where bunches of the fine substance had once streamed out in the wind. Some were worn by breeze and time down to the raw gold sheath that held them; of others just a stray thread or so remained; nearer the creature's head the bunches fluttered out thicker, and highest up a long thick mass floated out that time and rain had not quite robbed of its yellow tinge.

The wind came soughing down from the forest behind; moaned round the ruined walls, rustling the giant bell flowers coiled about the stones passing years had brought to earth, crept and murmured in and out of the few huge rudely carved slabs that remained upright, sighed through the ghastly temple and then on ahead, whispering of what it had seen. A little passing breeze got caught for a moment in the weird circle. It sobbed against the hard, cruel stones and back to the waiting altar, touching the fluttering hair tenderly, sighed, then went swiftly to a tent on the outskirts of the ruin, lifted the flap and called and wailed to one who sat inside with weary, anxious eyes.

Near by, a pale yellow fire tried to cast shadows of its own in opposition to the all-conquering silver flood. It danced on the faces of the porters who slept around, shot out little feeble fingers to where half-a-dozen silent black figures stood on the farthermost limits of the camp. Out of the forest came the long-drawn, moaning howl of a leopard calling to its mate, and the distant, quick, sharp, chorused yelp of a pack of bush-dogs on the track of a deer.

Inside the tent, with feeble hands moving restlessly over the blanket of the little camp bed, lay "The Babe." The lamplight flickered on his face thin and hollowed with the ravages of malaria fever in its worst form. For two days he had hovered on the verge in a state of helpless delirium, and only a few minutes ago had awoke from the sleep which had been his saving. A weary, anxious little face bent over him, whose heavy, dark-ringed eyes spoke of more than one sleepless night. A small hand smoothed back his mop of curls tenderly.

"Lord! Chrys, how long has this blasted caravan been halted here?"

"Three days, dear. I—I couldn't go on when you were so ill."

"Three days! Oh, damnation! Prop me up, Chrys, I can't think when I'm laid out here like a blooming corpse."

A pillow was brought from the bed behind the curtains dividing the tent. Chrysanthe slipped it under his head, lifted him gently and wrapped a shawl round his shoulders; then she turned to a box near, where some soup was heating over a spirit stove, brought it to him and watched him with big loving eyes as he attacked it with gusto—the first time he had had anything, but what she had coaxed into his mouth, for the last three days. The refreshment finished, she relieved him of the cup and sat by the bedside with one arm round him.

"Lord! Chrys, I've had a close shave this time. Quite sure my locks ain't singed? Rum go if I'd pegged out in the precincts of the family chapel! The gentle little pat Mungea gave me on the back of my curly head is responsible for this. Devil's own luck that I should have fever just now. Never had such a thing in the days of my evilness! It don't pay to be pious. Here I am, for the first time in my life going up to fetch goods belonging to me, and this is my reward! If it were not for that damned Sinclair; and that he knows enough of my wicked past to effect my prolonged detention at his Majesty's expense, I'd chuck looking for things that are really my own and go back to my bad wild ways. But there ain't any going back, my child. That route is closed to us forever! We must get our bag of pebbles and haste us towards the sunrise—a private exploring party that will cross this murky continent without advertisement! It ain't likely Sinclair will follow us across; but there's a chance he may get up as far as here—maybe with the Rev. Mungea acting as guide. If he does let him look out! I ain't partial to our ex-chaplain, or anyone connected with him. This infernal fever of mine has cost us a good week. It ain't likely they'll be here for a day or two yet. Beyond here no one knows the route save our two sweet little selves. I'll soon be fit to hold the reins again, and you'll be able to have a spell off. You're looking seedy, Chrys. I bet you haven't had much beauty sleep since I knocked up. Quite glad the devil didn't hook me under, ain't you, old girl?"

A soft cheek was rubbed against the thin white one and two arms hugged him lovingly, but not too tightly. There was not much of that bad wicked "Babe" left, and what there was looked very frail and shaky. A skeleton hand held and patted one of Chrysanthe's, and two blue eyes looked at her pleadingly.

"There ain't any whiskies going just now?"—anxiously.

She laughed and kissed the pleading eyes that were beginning to twinkle again.

"One very, very small one this time to-morrow, not before."

"Lord! Must I wait till then? I've been a bally blue-ribboner for the last week!—ever since I started this extra strong dose of fever and you got me nicely chained up by the leg. You're hard-hearted, Chrys, absolutely rocky, to refuse a poor ill devil a drink. It ain't Christian. Won't you let me have a smell?"

"No, dear, not even a smell before to-morrow."

"The Babe" laughed.

"Well, if you won't, you won't. There's no talking you round sometimes, Chrys. Now tell me what has been happening these three days I've been lost to the world. Any more of those blasted porters deserted?"

"Three went the day before yesterday. They slipped away in the early afternoon, when most of the camp was asleep. I always kept a good guard of our own men round at night; they got no chance then, so they tried this new tack successfully."

"That's the whole round dozen gone! This comes of scratching people together in a hurry. We can't throw any more ballast overboard. We aren't living high as it is and shall be reduced to native 'chop' before we reach the other side. It ain't no use sitting down weeping over the dear departed. I bet Mungea was at the bottom of their little scoot. He has filled their woolly heads with an almighty fear of what lies beyond. Lord! Chrys, ain't it just three weeks today since we started on our little jaunt? You haven't had a very happy time, I've been a blooming invalid most of the way. I lost too much blood the night Krua gave you the shock of your life. We're a week behind ourselves. To-morrow we must push on, my child. We can't afford to waste any more time this next hundred miles. You'll let me have the loan of your hammock for a couple of days longer, won't you? Fifty miles farther along the line is a big chief at Essuata Town, fifteen miles off the track. I'll hop across and get him to 'dash' me a score of porters; he's fearfully fond of me is that old sinner. I once kept a rhinoceros from tusking him, when we were out shooting together. He was very grateful-like, offered me unto half his kingdom, including a whole harem of dusky beauties. Said I'd rather have the choice of porters if ever I happened to be coming up here on business. Guess I'll keep him to his little promise. Then we'll jog along a bit quicker than these last few days. Now, this infant's going to sleep again. Captain Chrys, when you go the round of sentries and see that all's serene, tell Krua we're on the march at dawning. Then get into your own crib extra quick. No need to sit up nursing this baby all another night. I know you have these last three. I sort of felt you there though I didn't know much else. Lord! Chrys, if you hadn't been a she what howling times we could have had together, but still you manage very well considering."

Chrysanthe tucked him in and sat watching until he fell asleep again. It was a weary little figure that left the tent for its final nightly round. On her shoulders had fallen nearly the whole care of the expedition since its third day out. Sinclair might have smiled, though perhaps rather sadly, had he seen this small bird of his, in the short blue dress and floppy hat, go its round of sentries with a care and precision equaling his own. "The Babe's" unexpected illness, resulting from the scrimmage in the clearing, had made most of these duties fall to her lot, and she took his place much in the same way as she had taken it before, in less legitimate deals, but with the anxious knowledge that Major Sinclair was on the track of the beloved but sinful one. The only hammock, that had been told off for her special use, had very soon become the portion of her brother, who was too ill for walking. She and Krua combined, by persuasion and example, had managed to make the porters travel at the rate of sixteen miles a day, for the first week of their control. Afterwards, a scratch team of niggers had deserted one by one, and their burdens divided among the others had decreased the running somewhat, and the speed dropped. The last three days had been an enforced halt, and they were fully a hundred miles nearer their late residence than they had reckoned on.

She picked her way over the sleeping negroes, half of whom slept with guns as well as their daily burdens beside them. Eighteen of them were "The Babe's" specially trained handy men who had been with him on several gas-pipe and teeth-drawing expeditions, and were either porters or sharpshooters as the occasion demanded, and who would have shed the last drop of their blood for their reckless young leader. Six more of these picked men mounted guard over the camp. Although not popular with his own color the youngster had the hearts of all his dusky following, and a sigh of relief had gone round when the saving sleep came to him. Squatted on their haunches on the far side of the fire were Krua and "The Babe's" headman, Gola. They got up as Chrysanthe came towards them.

"It goes well with our brother, my flower?"

"So well, Krua, that we are to be on the march with sunrise. Gola, see your men are in readiness, we can lose no time."

The headman grunted complacently.

"The news is good, Golden Flower. It is a swift race to beyond and a sharp corner here. But we have turned many sharp corners, thy brother and I"—there was a wicked grin on the negro's face. "Once in Blenka's land, he who is now on our track thirsted for the blood of my master. He passed as close as thou art to me, Golden Flower; but I was a Mohammedan trader from the Northern Desert, thy brother my favorite wife, who sat shrouded and veiled in a hammock, on the shoulders of my slaves, and beneath the rugs were many guns of a pattern too new for my character. For a whole day we traveled with the one of the sharp eyes, and sometimes I feared the keen ears would hear the laughter of the one who sat in the litter; for he of the sharp eyes was hot on our trail and inquired which way we had gone. We said our way led to the party he desired, but he believed us not and departed on another trail before nightfall. Thy brother and I had donned that dress but two minutes before he came. It would have gone ill with us for he had a

large following, close on five score, and we numbered but two
dozen. That was a sharper corner even than this, and my master
won. There is no fear, Golden Flower, but what we win again," and
Gola smiled reassuringly.

"But then my brother was not ill, Gola."

"Now we have thee, Golden Flower. It is but one small blossom
yet it is of great courage and we are equally its servants. Krua is
thy great thorn, but I and my men are a tangle of sharp pricks, and
they who desire my master must fire break through these."

Here Gola threw a fresh supply of fuel on the fire. The crack-
ling blazes shot up and danced on the sleeping camp and on the
two black savage figures standing by Chrysanthe. It played on her
tired face. There was a worry and weight of care there that had not
been since the fourth day on the *Asabo*, when the fear that Major
Sinclair might have discovered her secret loomed over her. By trying to do the right thing then she had all but betrayed her brother!

Krua's hand patted her shoulder.

"Arru! Little flower, our brother's illness is over now and we
will make our way swiftly. The past weeks have been a burden beyond the strength of flowers. There is nothing more to fear now.
By sunrise everything will be ready, and soon many scores of miles
will lie between the pursued and the pursuer. These long hours
the forest blossoms have closed their petals with no thought of the
morrow. It is well if our Golden Flower do even as they, and stir
not until I announce all ready."

Chrysanthe left them and went slowly towards the tent. A few
yards away, between it and the forest, stood one of the sentries.
The long, pointed, wavering shadow cast by the tent reached up to
the nearest stone of the temple. Beyond, the great circle lay still
and lifeless, patched black and white in the silver flood, and on
the far side, some two hundred yards away, the rude stone altar
stood, shadowed by hanging trees and roped with a matted tangle
of creepers. She paused for a moment and gazed at the weird picture. What awful rites had been enacted there in times past. Each
one with the sanction of her people! Each in payment of an old
debt! She had refused to pay her dole. Once it seemed as if the old

gods had risen in their wrath and would take her brother's life as their due! Take it because she had refused to do her share! Two days he lay as dying in the shadow of this temple. She had brought no sacrifice as the old contract demanded. It was such a night as this the old gods claimed their due! Only last evening she had asked that this one precious life might be spared—the only one of her kindred left; the brother she had loved and cared for from her earliest days! She had not dared to go to the altar with the great stone horror, raised in the long-dead days—the facsimile of the one in that far-off mountain they were seeking. Perhaps there was some truth in that old scrawl! Perhaps this great evil beast heard and understood her!

Chrysanthe went closer to the moon-washed ring—a little flitting shape swallowed up in the black shadow of the tent. She stood with one hand on the first rugged stone. The wind came soughing down from the forest, filling the temple with strange, whispering voices. Almost unconsciously she went nearer the waiting horror—like a ghost in the mystic circle. She paused and gazed at it with dreamy, wistful eyes, then on again. The thick, dank leaves and heavy, cup-like flowers, growing on the worn, flagged way, rustled round her feet as she went swiftly towards the altar steps. She stopped with her hand at her throat, gazing at the fluttering mass of long, bleached hair nearest the head of the monster. Then she counted the gold bands, that glistened in the moonlight. Fifteen of them! Each killed by the hands of her people! And the last her own mother! How glad she would be when it was all over—when the devil claimed his own again! She could hear them calling to her down the years, those murdered women! There ought to be another bunch fluttering there! Another ghastly patch on the altar stone! Her toll!

Little feet went fearsomely up the broken steps, and Chrysanthe stood right under the hanging head of the awesome monster. The streaming, pale yellow hair touched her cheek lovingly—a gentle caress like a phantom kiss. She caught and held it tenderly, laid her face on the bleached strands and the slim, tired shoulders heaved convulsively. What devil's spawn they were! Thieves and murderers! But they had always hung together, always paid their due! All but she!

She looked at the hideous head. Wistful, dreamy eyes watched it with anxious pleading, and two small hands were stretched out to it imploringly.

"Great Asquielba! I bring no life but my own! Take it and let all this be ended!"

The moonlight streamed on a bowed curly head lying on the grim old altar stone. A passing wind toyed with the soft loose locks in the nape of the pretty white neck. Something rustled in the tall rank grass on the outskirts of the temple, crept stealthily along like a gigantic cat, with its glaring eyes fixed on the kneeling figure. The silver light gleamed on the great white fangs that the stretched-back lips showed in a ghastly, silent grin as the green eyes marked the slim bare neck. A breeze moaned round the altar, seized the long thick strand of pale golden hair, and it fluttered out, covering the bowed, curly head with an anxious, nervous movement. As it streamed out the leopard paused, crouched down on the old stone way and waited. The wind died down with a panting sigh, the long, loose tresses fluttered back and coiled round the hanging hungry stone head. Not a leaf rustled in the silent, waiting circle. A stray cloud floated over the moon, blotting out the flood of silver light. Nothing showed in the shrouded ring but the white neck and the glaring green eyes that watched it. The beast crept on again and paused at the altar steps, like a savage cat sure of its prey, its eyes on the bowed figure. A thin silver ray came trembling through the cloud, it glinted on the hanging stone horror and its repulsive shape seemed to move and droop nearer the patched stone as the uncertain, wavering light played on it. The leopard stretched its heavy paws, and the cruel, curved claws gleamed like old ivory in the flickering, silver ray. It looked at them with lazy speculation and then at the kneeling girl. The white fangs showed in the same silent, ghastly laugh. The long, hot, steaming tongue went round its lips; bending its head it licked first one paw and then the other. Something waiting in a crevice of the stone steps dropped on the lolling red mass. A wild yelp of agony made

Chrysanthe start up in terror. She shrank back into the shadow of the carved monster with big, dilated eyes on the spotted, writhing mass at the foot of the altar steps. Mad, tortured howls echoed and re-echoed through the temple, backwards and forwards from each of the gaunt upright stones to the hideous carved image, like shrieks of devilish laughter. A sigh went through the forest and the trees swayed down towards the mystic ring, their towering heads bent earthwards listening and wondering at the wild uproar. The camp woke with a sudden start. Black figures shot up and the firelight gleamed on steel gun barrels, and anxious, scared eyes were fixed on the ancient temple, waiting for some fearsome horror to appear. Suddenly a death-like stillness fell over everything, not a leaf rustled in the dense wilderness around, not a man moved in the camp, not a sound from the shrouded ruin! But only for a moment, then—an awful ravening sound and the mad devil's mirth broke out again.

In the tent "The Babe" woke with a sudden start, alert and wide awake.

"Chrys! Chrys! What's all this hellish row?" he called to the curtains.

There was no reply, only a whine from Grip, who lay in the screened division, tied to one of the upright poles. With an effort the youngster pulled himself up and one bony hand clutched a revolver from a box at the bedside. He listened for a moment and called again. Hurried footsteps came towards the tent. Krua and Gola loomed up in the flap with scared eyes on the ruin.

"Krua, you great, gaping fool, come and see if Chrys is in there," he called in quick anxiety, pointing to the curtains.

In a moment "The Babe's" worst fears were verified.

"Then she's in that devil's temple! By hell, I'll roast the lot of you if anything has happened to her!"

Before he had finished speaking Krua was out of the tent and heading towards the ruin, Gola close at his heels. The black faces went a curious, mottled brown as they reached the outskirts of the pile. The fear of every evil spirit that lurked by night in the uncanny ring was on them. Was not this the abode of the father of all wickedness? Was not that his laugh echoing through the forest? Was it not death to all who entered?

Two black statues paused just within the ring, scared eyes tried to pierce the shrouded gloom, gazing intently towards the spot whence came the hideous, shrieking laughter. The moon shone out full and clear from the passing cloud; the silver rays streamed on the ruined altar where a white-faced little figure crouched into the shelter of the silent stone god, with wide, terror-stricken eyes fixed on a great writhing, howling mass at the foot of the altar steps, not ten feet away.

Two shots rang out simultaneously. The tortured yelps died down to a sobbing moan, and all was silence as, with a few convulsive shivers, the beast lay dead.

Two shapes came swiftly over the worn flagged way, with unbelieving eyes on Chrysanthe, who stood, with one hand on the carved stone horror, gazing at the leopard. The negroes stopped at the foot of the steps and the white light gleamed on the steel gun barrels as they were raised in salutation.

"Ayati! Golden Flower!"

She started, looked at them with wide, dreamy eyes, then came down the steps, and, slipping her arm through Krua's, leant over, gazing at the dead beast. The men watched her with awed reverence on their dusky faces. A convulsive shiver ran through her.

"Why didn't it kill me? I heard nothing of it until that awful howl rang out, just at my back it seemed, and I saw it writhing there. It could have settled me without anyone in the camp knowing. It was very silly of me to come here at night. I don't know what made me do it."

"It would not dare to touch thee in the shadow of the Dread One, Golden Flower," glancing fearsomely at the carved image.

Chrysanthe laughed nervously.

"Nonsense, Krua! This battered old stone wouldn't have scared it away. It's horrible enough for anything, but not in the way leopards mind."

Krua made no reply, but knelt by the side of the dead beast and examined it carefully. The swollen red tongue protruded from the jaws. He opened them farther and gave a startled grunt. Gola bent over the carcass in round-eyed astonishment.

"Arru! Golden Flower, but see this!"

Chrysanthe crouched by Krua's side and gave a startled gasp. There, embedded in the beast's tongue, was a centipede! The thing that had dropped there as it licked its paws complacently, absolutely sure of its victim! She got up and her hand went to her throat as she gazed at the silent stone creature. A shower of white petals blew down from the creeper clinging round its many-legged body. They fluttered about her, settled on the curly head, touched the wistful red mouth, then crept on in the soft breeze.

"Golden Flower, do not the voices whisper that each of these is thy servant? Even as the dread God Asquielba!"

"Nay, Krua, they whisper only of the blood! Of a great red sea and the sound of much fighting! And over all, faint and distant, the wild golden bells are calling."

"Arru! my flower, but beyond the mist of streaming blood it was as I say."

"If each of these is my servant, why was it that one proved almost my master?—one whose scar I bore for many a day!"

"I know not why it was, my flower. But the voices whisper all these serve thee for thy good."

"I have no wish to be served by the jaws that have dripped blood these long years. I hate this evil beast whose poison has sunk deep into the hearts of my people, whose vicious, savage cunning has been our birthright, whose curse has been on us since the times the mists have swallowed."

"Have care, Golden Flower! It is not well to say these things in the shadow of the Dread One. The curse was the fault of the one who robbed it of the flower it loved."

"There is no love in that vile beast for anything save blood."

"But for this servant of the Dread One there would be fresh blood on the altar now. Even thy blood, Golden Flower!"

Chrysanthe gazed for a moment at the grim stone image, then turned away quickly and went from the old temple into the flickering firelight. It was a strained white face the flames danced on.

Many awed eyes followed her as she crossed to the tent. Inside, "The Babe" lay in impatient anxiety.

"Lord! Chrys, what have you been doing in the family chapel, raising hell? I got the shock of my life when Krua said you were not in your little crib. I guessed you had gone there; it always has had an awful fascination for all our lot."

She laid her head on his pillow with a stifled sob.

"What's the matter, old girl? Did your mutual godfather catch you trespassing and hop out on you suddenlike?"

A tearful voice explained what had happened.

"Lord! you don't say so!"—in vast astonishment. "A bit creepy, ain't it? Don't you get prowling about at night outside of the fire-light again, or maybe I shall be called upon to read the funeral service over my own twin. It ain't at all the sort of job I'd fancy doing."

"The Babe" kissed the tear-stained face in a half-shamed way, then laughed and said: "Now go to bed, there ain't anything more to worry about."

She got up and tucked him in afresh. He watched with something of the awed reverence that had been in the negroes' eyes. Then, when she disappeared behind the curtains, he sat up again lost in thought.

CHAPTER 14

"Sorry am I, yet my sorrow
Cannot alter fate."

ESSUATA TOWN WAS *EN FÊTE*. Was not the chief entertaining his blood brother? Huge bonfires blazed in the market square, and the roaring red flames shot skywards, playing on the bamboo palm-thatched huts surrounding it in untidy clusters of three or four, or groups of a dozen, intermingled with plantains, bread-fruit, lime and pawpaw trees. Great sparks flew out and were lost in the pitch-dark night, or settled on the nearer dwellings and caused some moments' anxious thinking to the more sober inhabitants. Giant torches flared on the rude stockading surrounding the village; cast long, dancing shadows into the dense forest, and threw suggestive shapes on a "devil-house" close at hand, just beyond the wooden walls; stained the blood-steeped rags fluttering around this abode of evil spirits an even deeper tinge; danced in and out of the bony orbits of the grinning skulls adorning it, and glinted on the bleached white bones that rattled and rubbed together as the wind swayed the slender pole they hung from. The smoke curled and mingled with the heavy, dank mist that rose from an adjacent patch of swamp. From all corners of the village came the sound of tom-toms, the bray of rude horns and the crude music obtained by beating a kerosene tin vigorously with a stout stick. Round the main fire a wild negro dance was in full swing. Dozens of savage naked figures twirled round and round in a circle; as the music quickened

185

so did their pace, until they went at an amazing speed—a jumble of arms and legs—uttering flesh-creeping shrieks and yells. The red light gleamed on their shining, perspiring bodies and on their faces, mad with drink and excitement; it played on the watching audience, who sprawled on the ground clapping their hands to the music and encouraging their friends with shouts and hideous cat-calls. Bowls of native palm wine, together with square, green gin cases, a profusion of empty bottles, well-chewed, scattered bones, denoting the remains of several whole goats demolished earlier in the evening, and the remnants of many local dainties, lay about.

Apart from the circle of merry-makers, on a raised mud daïs, surrounding the biggest of the huts, sat the chief—a picturesque old sinner clad in a long blue and white native cloth, worn toga-wise. A necklace, composed of bits of gold, coral and leopard's claws, and a profusion of charms adorned his neck; roughly made gold rings gleamed on the gnarled black hands; a handsome briar pipe was worn through the lobe of one ear, and a human tooth was suspended from the other by a serviceable piece of copper wire. Beside him sat one in khaki linen nethers and loose coat; a rough grey flannel shirt, floppy hat, leather belt, strongly made brown boots and putties completed the attire. In the shadow behind the two an ebony giant occasionally loomed; although its gait appeared uncertain and its laugh was as loud and drunken as one could wish, there was a remarkably sober, alert look about its eyes, and despite the several mad dances it had already indulged in, its armory remained complete. The firelight played on gilt-topped champagne bottles and glasses standing on a rough wooden block between the chief and his visitor, and on a tired white face with weary eyes and saucy, smiling mouth.

The pleased black face and tired white one were close together as the two talked confidentially. Was it not nearly two years since his white brother had honored him with a visit?—this small blood brother of his with the face of a child and a cunning beyond the lot of mere mortals! The chosen one had had the dreaded fever? Arru! he would have known, this small brother did not look quite the same as usual! He was traveling even to the far interior on a big trading expedition and desired more porters. Was not the whole of this village his, even unto the life of its king? Must he depart with the sunrise? He had but come with the setting of the same! But not too late but what the village made him welcome as becomes a king's brother! But there was reason for this haste! Here the old chief chuckled. Had not this small brother often deals that must be hurried.

As the orgies continued the two sat and talked of all that had happened since they last met. Many a time the fat black sides shook, and a great laugh passed from the wide, thick-lipped mouth as this small white brother recounted escapades calculated to tickle the local sense of humor.

By midnight the fun was running at its highest. The stockading torches had burnt down to their sockets and flickered in small uncertain crackles. The main bonfire blazed bigger than ever, and raised a great pillar of flame and smoke to the black, silent sky. All around, the forest lay still and lifeless; the noise and devilment in the village had scared the four-footed wanderers far away from its precincts. A few drunken figures still staggered round in the mazy whirl: the larger number snored loudly in the firelight. From the far side of the fire wafted the sounds of music where two beat kerosene tins, in competition, and sang meanwhile with a loud, discordant howl. The more seasoned spirits were gathered round the mud daïs. Was not the time at hand when the king and his white brother renewed their blood pledge?

Across the market square came the local pastor in full canonical garb, wreathed round and adorned with a multitude of dried reptiles, relieved here and there by shining white bones. A few smoked hearts, eye-balls, and other small but very necessary parts of the human anatomy, were threaded in a fancy necklace, a garland of teeth and knucklebones hung and clustered about his woolly hair, and a skull, other than his own, crowned this festive attire. He made a gruesome and most uncanny figure in the red glare. Behind him came an underling with a couple of goats that bleated in nervous apprehension. They stopped in front of the raised mud daïs, and the fetish priest saluted the chief and his visitor by name.

Then in front of each was sacrificed one of those protesting beasts, and the hot live blood allowed to flow into one and the same cala-bash. "The Babe's" face went a trifle whiter as the smell of the gush-ing blood reached him. One slim hand was put on the block, as if for support. The steaming bowl of thick red liquor was passed to the chief, who plunged his black paws into it with obvious relish, washed them up and down and let the slimy warm mess trickle through his fingers in patent enjoyment. For quite a long time he played about with the contents of the calabash, and his visitor watched with strained eyes and set, white face. Grunts of delight came from the assembled crowd. More fuel was thrown on the fire and the roaring red flames blazed sky-high, dyeing the whole scene a lurid crimson. A mad howl went up as the chief held the bowl towards his visitor; then all noise died down, as the watching circle waited for him to go through a similar performance, before the black and white hands met in the grip of blood brotherhood. The small hand on the block trembled. The king looked at him curi-ously. This white brother of his appeared to hesitate. The flames blazed up with a sudden loud crackle, then over the roar of the huge bonfire came another sharp crackle, but of something other than flames. The chief dropped the calabash in sudden alarm and a scared yell went up from the crowd.

A staggering ebony giant, on the outskirts of the waiting throng, tried to force his way through to the daïs. A dozen half-drunken figures barred his way, pressed him back and fought with him in terror. All was wild confusion. "The Babe" stood with wild, dilated eyes fixed on a full score of figures swarming over the stockade at the nearest point to the king's hut. Again that crackle, but well over the heads of the terrified people. A quick order from the chief. Each of his subjects was too muddled, with drink and excitement, to know exactly what was said; some fled in terror, others in obe-dience, and the two on the daïs remained alone. "The Babe" made a movement to draw his revolver, but a well-aimed knife pinned his hand to the wooden block. Gnarled black paws tried to remove it, but unavailingly. The youngster just looked at the knife and his strained white face went even more ghastly.

The fire blazed up afresh, and gleamed on the advancing party, now not more than ten yards away. It played on two other white faces, one stern and hard, the other with a look of triumph over its shifty cunning. The chief stood in front of his blood brother, and a red light flashed in his bleared old eyes.

"Who are you?" he demanded angrily. "I have no war with your color."

Sinclair waved his men back as he and Langfeldt came to the foot of the daïs.

"I have no war with you, chief, but with the one who stands behind you."

The negro started; looked at his scattered subjects, then at his guest in helpless anxiety. Sinclair's victory would not have been so easy had they met on fair ground.

"This is my blood brother. His foes are my foes."

"He has broken the laws of his country and he is my prisoner, chief."

A shaky black hand was laid on "The Babe's" shoulder.

"Little brother, this is none of my doing. I have not betrayed thee."

"I know that, chief. This one has been on my trail these long days."

As the youngster spoke Sinclair started and looked at him sharply, but the big limp hat shadowed the boy's face. He had wondered all along why "The Babe" made no attempt at escape or defence. The flames shot up again; the glare of the light fell full on his prisoner's face and on the knife that cut through the small hand, with its vicious point embedded deeply in the wooden block. In a moment he was on the daïs. At the same time the old king slipped away and was lost in the shadow of the hut.

"Good God! Which of your black fiends did this?" he said hoarsely to Langfeldt.

"Get his revolver before you loose him, or the young devil will shoot us before we know where we are," the German said in sharp anxiety as Sinclair tried once, but unavailingly, to remove the ghastly pin.

Ignoring his companion he tried again. Every wrench he gave it cut through his heart, and the bravely suppressed sobs of pain filled him with a red fighting anger. After about half-a-minute, that seemed an agonizing century, he succeeded in removing the knife. He took the trembling, bleeding hand into his, wiped it very gently and examined the wound. It was a clean cut, not at all serious, yet it filled Sinclair with a desire to hang whichever one of the German's kroo-boys had done it. From his emergency-case he took out some lint and a roll of bandage, and proceeded to bind up the cold, shaking morsel with an infinite tenderness.

Langfeldt came on the platform.

"You'd better rope him up, Sinclair. This quietness is all a game of his. We came on him before he knew it and that knife stopped him from doing any damage. He's sure to have firearms somewhere on his person. I'll relieve him of them before he does mischief, and those papers too. He'll be hell let loose when he finds he's really cornered."

The German's hands were stretched out to feel round the youngster for the revolver he feared, and the papers he desired. Sinclair's back was to "The Babe," without apology, and he faced Langfeldt with an air of suppressed savagery which made that worthy start back a pace or two.

"We've no time to waste for that. Any minute this place may be round our ears like a nest of hornets. Wentworth is beyond damaging anyone at present. All other things can be done when we get back to the camp."

As Sinclair spoke, a couple of rifle shots rang out from the shadow of a cluster of palms to the left of the king's hut. One bullet passed so close to his ear that involuntarily he moved his head a little as it whizzed by. Langfeldt ducked, and left the platform with unconcealed haste. Very hurriedly, and most unceremoniously, Sinclair hustled his captive beyond the lighted area, with his hand holding its shoulder firmly and himself between it and the group of palms whence came the shooting. The flickering flames made the attacking party's aim uncertain, for, although several shots followed them, no damage was done. A quick order to retreat was given. Sinclair had no feud with that village, and having got, not the man he thought was there, but something infinitely preferable, he was anxious to be off and away without doing further harm to these peaceful people whose premises he had entered in a really inexcusable manner, and whose rejoicings had been terminated by his purloining the guest in whose honor this high *fête* was being held.

The retreating party headed towards the darkest corner of the village, and presently were scrambling over the seven-feet-high rough stockading surrounding it. Without any preamble Sinclair seized his babe, perched it on the top of the wooden wall (it could not possibly climb with that hurt hand), swarmed up beside it, then lowered it gently down on the other side, where a moment later he joined it. And not too soon! For, as they disappeared over the boundary, a party, some twenty strong, headed by a gigantic negro, came tearing round the bonfire towards the point of their departure. There were those of Sinclair's following who were anxious to stay and make a free fight of it; under some circumstances he might have humored them, as it was a sharp order sent them forest-wards at a quick walk.

He held his babe in a firm but gentle grip, knowing full well it would be quite capable of slipping away did the opportunity arise, and might very easily be lost in the pitch-dark tangle. He went along with unpardonable haste for the first few hundred yards until they were well out of the vicinity of the village, and all sounds of their pursuers died away; then he eased the pace down considerably. Very often the prisoner stumbled, either from sheer weariness, fright or some unnoticed obstacle, but his hand kept it at the perpendicular. He wondered crossly why it did not faint in a sensible manner, so that he might carry it without arousing suspicion, instead of going along with uncertain, panting breath that spoke of overstrain, and white, defiant face trying to play up to its part. It was very foolish this small babe of his but in a way that made one love it all the more. For its foolishness was always to keep that young devil from his desserts. What was she doing in that village all alone, with the maddest of negro orgies taking place? Any slip on her part would have meant a fate too ghastly to consider! Where was that young devil of a brother? What did he mean by sending her there to run such an awful risk?

Only four days ago, under the able guidance of the negro who had come to his tent the night of the tornado, Sinclair had reached the ruined temple—the evening of the morning on which the party he sought had left it. He knew he had missed them by barely thirteen hours, and the fact annoyed him considerably. For the whole of the next day he followed hot on their heels, then two tracks confronted him showing equal signs of use. Instead of taking the one "The Babe" had used, he went along the main road to Essuata Town. Three days he followed this, and gradually it dawned on him he was on the wrong route. This same evening, after dinner, he had taken his headman and done a little skirmishing by night. Rather less than five miles along the line the lights and revelry of Essuata Town had taken his attention. The two advanced with stealth. The village force had joined in the "high jinks" taking place in the market square. From the shelter of a convenient clump of trees he had marked "The Babe," and straightway sent his headman back to the camp to return with a large and impressive force. He waited there and watched the *fête*, with the certain knowledge that, as the hours sped, the more fuddled and less capable of resistance the revelers would become. This pleased him because he had no desire to harm those light-hearted savages, only to catch his man. In every way he had succeeded beyond his wildest expectations. Not a single villager hurt, and by his side, in his very grip, was the one small bird whose existence had caused him more sleepless nights, more anxious thinking, more weary, cutting heartaches and more unspeakable joy than anything that had ever been in his life before.

The little feet beside him tripped again, and his prisoner would have fallen headlong, but his arm saved her. He called a halt.

"You'd better rest a moment, Wentworth. It's rough traveling here, and that gash has knocked the pace out of you a bit."

Sinclair was aware this babe must know, within the next few hours, that he knew who she really was; but it was not his intention that either Langfeldt or their guide, who called himself by another name than Mungea, should become acquainted with the fact if he could help it. He was not going to run any risks, and there were possibilities about the present situation which might lead to an easy victory for his side. But, once the German and his dusky confederate got an inkling as to who the prisoner really was, things might be very complicated. Whereas, if the two continued to think this was "The Babe," They might take an excursion to find the sister and perhaps capture the real article, with some trouble and considerable loss of life, leaving the whole of his force intact for the guarding of this small bird. Every man would be needed once the two were captured, and only himself and thirty men lay between Mungea's vengeance and the German's lust for gold. Mungea had a large following a few miles behind; so he and his headman had discovered during one of their nocturnal wanderings, and their combined forces must number fully seventy.

The prisoner stopped at Sinclair's command. A tree, brought down by some tornado, lay by the side of the track. He led his captive to what looked the most comfortable spot on the fallen trunk. "Sit down, Wentworth."

The youngster obeyed in silence. His captor drew out his cigarette-case and offered it to the prisoner, who was evidently "off" smokes, for a curt refusal was given. The former lighted up leisurely, then leant carelessly against an adjacent tree, but with one eye on his captive. Langfeldt came up to them.

"Keep a watch on him, Sinclair. He'll slip away in no time; he can find his way like a cat in the dark and run like fury. I tell you, you're risking a lot by keeping him loose. He has the devil's own cunning."

"There's not much left in the youngster. He looked fagged out before we got him, and that blood-spilling didn't make him any more lively. It's as much as he can do to keep up the pace we are going."

"That's all his little game. I've known him a few years longer than you, and I'm not at all anxious to lose either him or those papers. If you don't keep a hand on him I shall."

Langfeldt was about to act up to his words, but Sinclair elbowed him out with unpardonable rudeness and stood with one hand lightly on the object under discussion. The prisoner just sat with weary, drooping shoulders, and looked neither at one nor the other.

Chrysanthe had spoken no word since her capture beyond that brief refusal and was spending the most miserable time of her life. About twenty miles away was the beloved and sinful one, awaiting her return the following afternoon with a fresh supply of porters. A sudden relapse and severe return of fever had prevented "The Babe" from coming to Essuata Town in person. He knew the old chief would oblige no one but himself; therefore he sent his sister in his place with Krua, Gola and eight of the sharpshooters as escort, with orders to spare no one if there was any chance of the deception being found out, and full instructions what to do and say, how to act and what to expect. Chrysanthe was only too pleased to take his place. Anxiety to obtain more porters so that Major Sinclair could be successfully avoided, a desire to save her brother the arduous journey, and the precious day's rest he could have, whilst awaiting her return, a day's march farther along the line, made her fall in with his idea readily. Everything had passed off successfully so much so that Gola and the sharpshooters were recounting travelers' tales in a hut on the remote side of the village, at the moment of Sinclair's arrival. When the invading party appeared, Chrysanthe had just got her courage up to the pitch of plunging her hands into the blood she so abhorred. The whole thing would have passed off successfully, for with that the evening's proceedings terminated, and, at the next sunrise, they would have started their fifteen miles' walk to the meeting place with a new and reliable team of porters.

As Chrysanthe sat there limply, deadly tired and with an injured hand that throbbed and ached and brought her to the verge of tears, there was no one she hated more than Major Sinclair. Before long he would find out it was not Claude he had got! There was a certain amount of satisfaction in the fact although, curiously enough, it left her with hot and cold shivers and a desire to go and bury herself. What would he say? She would not tell him where Claude was, not if he cut her to pieces inch by inch. She would lie—lie as all her sort had done when the lives of their kindred hung on it. She would save him yet in spite of all Major Sinclair had sworn. What would this big, horrid, hateful man do when he found out? If he did not catch Claude he might turn on her. She had helped Claude in some of his deals and that was wrong, although he tried to make her believe it was not. Major Sinclair would guess she had played this game before, and would put a lot more things down to Claude hitherto not proved against him—things that might keep him in prison for the rest of his life. She would swear she had never done it before. Swear till the lies choked her!

Sinclair studied his prisoner in the faint starlight. He knew she was at the end of her strength, and three uphill miles still lay between them and the camp. There was a very tender look about his mouth as he watched the limp little figure. He had seen this babe in many different garbs; had loved it with an almost incredible suddenness the night it lay moaning in his cabin in highly striped night attire; had guarded and cherished it as it went about in white drill, and gave him much cheek and many heartaches; had worshipped it in soft, misty dresses and felt it was something that could not be his; but it had never been so adorable at as this moment, as it sat there listlessly a small replica of himself—even to the rough flannel shirt that had been voted scrubby—the missing little bit he had hoped to find some day, that he had always needed to make life complete, and without which the world would now be a hopeless, dreary place to be got out of as soon as possible.

A sound wafted down on a sudden cat's paw of wind roused him. It was faint and some distance away, but it said the enemy was still abroad and the sooner they put a few more miles between themselves and that sound the better. He gave the order to march. This time the prisoner did not obey so readily; instead a white tired face sank on the one whole hand, and there was no attempt at a move. Sinclair did not wait for any explanation of this rank disobedience but picked up his babe, who was too startled and weary to make any resistance, and settled her against his shoulder in the most comfortable position he could think of. This time Langfeldt evinced no desire to relieve him of his burden.

Instead he said shortly, "What's the matter with him?"

Sinclair kept the back of his charge to the German. He knew this small girl was trying not to cry, unsuccessfully (one big hot tear had splashed on his hand as he lifted her), and was just about scared to death.

"The youngster's more hurt than we know of. I suspected it as we went along, and I'm pretty sure of it now. The tiredness wasn't any sham; there's not another step left in him."

"Give him to one of the niggers, no need for you to fag yourself carrying him."

"I'd rather keep him. He has slipped through my fingers more than once, and I don't intend to let him out of my sight this time."

Langfeldt made no further comment. Chrysanthe lay there shivering, hardly conscious of what passed round her, trying to keep back the big, broken sobs and flood of tears that were slowly forcing themselves to the fore. The accumulated troubles of the evening, coming after the worry and anxiety of the last few weeks, proved a little beyond the strength of "The Babe's" lieutenant. Sinclair trembled lest others than himself should become aware of the prisoner's identity. A quick order sent Langfeldt to the head of the marching column—a place he did not mind having, considering they were the retreating party. As the last man filed past Sinclair brought up the rear, but a good ten paces behind. As he went along he felt the big, tearing sobs rise, but they were very well kept under, and the storm passed off in a few gasps and one or two damp sniffs. He knew the complete breakdown was bound to come sooner or later, but he wanted to get Chrysanthe safe in the shelter of his tent and screened from all eyes before then. He was well aware that more than one uncomfortable five minutes would have to be gone through before this wild bird and he arrived at a definite understanding. It struck him to wonder what sort of a figure he would cut, and how he would feel, if suddenly called upon to enter this little girl's presence, attired in a soft, fluffy dress borrowed from Marjorie's endless supply. He tried to picture the situation and the mere idea made him go cold. Although he liked his small bird's present plumage better than anything he had so far seen her in, she might not fancy facing him clad in garments taken from her brother's wardrobe. Would it be better to say straight out he knew, or better to let her come to that conclusion slowly and from her own observation? Which would be more comfortable for her?

Again Sinclair was on the horns of a dilemma. For a full mile he paced trying to make up his mind which of the two courses to follow. A head suddenly falling on his shoulder made him glance at his burden. It was up again in a moment, and two dead-tired blue eyes met his in sleepy surprise. He looked away at once, wondering what his little prisoner had been through within the last twenty-four hours. She was absolutely fagged out, and lay like a bit of limp rag in his arms. The head dropped again. He did not dare to look round but went along with greater care than ever. This time it stayed on the hard, scrubby shoulder. Was it possible this wild bird had gone to sleep in the grip of the captor! Very soon the regular breathing satisfied him. He studied his charge in the faint starlight. What a weary child's face it was! So wistful and worn—like a baby that had cried itself to sleep. Tears still glinted on the long lashes. The one whole hand was crumpled up into a fist, just in the manner of small infants.

A long convulsive shiver and little moan made Sinclair's arms involuntarily tighten round his prisoner; he watched, fearing his action would rouse the sleeper. Instead, this wild bird unconsciously nestled closer to him, and the small fist uncrumpled and gripped on to his shirt. Then Sinclair marveled at his own strength of mind. The greatest temptation of his life confronted him—to kiss this sleeping babe! He had wanted to do so ever since the night he found it. But he strove with this temptation and argued with himself at great length. It was not his babe to kiss yet, and such an action would come under the heading of theft. With wonderful self-control he turned his face away, knowing quite well he would fall if he watched much longer.

Chrysanthe was still sleeping when the camp was reached. The noise and the bustle roused her. She woke with a sudden start, and called for her brother, in quick alarm, before the events of the evening came back to her. The little cry shattered most of the rosy dreams Sinclair had woven during the last half-hour. He put her on her feet, and kept a hand on her shoulder conscious she was watching him scaredly, and knew she was wondering if he had heard. Langfeldt joined them.

"I'll take charge of him to-night, Sinclair. You've covered nearly double the ground I have to-day and must be fagged out. I'll tie him up in my crib and relieve you of the worry of him for a few hours."

"I'm afraid I can't take your offer. I must keep him under a guard of my own men," and Sinclair led a shivering mortal towards his own tent.

The German followed.

"Well, get those papers first. He'll destroy them in no time now he finds he's really caught."

Sinclair stopped and the hand on Chrysanthe's shoulder tightened.

"Have you any papers, Wentworth?"

A shaky voice answered in the negative. Langfeldt laughed coarsely.

"You're not going to be such a fool as to take his word for it, Sinclair. Of course he'd say he hadn't. I know him better than you do. Search him, and, if we don't find them, thrash him until he says where they are. If he hasn't got them I tell you he's dropped them on the way up here. He'd fool the sharpest man going."

Sinclair drew his prisoner closer to his side. There was an air of forced calm about him.

"Where are those papers, youngster?"

"Don't be a fool, Sinclair! What's the sense in standing on ceremony with one of his breed? Search him, and if they're not there, find a way of making him say where they are," Langfeldt broke in angrily.

"When I've settled with the guards for the night I'll see if he's speaking the truth. If the papers are not there I can do no more."

Sinclair turned away abruptly and hustled the scared, shivering captive along sharply. The German followed in a state of angry bluster, and caught them up just outside of the tent.

"I'd soon find a way of doing more."

"My orders do not permit of extracting information from prisoners by means of personal violence. If I find those papers you shall have them. As far as I'm concerned, everything is finished now Wentworth is caught. He's under arrest, and no one is allowed to enter this tent or converse with him except with my permission and in my presence."

There was a very stormy feeling in the atmosphere. Sinclair drew aside the curtain of the tent and pushed his prisoner in, with some lack of ceremony, saying: "Sit down, youngster, I'll be with you in a few minutes," then, dropping the curtain, faced the blustering German with the same air of suppressed savagery which had startled that worthy earlier in the evening.

Langfeldt climbed down with considerable haste—in fact, became quite apologetic.

"There's no need to get huffy, Sinclair. I only want you to understand you can't be too careful in dealing with the young villain. You can't take a tack with him like you would with an ordinary person. He's the very devil for cunning, will take advantage of any leniency and make fools of us yet. I know his little ways better than you do. He has got some deep scheme on behind all this quietness. If you come to grief over him, don't say I didn't warn you."

Sinclair took the advice in the spirit it was given, and, when the German left, called to his orderly to send the headman along to him. A strange nervousness grew over him as he stood outside of the tent awaiting the sergeant's arrival. Before many minutes had passed he would have to face his prisoner again, and he had made up his mind to acquaint her with the fact that her identity was known to him. It was far better to have it all over at once; then she could rest secure, not stay shivering in a state of uncertainty, not knowing what to do or expect.

The headman's voice brought him back to the thing of the moment, it might almost be said, with a jump. The sergeant received his instructions as follows:—a constant guard of five Hausas must be kept round the tent, but at a distance of eighteen feet from it; no one, on any pretext whatsoever, would be allowed within the guarding circle unless he, Sinclair, were with them, and the prisoner was not to be allowed outside the protecting ring unless under his escort: moreover, every night the remaining Hausas not on duty were to pitch their sleeping quarters just beyond the guarded radius, so as to be at hand in case of emergency, and day and night each man was to carry his full complement of arms. He waited until his instructions were carried out, and then went his usual round of the camp, setting a double watch at the nearest point to Essuata Town.

Meanwhile Chrysanthe sat shivering in the tent, wondering what was going to happen next and uncertain whether Sinclair knew or not. In any case she would have to tell him! But for those papers she might have faced it out a little longer and perhaps have got another day's grace for Claude. As it was— What would Major Sinclair think of her? She could feel his eyes fixed on her contemptuously, cutting right through her, with the partially smothered look of disgust that came sometimes on the *Asabo* when a certain woman with a notorious reputation behaved worse than usual, see his mouth go hard and stern like it did occasionally when he watched Claude. She was just as bad as Claude! Worse, because she had been to school and had a chance of learning the right way. Claude never had a chance—he had always lived up in the bush until he got in with Langfeldt—was only fifteen when that beauty crossed his track! Schmutz & Co.'s lot were the finishing touch. He was always wild and they made him a thousand times worse, encouraged him in every way and put him up to doing things he would never have thought of, left to himself. If only she had not been at school she might have kept him straight. He never took any notice of anyone else. As it was she got back too late, Schmutz & Co. had him tight! Claude had always wanted to go on this deal, but she had funked it at first; then he promised to settle down if she would go, and had been ever so much better these last few months. Now, just when everything was going on all right, Major Sinclair must come—come to take Claude to prison for things most people had forgotten about—come and upset everything!

A weary, aching head fell on the table. If she had done what Claude and Mungea had wanted her to do, Major Sinclair would not be here now. If Claude were caught and sent to prison it would be all her fault—all because she had tried to do the right thing!

A well-known step, just outside of the tent, made her shiver and start up in white-faced defiance. A moment afterwards Sinclair entered. Suppressed emotion made his mouth more stern than usual, and, the knowledge of the ordeal awaiting his prisoner, gave a hard look to his face. Every well-turned sentence he had thought of, every method for breaking the news gently, fled as those blue eyes met his defiantly, with tears, a dead weariness, and a great fear of himself in them. Sinclair was not in the habit of being afraid, but he was as that small replica of himself faced him in stony silence. It stood a head less than he did and was not more than half his shoulder measurement, yet he had never been so scared of anything. These awful five minutes must be got through somehow, or this worn-out, tired child would stay awake all night in a state of wearing suspense, worrying herself to death as to what was going to happen next, and might break down at an inconvenient moment and the whole camp become aware of her identity.

He came a few steps closer, searching vainly round his head for that neat speech. Chrysanthe watched him with strained eyes, then the grey flannel shirt started to heave in a most unmanly way. He knew, and was looking at her in the way she dreaded—as if she were the most despicable thing on earth! She sank down into the chair; the shamed curly head was laid on the table and an agony of wild, tearing sobs filled the tent.

Sinclair was at her side in a moment.

"What's the matter, little girl?"

A small hand pushed him away with some force—it was the hurt one, since he happened to be on that side—then a big note of pain crept into the shamed sobs.

He hung over his prisoner in a state of helpless anxiety, watching the red patch that quickly appeared on the bandage and spread rapidly. She would kill herself if she went on sobbing at this rate. He could not leave without explaining one or two things so that she would know what to expect. Her hand would have to be fixed up again, and, after all she had been through, she would require some sort of a meal before going to sleep.

"There's no need to cry, child."

This, instead of calming the storm, only provoked it. Sinclair was at his wit's end. Any one of those great sobs seemed enough to tear her into pieces. He stood with hurt, drawn face, wondering what to do. Then he did a bold thing. He took the small tornado into his arms, sat down with it on his knee, and its face against his shoulder. After all it was only a brokenhearted baby, scared and ashamed at being found out, and worried to death over the young villain of a brother. For a moment the remedy seemed worse than the disease. But he talked to the grief-stricken small mortal with the gentleness of a mother, smoothed back the soft curls and did all in his power to soothe her. After a time the big sobs died down to shivering gasps, and a limp, worn-out little figure, too weary to do anything but stay just where it was, lay in his arms. He watched the white face, and the world of anxious care on it pained him. It was so out of keeping with the childish innocence and roundness. Presently two tired wet eyes looked up at him with a world of pathos and pleading.

"You . . . you won't do anything to Claude, will you, Major Sinclair?"

It was the question he had been dreading and expecting, and he knew he was driving the nails into his own coffin.

"We won't talk about that just now, little girl."

"You could easily say he was not the man wanted. Nobody knows we change places but you."

"I couldn't do that, child."

"Why not?"

Sinclair's hand shook as he smoothed back the soft curls, but he made no reply.

The one whole hand played about with a button of his coat, and a tired face looked at him pleadingly.

"Don't bother about doing the right thing. I—I haven't got anybody but Claude. You've got a whole pile of brothers and a sister, and heaps of other relations, so have most people. We're just a lone couple that nobody ever cared a hang about except a few niggers. A pair of rotters! No good to anyone! But we're almighty fond of one another. Claude won't ever do any more deals that aren't square. It's hard lines you should come to nail him now"— the pleading eyes overflowed—"and it's all my fault: if I hadn't tried to do the right thing you would never have got as far as here. I shan't ever try to do the right thing any more!"

Weary, hopeless sobs broke out again.

Sinclair looked very strained and tortured as he sat with the pleading small mortal on his knee. Only Claude! Nothing else counted! Always the shadow of that devil's son between himself and all that made life worth living! He felt his self-control slipping away. He had taken this sobbing child into his arms for the frightened, hurt, lost baby she was, and so far had said nothing but what his own mother might have said under similar circumstances. He had just tried to soothe and comfort her, and make her understand she had done nothing to be ashamed of. Now all the other things came to his lips. Things he had wanted to tell this small precious girl for the last four months.

"Say—say you won't touch Claude. Say you won't take him to prison," came out in panting gasps.

"Chrysanthe, little darling, I must do my duty."

All the pent-up love and tenderness were in Sinclair's voice as he spoke. There was a moment of breathing silence. Wide, startled eyes looked at him. The sobbing, shamed baby, who had lain against his shoulder, vanished. Instead was a scared small girl who gazed at him in frightened dismay and tried to slip away. Arms suddenly tightening kept her where she was. Someone's face was very close to hers and a tender voice whispered, "Don't go away, my darling. There's something I want to tell you."

Then it was a trapped wild bird that struggled in his arms, with wide, frightened eyes, a heart throbbing to breaking pitch and hands that tried to break through to freedom.

In a moment Sinclair let that terrified bird go. He stood up feeling an abject brute. He had taken this child into his arms when she was too dead-beat to resist, too full of tears and pain to realise what was happening, too worn out with worry and anxiety to know really where she was, and she had stayed with a tired child's trust. He had broken that trust! Had held against her will! Had frightened her in a way that would make her uncomfortable for all the time she was with him! Had behaved in an unspeakable manner to an injured girl who was his prisoner and entirely at his mercy! Had been an absolute bounder and a cad!

Chrysanthe watched him nervously. What did Major Sinclair want to tell her? She had been frightened when he spoke. No one had ever spoken to her like that before. It had given her a terrible shock when she thought she could not get away. None of her sort liked being cornered. Then a hot cold shiver ran through her. She had been sitting crying on Major Sinclair's knee! She did not realise where she was until he spoke in that strange way! What must he think of her? A deep red flush of shame crept over her face.

Major the Hon. Tracy Sinclair looked, at the scared wild bird who stood in front of him. He had wanted to tell this little girl how much he loved her, forgetting for the moment how hideously out of place such a statement would be from him—the man she would look upon as her brother's murderer!—who, once "The Babe" was captured, could produce sufficient evidence to hang him three times over. He was sure she knew nothing of her brother's worst crimes. Nothing of three cold-blooded murders which could be laid at the young devil's door! To tell her he loved her! Tell her that and then go and hang her brother—the one she loved the best on earth! What a trick Fate had played! To give him what he once thought would be the greatest satisfaction in life—the clue to the clever, scheming arch-villain more than one man had been after in vain; to give it to him in the one small girl he loved to distraction, whose life was bounded by that devil's son—her twin! If he asked her to be his wife? She had no love for anyone except that fiend! A little liking and a great trust for him once, but he had shattered that now with his clumsy, boorish antics! If he bargained with her, promising to let her brother off if she would marry him, what would she say?

Sinclair's hands clenched.

She would marry him. Sell herself to the devil! Do anything to keep that young fiend from his desserts! He had only to promise that, in exchange for herself, and this little girl would be his. A trapped wild bird who would not dare to move when he held her, would shiver in his arms when he kissed her, because that villain's safety lay in doing just as he wished! A little slave whose price would be her brother's freedom and her husband's honor!

There was a tense, quivering silence, a feeling of self-suppression and overstrain. Then, in a curt, hard way, Sinclair told his prisoner it was advisable her identity remained solely in his keeping; gave a brief outline of the course he intended to take, in a short, sharp tone she had never heard him use before and left the tent.

Chrysanthe stood watching the curtain with wide, scared eyes long after he disappeared. It had dawned on her what Major Sinclair wanted to tell her, but he had remembered in time who and what she was—a rank outsider! The daughter of a race of thieves and murderers! Something utterly beyond the pale!

CHAPTER 15

"A horrid jumble on fighting men."

In his tent Carl Langfeldt sat awaiting the arrival of Major Sinclair and those papers. There was an unusually thoughtful air about him, as of one confronted with a most perplexing problem. It was very curious the way in which Sinclair had behaved regarding that map and document, and had refused to let him be in at the search for them—had put a spoke in his wheel every time he made an attempt at getting them. What was his little game? Claude never let the manuscripts off his person. If they were not forthcoming there was only one conclusion to arrive at—Sinclair had got them, and intended to stick to them and carry the deal on for his own benefit! It was not the sort of thing he would have suspected him of doing, but the prospect of obtaining such a vast amount of gold would alter the character of many a man beyond recognition. Sinclair had never shown any enthusiasm over the treasure-hunting part of the palaver, but that was nothing to go by, in fact it was all the more suspicious; it had probably been one of his little dust-throwing games.

The German poured himself out a good stiff whisky and drank it musingly. Sinclair was a deuce of a time. He had been over half-an-hour in the tent. Long enough to get them three times over!

A voice talking to one of the guards made Langfeldt settle himself in a negligent attitude, take up a book and wipe all suspicion from his face. He looked up with an air of bland friendliness as Sinclair loomed up in the open flap.

"Settled the young demon for the night?"

His visitor sat down without replying.

The German glanced at him covertly. There was a rum look about him. He had been having a good tussle with himself over something. If he had made up his mind to keep those papers there would be some difficulty in sailing round him. He always was one of the square-jawed breed, but more so than ever tonight—a flinty look about the eye and a tightness about the mouth! He had made up his mind just what his game was to be, and intended to play it.

"What's the matter with our young friend?" Langfeldt asked after a harrowing pause, anxious to get round to the subject next his heart, but not too abruptly.

"He's pretty well knocked about, and won't be much good for some time"—curtly.

"What's the chief trouble?"

"Too much strain when he was in no condition to stand it. He ought not to have walked as far as he did to-night. There'll be no walking for him for the next week or two. We shall have to take him along in a hammock."

Sinclair's sentences were rapped out in a hard, stiff way, not at all encouraging to his interlocutor.

"Seen anything of those papers?"

"No."

There was a moment of thoughtful silence.

"That's curious. Did he say where they were?"

"They are with his party."

For some time two people sat each lost in their own reflections; then Langfeldt said, "Did he say where his sister was?"

"He would hardly do that."

"Hardly. What's your next move?"

"We're too near to Essuata Town for comfort. Once they get over their carouse they'll be round our heads like a swarm of hornets. We must get away with the daylight, put twenty miles between ourselves and then, before the evening, try if we can cross country and pick up that other trail. We can't leave the district until we have both him and his sister."

"No, we can't leave her to the tender mercies of the niggers. You'll want pretty well the whole of your force for the guarding of our young friend. Essuata Town will send out detachments all over the place looking for him. You'd better let me scout round with my little tot and see if I can find her. That guide of ours is fairly good at tracking. It will leave you with a free hand; it will take you all your time to manage the prisoner, considering the high-flown tack you're taking with him. He's playing this quiet game purposely; he knows the old chief is on his side, and he's biding his time until they get over their drunk and come and stamp out the lot of us. If you take my tip, you'll get along with him out of their sphere and leave me to come along with the sister."

Langfeldt awaited his companion's reply with some anxiety. He was almost certain Sinclair had those papers; but if once he got hold of the sister, things would be about even. If he found them in the girl's possession, he would push on up country without returning to apprise his companion of his discovery. If she had not got them—! Well, he could soon make terms with Sinclair, once he held that taking little piece of goods as hostage.

Sinclair appeared to give the subject serious thought. It was exactly the plan he had expected the German to adopt. After a prolonged pause he said, "Yes; we could try your plan at first. We'll push along together until we find the other track, and make a permanent camp there. Then you can follow up the trail. Wentworth's party is sure to be halted somewhat not very far along the line waiting for him. There may be some fighting. His following would hardly deliver up his sister for the mere asking. If you can't manage, then I shall have to come along to your assistance."

The German heaved a sigh of relief. His and Mungea's forces, combined, could do the trick quite easily. The prospect of the fighting did not please him overmuch; but his anxiety concerning those papers, and the vast fortune the contents bid fair to lead him into, made him take greater risk than usual. After a little more conversation they parted, each entirely pleased with the proposed programme.

Shortly before sunrise the bustle and noise of the camp getting into marching orders roused Chrysanthe. She had lain down fully dressed, expecting they would be on the march with dawn. There had been no sleep for her during the brief hours, except a short, fitful doze into which she had fallen a few minutes before the preparations roused her. She washed, and then sat waiting for whatever orders might be issued to her. A well-known step outside made her start up quickly. It was a very proud, frightened face that Sinclair's gaze alighted on, when he entered a few minutes later, with deep dark rings under the tired eyes, and a haughty, scornful mouth. Chrysanthe took not the least notice of him as he stood there waiting until his orderly brought in a tray with her breakfast. He felt he deserved it all and more for his boorish behavior. He could make no excuse for his conduct. The circumstance was beyond apology. There had been no sleep for him during the brief hours since they parted. All the time he had spent wrestling with the temptation to take this little girl at the price he knew would make her his. As she stood in scornful silence, the demon assailed him again. It would be so until it was too late to make any compromise—until her brother had passed through his hands and was in the keeping of his country.

In the same curt, hard tone he informed his prisoner what time the march started, and how long she had for breakfast. Then the hurt hand took his attention. It had been on his conscience since he left her, but to have done it then would have been beyond his strength; to have held that limp, injured little thing would have shattered what self-control remained to him. There was a hard, uncomfortable look about the bandage, as if she had tried to fix it up herself as well as sodden lint and blood-stiffened wrappings would allow, and the slim fingers looked red and hot as if the wound pained her more than a little.

"Before we start I'll come and dress your hand."

A quick red flush came over Chrysanthe's face.

"It's not necessary. I did it myself a little time ago."

Sinclair's mouth went harder and his voice more peremptory.

"It must be done. You can't go through the day in that state."

As he left, Chrysanthe sat down listlessly. She tried to drink the coffee, eating was beyond her. How long would it be before he caught Claude? Which way would they march? So much depended on that. Would Claude be so foolish as to wait round trying to get her back again? If he got taken it would be all her fault. Enough could be proved against him to shut him up for twenty years at least. He could never stand that! Then she would be her brother's murderer! She might just as well have done it first as last, only then it would have been someone else, someone who did not count, not Claude!

A hopeless, weary face was propped up by one hand as she sat gazing blankly across the tent.

The breakfast was untouched when Sinclair came back. He made no comment, but the hard look on his face deepened. The best of the rough fare the camp boasted had been sent in to the prisoner. The coffee and crisp pieces of toast he had made himself, so that there might be something edible in the lot. Love and tenderness fate had forbidden him to lavish on this little girl, but all he could do to make the trying situation easier for her would be done. Chrysanthe stood in the same tired, haughty silence, conscious of not having spoken the entire truth about her hand. She had tried to fix it up again, but the bandage had stuck to the wound and hurt her so much she could not get it off. Pushing the tray on one side Sinclair put his fresh supply of dressings on the table, then, taking the injured hand into his, began to unwrap it, but with a stumbling clumsiness unusual to him. After one or two turns the true state of affairs dawned on him.

"You had better sit down. I'm afraid it will be rather painful."

Chrysanthe obeyed; she was beginning to feel deadly faint, and pain was undermining her proud front.

He cut through the whole bandage, and, turning back the ends, saw the condition of the hot, throbbing little hand. He made no remark, but sent for a bowl of warm water; then stood by the curtain waiting until his man returned, and watching the limp figure in the chair. Whatever he did he could only hurt this little girl. If he tried to touch the brother it was the sister who suffered. Whenever he tried to get that villain it always hit back at him—hit back and hurt him through this child he would give his life to protect—hurt him a thousand times more than if the blow were aimed direct. A one-sided fight! This little girl against him, and that laughing devil safe in the background, screened and sheltered behind the sister's love.

When the basin came he held the injured morsel into it, and slowly, piece by piece, removed the hard, caked bandage. Every twinge of the quivering hand, every moan that forced itself through the pale lips, every spasm of pain on the deadly white face, cut and bruised his heart. His behavior of a few hours previously was coming home to him with a vengeance. By his own ill-controlled feelings this child was made to suffer all this anguish.

Sinclair's face was nearly as white as his prisoner's when he led her outside. Langfeldt glanced at them curiously as they stood, just within the forbidden area, awaiting the arrival of the hammock. Why the best and most comfortable litter, with the only cushion the camp boasted of, should be doled out to that young thief he failed to see. It was just the way with one of Sinclair's breed. To risk his own life, put himself to no end of inconvenience and privations, for the sake of catching some villain who ought to be shot on sight, when he might be living comfortably at home doing nothing; then when he got him, instead of treating him in the way he should be treated, give up his quarters to him, keep the whole camp running after him, waiting on him hand and foot, the titbits of the stores sent in for his consumption, and as much fuss made over him as if he were some little god.

Very soon the prisoner was comfortably installed in her hammock and the procession set out. The look of anxiety on Chrysanthe's face deepened as the morning march went on. They were going along the very route she had used only the day before! It led right on to the track where Claude was. Krua could not get back much before midday, if he had started the minute she was captured. Before evening there would not be more than fifteen miles between Claude and Major Sinclair. Claude was in no condition for forced marching; it was only a matter of a day or two before he was taken! They had not more than thirty fighting men all told; these had good sixty, and half of them proper soldiers. If Claude were well enough to lead his own men the odds would not count. Krua and Gola would do their best but they were no match for Major Sinclair. If she had been there they might have done something, because she always understood at once just what Claude wanted, and could carry it out to the letter.

A sudden stop woke her to the fact the midday halt was called. By some patent process the hammock was converted into a comfortable lounge-chair. Just beyond the guarding circle the men off duty were lying on the ground, disposing of their rations before indulging in the sleep the three hours' halt allowed of: the heavy stifling heat made marching impossible during this time. Sinclair came to her side. He had seen hardly anything of his prisoner since they started out, although she had had a very good view of his back as he went along at the head of his men. Her litter had been carried by a couple of Hausas in the middle of a two-deep file, all armed to the teeth. This wild bird experienced the feeling of being really trapped, as she was carried along in the procession, headed by a tall, powerful figure in khaki, whose endurance seemed never-ending. Through the tired curly-head had run many schemes for escape, each one put aside as impossible as she glanced at her body-guard. If only she could reach Claude before Major Sinclair did, she might still be of some use in the last stand—things might even go their way.

Sinclair's voice inquiring what she would like for lunch put to flight a fresh plan for departure. "I—I don't want anything, thank you."

"This is rank foolishness. You had no breakfast. I must insist you have something now."

Chrysanthe's lips quivered as he spoke—it was the same curt, hard tone he used when issuing orders to his men, with an iron ring in it that cut through her—but she took no further notice of him. Sinclair watched her. The trembling little mouth did not escape him. He wondered how much more he could stand. How much before he promised her brother's freedom at his price!

"You're behaving like a very silly child, refusing your food in this manner."

A proud white face looked at him with brimming eyes and quivering lips.

"I—I feel as if it would choke me to eat anything just now, but I'll try since you insist."

He turned away abruptly. It was his orderly who brought a tray with a cup of soup, a few plain biscuits and the best of sandwiches that could be made with badly baked bread and tinned beef. He saw his prisoner had kept her word, for, when the tray came back, one biscuit had been broken in half and a scrap of it gone, the soup was an inch farther down in its cup and the sandwich just as it was sent. He wondered how long he would be able to keep this little girl alive once her twin was captured.

He and his prisoner met no more until the evening, then only in the presence of his orderly. The man stood at attention in the tent whilst his master redressed the hand, and his master stood by the curtain as his man took in and brought out the prisoner's dinner, then, very curtly, she was told she would be disturbed no more that night. After he left, Chrysanthe cried herself into a feverish sleep, because not many miles away was her brother, too ill to defend himself, and she could not break through the cage and help him. Outside, her captor went round in a state of raw-edged temper, wondering how long a girl could live on half-a-cup of coffee, a teaspoonful of soup, a square inch of biscuit and a shred of tinned chicken, and how long a man could stand seeing the one small mortal he loved to distraction slowly pine to death when the remedy lay in his own hands.

No noise of men getting into marching order disturbed the prisoner the following morning. A worn-out little baby, fast asleep in his own bed, greeted Sinclair's eyes as he drew aside the curtain of the tent, after some minutes' conversation with one of the guards. He dropped it quickly, and went to his breakfast in a much more cheerful frame of mind than had been his lot for the past twenty-four hours. The clatter of Langfeldt's expedition setting out to find herself, woke Chrysanthe some time afterwards. She looked at once, as she always had done since her brother's illness, for the curtain dividing their joint tent. It was not there. Instead, a folding-chair with Sinclair's name on it, in big black letters, met her gaze. The circumstances surprised her not a little. A sleepy bird sat up in natural astonishment, then lay back again wearily. A voice, talking somewhere at the back of the tent made her start up again in quick alarm. Major Sinclair always allowed her five minutes' grace before coming in, but she could not possibly get dressed in that time. She dare not say anything because the orderly might be with him. What could she do? Chrysanthe did a little sharp thinking. If she pretended to be asleep he would go away again.

When Sinclair drew the curtain aside gently, the prisoner still appeared to be sleeping. He stood watching with some anxiety. Just the same position as before, with one small fist limply on the coverlet. She had not moved at all! Was anything the matter with her? Being an ornithologist, he knew that trapped wild birds very frequently die of fright. The fact struck home with considerable force and brought him a step or two farther into the tent. She had been ill all yesterday and had eaten nothing. He must have a look and see if she were quite all right. Langfeldt had made enough noise to wake the average person. Probably it was only dead-tiredness, and she might go on sleeping for hours; but he must be quite satisfied.

He came noiselessly to the bedside and stood gazing down at his babe. She looked very much his, lying there in his bed, and wearing one of his white flannel shirts many sizes too big for her. Was she asleep or was she ill? He did not seem to notice her breathing. Only a crop of chestnut curls and part of a white little cheek to go by; all the rest was snuggled away in the pillow.

A thumb and finger laid lightly on her wrist made Chrysanthe look up in wide-eyed fright. She had heard the curtain drawn aside softly, but not the careful approach. Sinclair experienced the feeling of having been caught committing sacrilege. He had no business to be where he was, but this child, and anxiety on her account, led him into many hitherto unexplored realms, and he had been called upon to face situations which filled him with a nervousness the hottest corner of the battlefield had never succeeded in doing.

He could have explained his presence quite easily, but unfortunately the words refused to come. For some time the two looked at each other, he forgetting in the agitation of the moment, he still held the slim wrist.

"Is—is anything the matter, Major Sinclair?" The trembling voice and scared face untied his tongue.

"I'm sorry to have startled you. I was afraid you might be ill, and came across to see if there was anything you wanted. Would you like to have your breakfast now or when you are up?"

"I'd rather get up first."

"Very well, I'll send it along in about twenty minutes."

Sinclair went out, conscious of having given his prisoner another severe fright.

All day Chrysanthe sat in the tent. She saw nothing more of her captor, except when he came to dress her hand under the chaperonage of his orderly. She heard him outside when the man came in with her meals. All the books the camp boasted of had been sent in for her perusal and an order that she was to exercise within the guarded area, which however was ignored. After tea she sat, limp and listless, trying to read. Every plan of escape had been thought over and dismissed as useless. She knew she was well guarded, having become sufficiently versed, during the charge of her brother's camp, to tell how many men there were about her by the noise and movement in her immediate vicinity. There was no getting out pf Major Sinclair's grip. Why had he stopped here instead of following on Claude's trail? Perhaps he had sent a party out to head him off—she had heard a good crowd start out in the early morning—and was going to drive Claude down here and catch him between two fires. If Claude was well he could see through a trick like that in half-a-minute, would head along and chance it; but if he had a turn of fever, and was delirious, Krua and Gola might be taken in. If only she were there she could have pulled Claude through somehow. Nothing ever failed when they were together!

A step aroused "The Babe's" captured lieutenant from these warlike musings. She stood up, conscious of having broken orders by not exercising.

"Why are you not outside?" her captor demanded curtly. Anxiety for the prisoner, who stayed moping in the tent all day with no appetite, was straining Sinclair to breaking point. As his own temptation increased, his manner towards his captive became more harsh and peremptory.

The same frightened scornful face looked at him in silence. Sinclair's manner terrified Chrysanthe. She lived in momentary terror of what he would do next. He was so different from the sleepy, languid individual she had known on the *Asabo*, and the nice sort of elder brother who could be teased and laughed at with impunity, consulted and appealed to on all matters, during the time he was their guest. Then he seemed some big, quiet haven, someone to take all worries to; now he frightened her more than anything that had ever come into her life.

He repeated his query, watching her with the strange, smothered look she dreaded and could not understand.

"I didn't wish to go."

"I can't allow you to sit in here all day."

"I—I don't like walking up and down out there."

"Why not?"

The question was out before he thought. He felt an abject brute as a deep red flush came quickly to the childish face and said very plainly why. It is one thing to go about in one's brother's clothes when nobody knows, but another to sport this same attire conscious someone else is aware of the fact.

Sinclair was very anxious that his prisoner should have some fresh air, thinking perhaps it would give her an appetite. There was a faint, heavy look about her through sitting all day in the stifling tent. Outside a cool breeze was coming up with the approaching sunset. A few minutes' blow would do her a world of good after the dense, close atmosphere she had been in.

"I'll take you just beyond the camp. There's a good stretch of open country there, and you'll get a blow and perhaps an appetite for dinner."

"I'd rather not go. I'm very tired."

"It's not a minute's walk away. You'll be all the better for a turn outside." Sinclair's voice was even more peremptory; he knew it was not so much tiredness as fear for himself that caused this refusal.

Chrysanthe went obediently through the curtain and walked in silence by her captor's side. The camp lay on a ridge of hill, in an open patch surrounded by the usual dense tangle. Sinclair chose a narrow track, a little to the left, leading through the matted bush to where the hill, in steep, broken gorges, went down to the trackless, wooded country some two hundred feet below. Lichen-covered trees grew in the deep, dark clefts which were lighted here and there by stray fingers from the rapidly sinking sun; a noisy waterfall gushed out of the rocks about twenty feet below and plunged on, now lost to sight, now a torrent of molten silver, or a leaping mass of vivid red in the dying sun's rays, until it was lost to sight in the dense green beneath. To the west, the sun was sinking into a bed of indigo, edging the somber cloud a flaming carmine: a mist of red and gold came out from behind the darkness, spreading and swallowing up the amethyst pink and glowing orange that flicked and patched the sky.

Sinclair watched Chrysanthe, who stood a few yards away from him, unconscious of the glorious sunset, her eyes towards the east. Somewhere in that direction was her brother, the young villain whose freedom would buy her! He turned away abruptly, and gazed down into the deep, dark gorge, thinking of the first sunset they had witnessed together, when a ghastly trail of blood came down from the sky and linked them.

The sound of a short, sharp, desperate scuffle behind her made Chrysanthe turn in quick alarm. She stopped with one hand at her throat watching as Sinclair fought for freedom with half-a-dozen negroes. It was a very one-sided struggle. They had come upon him unawares as he stood lost in thought, forgetting everything but the little girl who was his prisoner. Powerful hands pinned his arms, and black paws gagged his mouth, before he had time to draw his revolver or give any alarm to the camp a stone's throw away. When she realized what was happening he was bound and gagged, helpless in the grip of his attackers. A sobbing, hysterical cry broke from her lips as a black giant turned quickly towards her, after giving a sharp, whispered instruction to his followers, which resulted in Sinclair being led briskly along a steep narrow path down the rocky hillside towards the forest below.

"My flower, there is no time to wait."

Black arms seized her and, a moment later, sure, unshod feet were going swiftly down the almost perpendicular track leading to the valley. Sinclair had a vision of a dusky savage dashing quickly past with a dazed-looking little figure in khaki clinging round its neck. Some minutes later, when the main body reached the bottom, Krua and his "Golden Flower" stood waiting for those whose progress had been impeded by the bound and helpless prisoner. The tables were turned. Sinclair was now in the grip of "The Babe's" following. So quickly had it happened, and without noise, that not one man in the camp was aware of this sudden alteration in the programme. Chrysanthe told one of the men to remove the gag (they were too far away from her late cage for any sound to reach there), then, waving the negroes back, came to her captive. Sinclair stood straight and stiff, with arms bound down to his side, looking at the nervous wild bird whose prisoner he was and, in spite of the really serious circumstances (he was sufficiently acquainted with "The Babe" to know his shrift would be a short one once they met), he could not help but smile.

"Major Sinclair, if I let you go will you promise to leave the country at once? Promise not to touch Claude in any way, or use any evidence you have against him. No one can prove anything but you. No one knows so much about us. Will you go back to England and say he's not the man wanted? Say you've been mistaken all along. If you will promise, on your honor, to do this you can go free."

Sinclair guessed she had a fair idea of what his fate would be once he and her brother met. Again this small maiden was trying to do the right thing!

"I couldn't promise that, child."

Blue eyes looked at him helplessly.

"Why not? It will be a fearful bother taking you along as a prisoner, and . . . and Claude might be very angry now you've found out we—change places."

"Then I shall have to risk Claude's anger, little girl."

Chrysanthe turned away drearily. Major Sinclair had had his chance and refused it—she could do no more. A moment later a procession, headed by Krua and "The Babe's" lieutenant, followed immediately by the bound prisoner, in the grip of a couple of negroes, and the remaining three filing up behind, was going swiftly into the rapidly deepening shadows that closed and gathered as the sun sank into its bed of indigo.

From the conversation of the two just ahead of him Sinclair learnt that Krua, with five of the sharpshooters, had followed him since the night of Chrysanthe's capture, watching and waiting round the camp for an opportunity like the one resulting in his capture. Also a certain Gola, at present unknown to him, had left Essuata Town, the moment after he had, to apprise "The Babe" of this undesired presence close at hand; likewise a man by name of Kudju, second in command of the sharpshooters, had remained in the village until the required porters had recovered from their carouse, then taken them along to their new master's camp as soon as they were in a condition to walk. "The Babe's" illness he learnt for the first time.

For hours they went along in the tangled dark forest, Krua pausing now and then to find the right track, a very difficult task in the faint starlight. After the first mile he picked up his "Golden Flower" and carried her lightly on one giant limb. A slim arm and small bandaged hand around the black neck, and a tired, trusting little face close to the smiling ebony one, gave Sinclair much food for reflection as he walked along behind the two. Before long he would have solved all problems. Fate had been one too many for him. That young devil had won. He would like to hold his little girl again before he went out—to kiss her just once! She had stayed in his arms like a trusting, tired child. He had shattered that trust. She would always think of him as a brute who had nearly frightened the life out of her when she was in his power.

As he went along silently through the dim aisle of trees, conscious that within the next few hours "The Babe" would keep his promise, there was nothing in his mind but the wild bird just ahead of him.

Midnight was well past when the glint of a smoldering fire, some way ahead, caused a grunt of satisfaction to run through the guard. Sinclair knew the time was at hand. Krua stopped. Three times the weird, sobbing cry, that had apprised Chrysanthe of her brother's presence in Rio del Rey, rang out. There were a few moments of eerie silence as the wail echoed and died away. Then, from the distant camp, came an answering cry—"The Babe's" sign and countersign. The party set off again and very soon came out of the forest into a clearing. When Krua appeared with his burden, a great shout went up. Fresh fuel was thrown on the fire, and a huge red blaze roared skywards. Sinclair stood, in the grip of a couple of negroes, watching the weird picture. The leaping fire gleamed on a sea of savage black figures with the red light flickering on their rolling eyes and massive limbs, and on Chrysanthe sitting wide-eyed, with weary, smiling mouth, high up on Krua's shoulder—a little bit of white foam on the crest of a great black wave. The flames danced on the gleaming steel barrels as a dense barrier of guns was pointed skywards in salutation. Krua raised his hand and fifty voices thundered, "Ayati! Golden Flower!"

Before the wild shout died down, fifty guns blazed up to the silent sky, three times in succession. A cloud of smoke, reddened by the flashing fire, hid the wild picture. As it gradually drifted away, the black savage mass spread and scattered, like a slowly opening curtain, and, in a tent behind, a little khaki-clad figure knelt with its arms round something white and frail that touched its curls with shaky, skeleton hands.

There was a lump in Sinclair's throat as he watched; he was very glad fate had taken the turn it had, since there was no chance for him.

The noise and excitement caused by Chrysanthe's return gradually died away. The fire was rapidly beaten out, and the camp lay in darkness but for the lamp in the one tent. Black silent statues, armed to the teeth, took up their vacated positions on the outskirts of the forest. The interior of the tent was screened by a couple of ebony giants who stood in close confabulation with "The Babe." Sinclair knew his fate was being settled. Presently an order came to bring him along.

The youngster was sitting propped up in bed when the prisoner was brought in. A nod dismissed the negroes. For a moment the two looked at each other. There was a malicious gleam in "The Babe's" eyes and a sweet smile of welcome on his thin, hollow face.

"Hello, old chap, who'd have thought of seeing you! I'd no idea you'd get up here so soon. It's jolly decent of you to look me up at once though. Tell me why you came. It ain't often my friends get up as far as here."

As he spoke, Chrysanthe came through the dividing curtain, no longer in her brother's attire, but in a soft, white dressing-gown. Behind her was Grip, who welcomed Sinclair with real friendliness and stood at his side with a cold nose in one of the bound, helpless hands. She came to her brother's side and smoothed back his curls tenderly.

"Claude, dear, Major Sinclair must be tired, you mustn't keep him up too late."

"The Babe" looked at her smilingly.

"Don't you worry about that, Chrys. I ain't going to keep him up. He'll soon be asleep sound enough."

"What are you going to do?"—watching him anxiously.

"You go to bed, Chrys. This palaver is between Sinclair and me. He came up here when I told him plainly I didn't want to see him any more. This little earth ain't big enough for both of us; one has got to shift off and make room for the other."

Chrysanthe watched her brother for a moment, then sat down by the bedside, with an arm around him. "What are you going to do, Claude?"

"Shoot him, same as I promised. Let him see I speak the truth sometimes."

"You . . . you've never done anything like—that, and you mustn't do it now, dear."

"You wouldn't like your one and only brother to spend the best years of his life in prison, would you, Chrys?"

"No, dear, but—murder ain't like thieving. You've never done it. Don't do it, now, Claude, when you've promised to live straight."

Sinclair watched the two. He knew quite well it was not his life Chrysanthe was pleading for—had it been Langfeldt, or any one of the niggers, she would have asked just the same—it was only to try and keep the young devil from his inborn evilness. To keep him from the crime she thought he had not yet committed.

For some minutes "The Babe" said nothing, but sat with a thoughtful, calculating air.

"And if I don't shoot him, Chrys, what do you suggest?"

Chrysanthe had no suggestion. Her brother laughed and looked at his prisoner with dancing eyes.

"Well, Chrys, I have—since you reminded me of my promise. I ain't in the habit of keeping them, but I make you an exception. What do you say, if we take Sinclair here along as our guest for the next couple of weeks or so, and then let him loose to find his way back alone. Ten to one he'll starve to death before he finds his own little lot again. Personally I think it would be kinder to shoot him straight out than to let him die a lingering death up in the wilds beyond. But if that'll satisfy you I'm more than pleased. Shall we put it to the prisoner, give him the casting vote like? What do you say, old chap? Shall I shoot you now and bury you nice and clean, or take you up there and let the birds pick your bones, eventually? Lord! it would be a fitting end for you, considering the crowd you've shot and trapped in your time."

Sinclair made no reply. He knew "The Babe" had no intention of letting him free, but would find a way of disposing of him quietly and without letting his sister know, once he was well enough to be about and take full control again.

"It seems you haven't any choice, old chap," "The Babe" went on as his prisoner made no answer. "Well, I'm with you there. Lord! if the thing lay with me, I'm hanged if I'd know which to pick. Chrys, decide! Is it better to die quick and painless with a clean Christian funeral afterwards, or better a few more days on this wicked earth with a lingering, gnawing end and all the vultures in the district sitting round watching you peg out?"

"Major Sinclair won't promise not to give evidence against you, so . . . so he must take his chance up there, dear."

"Right you are, Chrys. Ain't I always a good boy now and do just what you want? Lord! Sinclair won't ever believe a word I say. Promised faithfully I'd shoot him if ever I saw him again, and I ain't keeping my word! It ain't the first promise I've broken though, and I don't suppose it will be the last either!" and "The Babe" smiled a sweet, tired smile as he leant back on the pillows.

Chrysanthe watched him with relieved eyes.

"Now, dear, you must go to sleep again. All this worry and excitement will make you worse."

"Don't you worry about that, Chrys. It does me a world of good to see Sinclair here. Couldn't have had a better tonic! Never felt so gay since we left home." Then looking at his prisoner, "Now, old chap, I'm going to let you loose. It ain't hospitable to keep you standing tied up like this, but I tell you, if you make a move out of this tent without my permission, Grip will settle you before you know where you are. It's not the job he'd care about, because you're a pal of his, but he does as I tell him, does Grip, same as all of 'em, except Chrys here. Now, Chrys, unstrap our friend. Don't forget to remove his shooter first. You ought to have done it as soon as you caught him. You ain't trained up to your job yet, old girl. Still you can fill my place very creditably and I haven't much to grumble at."

Chrysanthe came to Sinclair's side, took the revolver from his belt and gave it to her brother. Then small nervous hands tried vainly to untie the knots.

"You can't make much headway with that lame paw of yours, Chrys. When I next see Langfeldt I shall have something to say to him about that. Have a knife to it, old girl."

"The Babe" searched round under his pillow and produced one, gave it to his sister and continued, "If you can't manage left-handed I'll have to trouble Sinclair to come a bit nearer and let me have a shot."

This however was unnecessary. Very shortly, stiff and numb, but free, Sinclair stood in the presence of his captor.

"Sit down, old chap, and make yourself at home. From what Chrys says you must have come away without your dinner so mighty anxious you were to see me. It's a good fifteen miles from your digs to mine, so I guess you are hungry. Chrys, scratch a bit of supper together—that is, if you don't mind taking pot luck, old man. You see I wasn't expecting you quite so soon or I'd have had the fatted calf all hot. Chrys worried herself no end as to whether we should ever meet again; was always talking about you—expected to see you turn up any minute. I wasn't so sure though, still I'm very glad you came, under the circumstances."

Sinclair accepted the invitation in the spirit it was given. He knew it was "The Babe's" intention to bait and goad him as much as possible. At least he would not give the young devil the satisfaction of seeing him in any way perturbed. Since he was to be treated as a guest it should be so. Any look or sign of discomfort on his part would only add to his captor's delight. For the little girl's sake it was better that everything should go on smoothly to the end.

It annoyed "The Babe" that Sinclair acquiesced so readily; it was his idea to make his undesired guest do a lot of dancing during the few days he was to remain alive; however, none of this disappointment showed on his face; instead he said, "Glad to see you're taking it sensibly, old man, it ain't any use kicking against fate."

The youngster chatted away in bland friendliness as Chrysanthe produced various comestibles from a tin "chop box." He watched his sister and guest with smiling speculation. The fact that no word had passed between them did not escape him.

Presently he said, "How long was it before Sinclair found he had bagged the wrong bird, Chrys? I bet you were a trifle disappointed, old man, when you found it was my sister you'd got and not me."

A red flush came to Chrysanthe's face as Sinclair answered, "I knew at once it was your sister."

"Did you though?"—in mock astonishment—"Well, I'm hanged! You're the first white who has ever marked the difference. Chrys in my togs can do me to perfection. Fancy you having spotted the neat little deception at once! Our best friends don't know us one from the other when we sport the same feathers—friends we've known for years! Here you come along, a raw new acquaintance, as you might say, yet you can spot us at once. How would you account for that, Chrys?"

Sinclair wondered why he did not strangle the mocking shadow that watched him with vicious, taunting eyes. The young devil knew the one spot to touch and make him twinge! Just how to hurt him! To make him suffer by seeing this little girl go red and white with shame and confusion.

"How would you account for that, Chrys?" "The Babe" asked again, watching the two with dancing eyes.

"I—I don't know, dear. But you mustn't talk so much, try and go to sleep now."

"Right you are, Chrys. Now, Sinclair, you get your supper. I hope you won't mind having a shakedown in here to-night, you came so late and I wasn't expecting you. It's hardly worth while running up another tent, we shall be on the move in a few hours. It ain't the first time we've shared the same crib. Captain Chrys, you run along and tell Gola there ain't to be any funeral to-night. He'll be grievously disappointed; he was looking forward to a little target practice."

Chrysanthe left the tent and went across the starlit clearing to where Krua and Gola were waiting to carry out "The Babe's" commands. Sinclair watched the ghostly little figure in its fluttering white robe, that stood talking to the two negroes. Then she went to the outskirts of the camp and spoke to a man there, for a time was lost to sight as each sentry was interviewed in turn, and finally stayed just at the edge of the forest, away from everything, looking up at the silent sky. "The Babe's" voice brought him back to earth.

"I say, old chap, if you've finished would you mind making up your own bed? There's a cane lounge behind the curtains in Chrys's crib, fish it out, and, with a pillow of mine and that rug, I guess you've been fixed up worse at longer notice. Then would you mind putting out the lamp. There are too many of my friends round and about the neighborhood, and the light might attract 'em."

He obeyed instructions, and very soon was lying down, fully dressed, with Grip to guard him. The tent had been in darkness for some time when something soft and white came stealing back. It leant for a moment over the bed and very gently kissed the sleeping boy's face. Sinclair watched, and he felt he wanted just those few days' grace to try and redeem himself in the sight of this little guardian angel.

CHAPTER 16

"Our parents of old entailed the curse
Which must to our children cling."

A GLOWING RED SUN was slipping behind a distant, misty bank of dense forest as a caravan, some sixty strong, came crawling down the side of a gigantic earth rent, more than five hundred feet in depth, that cut across the country, as far as the eye could reach, from north to south—a great volcanic slit, a quarter of a mile in width. On each side the matted bush reached to the edge of the gorge, which lay, a gaping black wound, between a jagged fringe of green. Already the shadows thickened in the wild, boulder-strewn chasm, and the huge rocks took weird and uncouth shapes of themselves in the gathering twilight. A wide stream, like an endless snake, crawled stealthily along between the rude blocks. Although it was nearly sunset, a stifling, oppressive heat still filled the giant cleft. Nothing moved in the shadowed depths, not a whisper cut through the heated silence, except the sudden, harsh, grating cry of the black, ill-omened carrion birds, perching round on the gnarled, stunted trees, when the slowly descending caravan disturbed their slumbers. By sunset the party reached the bottom. A strange green light came up from the west, flickered and played on the quickly purpling sky, cast an awesome shadow into the gloomy gorge, and died away as the moon rose over the dark forest. The silver ball soared higher; its white rays crept over the edge of the narrow valley, and shone on a couple of tents and a tiny

227

dancing fire far below. By midnight the moon looked straight down into the great earth rent, surprised at what it saw there. Several hundred years had passed since other rays than its own had lighted that wild chasm. Many generations had been since pale yellow fires had glimmered in this crevice in the forest. A long, inquisitive, silver finger played round the smaller tent, drowning the tiny lamp; it paused on an ancient document and very tenderly touched the one who leant over reading it.

A strong, tired face, with haggard eyes, gazed up for a moment at the passing silver orb. Before the moon looked down again, for him all things would have ended! The last night on earth! After three weeks of goading and ingenious mental tortures "The Babe" had informed his guest that to-morrow he would be free, and, for his amusement and perusal that evening, had given his prisoner the old manuscript which gave full details of the mission he and his sister were bent on. Twice Sinclair had read it through, and his own utter helplessness tortured him beyond all bearing, as he realised the awful fate awaiting his little girl in the hell her brother was leading her to. All the weird old tragedy lay before him; played down to its last act in the two now living, to be finished in the mystic peak about a month's march away. It was written in indifferent Greek, the last work of a man bricked up and left to die, by his own brother, in a secret chamber of the old fort, more than three hundred years ago. For a third time Sinclair went through the story, then he took a careful copy in English for his own keeping. Why, he did not know. By the next sunset "The Babe" had promised him freedom, and he was sufficiently acquainted with his captor to know what that meant. Very slowly and carefully he went through the whole thing, and the translated copy lay in front of him as follows:

"Fort Devereux,
"July 24th, 1597.

"I must haste me and write this before the light leaves this narrow cell for I fear by the morrow my strength will have sped and ere long I, Philip Devereux, will have passed to the hell that will be for all our kind from now until the blue-eyed flower comes again to serve at the golden altar of the Dread God Asquielba. The shadows gather quickly round me and out of the mist the wild distant bells are calling. I have heard them three times and this is the end! It is well, for Chrysanthe is dead and my brother Claude a traitor. Even as he deceived all others, so at last came my turn. Already the curse is working! By their own hands henceforth must every Devereux slay the wife he marries, even as Claude killed my wild flower with their newborn infant in her arms. Would the gods had been merciful and he had slain that too, for on it was the mark of the hidden devil! Would the cursed wine had not loosed my tongue to tell of all I saw in that far-off land, ere I started the voyage which kept me rotting for two whole years in a villainous Spanish prison! Even I broke the promise given before the great golden altar as I held Chrysanthe's hand in mine! Perchance I dreamt it all. God knows it was wilder than any nightmare!— right down to last night's work when my Golden Flower lay dead between us, slain by the sword that should have been my due—slain by her husband and my brother!—by the one who had deceived her equally with me, whom she had called 'Philip' and husband well nigh two years, loathed and feared because of a broken promise and the great red flood that swept away her people forever. My brother thought me dead or this would have gone on to the finish. But I escaped and returned to find my strange wild flower drooping on the terrace of our fort, rudely plucked by a hand so like my own she knew not the difference. Then she knew it was not I who had deceived her. For one brief hour Chrysanthe was in my arms, her weary, frightened little face against my shoulder and the traitor's child lay sleeping beside us. God knows I had loved my brother, but that was beyond all forgiveness! Claude came upon us, a very devil in his jealous rage, and the sword he thrust at me was sheathed in Chrysanthe's bosom.

"Chrysanthe! little Golden Flower, even now I hoar the faint sweet bells whispering as you came, like a red mist in the moonlight, to meet me where the palms sighed by the stream in the grove behind the temple. I can feel your small white hands on my heart still, as when you brought me back to life after the great golden god stirred and moved on his altar. Little wild flower, I can see you with the red stream flowing from your breast and your dead, peaceful face against that traitor's shoulder. He held you tight against him as we fought for you—a last mad round till I slipped and fell in the red pool that dripped down from your bosom, and my own blood mingled with it. For a time I was forgotten as he paced up and down with you, limp and bleeding, in his arms. The gold of your dress was lost, wild flower, and a wet shroud was around you. Now I am bricked up here to gnaw off my fingers in slow starvation. Would I had slain that traitor first, then the worst tortures hell can hold would not have deadened my satisfaction. Chrysanthe, I forget and hear you coming. All day I have sat in this cell and watched the gaunt skeleton confronting me. Now, before my brain grows feeble and my eyes dim, I would fain write down everything. My history and yours, wild flower! Perchance I dreamt it all, I rotted overlong in that Spanish prison. Even now the mists close around me. Perhaps they will clear some day and the tangled skein be straightened. Perchance I only dream this wild end, and will wake again to find you beside me at the altar of the Dread God Asquielba. Maybe I have had a fever, and, when the delirium goes, I shall find Claude, my brother and twin, with me as we have always been, loving and trusting one another.

"I, Philip Devereux, do give this as the true history of myself and Claude, my twin, one time of the Royal Navy, the only sons of Philip John Devereux, squire in the county of Cumberland, England.—So alike are we that even our own parents knew us not one from the other.—And of Chrysanthe, priestess at the altar of Asquielba, in a land lying beyond the devil-haunted forest, many hundred leagues away, in the heart of this ghastly country.

"I, Philip, and my twin Claude, followed the sea after the manner of all our people, and were but young men when he was given command of the swiftest frigate in the service and I appointed as his chief lieutenant. That voyage we sailed with the fleet to the Spanish Main. Claude was no favorite with our admiral. I know not how or when the quarrel rose, but it ended on the quarter-deck of our vessel when my brother, in a fit of temper, slew him in the presence of his staff. For some minutes all was confusion as back to back we fought for life and freedom. Our officers were against us, but the crew were for my brother. Before the rest of the fleet knew what had happened, we had slain our opponents and were showing a clean pair of heels—a crew of mutineers, outlaws and murderers, who henceforth sailed the seas with the skull and crossbones where so lately had flown an honored ensign. We did well at our new profession. It was a wild life and a merry! Our harbour was a well-screened haunt in the depths of one of the many mangrove swamps skirting the coast of Africa. Some two weeks' march away was our stronghold up country, this fort armed with captured guns and cannon, ready for any siege. All countries were hot on our track and our name a terror to the seas.

Then we tired of the sea, lived ashore with our following and many wild orgies held riot in this fort.
There came a time when I sickened of the life, but
no country was open to me, so I turned my steps to
discover more of the savage unknown continent we
had made our home. But this Africa is a devil-
haunted land! Often I had heard it whispered the
master-fiend himself, in the shape of serpent with
many legs, still dwelt in a temple lost beyond the
trackless forest. Methinks I have seen an old painting, in my father's study, where the author of all evil
comes to our mother Eve in this guise—an awful
beast more fearsome and horrible than the most
deadly of the forked-tongued reptiles that glide in
the forest.

"Several weeks I travelled in this strange country and came to a great stone temple some hundred
leagues or thereabouts inland. A hideous, awesome
place where a monster, many-legged serpent, carved
from the virgin rock, lay coiled round and about a
rude stone altar. For a time I stayed in the land, the
guest of their priest-king Mungea. There was much
strife and dissatisfaction throughout the tribe because of a whispered message that had floated down
from the far north-east, purported to have come
from a new priestess who served at the long-lost altar of the great golden god Asquielba, whose stone
image lay in their temple. A strange and beauteous
woman, the beloved of the Dread God, at whose desire all things were changed, and only white flowers
to be strewn on the altar that had dripped blood
since times lost in the mists. Now Mungea and his
ancestors had held sway at this temple for time further back than the mind of man can go, and had sacrificed according to ancient rites. This message
pleased him not and he ignored it, declaring it to be

a false one. Each night, at the full moon, it had been the custom to sacrifice a maiden at the stone horror in the great round temple. I was present the night when, one after the other, six priests went up to slay a girl who was bound in the jaws of the monster, and each was bitten by a swarm of loathsome, wriggling insects, and died in writhing agonies but shortly afterwards. Then the high priest Mungea grew afraid and with his own hands unbound the maiden; as he did so the vicious wriggling mass of copper-coloured creatures disappeared, and neither he nor the intended sacrifice was injured!

"That night I was with Mungea as he sat deep in thought after the fiasco in the temple. In his heart was a great hatred for the unknown priestess, for he had lost prestige with his people, having boasted that his power was beyond this new prophet's. All the tribe had gathered together to see if the old creed still held sway. I inquired more of this priestess from whom the message was purported to have come, and the land where she dwelt, but he could tell me little. Tradition had it that, in a land far beyond the sunrise, the Dread God dwelt, whose priest and servant his people had been from days forgotten. He had stayed silent since the time the moon was young, and the old rites had gone on according to the rules laid down in those old days. Then this message came wafted out of the shadows.

"I had heard something of this beautiful woman who ruled in a forgotten country, and rumours of a vast temple containing wealth beyond the desires of nations, piled round the altar of a long-lost god whose weird stone images remained in one or two temples throughout the land. Now life held nothing for me, and in my heart I cared but little for the way Fate had led me, but I had loved my brother Claude

and sworn that his way should be my way; so I determined to set out and risk all the evils of this devil-
haunted continent, and prove for my own satisfaction how much of these wild rumours were true. Of
late years I have drunken much; wine drowns all
memory and I care not to think of the good name we
have dishonoured. Perchance I saw all that follows
through the fumes of the brain-clogging spirit. Yet
methinks it true, for, but yesternight, I saw
Chrysanthe dead on the terrace of this fort which has
been our home these twelve years.

"For months I travelled in this savage land, heading always to the north-east; for days I skirted a desperate earth crack, too steep for descent and of a
width too great to span, and much time was spent
ere I succeeded in crossing this chasm, and then
again the forest. Weeks I passed in this, and beyond
was a desert where death from thirst well nigh over-
took me. Would to God my bones had bleached in
that and waste! Then one morning, with the sunrise,
a great golden hand rose on the horizon, belted
round with a cuff of green. It vanished as the morning mists melted, but I went towards the spot. Again
at even, blood red in the setting sun, the great weird
shape confronted me. This time it stayed, until the
black shades of night shut it from my sight. By the
next sunset I reached the forest surrounding it.
There a party of gigantic negroes, whose language I
know not, seized me and held me prisoner. For days
they took me through the forest's gloomy depths, till
we came to a low fringe of hills circling a high plain
where stood the mystic peak—the rough-hewn hand
I had seen those times in the desert! A stretch of
beautiful country lay round it, like my father's park
but larger; a silver waterfall gushed from a wound
below the colossal pointing finger and flowed on, a

placid, shimmering river, through the peaceful wooded scene; groups of feathery palms and groves of yellow-fruited trees grew on its banks, and under their shade were scattered native huts. Some way beyond was a huge natural gate, and, from that roughly hewn steps led up a steep incline to a narrow opening some hundred feet above, apparently leading to a gloomy cavern in the depths of the great clenched hand.

"My captors led me towards a large hut, set a little apart from the others—a snowdrift in the green, so wreathed and festooned it was with white flowers. Behind, flame-flowered trees dripped blood-red petals on this dainty nest. It came to me I had reached the Land of my Desires, so quiet and peaceful was it all. God knows, I had never been nearer hell!

"It was then I saw Chrysanthe, clad in a misty, shimmering, red-gold robe and girt about with awesome jewels, the like of which I had never seen. She was seated on a bank of white flowers and around her were negroes of gigantic stature. Some my brother brought down as slaves when he plucked my flower so rudely. I knew I had passed through the shadows to the land beyond the sunrise. I was in the presence of the priestess who served at the altar of Asquielba! I gazed in a dream. To find one of my own colour in the heart of this devil's land was beyond comprehension, and that a girl, hardly more than a child! It was a wistful little face that looked back at me in timid curiosity, with wide, dark eyes, clear and pure as the far tropic sky they resembled. Rippling chestnut hair, crowned with a wreath of golden flowers, reached far below her waist. A red stone, like a drop of blood on her finger, flashed in the sunlight as her hand went slowly to her throat. She came, a gliding, misty little thing, a few steps closer to where

I stood, bound and a prisoner, in the hands of her people. It was my wild flower! Chrysanthe who loved me as I worshipped her, who would not leave that devil's temple for the curse that would fall on me and mine, on her and all her people if she went from the altar of Asquielba—a great golden horror, shut away in the depths of the awesome hill, that no eyes had seen save her own and mine, and whose whispered name sent a shudder through the country.

"I stayed in the shadow of the peak. Why those black giants let me live I knew not until afterwards; of a truth there was scant friendliness between us. It was a timid wild flower I had found; for a week I saw nothing more of her, save once when she stood at the head of the steps, like a fleck of gold in the black opening leading to the heart of the hill. The dying sun's rays played on a dreamy, wistful face as she watched the great orb sink to rest. The vivid rays dyed the white flowers she held a flaming carmine, and, even as I gazed, she disappeared, washed into the gloomy depths on a red sea that swept down from the heavens.

"One night I wandered by the river lost in a dream of this maiden I had seen but twice, wondering who she was and whence she came. Sweet whispering bells caused me to turn and I saw her coming towards me. I stayed, not daring to move, she had not yet marked me in the shadow. She stopped with a frightened gasp, and looked at me with the startled eyes of a forest fawn. I trembled lest she should go and leave me, it was such a timid, gentle little girl, and I such an uncouth, rough brute that I feared to scare her. For a moment she watched me with wide, frightened eyes, then spoke in the dialect of the country. This I could not understand and replied in English, then French and Spanish, with both of which I was well acquainted, but this dainty forest blossom had no knowledge of them. Then I bethought me of Greek, of which I am but an indifferent scholar, yet it pleased me to write in this for it proved Chrysanthe's language. As I spoke she came a little closer, and looked at me with listening eyes, like one who hears a once familiar sound, now almost forgotten. My wild flower had once known that tongue, for she replied haltingly, and in baby words such as would have been used by a child not more than five. She knew nothing beyond her name and once she had lived with people of my colour, but so far back she had forgotten it until she saw me. I surmise she must have been stolen as a child, perhaps brought across the Great Desert and may have strayed and been found by this tribe.

"That was the first of many nights I met Chrysanthe as she came from the temple. She would stay but a minute and ask me some timid, curious question of the unknown world beyond. I had been a drunken, vicious brute those past years, and knew not that I had the careful tenderness left in me to win such a shy wild flower each night a moment longer at my side. And she trusted me, a savage, bloodstained pirate, with a name cursed by all who heard it! Even now I can hear the faint golden bells whisper, as a slim white arm crept through mine, and a tiny hand, like a scared mouse, would stay for a moment on my sleeve. There came a time when I told Chrysanthe of the love that filled my heart, which had grown with a suddenness incredible from the moment I saw her. But it was a strange small flower, it knew not what I meant! Did not everyone love her? Even the Dread God Asquielba, who from times forgotten had loved nothing but blood and gold! God forgive me, I took that innocent little thing into my arms, and kissed her as she tried to break away. Kissed her till the shy, moist eyes refused to meet mine, and a slender, quivering form stayed with its face hidden against my shoulder.

"The next night she came not to the grove, and I tarried till the sun rose. As the moon came up in the evening I went through the forbidden gates, and waited by the slit in the hill till she came from the hidden temple. But it was a terrified little flower that hurried me quickly back to the grove, with nervous, loving hands, and made me promise never to go through those rocky gates. I was a man and a lover, and would give no promise unless she in return would come to me every night as usual. I cannot write of the days that followed. Was I not the most blessed of mortals! Chrysanthe loved me, and the great old god stirred in the depths of the hill and grew jealous! This wild flower stayed always longer with me, and at times neglected the temple. Much as I pleaded she refused to leave the land and return with me. I knew she feared the wrath of that which lay in the hill. I desired to face the Dread God, and ask boldly for my flower from the one whose priestess she had been since childhood. For a time she would neither let me enter nor tell me what lay therein.

"There came a day when Chrysanthe said I must return, and alone; she wept when I refused. I knew she feared to bring evil on me. I pleaded but to stand before the altar and state my desire, then, if she still wished it, I would return alone, for, 'twixt love of me and fear of that which lay in the hill, my wild flower drooped. That night it was a silver moonbeam that met me in the grove, and a white, tearful face was laid against my shoulder. She had asked that I might go with her into the depths the next night and hear what had been said to her, and the reasons she dared not leave the altar. I write what follows as it appeared to me through the red mist, even now it comes to me I may have dreamt it, for, when life returned to me, I lay beneath the jaws of the Dread God with my head on Chrysanthe's bosom, and her shaking little hands warmed my heart. There was nothing but the gloomy, shrouded cave, the lamps flickering on the ruby-studded altar, and the vast, fearsome, glittering creature that coiled round it—a monster of pure gold for I touched and felt it.

"The next even at sunset I met Chrysanthe by the rocky gates as she came with the offering of white flowers to the temple. She was clad in a misty cloud of silver, the dress she wore at the altar of Asquielba when asking some special favour. Gathered round were many of the giant blacks who gazed at me with awe, as it was death to all who entered that dread cave, save my blossom. Together we went up the steps. A great red ray came out of the west and shone full on us twain as we paused to watch the dying orb before entering the narrow slit. God knows it was ghastly! As I gazed round, the plain between the hills filled with a lurid flood. A sea of blood drowned the peaceful landscape. It swept right up to the very step where we stood; but for a moment, and, as it died away, the placid scene lay bathed in a sheen of gold. Then a cold little hand was slipped into mine and we passed into the gloomy cavern.

"But it was the devil's own land I had entered! Vast black depths lay ahead filled with a curious faint scratching sound as of the moving of a myriad of tiny feet. Things the shape and size of serpents, but with an uncanny movement, darted like quick shadows across the narrow path we descended. Weird forms deepened in the blackness and wafted the still thick

air as they circled round us. Gaunt leathery wings
touched my face and phantom, clammy hands seized
me. The heavy splash of unseen, dripping water cut
through the murky, breathless silence. Anon was a
gust of fire-heated wind like the breath of a hidden
furnace. God knows I am no coward, yet I held the
tiny cold hand closer, and my heart was filled with a
great desire to seek again the way by which I had
entered. But I wanted my wild flower above all
things, even as every one of our people shall want it,
and go out to the fiend who now owns us with that
name on our lips, and, though a vast fear entered
into me, there was a love beyond it.

"How long we traversed the narrow passage I
know not. Then a faint light grew ahead of us and,
in the dim glow, I saw an endless cavern. In it was a
mighty altar hung about with a score of lamps—a vast
golden pile studded with rubies that lay wet in the
feeble light, like clots and splashes of blood. Coiled
around this weird shrine was a great, glistening,
golden horror, a serpent of a size too huge to conceive, with legs to the number of two score, a horned
purblind head and fearsome, gaping, red-dripping
jaws. It hung, head downwards, to within an arm's
length of a gem-studded, flower-strewn slab. A thing
fearsome beyond the sight of man, yet of a wealth in
gold and gems outside of comprehension! A glittering path edged with a bank of golden lilies, which
swayed at a touch and whispered as tiny bells, led
from where we stood to the foot of the awesome pile.
There was a dreadful whispering silence over everything, as of a multitude waiting, as of many watching whom I could not see, for my eyes were yet dim
in the red gloom. Still in my ears was that faint
scratching sound, but louder. Then I wondered that I
retained my senses, for, as I peered into the shadows,

the whole place became a moving mass of deadly, loathsome, copper-coloured insects, such as I had seen that night in the temple of the priest-king, Mungea. God! How they closed round me! A vicious army of legged reptiles in number as the sands of the sea. Chrysanthe drew me closer and spoke. The myriad vanished again into the shadows, a wriggling, writhing mass, and there was naught of them, only the sickening, scratching sound. It came to me I had reached hell and my knees grew weak beneath me as we went up the golden path. At the foot of the ruby-flecked steps Chrysanthe left me. That was a most desperate time, for beyond the bank of golden flowers the multitude awaited me. At the altar she stood with her hand on the hanging golden horror, turned and smiled at me and spoke again to the devil's army. I knew they thirsted for me, for one brute, of a fearsomeness that turned my blood to water, came through the lilies. God! I can see it now as it crawled slowly upwards to my throat. My terror was such that I stood frozen. But my flower saw and came quickly towards me. Little hands took it with a quick carefulness, and the vile, death-giving thing lay coiling around her wrist like a fiend's bracelet; she talked to and chided it, then put it behind the bank of whispering lilies. As she did so all light died away, and there was nothing but a still blackness, and out of the depths a sudden peal of wild bells, which henceforth each Devereux shall hear three times before the devil claims him.

"Then all was awesome silence. The icy cold hand in mine trembled. The shaking morsel took all fear from me. I would have faced the master-fiend himself! It was a shivering little flower I held against my heart as I boldly stated my desire. There was no sound until I finished. Then a low chuckle of hellish laughter came, as it were, from the bowels of the earth; it rose and grew to the sound of thunder, echoed and rang through the cavern till the very hill shook and the path we stood on heaved like a tempest-ridden sea. All was blackness, and through it thundered the awful mocking laughter. There was naught on earth so horrible! My flower wept in terror. At the first frightened cry the mad mirth died down, and there was nothing but the stifled sobs and the feeling of a hidden Thing listening. Then a voice spoke. God! That hideous devil's whisper will ring in my ears for ever. Yet a note of utter tenderness mingled with the fiendish hissing. It came from but a few feet away, from somewhere about the shrouded altar. It called my flower by name. She would have gone but I held and would not let her. A frightened voice pleaded with me and a weak girl's strength was pitted against mine. I drew her closer and kissed her as the unseen Terror called again. Then, out of the darkness, something swooped on to us. What, I could not see, for all was blacker than the deepest night. It held us in a metal vice, for my hands felt and fought with it. A fear past earth seized me. I held my flower faint against me. It came to me the end of all things was upon us, for slowly the nameless Horror lifted us. God! But the pit of hell lay spread beneath us! There was nothing but Chrysanthe's unconscious face against my heart and the great, red, roaring flames sweeping towards us. Hell's blackest night lay around; beneath was the seething pit, and through all thundered the shrieking devil's laughter! I can see it now! An endless ocean of boiling blood with a stench indescribable! In it writhed the damned, girt about by hideous, legged serpents with a poison that tortures for ever. Racked with a thirst eternal and naught but the red blistering blood to slack it! The place for me and mine if the flower was taken from the altar of Asquielba! For her, if she went from the golden Horror! A curse would be on her children; each to be born with the brand of that Dread Monster, with an inheritance of evil viciousness that would make them banned by all, companions only of hell's refuse. Offshoots of the devil! Murderers, thieves and liars! Till their bloodshed turned the slow grinding Wheel of Time, and out of the unborn ages Chrysanthe came again to serve at that devil's altar!

"Even as I looked it passed from me. The golden lilies whispered about the unseen path as the deadly waiting army crawling among them. I stood with my limp wild flower in my arms, and only the fiend's voice echoed and drifted away in the darkness. I pray to heaven it was but a ghastly nightmare!

"A gust of wind, chill as death, came moaning through the cavern. My flower stirred. God knows I loved her, but the dread curse fell on her equally. For myself I cared not: I could get no lower, but I would leave my pure white blossom even as I found her. I whispered I would return whence I came, alone. As I did so, the lamps flared up again and the great Golden God lay coiled round the jewelled altar. Chrysanthe led me up those blood-flecked steps and, with my hand in hers, I swore to leave her, and that very hour, to say naught of what I had seen, and turn no more to that forgotten country. God! As I stood there I swear that legged serpent moved and the red-dripping jaws closed round my flower's waist! It was horrible beyond all hell! I knew nothing till I woke with my head on Chrysanthe's breast, and her little white hands on my heart. Through the temple the wild golden bells were pealing. Yet, with a repugnance beyond all words, I examined the awful creature. It was but a huge thing of gold and from the hideous pincer-like jaws dripped a cascade of marvellous rubies. A vast fiend's pile of gold and gems! A wealth beyond all comprehension!

"I know nothing of how I left the cavern, saw nothing but the endless devil's army that closed up to us, so thick I could not stir for them. Nervous little hands tightened on my arm, and Chrysanthe spoke to them. The path cleared, and I stood alone in God's pure moonlight, by the rocky pillars which in truth had been the gates of nethermost hell! It came to me I had had a ghastly nightmare. When the wine has been strong within me I have seen desperate horrors, but naught like that! Yet in my hand I held one great ruby taken from the dripping jaws of that devil's effigy!

"I looked in the grove for Chrysanthe. As I waited by the placid stream the horror of the temple died away. It was naught but a wild, mad dream, a thing of my brain's own conception! I had promised to leave the land that very hour, yet I must see my blossom but once again. With swift, quiet steps I went to the white nest where my wild flower slept. I can see her now, as she lay on the soft cushions in her silvered robe, like a ray of moonlight, with a girdle of rubies round her waist where dripping red jaws had held her. Small hands were crumpled into baby fists as she slept—a little thing of mist, half buried in her own sweeping hair. One white arm bore the image of the yellow-legged devil, and the Horror's blood-red ring flashed on her finger. She awoke with a startled cry, for my arms were round her and my lips on hers. In a moment a crowd of gigantic blacks were on me. They would have killed me, but I drew my pistol and slew two ere I escaped. I think the arch-fiend must have whispered in my ears to enter the bower, for from the first I broke my promise.

"Several months passed before I again reached this fort, with naught to show for my travels save the one great ruby. Claude wished to know more of it, but I would tell him nothing. God! But life was dreary, for all sweetness lay hidden far beyond the forests! There came a night when my lost flower's face haunted me past bearing, and I drank as I had not since that journey beyond the sunrise. Claude sat with me and filled my glass again and again. The warm wine roused me, my tongue was loosed and I told of all I had seen. I trusted my brother, yet I know now that even as we sat there in his heart grew intention to deceive me. He would hear more of my strange wild flower. I was a love-stricken fool in drink, and told him all he asked. Then it was my brother and twin who had always shared my sorrows! He it was who said I must take the next buccaneering voyage, even though it was his turn and he loved the mad life, for in that way might I find forgetfulness of Chrysanthe. It was an evil to sorrow so long for one girl in a life that brought us many! With him no love had lasted longer than a night; yet, when he plucked my wild flower, he touched her not till a holy priest had joined them, and loved her with a fierce madness that would scarce let her stray an instant from his side.

"It comes to me now that even as my brother planned the voyage for me, likewise he planned my death and capture. For, during the expedition, I boarded a Spanish craft with a portion of my crew; they deserted me suddenly; my vessel sheered off at once, and I fell wounded sorely, fighting one to fifty. Two years I rotted in a villainous dungeon, and escaped to reach this fort well nigh three years after leaving it.

"The following I set down even as Chrysanthe told me during the brief hour yesternight, and what

the traitor mocked me with, as he watched our servants brick up this narrow cell where I shall suffer
till hell claims me.

"I had left my flower's country scarce a year,
when a rumour reached there that I had returned,
with many of my own colour and an army of a strange
tribe, and was camped about the vast tangled forest
beyond the hills. A message came through, by one
of her captured people, asking that she would come
to me and speak more of the compact made in the
temple. This she would not do, for it was forbidden
that she went beyond the circling hills. But her heart
was filled with love towards me, though she sorrowed
much over the broken promise. She wished to see me
again and reason with me, for the multitude I had
returned with spoke of evil intention. My flower sent
several of her people with gifts of gold and rubies
for my following, and a message to me to come to
her, and alone, under the escort of her people, who
would guide me through the dense wild. To me was
sent a glittering golden insect which meant safety
wherever the Dread God Asquielba held sway.

"Chrysanthe told me she was sitting among her
people when my brother came to her in my name and
face, even as she had been, the first time I saw her.
But from that moment all love went from her, and a
great and shuddering fear took its place. For, even
when he saluted her in the words all gave her as
queen and priestess, there was a mocking, laughing
echo in the voice which had not been before. Yet she
had no doubt but what it was I, for all that had
passed between us, and in the temple, was mentioned. It came to her the evil desire that filled my
heart had changed me beyond all knowledge. As she
spoke longer with me the fear grew, and when I
wished to wander with her in the grove she refused.

Then it was my brother swore to have her, to take her from the devil's very grip! For, even as with me, a great and passionate love grew suddenly in his heart for this innocent wild flower, but of a fierceness and uncontrollable madness as of the savage rages that do at times come to him. My flower wept, and promised great wealth in gold and gems if he would but leave the land. But he laughed, saying he had all jewels he wished save one—a golden flower—to wear upon his heart. The people murmured loud against him, but he had the sacred symbol and none dared do him hurt. Then my flower would see him no more, but stayed always in the temple, and he departed, for he feared to enter that place.

"But that was the end of all peace. Slowly the traitor crept up through the maze of tangled forest, with his whole force. The sweet plain ran blood for many a day, till my flower could stand no more, but came and knelt at his feet, pleading for the lives of her people. All that followed was one long shudder, and, when reason returned, she was well nigh two hundred leagues away, in the town of the priest-king Mungea. This man's help my brother had asked when he went up to that forgotten country. There was some contention in the place, for Mungea had wished to kill my flower, through whose gentle decrees his tribe had lost much caste, and, by this sacrifice, all honour would return to them. Now Claude had promised this, for at first it was only treasure he sought. But, once he saw Chrysanthe, earth held naught else. His following had clamoured for gold and gems such as he had promised them; he led them up to the temple gates, and they went in, one by one, to the number of half-a-score. But not one returned! They who remained grew afraid, and desired to leave the land at once. That traitor laughed; he cared not for all the gold, since he held my white blossom faint against his shoulder. It comes to me now the devil's army I saw there may have been no nightmare.

"Now this Mungea was wise. He saw the forest flower was not for him. Moreover he knew that willingly she would have died at the stone altar rather than stay in the arms that held her. Even then the devil's curse was working! For the priest-king made a compact with my brother of a ghastliness born only in a fiend's mind. Every year the traitor held my flower there must be sent up a golden-haired maiden whose blood must wash the fearsome stone altar. Each Devereux as they came in generation must, at that place, sacrifice the wife he marries, when she had been with him for a space of not more than two years, even so might the wrath of the golden Horror be appeased. For into Claude had entered a great fear of that hell, but beyond it was a mad love for my flower. This devil's truce came back on him, for, with his own hand, he slew Chrysanthe! Also, when the blue-eyed flower came again, she must make sacrifice of a maiden with hair of the colour of the hidden god, at that, his stone image, or her own life should be forfeit. So that, in the hidden times to come, Mungea's children's children would have the unborn flower's life, unless she spilt blood at the altar of Asquielba, and proved her own decree a false one. God! But there was nothing that black fiend loved as blood! Moreover he was a seer of visions, and one who could probe the future. His was a vengeance that would keep, though its finish lay hidden in the days still before the sunrise. There was naught he hated as my flower, and he knew the price in blood paid for her would grieve her gentle heart beyond all tortures his hell's mind could conceive.

"There is nothing more to tell. Chrysanthe, little Golden Flower, through me your gentle life is ended and a curse on you and yours for ever. Would I could suffer in hell for both! I have been an even greater traitor than my brother, for he saw not what I saw. But your love was mine, wild blossom, even though he called you 'wife.' May the Dread God judge you kindly, for you went not willingly. Your face was very peaceful when last I saw it, sweetest, even as the time I found you, since when peace left your life for ever.

"The day is fading, and, through the narrow slit of my cell, comes a ray like a blood-red finger. It falls right on me, even as that time it shone on us twain ere we entered the temple together. In the unborn ages will it glint on us again—some day when this ghastly thing is finished? Who knows? There may be a heaven beyond the nethermost hell. Even as I write this, Chrysanthe, there comes one of that devil's army crawling through the slit where the sun now glints in gold. God! It is a loathsome beast, yet preferable to the gaunt skeleton watching me. Its poison is a quick and a swift. I will have it, and in this last is that traitor defrauded. Better an hour's agony than a week of lingering torture. I am going now, wild blossom, to hold it even as you did. It loves me not, for, when I seized it, it sank deep into my hand. The end is swift, and I am glad, for the sooner do I join you. The wild golden bells ring loudly, right overhead, a joyous, merry peal! There is naught but the grove where the silver stream whispers behind the temple. And you are there before me! Methinks it is the first time, little flower!"

Sinclair folded the document carefully. It was a wild, mad thing, written by a man who, from his own confession, was more than an average drinker. Yet there was an echo of truth through it all, like one who had tried to persuade himself it had all been a ghastly nightmare. In his heart was a great pity for the long-dead buccaneer, who, for the love of his vicious twin, had followed his way, in the end to be deceived.

Sinclair's hands clenched in an agony of feeling as the utter fearsomeness of the place "The Babe" was taking his sister to came to him with redoubled force. Not that he would not let himself believe the whole of the weird old manuscript, but certain parts he knew were true. The long-dead Chrysanthe had looked back at him with his little girl's face; he had seen the uncanny birthmark on her arm, and she had said she could handle those vile insects, when she wore the jewels, and they did not harm her. Heaven alone knew what monster waited for her in that hill! It was impossible! A thing to be laughed to scorn! In England Sinclair would have scoffed at it all, but ghostly, devil-haunted West Africa had him in its grip; there was no laughter left in him, only a great fear of what might be. So much of it was true! Why not the rest? The thought tortured him beyond all bearing.

"The Babe's" entrance roused him. The youngster's appearance had altered considerably during the last three weeks. All traces of fever had gone and he with his usual round-faced, saucy-looking self, with a greater innocence and cherub-like air than ever. He seated himself opposite Sinclair and glanced at him with a sweet look of inquiry.

"Well, old chap, what do you think of that scrawl? Philip must have had worse D.T.'s than ever I've had. Lord! But all my green snakes come with legs, so evidently it's in the family. Ain't it just the cutest idea for keeping off trespassers? Chrys ain't over-keen on this deal, but she wouldn't let me go smelling round there on my own. She's superstitious-like, is Chrys, and believes far more of that than I do. Still I can't say I'd fancy going into that cave unless she was there to hold my hand, especially after that little do in Mungea's temple. Did I ever tell you how a centipede kept a leopard from 'chopping' her there? No?"—in reply to Sinclair's look of surprise.—"Lord! you mustn't miss that! It'll be something to tell your folks when you get home."

"The Babe" gave a graphic description of the incident, watching his victim in an ecstasy of malicious delight. It struck Sinclair to wonder how much of the old document Chrysanthe understood. Her brother had a fair knowledge of Greek, he knew, from the books he had seen him reading at times, but whether she could read it for herself or only knew as much as this young devil liked to tell her, he was uncertain.

During the past weeks Chrysanthe had avoided him, only speaking to him when they met at meals, and then to escape her brother's remarks. Sinclair felt he had erred beyond forgiveness, and "The Babe's" promise of freedom brought only a sense of relief. Long after his host left, he sat thinking over the past five months—from the first time he had seen Chrysanthe, that brilliant afternoon in the Mersey, when she came up the gangway in her brother's name and place, right down to now in this gloomy African gorge. He thought of the first sunset. A deep red ray had come out of the sky and joined them! Before the next she would be lost to him forever.

CHAPTER 17

"All is over! This is death!"

THE TROPICAL AFTERNOON was slowly waning; over everything was a still, oppressive heat—the sleepy calm that comes after the broiling midday hours. Nothing moved except a few faint specks high up in the heavens, like tiny black marks against the deep blue sky. They appeared in ones and twos from every direction, all making for the same point. There was no hurry about them; they flapped along on untidy ruffled wings, with repulsive, featherless, raw-looking necks outstretched, and eyes fixed on something far below in the gorge. The time had not yet arrived, for, on reaching the ravine, they perched clumsily on jutting rocks or the branches of some stunted tree and waited—a horde of Nature's undertakers. A few, evidently young hands at the game, swooped down into the chasm, which at this point had a fertile look that had not been at the point where the expedition camped the previous evening. There was an impatience about this younger generation of vultures not noticeable in their elders. They circled into the gully with harsh cries, then up again a little way, and, finally, down towards a cluster of palms that grew round the stream; there they sat and preened their feathers with vicious hooked beaks, wondering how long before the thing standing beneath, bound to a battered stone image grown about with and almost hidden by trailing white passion-flowers, could be attacked with impunity. It was a long time since anything of the sort had been seen in the carved jaws of the flower-decked monster; a long time since they had come in at the death, and feasted on the body after the blood had washed the altar! So long that it had become a matter of tradition, yet they had always hovered round the gorge through an instinct that had come down to them. Now there was something alive in the place again!

With harsh, discordant cries the crowd of draggled-looking scavengers sat round and told a garbled tale to one another, based on the ancient rites of the ruined altar beneath. There was considerable difference of opinion among them, and some inclination to quarrel as to which version was the correct one. Finally, the most bald-headed and hideous old bird, whose strident voice was listened to with deference, was appealed to. He said this was not the ancient custom. The thing standing there now, bound and helpless, was a man: in the lost days, so said tradition, it was a girl. Maybe the tale had drifted through wrongly, in any case it did not matter, the taste was much the same! Here the old ghoul stretched his shabby, well-worn wings, and flapped farther down into the gorge to get a better view of the coming feast.

As the afternoon wore on, the one who stood bound against the battered stone monster turned dreary eyes towards the departing sun. This was the promised freedom! To stay helpless against this ghastly rock, unable to move hand or foot, till thirst, the knowledge of his own lingering, awful end, and the swarm of vicious insects buzzing round and crawling over his bare flesh, brought madness, then, when weakness overtook him, the horde of carrion birds hovering round would come and tear him piecemeal, alive. He had been there barely three hours; yet the heat had dried his tongue, and already the sound of the cool stream so close at hand was beginning to torture him. A dew would come up with the night; that would ease him for a time, and make him able to endure longer agonies. How long would he last?

For once Sinclair cursed his own great strength and iron constitution. He might linger for a week! A week of hell's tortures! "The Babe" had mocked him with it as his servants bound him, and had fixed him so that the sun only reached him in the waning afternoon, after its maddening midday heat was spent. It came with just enough force to bring an awful thirst whilst the ripple of the stream was in his ears; not enough to take reason, for the first day or two, as, soon after, came the heavy night dew, with sufficient moisture to keep him alive for a time. And his little girl thought he was free! She had talked to him for a few minutes before saying "good-bye" and her hand had rested for a moment in his.

After a midday halt, Chrysanthe had gone on alone with the caravan, leaving Sinclair with her brother and a trio of negroes. "The Babe" had sent her on, promising to see his guest safely back to the path by which they had descended the previous evening. Three porters were to go with him, with a supply of stores, so as to give him a chance of getting in touch with his own men again. This had been one of Chrysanthe's stipulations. Sinclair had overheard her, only a few days before, asking her brother to do it, and he had agreed heartily. Even then this end had been planned, for "The Babe" mocked him with it before setting off to join his sister. Shortly after Chrysanthe left, the negroes had overpowered and bound Sinclair to the old stone altar, at "The Babe's" command; then they were told to put the stores where his guest could see them in case he should get hungry. When the instructions were carried out, the youngster shot the men before they had time to resist or realize, and dragged the bodies into the stream, where they quickly drifted away down the gorge. Then he sat down and talked to Sinclair for some time; said he regretted having to kill three of his best porters, but he could not have explained their presence to his sister had he returned with them; and, after bidding his late guest an affectionate farewell, left him to slow starvation.

As "The Babe" disappeared round a bend in the gorge, to follow up the ravine leisurely to where his sister would be camping, not more than five miles away, the first vulture came like a black speck in the sky.

Sinclair's gaze was on the sun as it left the gully: then his eyes went to the carrion birds that watched him speculatively. Around him buzzed a swarm of biting flies, that settled on his face, crawled about his neck, and on to his chest the open shirt left exposed. Loathsome winged things, with sticky legs, got caught in his hair and buzzed angrily. Now and then a sharp bite came as a relief from the torturing host of tiny clammy legs that crept about him. Sometimes, by moving his head a little, a friendly leaf could be persuaded to flick off an almost unendurable insect. As the twilight thickened, this agonizing horde left him. Huge bats came flitting up and down the gloomy gorge, circling under the drooping palms till their wings rustled the leaves around him; big horned beetles butted against him in blind clumsiness; bloated night moths with fat, repulsive bodies settled on him for a moment, then off again with a quick flutter. The flower-wreathed stone glittered with a hundred tiny moving silver lamps as the fireflies danced about the trailing creepers. A white mist rolled up the gully, and its heavy dampness eased his parched throat. The shadows deepened till the trees stood like an array of phantoms. The night was full of strange whisperings—the wash of the deep stream close at hand, the sudden rustle of one of the carrion tribe roosting round, the rush and rattle of a loose stone falling into the depths, and, wafted down from the forest above, came the faint moaning howl of a leopard.

Slowly the moon came up, a great ball of light in the deep purple sky; the silver stars vanished, one by one, as the white flood swept them into the black vault beyond. The molten orb soared higher, and stray rays reached down into the wild valley. They washed round the grove of palms, silvered the swift-running stream, turned the flowers on the altar a transparent ghostly whiteness and put out the tiny moving lamps. The weird chasm lay stretched out in black and white, a study in deep shadows and pools of moonlight, a picture in indigo and silver. Strange shapes flitted and moved as a warm breeze came sobbing down the gorge, stirring the drowsy palms and the distorted trees growing on the sides. The movement roused one of the roosting ghouls; great wings flapped clumsily, and, with a sleepy, discordant cry, it flew farther into the valley— a gaunt hell bird in the flood of silver. A spray of white passion-flowers streamed out as the wind came moaning round the ruined altar; it touched Sinclair's haggard face with gentle, sympathetic fingers. He gazed at the scene drearily. How many nights would his eyes rest on this weird, beautiful picture before madness brought relief, or death came and ended all tortures? Alone in this unknown chasm, where no soul had been for the past three hundred years, until the last Claude Devereux led his party into it!

Something stirred in a crack of the broken altar close to his arm. The noise of tiny pebbles falling roused him. He turned his head a little, and watched as a centipede crept out of a crevice. It waited, with antennae waving backwards and forwards, uncertain which way to go. Sinclair envied the long-dead Philip Devereux. At least he had been free to pick up the brute! He watched it eagerly, praying that it would crawl on him—on his face or neck, the only part he could move, so that he could knock it against the stone and let its poison end his life too—end it before the daylight brought back the vile horde of torturing flies. He glanced up at the moon. He had been tied up barely eight hours! Eight ghastly, torturing centuries! He was strong enough to stand a hundred!

A hoarse laugh rang through the gorge, echoed from side to side, resounded up and down the cliffs—the place seemed convulsed in an ecstasy of wild mirth—and finally died away as the wind swept it onward. Sinclair stood listening to the commotion he had caused and the stealthy whispers his own ghastly end brought to his brain. He looked again for the deadly insect, but the noise had evidently frightened it away, he could see nothing of it. His little girl was sleeping, not more than five miles away, and he could not keep her from the awful army of those brutes that might be waiting for her! Could not save her from that ghastly end! She might have said she could handle them, just to screen her brother! How she loved that fiend! There was no one, only Claude! Her twin! The devil's own offspring.

A light touch, like a hair wafted across his hand, made him glance down to see the antennae of the purblind, legged worm playing across his fingers. It paused hesitatingly, undecided whether to come on him or continue its journey up the rock. A shiver ran through him as it crawled on to his hand. Forty poisonous little legs, like so many red-hot pins, moved slowly across his bare flesh and on to his shirt sleeve. He watched it breathlessly, with a shuddering eagerness, praying that it would come up to his neck, when a quick movement would mean those pincer-like death-dealing jaws and forty hooked legs, embedded deep in his flesh. A ghastly enough death, but heaven compared to the hours of hideous torture confronting him! The thing paused halfway up his bound arm, took a quick turn and crawled across on to his chest. It stopped about six inches below his neck; curled itself into an ill-shaped S and stayed there, just on his heart. The great muscles heaved, and the tight ropes cut deeper into his flesh, as he tried to move sufficiently to scare the motionless insect and make it attack him. "The Babe's" men had done their work well: much as he strained, he could scarcely move in the network that bound him. For some time he gazed at the creature, with hopeless eyes. Quick death lay there, and he could not reach it! Little white hands had warmed the long-dead pirate's heart! This thing slept on his! Soft small hands like the ones he had seen so often flutter round that young devil with such gentle tenderness. Baby hands with a touch that thrilled him as nothing else had ever done. This vile creature lay on his heart, yet it would not touch him! Just stayed and mocked him! Mocked him as Fate had done since the time he swore to have that villain! Mocked him and showed him life's dearest treasures, that lay just beyond his reach!

Haggard eyes watched as a greater flood of light filled the valley. The wind swept along with a ringing sound, like a sudden peal of wild bells, and died away almost before it reached him. What strange tricks the moon plays, casting shadows like white shapes flitting in and out of the boulders! One, a mist-wreathed little form in a cloudy robe of silver, had just crossed the bend in the gorge, and was swallowed up at once in the deep black shadows. What was that coming through the palms? Strained eyes watched it. She was in the grove before him, and he could not get there! Not till this devil's agent brought death, so that he could cross the silver stream and reach her! She was waiting there under the drooping palms, and only life divided them! His life! And this vile insect would not kill him and let him go to her! If he called, would she hear him?—right across the great black flood that rolls between earth and heaven!

"Chrysanthe!"

The misty shadow stopped abruptly as the hoarse, strained voice wafted across the stream. White rays gleamed on a great red ring as a hand went slowly to a slender throat. The moonlight flickered on a glistening yellow ornament circling a slim bare arm, and on a girdle of blood-red stones, like wet drops, round a girlish waist. The soft breeze fluttered the gleaming robe, and it swept round her like a veil of moonlight. Chrysanthe as she had crept out alone and unattended from her brother's sleeping camp, down to this ruined altar to ask a long-forgotten god that one whose life was dear to her might return safely to his people. No one knew she had gone, for all moonlight excursions had been forbidden. Only Grip came with her.

A low pleased whine, and a warm scrubby tongue licking his hand, made Sinclair start with a violence that roused the sleeping insect. It crawled an inch or so higher, and its antennae waved with a spiteful viciousness. He glanced down to see a tawny beast looking at him anxiously, and a cold friendly nose vainly tried to snuggle into his bound hand. In a dazed way his eyes went back to the shimmering slender figure that flitted lightly from boulder to boulder across the stream, and came with a quick nervousness up the broken flagged way leading to the altar. A small face looked back at him with wide, unbelieving eyes. The wind stirred the white blossoms, a shower of petals blew down, touching the wistful, quivering mouth, and lingering for a moment in the soft chestnut curls. A frightened gasp broke from her lips as her eyes fell on the insect that waited, in stiff expectation, on the strong, heaving chest. A trembling hand laid on his heart roused Sinclair.

"Chrysanthe, darling, don't touch it! Don't touch it, little girl!"

The hoarse whisper echoed round the listening altar with a world of hopeless love. The shivering morsel struck a chill of awful fear to his heart. She was going to entice the insect on herself, as she had done once before! But the hand stayed where it was as she talked to the loathsome thing with low crooning voice.

The creature raised its head and listened as the soft murmur went on, then turned its vile length slowly and crept towards her hand.

"Good God! Don't do it, darling!"

The harsh, broken cry came out in an agony of feeling, as Sinclair watched the deadly insect crawl towards her. Then he gazed with helpless, agonized eyes. A little gasp reached him at the first touch of the centipede. The other small hand came and clutched one of his bound arms, with a tight frightened grip, as it crept slowly on to her fingers, then up and coiled round her wrist— an awful, poisoned devil's bracelet! Chrysanthe looked at him in helpless terror and back to the living, writhing bangle. She moved a few steps, still watching the thing on her wrist. There was a movement of breathless silence. Each tree stayed stiff, with an air of dread expectation. Grip whined with an uncanny note of fear. The red ring flashed in the moonlight, and the great ruby seemed to break up and wash the shaking hand with a stream of blood that reached up to the squirming bracelet. A wild wind came tearing down the gorge, screeching up and down the cliffs. Not a tree or leaf moved as the shrieking Terror rushed along with an Arctic chill, and, as it swept past them, Sinclair seemed to hear a fiend's voice call "Chrysanthe!" The waiting insect uncoiled, fell from the slender wrist and was lost among the surrounding greenery.

The mad gust died away as suddenly as it came. There was nothing—only the palms drooping in the still, warm night air, the silver stream rippling among them, a slim girl standing, like a ray of moonlight, who watched the battered image of a forgotten heathen god, with terror-stricken eyes, and a man bound and helpless, whose strong face had whitened under its tan, for that fiend's voice seemed to have been in his ears before!

A short pleased bark, and a cold nose on her arm, aroused Chrysanthe. She went to Sinclair's side. He watched as she struggled with the tight ropes. It was very slow work for small fingers, and the bent curly head was a whirl of agonizing thoughts as she wrestled with the stiff, hard knots. Who had done this thing? Not Claude! He would not have done a dreadful thing like this! Would not have left Major Sinclair to this terrible death! It must have been the porters. They were three of the Essuata Town lot; and may have had a grudge against him because of that affair, set on him unexpectedly, after Claude left, brought him back here and left him to die. Claude could not have done it, it was too horrible!

The moonlight glinted on tear-filled eyes as the little fingers, sore and almost bleeding with the hardness of their task, attacked the knots that bound Sinclair's shoulders. So far he had seen nothing but the bent curly head, which had been kept lowered as she worked away at the ropes. Now the position of her task brought her face into view. It was very shamed and white with a world of awful dread. Much as Chrysanthe tried to persuade herself the porters were responsible for Sinclair's present position, there was a pressing, growing fear it might have been her brother. He watched her in stunned silence. It was some wild dream like all the dreams he dreamt of this little girl! He would wake up soon, stiff and cramped, tight bound against the rock, with nothing but the moon shadows flitting round him and a gaunt, hideous vulture soaring high up in the soft white light. Gradually the ropes loosened.

"Will . . . will you unfasten the other knots, Major Sinclair? I don't think I can do any more."

The faltering voice awoke him to the fact his arms were free but too cramped and numb to be of much use to him. Gentle hands rubbed them till life and feeling came back with a painful, tingling rush. With stiff fingers he attacked the mesh. Chrysanthe watched him for a moment, then drifted down to the stream. Sinclair worked with feverish impatience. He must get loose and join the moonbeam before she melted away. Must take her back to England! Away from this devil-haunted land!

A step made Chrysanthe turn. Her hand was laid on Sinclair's arm with quick anxiety.

"You must start back now, at once. Try and find your own men again. Pick out the most useful of the stores. Follow the stream down the gorge till it takes a big twist like a double S. The way up is there. I . . . I hope you'll get back safely."

He drew the quivering moonbeam close against him, and held it with a loving tenderness.

"Will you come back with me, Chrysanthe? Come back and be my little wife. I've loved you always, darling, will you try and love me too? Can you forgive and love your worst enemy, who has done nothing but hurt and love you?"

Beneath Sinclair's gentle hold a wild bird's heart was thumping.

"You mustn't stay here. You must start right back at once before anyone comes and finds you," a scared voice gasped.

"If anyone came and found me, what then, darling?"

"They might—kill you. Please go. Do go!"—the anxious little face was almost hidden by another that bent over it, watching it with a great gentleness.

"And if they did, would you mind, Chrysanthe?"

There was no reply, only a frightened heart beating against his. Sinclair held his wild bird close against him and kissed the soft dark curls.

"Say you will come back with me, darling."

Small hands endeavored to loose the careful strong ones, but it was no use; so they stayed, and instead nervous fingers tried to span round a sinewy brown wrist, but at their biggest stretch there was fully two inches of uncovered brown between the small thumb and the longest of the slim fingers.

"Well, darling, what are you going to tell me?"

The fingers stopped their measuring. A wistful face looked up at him with sad, tear-filled eyes. A soft wind caught the moonbeam dress, and it fluttered round him like a cloud.

"Major Sinclair, if I asked you to let Claude off—asked you very much and promised to do and be all you wished, what would you say?"

A cold flood came suddenly over him, sweeping away all the unspeakable happiness of having this trembling little girl in his arms. Only an awful, gnawing heartache was left. He had forgotten that devil's son!

"Chrysanthe, darling, don't!"

There was a low, sad laugh, like a ripple of the stream close by.

"I'm not going to ask you—dear. I want you to do the right thing. To stay just like you are. Quite different from anybody I've ever known. But you mustn't ask me either, for I must stay with Claude. Now will you stoop down a bit, you're so big I can't reach and—I want to kiss you just this once and say 'good-bye.'"

For a moment a quivering mouth rested on his. Then Sinclair was kneeling by the moonbeam, with arms round the girlish waist and his face buried on the misty silver cloud.

"Chrysanthe, don't make me go back alone. Claude can go free if only you will come with me."

Trembling hands smoothed the bowed head.

"You mustn't talk like this, dear. You mustn't forget your duty. By-and-by you'd think of it, when you got back among your own people, with your own sort. I want you to do the right thing. I couldn't love you if you didn't, and I couldn't be your—wife if you took Claude," slim arms crept round the bent neck. "Say you will go back alone, and do just the same as if you hadn't known me. It's the first thing I'm asking you to do, dear, don't refuse me."

There was silence for a moment, then a broken voice, said, "Chrysanthe, little angel, I'll do just what you wish."

"I want you to kiss me again, dear. To hold me in your arms just a minute. I always feel so safe there. Then you must start straight away back, not even come one little step with me."

Sinclair's arms shook as he lifted the moonbeam. A sad small face lay against his shoulder, watching him with big loving eyes.

"Will you take me across the stream, into the grove on the other side. Then you must put me down, dear, go back and forget you ever knew me. For it's always war between my sort and yours, but we'll make a truce just for this minute."

Presently Sinclair stood alone. There was nothing to prove it had been but a dream, except his own loose limbs and the scattered ropes around the altar.

CHAPTER 18

"I crawl'd safe into the cave—
All silent—
All dark as the grave."

A FLASH OF FORKED LIGHTNING suddenly lit up the pitch-dark night. It played round a rugged peak and on a vast black column of rock, which stood like a giant finger against the lowering sky. The lurid fire gleamed on the lake surrounding it—a stagnant sheet of muddy water with a curious red tinge, stretching to a circle of low hills about half-a-mile away. Not a thing grew on the weird pile in the middle. Nothing moved, except a thick stream oozing from a gash just below the giant finger. There was no sound beyond the heavy splash of the reddened muddy water dripping into the circling waste. As the vivid flash lit up the sky the uncouth pile cast a shadow, like a colossal hand, and a menacing forefinger was laid on a tent away on the low surrounding shore. Only for a moment. Afterwards there was nothing but total blackness, and a pale yellow flicker on the farthermost edge of the lake. This light did not penetrate very far; not far enough to reach the ghostly mass in the center of the stagnant waste. It cast dense shadows on the water close at hand, and danced in and out of the grotesque, poisonous cacti growing among the sand and rocks. One or two gaunt, blasted trees stood like hell's sentinels over the weatherworn tent, and, nearer the fire, low, stunted shrubs, grown with orange and grey lichen, formed some slight cover for a good score of sleeping negroes. Three others were on guard round the camp, and beyond, seated on a boulder, gazing across the shrouded lake, and waiting for every lurid flash that lit up the uncanny pile, was their leader. His was a haggard, worn face, with a hopeless misery in the keen, watching eyes. At last he had reached the devil's hand! What had happened in there? Was the wild old tragedy finished?

A low sigh came over the black water. There was a slow oily movement, and the whole of the lake heaved as if a great creature were crawling beneath it. Another flash came out of the heavens. It lit up the cut below the giant finger, and Sinclair saw a sudden stream of thick heavy matter gush from the wound. What had Philip Devereux seen? Tomorrow he would know. He would go into the hidden temple—probe its secret—find out if his little girl had been there! Nearly four months since that misty dream thing had come to him in the gorge—come and gone before he could realize it was a little girl and not a moonbeam. He had held and kissed her, then she had slipped away from him, back to dreamland. There was no girl-babe at all. Only a misty silver shadow that melted into moonlight. He ought to have taken her back with him, but he had been too dazed to do anything but just what the strange small moonbeam told him.

Sinclair sat thinking over the past dreary months, from the time that seemed like a sweet wild dream, when Chrysanthe saved him from the end her brother had planned, until now, when, only two hours previously, he had reached the peak which had been their destination. It was nearly six weeks before he succeeded in finding his own men. Since his disappearance the Hausas had remained at the same place, according to instructions he had given his headman, in case of such a contingency. He learnt from his sergeant that, the day after his capture, Langfeldt and the guide had come back, but left again immediately, and nothing more had been heard of them. Sinclair allowed himself no rest, but, the morning after his return, was on "The Babe's" trail, and less than a month afterwards camped by the altar in the gorge where he had so nearly met his death. Then followed a long dreary time as, slowly, he worked his way up to the mountain. The trail of those ahead was completely obliterated and he had only his own knowledge to guide him. For a full week he had skirted the miles of quaking bog and dense matted forest surrounding the mystic peak. A block of rock, with a rudely carved χ on it, had given him the clue. From point to point he had followed the letter until the whole word χ-ρ-ι-σ-α-ν-θ-η brought him through the dark swampy waste to the circle of hills. The beautiful plain the old document mentioned, no longer lay beneath. Instead was a weird, volcanic lake—the sea of blood he had once heard Chrysanthe speak of—and in the middle a black rocky hand rose menacingly. There was no trace of "The Babe's" party. In the short twilight, whilst the camp settled for the night, he had searched round but seen nothing. He pondered over it all as he sat gazing over the darkened lake. Had they been and gone?

A heavy flop in the water close at hand made him start with a nervousness unusual to him. He peered into the murky gloom and waited. A wide, sullen ripple came within the area of the firelight. Something was washed up a few feet from him—a little gleaming yellow thing. His hand shook as he stooped to pick it up, so much so that the tiny bells whispered like fairy voices. A bangle of golden flowers! Part of a wreath of bell blossoms he had once seen round Chrysanthe's wrist! What was it doing there cast up from the ghastly depths? He held the trinket with shaking hands. Was Chrysanthe in there? What was the secret of that clenched hand? Did some unknown Horror lie within its depths?—some thing that had taken his little girl? What a hideous, impossible yarn it was— yet so much of it true! What would to-morrow show him? Would he find her there?

Sinclair got up from his dreary musings, and stood twisting the broken bangle in and out of his fingers with a careful loving touch. How the sweet tiny, voices mocked him—just as they did the night she was snatched from the veranda! What ghastly Horror held her now? His little girl! The daughter of a long-dead priestess who had served in this buried temple. A little thing draped in a mist of blood and gold, with a hideous monster coiled about her. A dream child in a silver cloud, with a red girdle round her waist where dripping bloody jaws had held her. Something that always slipped from him.

For a time he stayed peering across the lake. An eerie silence was over the hidden peak. No further flash of lightning came out of the pitch-black sky. Nothing! Only Chrysanthe's bangle in his hand to tell him she had been there.

Sinclair went back to his tent, and before retiring filled several empty shells with an explosive compound, then he lay down waiting for the daylight. Before the sun rose he was about superintending the unpacking and fitting together of the one collapsible boat his baggage boasted, and stocking it for his solitary journey across to the cavern. When the light came up from the east, the giant hand grew from a threatening shadow to a glowing mass of vivid red. He studied the peak in the growing light. The stagnant water reached nearly up to the opening of the cavern—another slit, on the side remote from the gash by the giant pointing finger. The old manuscript had been truthful again! There were still about half-a-dozen rough-hewn steps between the sullen water and the deep black entrance. The volcanic flood covered the others and the rocky gates mentioned. How much more of the wild old yarn was true?

There was a curious feeling about Sinclair as he rowed across to the waiting hand—hardly fear, but an awful dread of what might be within. On reaching the steps he tied the boat securely to a rock, examined his revolver carefully—not that it would be much use against the devil's army waiting there—then took some torches and a small packet from the boat, and went up the steps to the entrance. Here he paused, conscious of a sudden cold feeling, for out of the screened black depths came a long-drawn sigh, like a vast creature slowly waking! He noticed his hands were shaking as he drew a torch from the bundle. For a moment he hesitated, then, taking a broken bangle from his pocket, pressed his lips against it. His little girl had been in there. He would find out what had happened to her if it meant going into hell!

His eyes went to the rising sun, and he watched it as it hung, like a crimson ball, over a sea of distant green forest. Would he ever see it again? A broad powerful back was turned on it deliberately, and he entered. After going a few steps, he paused and lit a torch. The light flickered on the damp rugged sides of a narrow

passage, hardly wide enough for two people to go abreast. Stalac-
tites hung from the roof. A myriad of bats swarmed in the place,
fluttering round him like a host of hobgoblins. The torch cast uncouth shadows, and wild shapes danced in the semidarkness just
ahead of him. A heavy drop of water; coming unexpectedly on his
hand, made him start with such violence that the torch fell. The
light went out and he stood in utter darkness. He groped round
trying to find it, and a cold clammy body slid over his hand. He
shuddered, drew back quickly, and his foot struck against something that rolled along with a curious sound, like a hollow wooden
ball. The same awful heaving sigh came wafted from the depths
beyond. His hands shook to such an extent he could hardly light
another torch. He looked for the thing he had kicked. A bleached
skull stared back at him, and out of one of the vacant orbits, a centipede crawled! how many waited for him? He examined the bony
relic carefully. It was no negro's skull but a European's! One of the
ten who had entered to look for treasure when the first Claude
Devereux raided the buried plain and stole the first Chrysanthe!
He looked a little farther. A heap of white bones met his view, a
sword rusted down to the hilt, and a heavy clumsy pistol of the
period. He picked the latter up, curious to see whether this ancient buccaneer had died fighting against a devil's horde. There
was no bullet in it, nor round the scattered skeleton. The long-
dead treasure-seeker had fired his last shot into the multitude chas-
ing him, before he fell poisoned by the ones swarming over him!
Sinclair shivered. Who would be the next in this ghastly place? Who
would find his bones, and mark his race and period by bleached
skull and empty firearm?

A sudden shriek of mad laughter came tearing down the
shrouded passage. Sinclair's hand went to his revolver and he stood
waiting for—he knew not what! The torch flickered wildly and all
but went out as it swept by. What a fool he was! It was only a gust
of wind howling down some hidden hole in the hill. Reading the
old manuscript had made him as nervous as a girl.

Pulling himself together, he continued his journey along the
eerie passage. One by one he passed the round white balls, to the

number of half-a-score. It had a weird fascination for him to count
these skulls. Every step was further proof of the truth of the wild
old yarn. On reaching the tenth he paused. There the passage widened considerably and a faint distant whispering sound reached
him. Whatever it was had killed the followers of the long-dead
Claude Devereux waited for him in the depths beyond. There was
proof that one of the pirates had reached as far as this. A scrap of
white lying just ahead, brought into view by a sudden flare of the
torch, attracted his attention. He went forward quickly and picked
it up. It was a handkerchief, with an ominous dull red stain over
more than half of it, knotted as if it had been tied hastily round a
wound. On it were the initials C. W. Which had dropped it, Claude
or Chrysanthe? It was a medium-sized piece of hemstitched linen,
such as either might have had. How came that mark on it? Sinclair
stood holding the bloodstained handkerchief till the torch burnt
down and scorched his fingers.

A long-drawn moaning sigh came echoing down the widening
tunnel. As it died away, a faint scratching sound reached him, like
a myriad of tiny feet rushing over pebbles. He stuck the torch into
a crevice of the rock and waited. How long before the devil's army
reached him? Keen, strained eyes peered into the flickering shadows, as he stood, with drawn revolver in one hand, and an explosive shell in the other—the first thing to hurl into the advancing
horde. He would send many a hundred back to the fiend who made
them, before they settled him! The distant noise died away. Only
silence and a darkness deeper than the grave!

He waited a little longer, then lit another torch and threw it as
far as he could into the depths ahead. His eyes followed the light
with an awful anxiety. It struck the ground, flared up for a moment and then went out. Nothing, only damp walls gleaming red
in the sudden blaze. Not a sign of the devil's herd! Not a sound
from the waiting hell beyond!

Sinclair drew his torch from the crevice and proceeded. For fully
ten minutes he went along, until the passage widened and stretched
away beyond the lighted area. A great broken sob came out of
the darkness, and the whispering, scratching rush he had heard

before, but much closer. He was conscious of his flesh creeping as he paused and waited till the scrambling, rushing army came within sight. It died away with a long-drawn sigh, and a feeble lapping sound reached him. He lighted another torch and threw it into the depths beyond. A vast red sheet lay ahead. A splash and darkness! He went quickly forward, and paused at the edge of a subterranean lake. There was nothing, only the great black cave, and a sullen, silent sheet of water. What secret lay beneath? What tragedy had this red flood swept away?

He skirted round the water until a wall of rock stopped further progress. Out of the darkness came the same sighing moan; the lake heaved as if some vast Horror were writhing beneath it; there was a dull heavy splash, and a great red ripple swept towards him. He waited breathlessly. What hideous monster was swimming behind the advancing wave? Nothing. Only the whispering rush of scaly feet as the water moved the tiny pebbles scattered around the edge. He turned and skirted the lake until a further wall stopped him. A narrow shelf, a foot or so above the water, ran along the rock, stretching away till darkness swallowed it. He climbed along this carefully, shuddering when his hand touched slimy, sticky things on the side. A large piece of rock, that he had stumbled over, fell with a dull heavy thud into the water—there was no sound of it reaching the bottom! For some time he went along the ledge, then it turned an abrupt corner. Even greater depths beyond! He paused, lit a floating light, and pushed it out on to the lake. For a moment it stayed just where it was, then some unseen current caught it and took it round in a gigantic circle, till it looked like a tiny pinprick of yellow in the black distance. It grew bigger and came back to him, but on an inner ring; round again, not in such a big sweep but quicker. He watched it, fascinated, as it swept round and round with an ever-increasing velocity and an ever-lessening ring, and finally was sucked down an awful whirlpool's throat. That would happen to him if he slipped from his narrow perch into the water.

A sudden stifled rumble, coming as it were from the bowels of the earth, made his fingers stiffen round the torch. Good God! What was going to happen now? The noise grew and increased like a roar of fiendish laughter, till the very hill shook and the path he stood on trembled. Something shot up out of the darkness, with the sudden rush and whirl of a monster darting serpent. What, he could not see, for a wet flood swept over him, extinguishing the torch. With both hands he gripped on to the jagged rocky wall, waiting for the end. The thing dived down again with a great broken sob. The thick muddy waters of the lake heaved in wild waves, reaching nearly to his middle. The darkness was so intense he could see nothing, only feel the thick warm water washing round him, like a sea of blood. How long he held on there he did not know. When the mad flood subsided, he lit another torch, and groped his way back to the edge of the lake. Then stood frozen! The light gleamed on something thrown up by the last volcanic outburst, flickered and played on a white, dead face, on a mop of dripping chestnut curls, on slim hands clenched in awful agony, on a slight form lying there cast out from the nethermost hell! Claude or Chrysanthe? The clothing was nothing to go by. He knelt by the limp, khaki-clad figure, and his hands shook as he examined the body. "The Babe!" Then he drew back in sudden ghastly fear. Under the boy's arms was a great round hole as if a sharp metal bat had been thrust through his body—WHERE SOME HIDDEN, WAITING HORROR HAD SEIZED HIM WITH GIGANTIC, PINCER-LIKE JAWS!

Like one stunned, Sinclair knelt gazing at the dead agonized face. What lived beneath this fearsome lake? What monster beyond all comprehension had taken the last Claude Devereux to the hell he deserved?

A glint of gold in the clenched hand took his attention. He opened it carefully. A spray of crushed golden flowers, broken in the death agony! The missing part of the whispering bangle that had been cast up at his feet! Where was his little girl?

"Chrysanthe!"

Sinclair's grief-stricken voice rang through the vast cavern.

"Chrysanthe!" the echoes called to him with a wailing moan. He stood listening till the sound died away in a broken-hearted sob. There was nothing, only eerie darkness, and the corpse at his feet. That hidden Horror had given him the man he had sworn to have alive or dead. Given him "The Babe" and kept Chrysanthe.

For hours Sinclair searched round the gloomy cavern, following the narrow ledge to the far side of the lake. No sign of his little girl. All ghastly, whispering silence, broken by an occasional sigh or rumble. She had been with her brother when the Horror seized him, the broken bangle proved that. Where was she now?

He groped his way back round the lake to where the dead boy lay. Very carefully he picked up the limp body. His little girl had loved this youngster, yet her love had not saved him. There was nothing he could do, only go back—his mission was completed with "The Babe's" death or capture.

The sun was setting into a mist of gold when Sinclair again reached daylight. He put his burden into the boat, and rowed across to the far shore. Before darkness fell, the last Claude Devereux was laid to rest in a narrow sand bed on the circle of wild hills where, centuries before, his ancestor had camped when he came to raid the temple of Asquielba. Inside a tent, near at hand, Sinclair sat gazing at a broken bangle and a battered sweet in silver paper. All left to him of Chrysanthe!

CHAPTER 19

"All silent—they are dumb, and the breezes go and come
With an apathy that mocks at man's distress."

SOMETHING UNUSUAL WAS HAPPENING in the gorge—in the palm-grove by the old stone god. The black carrion specks, high up in the sky, watched with glad expectancy. There was a good time coming for them! But it was not safe to venture down till all noise and smoke had died away completely, and things were quiet again. The fight had been going on since noonday and now it was past sunset. It was a very one-sided affair. Two to one, and the weak side had fought like demons, and were still fighting, though only a handful were left. Fighting like fury round something lying on the altar stone—something quite different from anything in the wild, jumbled crowd. The losing side had been waiting for the nightfall; that was plain to see by the way the giant leader had glanced occasionally skywards. Waiting to rush through the attacking force and make off, down the darkening valley, with the limp thing they were quarrelling over. What a fuss to make over a half-dead body. Much better to let it stay where it was, and they could finish it off when all was quiet again!

The vultures swooped a little lower and watched excitedly. Would or would not the twelve get through? They were going to try now, for the biggest of the men had picked up the limp thing, and the others formed a square round him. The audience held their breath. Was there ever such a man-killing scrimmage! Yes, they were through, only six though! Through, and running with the swiftness of wings down the darkening glen—running with sixty after them! There was no chance for them! They never had a chance! The other lot came on them unexpectedly. No, they are not going to give up hope yet. The five are going to make a last desperate stand, so that the giant can get a good start with the dead-looking burden he carries. Five to sixty! Long odds! But there are ten dead before they die! One to fifty! He does not pause, but flies straight on, with the crowd some way behind him. He may do it yet, he has a good start!

"I say, that's not fair!"—a hundred vultures chorus disapprovingly, for a man in European dress kneels and takes careful aim at the flying negro. Hits him, too, for he drops the thing he is carrying, falls backwards into the stream, and the waters rush along with him down the gorge.

An army of interested spectators swoop lower, anxious to see what will happen to the limp thing lying there by the stream, that all this fuss has been about. Most of the crowd rush on and swarm around it with a mad, blood-curdling howl which made the winged watchers dart up again. One of the swarming horde, their leader, picks it up and holds it high above his head. There was a dead silence. The audience swoop down again. Only for a moment, and then a great mocking yell reached up to the heavens, with such a note of awful menace in it that the vultures shivered as they watched eagerly, wondering what would happen next. It took all this howling mockery to make the limp thing open its eyes! Why don't they kill it instead of standing round it raving like an army of maniacs? The big man in European dress, who shot the giant, seems to think so, too, for he comes and speaks to them. How they laugh! A hideous yell of devil's mirth! His face whitens, and he looks towards where his men are. Only a handful of them against an army of shrieking fiends! He speaks again and an ominous silence falls on the raving mass.

The vultures fly down, with their raw heads on one side and their keen ears strained—curious to hear what is said. Something about a bargain! They let him finish, then the same howling laugh!

He runs quickly back to his men, thirty-seven fiends after him! Their leader stays with the limp thing on his shoulder, laughing. It is moaning now and he is talking to it, watching it with an evil smile and mad, fanatical eyes. Why are they fighting again? Fighting with the big European who had so lately been their ally—still fighting over the half-dead, moaning thing! There never had been such a feast as this!

Darkness closed round the valley; the winged spectators drew off with disappointed cries, and flew to roost farther down, beyond all noise. They would have liked to see the finish, see what really happened to the limp thing all this fighting had been about!

Before sunrise the carrion horde were again hovering over the palm-grove, looking into the gorge with sharp, hungry eyes. All silent! Only a lot of dead bodies scattered through the trees and around the altar. The dingy crowd of scavengers swooped down, and up a little way, then a farther drop, and back, not quite so far, until they were perfectly satisfied there was nothing to disturb them. Then they settled down to a comfortable meal, discussing meanwhile what had happened to the limp little thing; it looked a very dainty morsel, and nothing of it could be seen lying about. One, a sharp young bird, spied a light-colored object lying, nearly hidden, in the mass of broken vegetation behind the altar. It went clumsily across and pecked at it. A tawny beast, with dim, bloodshot eyes, snarled weakly, and kept its paws on something just beneath its nose. The enterprising and observant bird backed with haste, and flew to a remote corner of the battlefield where a trio of its sort were tearing away at a corpse.

When the sun went down the carrion horde were still feasting in the valley. During the night, whilst they slept around the festive board, a shadow crawled painfully down to the stream, stayed drinking for a time, then crept back to the altar, and lay there moaning. The next day high riot was held in the grove, and the next and the next; then a yellow beast limped down to the stream and snarled at the carrion crew, who took but little notice of it. They had seen it several times during the past few days, and it made no attempt to touch them unless they tried to sample the thing it always stayed against. As if they wanted that! It was not flesh and blood, with a nice ripe smell which gave piquancy to the appetite and encouraged the eater beyond the limits of discretion.

The following day the animal nosed round in weak hunger, looked at the putrefying, partially-eaten corpses with disgust, had another long drink, and crawled back to its precious charge. That night, whilst the vultures slept, it sneaked out stealthily ashamed of its mission, smelt one of the almost-demolished bodies hungrily, drew back with repulsion, then went and cried itself to sleep on its treasure. The next day a gaunt yellow beast quarreled with the vultures over the most meaty of the bones. A week after the fight the sun shone down on an array of clean-picked skeletons, and on a gorged horde sleeping round, who scarcely moved when a snarling brute limped among them, nosing round for a bone which it ate with the greatest repugnance.

Late that afternoon, a sound drifted down the valley, causing the less satiated of the carrion crew to open their eyes in alarm, flap clumsily along for a yard or two, then drop heavily to the ground and sleep again. The dog lifted its head, growled and held its treasure more firmly. Whatever was coming down the valley was not going to have that! As the noise grew, the brute listened intently. This was not an ordinary nigger train, they went along all out of step, with an uneven shuffle: these walked very differently, with a steady tramp, just like one man! Yes, he had heard the sound before, the day he had started on this ill-fated expedition, but the feet that walked as one had gone in another direction. He had seen their owner since though! The last time here, by this very place, when she who had worn this hat he held brought him out one night. The owner of the feet that walked as one had gone away down the gorge, and she had gone up, with a finger through his collar, crying all the time—crying till she hardly knew where she was going, and he had had to nose along very carefully, lest she should fall over any stones. Then he had crept quietly back into her kennel, and no one knew they had been out, no one knew what had happened. She never cried in the daylight, only at night when they were alone together. The dog's brow wrinkled perplexedly. She had not cried lately, not since she came alone from that water journey where she would not take him, much as he asked. She had just stayed all day looking straight in front of her, and knew no one, not even him!

The faint, distant tramp came nearer. A tail wagged feebly. Through the noise of the men who marched as one came a well-known footstep. Yes, this one might have the treasure! It should be taken to him! A gaunt yellow beast got up slowly and limped painfully through the grove and on towards the bend. Perhaps if this one coming found her, she might know people again!

As Sinclair swung round the corner, at the head of his Hausas, a gaunt yellow beast came limping towards him. He stopped abruptly, staring at it dazedly. In the dog's mouth was a floppy felt hat, with a blue gauze veil around it. The one he had so often seen Chrysanthe wear!

The treasure was laid at his feet with a pleased bark, and faithful eyes looked at him pleadingly. He picked it up with shaking hands, and turned it round and round, hardly conscious of what he did. What was it doing here? On the very spot where he had last seen her, as she flitted round the bend like a moonbeam! His little girl was drowned in the depths of that awful lake—in the ghastly peak more than two hundred miles away! He stooped by the dog's side with an arm round it and his haggard, working face hidden in its neck.

"Grip, what does it mean? Can't you tell me?"

The weak, pleased bark was very reassuring. The animal seized his hand, and tried to lead him towards the grove. He followed mechanically, then stood staring blankly at the ghastly sight—the clean-picked skeletons, the carrion horde sleeping round, the scattered baggage, and the trampled vegetation round the broken altar. Over all was silence; the palms drooped lazily in the afternoon sun, and the silver stream lapped softly by. What had happened here? Sinclair searched round, in white-faced anxiety. More than seventy corpses must have been there, piled three deep round the broken altar. Baggage was strewn all over the place, some "The Babe's," some Langfeldt's. What did it all mean? He opened one of the boxes. It was full of the dead youngster's things—the boy he had buried nearly a month ago! He looked through the others. Not a sign of anything belonging to Chrysanthe, except the battered hat Grip had brought to him! The dog watched him impatiently as he searched among the debris looking for a clue. Nothing, only a jumble of bones and the grey felt hat his little girl used to wear!

Grip seized the hat, and tried to draw him farther down the valley. He followed. The dog went limping on past the farthermost skeleton, beyond the battlefield, away from all scene of slaughter, into the quiet depths below. Sinclair gave up his command and obeyed the new leader. That night he camped five miles from the grove, and in his tent an almost dead animal lay. It had all but killed itself in trying to make him understand he must go on, and quickly. He knew now, for he had found signs of others who had stayed on this spot not more than a week ago. Those ahead had no tents, yet they had something with them they were taking care of for some reason. A shelter of branches had been fixed up, and on one of the sharp thorns was a scrap of blue drill. The dress that always went with the hat!

Sinclair sat by the dog's side coaxing pieces of soaked biscuit into his mouth, and talking to it the whole time. He knew Chrysanthe had escaped from the drowned temple within the peak. But to what fate? The returning party had fallen in with Mungea, and he was taking her down to the ruined temple where, centuries before, his ancestor had bargained for her life.

Only the vultures knew where Carl Langfeldt was!

CHAPTER 20

"A life like a shuttlecock may be toss'd,
With the hand of fate for a battledore."

THE NEARLY FULL MOON came up on the horizon, and soared slowly above the fringing trees, turning the black night into a soft shimmering whiteness and steeping the forest in a flood of silver. Ghostly fingers crept between the matted, overhanging vegetation on to a narrow track leading, like a broken thread, through the tangled waste. The bright rays touched a tiny lake, and turned it into a smooth, burnished mirror, barred and blurred by the shadows of the creepers and massive trunks around. By the pond the path widened a trifle, and the moonlight filtered on a score of black shapes sleeping, in dead fatigue, round a pile of baggage. The loud shrieks of a couple of bush-cats engaged in a death scrimmage nearby did not disturb them, nor did the sudden roar of a leopard, on the other side of the lake, that had come to drink, unconscious of the party close at hand. The brute skirmished round to within ten yards of the sleepers, then stood, stiff and motionless, with green eyes peering through the undergrowth at the easy victims lying about. A sudden movement startled it, and a stone came crashing down within a few inches of its head. It backed with a howl, and slunk away beyond the danger zone. The one who had caused this hasty retreat picked his way carefully over the sleepers to the outskirts of the ring, round and back to his seat, this sole guardian of the camp. A soft wind came soughing through the forest, bringing with it the distant, tortured sob of a tree-devil. Sinclair shivered. The dog sleeping at his side woke with a start, whined, then lifted its head, listening intently. He watched the animal for a moment, then glanced up between the tangled branches to where the moon shone bright and clear. The party ahead of him must have reached the temple by now. Would they kill her at once, or wait till the night of the full moon as the old custom demanded? She was alive when Mungea reached this spot, for the same shelter of branches had been erected. Thirty miles still between him and the place, and not twenty-four hours to cover the distance in! But he could do it.

It was barely a fortnight since Sinclair had left the grove, with the idea of reaching the ancient temple by the night of the full moon. He had pushed on, scarcely allowing himself or his men time for rest, marching every possible hour by day or night. Now, the last night, Sinclair guarded his own camp, so that every man might have a good rest for the heavy day before them and the fight to the death that must finish it. He had no hope of rescuing Chrysanthe, for the moment of his attack would mean her death, if this had not already happened. His only desire was to stamp out every one of the fiends who had assisted at her murder, his only prayer, to hold the crushed little flower in his arms again and kiss the dead face before the dark, devil-haunted continent held her, as it held her brother and all her people since the time the first Chrysanthe was stolen from the altar of Asquielba.

The dog got up, stiff and listening, with eyes on the twisted path down which they had traveled until darkness overtook them. He watched curiously. It was no enemy, or Grip would have growled. Not a sound drifted through the forest, except the usual whisperings and distant, howling calls. He made another turn round the sleeping camp, and came back to his seat again, still watching the animal. There was a low, pleased whine and its tail wagged, then, crouching down with its heavy head on its paws, stayed with eyes on the track that twisted and coiled away, lost in the dim aisle of trees. Sinclair waited. Something was coming— something this animal knew and liked. What? Not his little girl

escaped from those fiends' clutches. He stifled the wild hope even
as it rose. Grip would not have stayed with him, but would have
gone to meet her at the first sound. Who was it?

A shadow loomed up, picked out very clearly in a patch of moonlight. It came along at a steady trot, with eyes for nothing but the
track just ahead. Another making for Mungea's temple, anxious to
be there by the night of the full moon, before the ceremony was
over and the high priest departed. The dog's welcoming bark made
the runner stop abruptly. A black hand went to a gleaming knife,
and two men, whose mission was the same, stared at each other in
silence for a time.

"Let us make a truce, Krua, till the night of the full moon be past."

The hand dropped, and the giant came quickly towards Sinclair.

"What know you of the full moon and what happens then? How
came you here?"

"I came down from the gorge swiftly, even as you, to save the
flower from Mungea's hand."

"But for one who was your friend the flower would not be there
now."

Sinclair started.

"What do you mean?"

"As I returned from the drowned temple with my flower, alone,
we fell in with the German and Mungea. There was a great fight
and they slew all but my flower and me. Even then we should have
escaped, but as I fled the German traitor fired with a sureness of
aim beyond all his following, and I fell. Before I had time to seize
my flower again, the swift stream caught me and carried me far
into the valley beyond. When consciousness returned I was miles
below, and my flower in the hands of Mungea. Since then I have
followed; at first slowly, for my strength was spent, and now
quickly, for with the morrow will all things end—for my flower, for
me, and for the priest Mungea. I have still two knives, one for the
Golden Flower that she die quick and painless—a swift death, not
the one Mungea would have for her, and one for him, even as I
promised. I am alone against many, yet I would do this before I
join the shadows."

"Our paths are the same, Krua, for I have sworn that not one of Mungea's people leave the temple alive."

The black giant came nearer and scanned him closely.

"I do not understand you, nor have I from the first. I have seen you with all: as a friend of my brother who now lies in the red lake beyond, with the German dog, and with Mungea, both his enemies. Now you hold out the hand of friendship to me—when through these two, your friends, my flower lies crushed."

"I have always desired to protect the flower."

There was a short, scornful laugh.

"It is a strange protection, friend of traitors, to follow on in the wake of a girl flying from you with the one she loves ill and almost dying—flying from the protector who would take this one treasure from her. A strange protection indeed!"

"You know why I followed. But that one is dead."

"How do you know this?"

"I, also, have been up to the devil's temple. The waters of the lake gave him to me, and he lies buried in the shadow of the peak. Now, my one desire is to save the flower my hands have helped to crush."

"Arru! It is a white flower, yet there is an evil about it, for once the Evil One loved it, and since then evil has come to all who touch it. Yet, when I went into the dread cave, it was my flower I found white and limp as the blossoms she held, and my brother whom the Evil One had taken! There was no trace of him in that devil's hole. Naught but my flower lying there as dead, and since then she has been as dead; for she knows nothing. And it is well, for she knows not Mungea holds her prisoner nor the end that will be hers to-morrow. No further harm can happen, it matters not whether we go on singly or together."

"Let us go on together."

"As you will, for I would see the end of Mungea's tribe, even as in the dead days he saw the end of mine."

Sinclair sat down again and Krua squatted beside him, telling of all that had happened since the afternoon, nearly six months ago, when "The Babe" left his undesired guest bound to the old stone image in the gorge. He learnt how Chrysanthe and her brother had crossed the lake, with Krua as boatman, and had gone into the cave together, leaving the negro outside. The day passed and they did not return, a night, and still he waited for them. With the next sunrise he entered the buried temple, with a dreadful fear at his heart, for the story of the hidden Horror within had been handed down from generation to generation, from one to the other of the descendants of the first Chrysanthe's people, whom the first Claude Devereux had taken back with him as slaves. Like Sinclair he had seen nothing but the lake, and by the side of it, with the red-gold dress clinging wet around her and the water dripping from her curls was Chrysanthe; just as she had entered, except that the whispering bangle had gone, and round her torn wrist, was a knotted handkerchief. Whatever had happened in there had taken her reason, for she knew nothing and recognized nobody.

Sinclair listened in dreary silence, wondering what awful sight had fallen to Chrysanthe's lot in the cavern, what ghastly end the fanatical priest had in store for her, and what fate may have been hers before now.

Something of his thoughts reached Krua, for the black face watched the white one speculatively for some time, and then he said, "There is one who would pluck the flower for its own sake, not for treasures in gold and rubies or a vengeance which has slept for ages. It is even as my mother—who, the voices whisper, now awaits me in the shades beyond—said; then I did not believe her, for this same one would have my brother, but I know now the truth was spoken. No hurt comes to the flower before the night of the full moon, for Mungea sacrifices according to the ancient rites, but with this difference: in the old days one stroke of the knife and the maiden lay dead in the jaws of the stone god, now there is a stroke for every year since the Golden Flower ruled as queen and priestess on the buried plain. More than three hundred strokes before my flower dies! Who knows but what the old god may refuse this sacrifice? Even as the first flower came back from the Dread Golden God, who dwells in the drowned temple beyond, so may the last from this, which is but his stone image. Arru! for again to-night the voices whisper, and to-morrow I shall be but a voice calling out of the mist. There are none of the flower's kindred left, none of her slaves save one who soon joins those who wait beyond. When this one is gone she will be as before my dead brothers, the thorns, found her—a small thing alone in a great desert. Who knows? What is the end of the Golden Flower? In the lost years the Evil One loved it with a. love passing all else, yet, when it returned to him, it was my brother who stayed, not the flower."

Krua lapsed into silence again, and, taking his remaining two knives, started sharpening them for the last time. Sinclair said nothing, and, until the moonlight faded into dawning day, sat thinking of the wild old tragedy that would end before the sun rose again.

THE DYING SUN LAY LIKE A DRIPPING BALL of red in a bed of soft golden clouds, and, as it slowly sank behind the wall of deep green trees, lurid fingers shot out, bathing the forest in a flaming carmine, till the whole country was a mass of fire and the night mists rolled up in wreaths and pillars of reddened smoke. When the sun disappeared there was a golden gleaming, a shimmering, moving, yellow sheen over everything, and, away on the horizon, a giant black hand came creeping up, red-stained where the rays of the lost orb touched it. As it grew bigger the hidden light caught it, and broke it up into little clouds that floated away like flecks of blood; they changed gradually and turned into masses of soft pink, until finally the ominous shadow was gone, and behind lay a deep dark blue where the first of the stars twinkled faintly. Then there was nothing but a purple void and a scattered host of flashing, dancing, distant silver lamps, that sported, played and twinkled, anxious to have their turn before the full moon rose and swept them back to the eternity they sprang from.

Others besides the stars awaited the arrival of the moon at its zenith—two separate parties, and still seven miles divided them. Nearly two hours before the silver ball came up over the fringing trees, before the first long, cold finger was laid on the stone altar in the temple of Asquielba—a broken ring, in the heart of the forest, with meaning lost to all but a few. Several centuries had passed since there had been so much life and stir in the clearing around the shattered stones, or so many weird figures flitting within the uncanny circle; for there was a great "ju-ju" on the place, and few dared venture there unless under the escort of a priest. One or two parties had camped about it during the past months, but no one had ventured within the ring, except the leaders, curious to see the stone monster coiled about the altar, for, although the old religion had died, the superstition had remained. But now the ancient creed was to be revived! As of old, at the full moon, human blood would drip from the jaws of the silent monster, and wash the altar stone beneath. The whisper had gone through the country, as these whispers do, and the old lust stirred. With the setting of the sun a few spectators came to the clearing, as the shadows thickened so did they, and, long before the moon rose, a dense throng surrounded the temple, anxious to witness the sight. Within the ring black shapes went to and fro in the faint starlight, underlings of the priest Mungea, each with a red, legged horror painted on his chest; all with mad, fanatical eyes. This was more than sacrifice, it was revenge as well! An old debt paid at last, washed out by the blood of one who had broken this religion. It was whispered through the waiting crowd, passed from mouth to mouth, till the murder lust filled all. A sea of rolling eyes and thick, moving lips surged round the outskirts of the temple. The smell of hot blood was already in their working nostrils. But it had been a good religion that! With much blood! Red human blood! A girl's blood! What better could the gods desire? Blood and vengeance! This night the forgotten Horror claimed the one who had been his spoiler.

A wild howl greeted Mungea's appearance, as, with about three dozen of his kind, similarly attired, he crossed the faintly lighted ring. The stars twinkled on the uncanny figure, and marked out the white bones in his girdle of dried atrocities. When he raised his hand for silence, the string of eyes, ears and hearts around his neck moved and whispered together. What is he saying? The dead ears listened. Before to-morrow another heart would join them! The heart of a false priestess who brought dishonor on his tribe, and a yoke to the neck of his people. In those days they were free to shed blood, to pour out to their hidden god the warm red stream he loved. Now the land was fettered, and the old religion broken. But revenge still lived! Though it had slept for centuries it was awake at last, and, to-night, blood would again drip on the altar. The blood of this false priestess! At first slowly and with but a small cut, till each of the lost years was paid, and, with his own hand, this false heart was torn alive from its resting place

A roar greeted the finish of Mungea's speech. The moon came up over the trees, and shone on three hundred blood-maddened fiends howling round the temple—a great mad howl, that the passing wind caught up, and carried away into the forest, until it reached the ears of those coming swiftly through the matted depths. It had hardly died down when another roar reached them. This time, wafted on the breeze, with an awful note of mockery and menace. Sinclair shivered, for the moon was up, and the ceremony in the temple beginning. For a time all was silence, and the quiet forest lay marked out in patches of black and silver. Then a faint sob came with a sighing wind, like a moan from a tortured baby. It was drowned at once by a howl of fiendish laughter. Silence again! A breathless, throbbing silence, and the party pushed on with desperate, feverish haste. A moaning scream of girlish anguish! The howling mirth of three hundred devils! Silence again! For a third time the tortured cry sobbed through the listening forest, but no shriek of fiend's laughter followed, instead came the sharp crackle of guns. Again and again, till the clearing round the temple was a tearing mass of scared negroes, brought back to reason by the sound of the blazing firearms, all anxious to escape lest their lives and property paid forfeit for the blood orgy their innermost souls rejoiced in.

The moon shone down on a little red-gold figure lying, gashed and bleeding, in the dripping jaws of the silent stone god; on a group of nearly forty priests who waited on the opposite side of the temple, and on three of their kind who stood on the altar steps. These fell with Sinclair's first volley. For a moment all was chaos, and the fanatics stayed petrified. The attacking party took no notice of the surging crowd in the clearing, but kept a constant stream of bullets between the limp, moaning figure and the forty fanatics who now darted across the ring, ignoring the death-dealing stream that swept away more than a third of their number. A shower of knives was hurled at the sacrifice, but a black shield was there, and only one sank home in the white shoulder. There was a brief hand-to-hand scrimmage as Sinclair and his men fought with the maddened priests, trying to get through to where the black giant and a yellow dog struggled against half-a-dozen fanatics on the altar steps, anxious to kill the victim before their own turn came.

As Sinclair broke through, Krua turned suddenly, faced the red-dripping figure, with a shaking hand raised in salutation. "Ayati! Golden Flower!" and sank across the broken slab with his dead face on the sweeping dress. As he fell, his last knife found the resting place it had wanted since that night in the Rio del Rey swamp—the steel blade, clutched tight in death grip, reached the heart of Mungea, who lay across the altar, with the dying dog's fangs in his throat.

The moon shone down on the empty clearing, on the remaining Hausas in the temple—a third of them lay dead among the array of silenced fiends—and on their leader, who stood by the grim stone head, with something limp and bleeding in his arms. Yet it knew him, for, as he took it from the monster, the moans died down for a moment, two tortured blue eyes opened, and his whispered name reached him like a sigh as they closed again.

The sea of blood was crossed; the last red wave had brought his wild bird back to him, and swept away all belonging to her. She was now as the first Chrysanthe—a little thing alone in a great desert.

That night Sinclair knelt by a little girl who lay moaning in his bed, too weak to move, barely conscious yet just alive. His own babe! His to tend and care for, as she had been that time she lay helpless in his cabin nearly a year ago. And, as he knelt there, it seemed he had loved this little girl not one year but centuries, for many things were whispered to him on the wind that came soughing through the fort down from the far northeast.

CHAPTER 21

"How queer that such a difference should be
Between a human he and a human she."

THE S.S. *ASABO*, HOMEWARD BOUND, swung at anchor opposite the
English factory in Rio del Rey. It was a breathless, tropical morning, and, beneath the white awning that screened the vessel from
the sun's rays, the heat was stifling. On the shaded upper deck
Captain Morton sipped his before-breakfast cocktail, attired in the
light and airy costume, and stretched out with an ease and lack of
dignity which betokened absence of passengers; he was watching
the German side of the river with idle speculation, wondering why
a flotilla of native "dugouts," that had just emerged from one of
the waterways on the left of the trading station, should cross the
mangrove-circled lake towards his vessel, instead of going to the
factory. The fact aroused his curiosity to such an extent that he got up
lazily, shuffled along the deck in a battered pair of carpet slippers,
into which were thrust feet devoid of socks, and went into his cabin
for his binoculars. For a time he gazed at the distant array of canoes.
A soft whistle escaped him, and he became conscious he wore but a
pair of trousers and a shirt, and there was nothing about his present
attire to uphold the dignity of his position or the company he represented. He retired hastily to his cabin to complete belated dress-
ing operations, and a few minutes later emerged spick and span.

The canoes by now were considerably nearer the *Asabo*. There
were about half-a-dozen of them; the first contained a powerful,

soldierly-looking figure, an orderly and something wrapped up in a blanket; the back ones, travel-stained porters and battered baggage. When the procession rounded the vessel's bow, Morton left the upper deck, and went along to the gangway to welcome the new arrival. He leant over the rail, watching the approaching party with the greatest interest, wondering what lay within the blanket, for he had never seen anyone take quite so much care of anything as this big, khaki-clad man did of the bundle he held in his arms. He hailed the coming passenger, with great cordiality, as the canoe stopped.

"Why, Major Sinclair, you were given up for dead months ago. No one heard a word about you after you left Dwala with Langfeldt. Rumor said he and Wentworth had settled you, for nothing has been seen or heard of them since."

"Rumor is wrong again, for here I am, and they are the ones settled."

The speaker stepped on the gangway with his burden. Morton met him at the top of the steps.

"What have you got there?" he asked with undisguised curiosity.

Sinclair lifted a corner of the blanket. A small white face lay beneath, fast asleep against his shoulder. Such a worn little face, thin to transparency, with a halo of chestnut curls around it.

"Why it's 'The Babe!'" looking at the bundle with rank unfriendliness.

Sinclair smiled.

"No, it's his sister, a little girl-babe. My wife."

Morton's amazement was beyond words. He stared at the sleeper in blank astonishment, peering into the blanket, speechless for a few moments, and then whispered, "No one ever knew he had a sister. Why, they're as alike as two peas. Where is he?"

"He was drowned some months ago, nearly a thousand miles up country!"

"You don't say so! Where did you find his sister?"

"She was up there with him."

"The devil!"

The exclamation roused the sleeper. Two blue eyes opened with a start, gazed at him in some alarm, and a small hand crept out and took hold of Sinclair's shirt in a weak, nervous grip. Morton looked at it for a moment, and then a gnarled forefinger touched it with a clumsy tenderness.

"What do you mean by boarding my vessel in this manner, Mrs. Sinclair?—Without giving me any notice or time to get things ready for you?"

Sinclair held his babe closer and watched the white face tenderly.

"Once I doubted if you would get as far as here, didn't I, little girl?"

Morton turned away, blew his nose vigorously, and then said, "Will your wife object to coming into my cabin? The berths below are not straightened up yet. We were not expecting anyone on board before Calabar, certainly not lady passengers, and I've no stewardess till we get there."

"Your cabin will be luxury after the rough times we have had. I've been my wife's nurse for the last nine weeks, so I fancy I can do stewardess for a day. What do you think, Chrysanthe?"

A white little face smiled up at him. Morton started, and cast many curious glances at the bundle as they went along together. On reaching his quarters, all the pillows and cushions were arranged on the couch, for the propping up of this same precious bundle. It looked a very quaint small thing, as it partially emerged from its blanket cocoon and glanced at him with a shy smile. He watched it with the deepest interest, still a trifle undecided as to its sex. A big soft white shawl, of the kind usually used to wrap up very young infants, draped its shoulders, but the weak-looking little hands, lying on the blanket, emerged from the wristbands of an obviously masculine shirt, pinned over with surgical safety pins to keep the morsels from getting lost in the depths beyond. In spite of its married state, it wore no proper wedding ring, only a rough gold twist, of native manufacture, around that special finger, with a very new look about it, too, and at which the wearer glanced now and again as though the sight were still an unaccustomed one. Its hair was short—a mop of dancing curls.

There were a hundred and one questions Morton wanted to ask, but they all verged on the ultra-inquisitive, so he refrained and instead he said, "I knew your brother very well, Mrs. Sinclair, he traveled with me occasionally. You're very much alike."

The blue eyes suddenly filled with tears.

"He was my twin and . . . and was drowned in trying to save me."

Morton became conscious of all the uncomplimentary things he had said concerning the duplicate of the small personage who lay on the couch, trying to keep back the rising tears. It was evident she had been very fond of the young reprobate, and that he had touched a tender spot, for a sinewy brown hand crept surreptitiously underneath the shawl, and there was only one thin white morsel left on the blanket. He changed the conversation quickly by inquiring if they had had breakfast, and, on finding they had not, seized the opportunity of escaping to give the order in person instead of ringing for a steward as was his wont.

Morton was very anxious to hear further details, but no chance occurred until well into the morning, when Sinclair left his babe asleep and came for a turn on deck. The captain approached and opened fire.

"Your wife looks very fragile, Major Sinclair."

"She had a rough time up there; got hurt more than a little, and finally had a bad attack of fever."

Sinclair lapsed into silence, thinking over the time since he had rescued Chrysanthe from Mungea, of the moaning, bandaged little thing who had been his care and charge for the wearing, anxious days that followed; then, when he had coaxed her back to a semblance of life, a bad attack of fever had nearly taken her from him. By then he was a week's journey from the coast, near the Elingo Mission Station, the point he had been making for all along, the only place in the district where a doctor could be obtained. For more than a fortnight she had flickered on the verge, calling for the brother who lay buried hundreds of miles away in the far interior, and only his own arms around her could soothe and quiet her. They had been married there but a week ago, and he had sworn to love and cherish the little girl he had had to carry into the church—

only repeating the vow he had made more than a year before, when Fate first put this same small mortal into his hands.

Morton's voice roused him.

"How was young Wentworth drowned?"

"He was on a treasure-hunting expedition, looking for some hidden temple supposed to lie in a mountain away in the interior. I was there some weeks later and found the youngster's body; some agent in the water had preserved it, it might have been there only a day. Instead of the gold he expected to find, was an underground lake. The temple was all swept away. My wife told me they went in together and, whilst going along a narrow shelf of rock to reach the other side of the water, a volcanic outburst occurred; the force of the first wave swept her into the seething lake; her brother plunged in after her, a strong undercurrent seized him, he clutched at her wrist, just caught hold of a bangle she was wearing, and they were both dragged under. She remembers nothing more until some time afterwards when I found her. Probably, when the bangle broke, the backwash caught and carried her to the shore."

Sinclair said nothing of the ghastly wound he had seen on "The Babe's" body. This he kept strictly secret, and tried to persuade himself, but unsuccessfully, it was the result of a piece of rock forcing itself through the corpse as it lay at the bottom of the whirlpool, until a further upheaval sent it back to earth.

Morton looked at him for some time, as they paced along in silence; he was thirsting for more information, but there was that about his companion's manner which forbade further questioning. Evidently there was some mystery about the girl who was now his wife—something he intended to keep to himself. The captain sighed. He would like to know more of what happened during those months when no word came through to the world of Major Sinclair or his doings.

After the *Asabo* left Calabar there were others beside Morton curious regarding Sinclair, for a cablegram reached England, which when it appeared in the morning papers, caused some excitement in various families:—

"On August 2nd, at the Elingo Mission Station, West
Africa, Major the Honorable Tracy Sinclair, of "The
Kite's Nest," Earlsden, Cornwall, second son of the
late Lord Malstan, and brother of the present peer,
to Chrysanthe Devereux."

No mention was made of whose daughter she was, where she
had previously resided, or anything of her former history. A month
later, when the *Asabo* arrived in Liverpool, six of Major Sinclair's
brothers came on board, the moment the vessel dropped anchor,
to inquire further into the matter. Half-a-dozen big men went along
to where he stood with a slim, delicate-looking girl in pink, who
hung on to his arm watching them, from under a broad-brimmed
hat, with rather scared eyes. There were so many of them and they
were all so big!

For some time, Chrysanthe was lost, and voices could be heard
asking if she had any sisters, and great disappointment was expressed when it was discovered she was the only one of her sort
left, for they had all decided to go to West Africa and hunt for similar birds. Sinclair watched her hoping that, in the six new brothers
who clustered around her, she would forget the one who slept in a
narrow sand bed by the lost temple of Asquielba.

A few days afterwards two people were walking in the grounds
of a quaint old country house. It was built in a wood, as a nest
should be; trees surrounded it on three sides, and, in front, a sweep
of lake and lawn ended in a steep gorge, leading down to where
the sea broke on a stretch of yellow sand. All kinds of curious wild
songsters whistled and called in big cages built among the shrub-
bery, rare and wonderful waterfowl splashed about in the rush-
grown, shady ponds, peacocks strutted on the terraces, and all
looked askance at the two strolling towards the glen. There was
much jealousy and heart-burning among these feathered inhabitants. Only the day before their owner, whom they had not seen for
over a year, had returned, and with him he brought a strange wild
bird! So interested was he in this new specimen, that he had hardly

deigned to notice them. There were many disapproving voices; so far no one bird had been any more to him than any other bird. But now—!

A hundred pairs of jealous eyes are fixed on the two who stand by a big rock at the head of the glen watching the sun set over the sea. The newcomer is evidently a rare sort and of great value to its owner. It is whispered that it got hurt in the snaring, and is still far from strong. But, with the catching of this same small bird, Major Sinclair's aviary is complete.

COACHWHIP PUBLICATIONS
COACHWHIPBOOKS.COM

Bestiarium Cryptozoologicum

Mystery Animals and Unknown Species in Classic Science Fiction and Fantasy

ISBN 978-1-61646-009-9

COACHWHIP PUBLICATIONS

ALSO AVAILABLE

zoologica
fantastica

ISBN 978-1-61646-163-8

COACHWHIP PUBLICATIONS

COACHWHIPBOOKS.COM

ISBN 978-1-930585-74-4

THE LAST
MAMMOTH

Manly Wade
WELLMAN

ISBN 978-1-61646-245-1

COACHWHIP PUBLICATIONS

COACHWHIPBOOKS.COM

THE MUMMY
CASE MYSTERY

DERMOT
MORRAH

ISBN 978-1-61646-250-7

THE QUINNY HITE
MYSTERIES

CHINESE RED · HERE LIES THE BODY

RICHARD BURKE

ISBN 978-1-61646-247-5

www.ingramcontent.com/pod-product-compliance
Lightning Source LLC
Chambersburg PA
CBHW020946260626
47169CB00006B/1852

VALENTINA CANO

ALEISTER
BLAKE

ISBN: 978-1-950305-50-6 (sc)
ISBN: 978-1-950305-51-3 (ebook)
Library of Congress Control Number: 2020937693

First printing edition: September 25, 2020
Published by Trepidatio Publishing in the United States of America.
Cover Design and Layout: Don Noble
Edited by Sean Leonard
Interior Layout and Proofreading by Scarlett R. Algee

Trepidatio Publishing, an imprint of JournalStone Publishing
3205 Sassafras Trail
Carbondale, Illinois 62901

Trepidatio books may be ordered through booksellers or by contacting:
JournalStone | www.journalstone.com

TREPIDATIO
PUBLISHING